S0-CBG-533

UNIVERSITY OF ALBERTA
QUAECUMQUE VERA
EX LIBRIS
UNIVERSITATIS
ALBERTENSIS

the substance of things heard

Eastman Studies in Music

Ralph P. Locke, Senior Editor
Eastman School of Music

(ISSN 1071–9989)

Additional Titles in Music Criticism and Twentieth-Century Music

Analyzing Wagner's Operas: Alfred Lorenz and German Nationalist Ideology
Stephen McClatchie

Berlioz: Past, Present, Future
Edited by Peter Bloom

Berlioz's Semi-Operas: Roméo et Juliette *and* La damnation de Faust
Daniel Albright

"The Broadway Sound": The Autobiography and Selected Essays of Robert Russell Bennett
Edited by George J. Ferencz

"Claude Debussy As I Knew Him" and Other Writings of Arthur Hartmann
Edited by Samuel Hsu, Sidney Grolnic, and Mark Peters
Foreword by David Grayson

Concert Music, Rock, and Jazz since 1945: Essays and Analytical Studies
Edited by Elizabeth West Marvin and Richard Hermann

Debussy's Letters to Inghelbrecht: The Story of a Musical Friendship
Annotated by Margaret G. Cobb

Elliott Carter: Collected Essays and Lectures, 1937–1995
Edited by Jonathan W. Bernard

Historical Musicology: Sources, Methods, Interpretations
Edited by Stephen A. Crist and Roberta Montemorra Marvin

The Music of Luigi Dallapiccola
Raymond Fearn

Music Theory in Concept and Practice
Edited by James M. Baker, David W. Beach, and Jonathan W. Bernard

The Musical Madhouse (Les Grotesques de la musique)
Hector Berlioz
Translated and edited by Alastair Bruce
Introduction by Hugh Macdonald

A complete list of titles in the Eastman Studies in Music Series, in order of publication, may be found at the end of this book.

the substance of things heard

writings about music

paul griffiths

University of Rochester Press

First published 2005

University of Rochester Press
668 Mt. Hope Avenue, Rochester, NY 14620, USA
www.urpress.com
and Boydell & Brewer Limited
PO Box 9, Woodbridge, Suffolk IP12 3DF, UK
www.boydellandbrewer.com

ISBN: 1–58046–206–5

Library of Congress Cataloging-in-Publication Data

Griffiths, Paul, 1947 Nov. 24–
The substance of things heard : writings about music / Paul Griffiths.
p. cm. — (Eastman studies in music, ISSN 1071-9989 ; v. 31)
Includes bibliographical references and discography (p.) and index.
ISBN 1-58046-206-5 (hardcover : alk. paper)
1. Music—History and criticism. I. Title. II. Series.
ML60.G845 2005
780′.9—dc22

2005018351

British Library Cataloging-in-Publication Data

A catalogue record for this title is available from the British Library.

This publication is printed on acid-free paper.
Printed in the United States of America.

for Anne

contents

preface

The Greeks had a word, *ekphrasis*, for the description of pictures, but none for writing about those other images we make, in sound.

We cannot say what music is. Yet we are verbal creatures, and strive with words to cast a net around it, knowing most of this immaterial stuff will evade capture.

Description invariably becomes commentary, invoking previous experience of works and performers as well as more general notions of style and, at the abstract horizon, ideas about music's fundamental nature, its possibilities and purposes. For the professional writer, the response—the net throw—has to be made in public, and this introduces other considerations: of language, of the limits of the personal, of morality, and indeed of the pressing need to come up with what is, in the newspaper world, aptly called a 'story'.

The stories that follow cover a wide range of events over a period of great change. Yet the net's aim was always the same, to catch the substance of things heard.

◆

What is heard is not the same as what is performed. A recording may perpetuate the latter, but only written testimony can tell us how music sounded at the time, how it felt and how it was understood. The history of listening depends on such testimony; the furtherance of listening, and of music, is rooted in that history. In this is the justification for the present volume, selected from a bulk of material ten times greater in size, produced for newspapers and magazines in just over thirty years.

Much of the rest is ephemeral. Criticism generally has to be, for it has to keep track of the everyday: a newspaper critic will probably be attending five performances a week, on average, and writing about nearly all of them. The pen cannot wait for the extraordinary or significant—whose extraordinariness or significance may not, in any event, emerge until later. Besides, criticism is subject to other hazards: a skimpy assignment of space, insensitive editing, and all the critic's own fallibilities.

Until newspaper production was slowed down by computerization (effectively until 1987 in terms of the pieces collected here), reviews were customarily written as 'overnight' pieces, for publication the next morning, which might mean scribbling nine hundred words in forty-five minutes. The notice had to be there, and at the prescribed length. There was no option to ignore a dull event—or, contrariwise, to expand on a great one. Nor was there much time for consideration: one seized gratefully what words came to mind.

The more relaxed schedule of newspapers subsequently, or of magazines generally, alters the task. A critic will be influenced as well by the voice and needs of the publication in which the piece is to appear. Criticism comes not just from an individual but from an individual within a context. And that context includes—besides editors and colleagues—readers, the known and the presumed, among them the musicians under review.

That is one way in which criticism differs from the kind of opinion we might all want to articulate, with friends or just for ourselves. It is tuned by responsibilities—including the responsibility to make sense, to support description and judgment by argument and explanation. A concert notice is not just a point of view but a line of approach—to the music, the performers, the conditions—and its source is in concerns that include but outnumber personal taste.

◆

Criticism arises within another context, that of language. Music is often said to be beyond the reach of words, but it is so no more than a sunset or an emotion, to mention two things that share both its constant fluidity and the meagreness of the available vocabulary.

The language of criticism includes very few specifically musical terms that can be taken as common currency: chord and chorale for sure, tritone and triad probably, but not dominant seventh or heterophony. Criticism therefore has to work largely by analogy and metaphor.

This is no limitation. It is largely through such verbal ties that music is linked to other sorts of experience, not least the natural world and the orchestra of our feelings.

◆

Embedded in a society of readers and in a language, the critic is at once a cultural observer and a part of the culture observed. Inevitably, therefore, this book is marked by changes in western culture during the closing decades of the twentieth century—in particular, the declining belief in such an entity, or at least in its homogeneity.

In the early 1970s the universal value of 'classical music', at least within western societies, was still largely unquestioned. A serious newspaper would have a substantial force of critics for this area: three staff writers, for example, at *The* (London) *Times*, plus an arts editor who frequently reviewed opera and four 'stringers' (writers paid by the piece, or retained by monthly payment), contributing altogether three or four notices in every morning's paper. Moreover, a critic could write unhesitatingly for everyone, in the belief that everyone would be interested in, say, the latest work by Steve Reich.

As in the political world, solidarities were strengthened by opposition—between the avantgarde and traditionalists among composers, or between period style and received custom in the performance of older music. In both cases the 'left wing' was the junior: most of the adventurous composers were in their thirties (Reich, Birtwistle) or forties (Berio, Stockhausen), while the scholar-performers of the early-music movement were barely out of university. Borne by the certainty of youth, progress seemed sure.

By the year 2000 such confidence was gone. The same composers were at work, but in the full afternoons of their lives and absorbed by the mainstream. As for those now in their thirties and forties, they were legion, striving not for general change but simply to be heard, and striving in innumerable directions.

So it was with performers and performances, that the intensely personal was increasingly being manifest, and prized. Among musicians basing their work on studies of period instruments and practices, for example, the aim was not so much to recreate an 'authentic' sound as to have the music speak to the utmost.

One marker of changing criteria—of the rising value of the personal, the immediate, the expressive—was the growing recognition of, among composers, György Kurtág.

Any culture has to balance the individual with the communal. In western culture, as measured by its music, this balance has shifted, and not only in how the producers—composers and performers—are assessed. The standard listener now is not the concertgoer, a member of a group, but the record buyer, alone. Discursive prose, the sharing of response within a population of listeners, is replaced by the awarding of stars.

◆

A note, finally, on the contents and structure of this book. Most of the pieces are reviews of performances or, in a couple of instances, recordings; a few other pieces have been included for variety, to fill gaps or because they consider topics raised more glancingly elsewhere.

Sections devoted to composers, most of them living, alternate with others that, implicitly or explicitly, turn to other concerns: the music of non-western cultures, how composers present themselves in interview, how singers present themselves in recital, some moments in the collapse of the Soviet empire, some approaches to operas of endless fascination. There is also a symmetry at work. And there are those ideas, obsessions, that will not go away.

An anthology is a collection of bits and pieces—of scattered individuals. They also—this is the hope—belong together.

Manorbier—New York
January–February 2005

acknowledgements

This project was made a pleasure by the encouragement of Ralph Locke, Mark Klemens and Daniel Albright. I owe a lot, from further back, to those editors who gave me help and support as a working critic: Stanley Sadie, who accepted my first review for *The Musical Times* and remained a guide for many years; B.A. Young, who smiled on my toddler efforts at newspaper journalism in *The Financial Times*; John Higgins, who taught me much through nearly two decades at *The Times*; Robert Gottlieb, who introduced me to different rhythms and disciplines at *The New Yorker*; and James R. Oestreich, a beacon at *The New York Times*.

Articles are reprinted by permission of the publications in which they originally appeared: *The Musical Times*, *The Financial Times*, *The Times*, *The Times Literary Supplement*, *The New Yorker*, *The Opera House*, *The New York Times* (copyright in all articles rests with The New York Times Co., © 1996–2002), *The Hungarian Quarterly*, *The Full Score, Classic FM Magazine* and *andante*.

a debut

Each new work by Alfred Schnittke establishes him more firmly as Shostakovich's heir, a composer at once overtly rhetorical and deeply mistrustful of his own rhetoric, at once greatly daring in his expressive range and force and highly sophisticated in his ironic self-observation. His Viola Concerto, written last year, is a typical nightmare of the Romantic spirit, and it had a suitably full-blown, fiercely varied and dramatic performance from Yuri Bashmet and the BBC Philharmonic under Valery Gergiev at the opening concert of the Lichfield Festival.

Playing continuously for over half an hour, the work begins and ends with ruminative solo playing, punctuated at intervals by explosions of sound. At times the viola fantasizes about being a violin: an instrument of slightly uncertain character is especially valuable to a composer concerned with questions of authenticity, and the work has its main climax in an extraordinary passage of banal salon music for the viola in violin guise with piano accompaniment, further accompanied by dizzying layers of doubt in the slides and harmonies of the orchestra.

Bashmet's large-toned, noble performance, strictly in tune, added to the concerto's immense power in not over-playing either its elegiac monologues or its keen parodies. Gergiev, making his British debut, was also magnificently in control. There was a fizzing *Ruslan* overture to start, and later an account of Tchaikovsky's Fifth given with epic sweep, a Russian thrill and abundant life in subsidiary parts. It found the orchestra at full, hearty strength. (*Times*, 4 July 1987)

Berio

Time and again, through the second half of the twentieth century, Luciano Berio showed how fully he understood music's intimacy with gesture, memory, language and voice. Among the works considered below, his opera *Un re in ascolto* ('A King Listening') takes place in a theatre, where Shakespeare's *Tempest* is at once being rehearsed and undergoing disintegration. His *Sinfonia*, for orchestra with voices, is one of the period's classics, not least for its middle movement, in which the scherzo of Mahler's 'Resurrection' Symphony sparks off quotations from throughout the western repertory since Bach. He also gave the age its hallmark studies in solo virtuosity, of which that for cello (*Sequenza XIV*), was one of his last compositions.

Un re in ascolto

It is like looking at the disturbed surface of a pool: if you try to make out what is reflected, you may miss the pattern of the ripples. The important question concerning Berio's opera *Un re in ascolto* is not what it is about, but rather how it goes about the business of being about anything. For the director, this is a marvellous liberation, since there is very little action or motivation that needs making plain. But the impalpability of the piece also presents a challenge, a challenge not to use ambiguity as an excuse for recklessness; and the first thing to be said of the Covent Garden production is that Graham Vick directs a wonderful show that is also intimately responsible to the work.

Perhaps sensing that it would be risky to go too far with the dream imagery, Vick places the action decisively in a theatre and keeps the listening king, Prospero, almost entirely within his persona as a theatrical manager. As far as possible the activity is naturalistic, but there is often an awful lot of it going on at once, especially in the opening half of the first part, where the *Tempest* rehearsal proceeds with acrobats, chorus members, dancers, principals and trapeze artists all in wild, contrary motion. Far from diverting attention from the music, this superfluity of bodies and gestures intensifies one's response to the score: so much is happening so fast that the stopped movement of Berio's music, where ideas go on rebounding with built-in echoes and long reverberations, becomes all the more remarkable and enticing.

Of course, it helps that the orchestral music is splendidly played under the composer's direction. The calamitous huge chorale (the hallmark of the four big multiple ensembles) gains in potency even though its repetitions become more tenuous; the tall, dense chords of the second part go by like a sombre parade; solos for violin, clarinet and piano rise up through the orchestral flood stylishly and with character. But perhaps the most intense moments in this production are those where the stage thins and the music comes to underlie some particular action, as when Venerdi (the Caliban figure, a savage, hairy performance from Graham Valentine) brokenly remembers an earlier dialogue for the Mime, a boy (Memnos Costi) who replies in sign language, while the orchestral wind also wander in search of past richness. This extraordinary scene of misremembering and malassimilation stands revealed as crucial to the nature of the opera. Other striking instants include those where Prospero tears down the backcloth at the end of the first part to disclose only ice outside (this rather contradicts the hammering and siren of incipient revolution, which we could do without), or where he is robed and crowned to the strange, marvellous orchestral 'Air' as a pathetically absurd monarch, or where the Protagonist (stirringly and fiercely sung by Kathryn Harries as a La Pasionaria Miranda) arrives to condemn all levels of the action.

There are nice jokes, too, like the portrayal of the first and third auditionees (Penelope Walmsley-Clark and Rebecca Littig) as flighty little misses, while the second (beautifully sung by Elizabeth Laurence) is altogether more serious. The 1950s setting, designed by Chris Dyer, also allows Robert Tear to give a seething performance of the Director as intemperate existentialist. And it provides the most solid possible framework within which *Un re in ascolto* might be seen as a realist opera. If nevertheless the doubts and disparities and the ripples prevail, that is due partly to the orchestra and partly to the strong central performance of Donald McIntyre as Prospero. The potential grand rhetoric of the part is effectively conveyed: just as important is the straining for sense and memory, the scratching of the mind's fingernails on a world that has gone smooth and slippery. Here is the urgency of the work, while from the pit we hear the solemnity and the beauty. *Un re in ascolto* stands with Stockhausen's *Donnerstag* and Birtwistle's *The Mask of Orpheus* as one of the major operatic explorations of the decade. (*Times*, 11 February 1989)

◆

Un re in ascolto is one of the great operas, and its US premiere on Saturday night was a breathtaking occasion. Lyric Opera of Chicago wisely imported the production that Graham Vick created for Covent Garden in 1989, complete with trapeze artists, dancers, choristers who gently ascend on wires while singing, a magician, baleful birds and, most important, a moving presentation of the personalities and antagonisms at the heart of the drama. Berio asks us, with his king, to listen. Vick makes us listen well.

To take one small, beautiful and touching example, there is a moment where, among various fragments and figments from *The Tempest*, a monstrously costumed actor (who might be Caliban; nothing in this opera is quite definite) is being calmed in his confusion by a mute boy (possibly Ariel). Here the two, with Claudio Desderi a sympathetically unkempt monster, play the scene as comrades in affliction, under a moon that waxes as it sails up, and the eye cues the ear to the poignancy and grace in the orchestral music: slow, wide curves from strings, flutes and clarinets.

The central metaphor throughout is that of rehearsal. A director (Kim Begley in scathing frustration) is trying to deal with an unruly cast and an uncertain boss, Prospero, who is at once creator, impresario and lead. Singers turn up to audition; as portrayed by Sheryl Woods, Emily Golden and Sunny Joy Langton, they neatly enact Berio's humorous and human caricatures of dumb diva, seductress and nervous ingenue. Other performers exercise. Even the conductor and orchestra (roles magnificently achieved by Dennis Russell Davies and the Lyric Opera musicians) seem to be trying things out: changing the colours of chords that sound like long echoes, repeating a swirling waltz figure (one might think of Ravel), practicing as soloists or in sections, so that we hear just the outline of a wave or a surface shimmer from what the libretto calls 'the sea of music'.

Most often a performance—play, opera or whatever—is a narrow, perfect doorway between two areas of vast irresolution: the preparation of research and writing, and the aftermath that is the mess we make of the experience in our memories. *Un re in ascolto* forgets the doorway and puts before us what might be yet to come or is already jumbled and half-forgotten. Potentiality folds into reminiscence; only the present is missing. Action, in Berio's theatre, yields to interpretation and imagination. Our lives, he thereby suggests, are determined not so much by what we do as by what we think we have done and what we hope to do next. This is why *Un re in ascolto* is not only an aesthetic but a moral achievement. Berio's worry, as an Italian who grew up during World War II, is that the world of action in the present, specifically of political commitment, is important; and the ultimate arrival in this opera, as if from the barricades, of the female Protagonist (strongly embodied by Kathryn Harries) might appear to confirm that this is so. But of course the Protagonist, too, is part of the show. Attendance to the outside world is not an alternative to self-understanding but a necessary step.

On one level, the opera is pessimistic. Prospero dies, beset by unassimilated delusions and unfulfilled obligations, even if Jean-Philippe Lafont, in a superb and sombre performance, makes him go to his death with growing decisiveness. But he dies because his listening comes too late, and his tragedy offers us challenges and opportunities that are not hopeless at all. (*New York Times*, 12 November 1996)

Barbican 1990

This was the right way to start the BBC's four-day Berio festival: a concert leading up to one of his most festive works, the *Sinfonia* of 1968–9, attended by a large and enthusiastic audience. And though there may be some doubt whether Berio is his own best servant as conductor, his account of *Sinfonia* was fascinating, not least in the light of the brief comments he had made to the audience beforehand. Deprecating the fashion for collage, which he suggested he had initiated with the Mahlerian riverrun at the centre of this work (though surely Ives was there half a century before), he proceeded to underplay that aspect of the piece. There can hardly have been a performance in which so few of the quotations were clearly audible, and those few, perhaps with the exception of the waltz episodes appearing by courtesy of Richard Strauss and Ravel, weakly characterized. The running commentary provided by the eight amplified vocalists was also depressed, at least until the 'Mayakovsky' outburst towards the end of the movement. The effect was to concentrate attention on what one might naively call the 'original' substance of the music—naively, because the hauling in of verbal and musical references, explanations and undercuttings, is surely the work's most original feature. However, Berio and the BBC Symphony players made a good case for hearing all the allusion and glamour of the music as surface chatter on a line that begins as Berio, continues as Mahler subverted by Berio, and ends as Berio subverted by Berio. That line was made particularly prominent by the playing of the five movements as a continuous half-hour whole, and by the pointing of the strands from the first and second movements that are drawn into the fabric of the last, so that the work ends by racing backwards towards its beginning. The notion of the work as a single utterance was also strengthened by the effect at the start of an orchestra stuttering into speech, and then, in the later stages of the opening movement, sounding great phonemes of clattering and richly-coloured sound. Here was *Sinfonia* as a story for orchestra.

Earlier, there were other stories: the uncharacteristically broad joke of the four discrepant versions of Boccherini's night portrait of Madrid superimposed on one another, the nostalgia for Russian nostalgia in *Ritorno degli snovidenia*, with Rohan de Saram tracking a lean path as the cello soloist, and the pencil-drawn mirror play of *Corale* around Carlo Chirappa's crisply virtuoso performance of Berio's own violin *Sequenza*. (*Times*, 15 January 1990)

◆

By far the outstanding piece in this second Berio evening was the last, and the latest we shall hear during these four celebratory days: *Ofanim*. The Hebrew title, meaning 'wheels', is a reference to the eyed wheels of Ezekiel's vision, extracts from which are interspersed with verses from the Song of Songs to suggest a forthcoming catastrophe, a love scene in a garden with terrible things about to move in from the skies. But the wheels are also those engineered by the computer-driven sound equipment, which flings the often colossal sonorities of the piece around the hall. As so often with Berio, the work seems to spring at once from a material notion—concerned here with using the facilities and expertise of his Tempo Reale studio in Florence—and from an immaterial expressive possibility, from a 'how' intimately and brilliantly fused with the right 'why'. Berio is classically a master of the ambiguous, but this is one of those works, like *Coro*, where his sweep is implacable, so that half an hour is contracted into a strong, hard, monumental instant.

The bulk of the piece consists of choral acclamations, for children's voices with antiphonal orchestras of wind and percussion, alternating with verses for the instruments alone. Berio wonderfully accommodates the simultaneous freshness and urgency of children singing, and also the ancientness: for all the sophistication of its hardware and technique, this is music restored to primitive origins, born from a simple three-note motif, and supported by a group of clarinets, brass, drums and gongs echoing back into antiquity. Many of the most magical inventions in the score also have the sudden authority of deeply ancient gestures newly made: the opening for rival drummers, the beginning of the chant by two child soloists, the shattering metallic eruption of the whole amplified ensemble, or the long-delayed arrival of the flutes in forest twitterings and glissandos. At other times, for instance in the solos for clarinet and trombone, Berio seems to be catching moments from his own creative history, and nowhere more so than in the closing minutes, where the children fall silent, the orchestra holds a chord, and Esti Kenan-Ofri rises up from huddled darkness to deliver, with fervour, Ezekiel's prophecy of the fruitful mother uprooted into the desert. This at last is the catastrophe, the barrenness after so much sonic excitement. But because it is voiced with such naked intensity and because it projects the image of a solitary female voice central to so much of Berio's music (here surely is another lament for Cathy Berberian), the catastrophe becomes a defiant triumph. This is what Berio perhaps most essentially is about: searching into the uprooted state of music (and not only music) to find a new beauty. (*Times*, 16 Jan 1990)

Sequenzas

Since 1958 Berio has been fathering a series of solo pieces, the *Sequenza* siblings. There are now nine of them, but the baby of the family, for percussion, is not yet ready for outings, so there were eight to be introduced in turn during last night's festive celebration at the Queen Elizabeth Hall. Berio himself was present to keep a paternal eye on his offspring, and most of them were in the care of the virtuoso musicians for whom they were created.

The oldest is a flute line, now quite an elegant young man, but often dreamy or puzzled in expression. Next came a harp solo, unpredictable as any seventeen-year-old, rippling and graceful, but given to fits of spiteful bad temper which quite belie her appearance—though none of this bothers her fourteen-year-old sister, the vocal member of the family, who flamboyantly parades the special attributes of song and speech. The fourth, fifth and sixth members are all in their early teens too, but utterly different in character: the athlete at the piano, the clown at the trombone, the bookish child who worries at trembling chords on the viola. A little younger, the seventh is a bright lad gambolling around a single oboe note. The violin eighth is a difficult infant, at first going on and on with regular insistence, then running off in playful pirouettes, but finally settling into ominous, quiet repetitions.

This last and longest of the set made an upbeat finale in a brilliant performance by Carlo Chiarappa, who awakened the memories of Bartók and Paganini and Corelli that lie in what is an aural portrait of the violin. But there was delight and astonishment, too, in the more familiar items: in the snappy attacks and luminous resonances of Katia Labèque at the piano, in the pure tone and intelligent phrasing of the flautist Alain Marion, in the wit of Heinz Holliger's oboe and the humour of Stuart Dempster's trombone, the sheer abundant virtuosity of Cathy Berberian, Francis Pierre and Walter Trampler. It was an all-star evening. (*Times*, 1 April 1980)

◆

There should be more concerts like the one at the 92nd St Y last month, when a programme of masterpieces, mostly in masterly performances, was played before an enthusiastic audience that included the composer: Berio. So many concerts are commemorations, of composers gone. Here, we could be celebrating. Berio's presence provided at once a pattern and a focus for general delight, since we could share in his appreciation of what was performed, if in the chastened knowledge that our participation couldn't be more than partial (a remark of his during the pre-concert discussion—'I am my own best listener'—conveyed not so much pride or defensiveness as a melancholy recognition of what in music cannot be communicated), and, at the same time, direct to him our gratitude for what had been written.

While the music was happening, though, this distinction between the written and the performed was largely effaced. What we were hearing was the full complement of Berio's *Sequenzas*, a line of solo pieces composed at more or less regular intervals through the last thirty-seven years. But what we were hearing was also a succession of musical moments occurring now. Because nearly all the musicians performed from memory, nearly all of them released themselves from the encumbrance of the past tense represented physically by printed paper. This was useful in many ways that can be applied to music other than Berio's: a musician without a script can perform entirely to the public, not to the page; to commit music to memory is to take possession of it, and also to pay it homage (both highly positive gestures); and performance is liberated from such extraneous and bathetic actions as turning pages. Beyond all this, however, the *Sequenzas* benefit from extemporaneity quite particularly. Visual attention is fixed on performer and instrument, and this is where the musical attention is, too. Though the *Sequenzas* require consummate musicianship, they are not primarily showpieces—like, say, Paganini caprices—in hearing which we can usefully be kept aware that the performer is fulfilling prescribed obligations. The dialogue in which Berio has his virtuosos engage is much less with note-blackened texts than it is with their instruments and with themselves. The notes are there to activate the instrument and the performing persona, not the other way around. The music points towards a condition in which we might say not that Claude Delangle played *Sequenza IXb* on the alto saxophone, but rather that *Sequenza IXb* played the alto saxophone as handled by Delangle, or even that the piece played Delangle as saxophonist. Difficulties in the music are not just acrobatic feats to astonish; more important, they are opportunities to display new aspects of the instrument—its sound, its technical possibilities, its weight within musical history—and of the performing self. The work is not so much object as means.

There was a splendid demonstration of all this when, some time after Delangle's performance, David Krakauer returned to the same text in its clarinet version, *Sequenza IXa*. Some of the differences had to do with differences between the instruments: how the player's two hands are more widely separated on the saxophone, so that they seem to behave almost like separate animals as they tremble on the keys (tremolandos and quick figurations being thick on the ground in this piece); how the saxophone has associations with music and venues different from the clarinet's; how the saxophone's habitual tempo is slower; how its tone works to draw the listener in, whereas the clarinet is more inclined to project out. Differences between the players must begin here too, since people choose instruments with which they are in sympathy, and in turn have their performing personalities moulded by the instruments they play. Delangle could find his way to a comparative reticence and a sly sensuality, whereas Krakauer was more abruptly present. The emphatic high note that keeps punctuating the middle part of the piece was a beautiful, abstract musical effect from Delangle—a hard ceiling above soft, malleable activity—but became a strident alarm call from Krakauer, who swung his instrument up, bell forward for each attack. (Here was another difference between the instruments: the clarinet is more mobile.) The melody a little later was smoothly modelled by Delangle, yelled as something like an Eastern European folk tune by Krakauer, who surely showed here his experience as a klezmer musician. That a player could be provided with the opportunity to fashion so vivid a self-portrait—some of whose features (klezmer, in particular) cannot have been known to Berio in 1980—was a remarkable tribute to the provocative, evocative power of the *Sequenzas*.

If what was practically the same piece could give rise to two such divergent performances, variety abounded in the programme as a whole: variety enough—and also joy enough—to lift the occasion above the potential disaster of interleaved poetic messages on tape from Edoardo Sanguineti. The one comedy item, *Sequenza V* for trombone, was as funny and touching as a clown show ought to be; the performer was Michele Lomuto, in white sneakers, with an enormous red flower in the lapel of his tailcoat. Alice Giles, in a highly acute performance of the harp piece *Sequenza II*, revealed how Berio typically discovers new possibilities in the instrument, especially in its spiky top range. Sabrina Giuliani, playing *Sequenza VI* for viola, gave an unusually unflustered account of its quadruple-stop scrubbing, which was the more intense for being exact; the tune at the end, after all this wire-brush music, sounded like the first melody of the world. The trumpeter Gabriele Cassone, in *Sequenza X*, was superbly in command of the physical swivels from brilliant, forward ejaculations to notes played into the open grand piano behind him, played to make echoes that seemed to be disappearing down long hallways. Luisa Castellani made a powerful dramatic vignette of the voice piece *Sequenza III* in her own terms: not flamboyant in the manner of Cathy Berberian, for whom the piece was written, but centred, with eyes narrowed, in obsessive muttering. This was another demonstration of how the *Sequenzas* are designed to accommodate the signatures of those who perform them.

Diverse as they are (because matched to the natures of diverse instruments), the *Sequenzas* are also a family, though with one odd man out: the flute solo that was the first of them. This wanders and darts and skitters, as if touching on and sometimes exploring different parts of a landscape, whereas all the others take paths that include movements in circles, even in whorls, and turnings back to branch out again. They move as memory moves, mimicking the course by which they arrive in performance: from the musician's memory, and from the memory of the instrument. The guitar's *Sequenza XI*, for example, is an exhalation from flamenco, while the violin, in *Sequenza VIII*, has an image of Bach's D minor Chaconne at the back of its mind—though with its front brain it can spin off on new courses, such as the pianissimo evolving melody that was simply and magically spun here by Carlo Chiarappa. *Sequenza I* comes from a moment before the series knew quite what it was about, but in the context of so many predecessors, the piece's capriciousness is cherishable, and Paula Robison made it specially so.

At the other end of the line, *Sequenza XII* for bassoon was being played for the first time in the US, by Pascal Gallois, for whom it was composed earlier this year. Perhaps because this is an instrument with rather little solo history, Berio treats it in an utterly new way, writing long slow glissandos that have the massive substance and strain of some great piece of wood being bent. This astonishing piece—which was astonishingly played—demands that tone be sustained for much longer than the span of a breath, and indeed Gallois, using circular breathing, barely moved his lips from his reed in all twenty minutes of the work's duration.

Next to come will be a *Sequenza* for accordion, on which Berio is now working, and there have been intermittent reports of one for percussion. Other candidates for the future must include cello, horn and harpsichord. And maybe there should be a piece too for the virtuoso Berio honours and obliges throughout the series: a piece—possibly made with electronic sounds, so needing no performer—that would be a *Sequenza* for listener. (*New Yorker*, 18 December 1995)

paths to Montsalvat

Wagner's *Parsifal* is the story of a hero who brings new life to the knights of the holy grail, gathered in their castle of Montsalvat and hitherto languishing under a sinning, wounded king, Amfortas. In accomplishing this regeneration, Parsifal also destroys the magician Klingsor and heals the single female character, Kundry. Gurnemanz, one of the knights, is both narrator and observer, at an action that, like a ritual, will have to unfold again and again.

English National Opera 1986

The terrible tragedy at the heart of Wagner's last opera is that of a work which knows it cannot fulfil itself, and Joachim Herz in his new production is right to identify one of the main reasons as the composer's presence in the drama in the guise of Amfortas. This was the character with whom he felt overwhelming sympathy: *Parsifal* was to be his redemption of himself just as Parsifal would be the redeemer of Amfortas.

If Herz offers a plausible diagnosis of the opera, however, he does so with little subtlety, though it is unfair to give a definitive judgement on the production as yet, since on opening night it was not running at all smoothly, and also since the title role was taken over at very short notice by Siegfried Jerusalem. He did a splendid job in entering a new production cold, and sang magnificently, particularly in the third act; it even seemed appropriate that this Parsifal should be singing his own language, with everyone else onstage too polite or too mystified to mention the fact. Nevertheless, the production had evidently been shaken by recent trauma.

But, even allowing for that, to clothe Amfortas in a Wagnerian dressing-gown trivializes the point, just as it trivializes the moribund authority of Titurel to have him appearing, if tottering, onstage in cope and dalmatic: of course these two represent on one level the exhausted old church and the tainted new, Rome and Bayreuth, but the suggestion can be made less explicitly. Nor is this a lone example of heavyhandedness. The stuffed swan flatly plopping to the ground raised an inevitable laugh; equally disappointing was the appearance of the flower-maidens in quite unseductive close-fitting caps, or the knights parading as a schoolboy chorus, or Kundry's call on Parsifal from a position where she was invisible, or Klingsor's trapezing on a pink hulahoop with a mirror that obscured his singing, or the destruction of his domain that could be predicted a full hour ahead, or the lowered curtain for the final transformation, or the unnecessarily complicated grail machine. In short, Herz bungled every intervention of the fantastic. The blame must be shared by his designer Wolf Munzner, whose first-act forest is an ugly mess of leaf-green piping. With the ultra-violet lights turned off, this becomes the contents of a giant ashtray for the third act. The flower-maidens operate from within a bowl of pink rags, and return at the end as vestal virgins (or perhaps snowdrops), though the feminist point would be stronger if the music were not by this stage thoroughly unconvinced by itself.

Sir Reginald Goodall, however, sounds convinced, indeed possessed, by every bar: he conducts a performance that is both searing and grandiloquent. Also excellent is Gwynne Howell's refreshingly human Gurnemanz, a young man of limited imagination but touching vulnerability in the first act, and still green as the aged hermit. Neil Howlett as Amfortas sings with a passionate sense of great strength in travail, and Anne Evans as Kundry has a candour and fragility that worked rather well in her dealings with Parsifal. Rodney Macann has been encouraged to play Klingsor too much as the demon king. (*Times*, 17 March 1986)

Proms 1987

Parsifal, so actionless, might seem to be the ideal concert opera, but yesterday's Prom performance of just the third act showed by omission how important the action is: so much in the music supports and echoes from those crucial liturgical gestures of anointing, baptism and procession. But there were huge compensations, most especially in the rare privilege of being able to watch Sir Reginald Goodall at work.

There must be the fear, now that he is aged eighty-two and evidently frail, that he will not conduct this music in the theatre again, but his ability to command a single act is awesome and undimmed, and gained an unstinting response from the English National Opera Orchestra. It was a performance to justify Debussy's remark about the orchestra in *Parsifal* sounding 'as if lit from behind': the light glowed through the chording of the woodwind, or that of the quartets of trumpet and trombones. And it was a serene, mellowed light. Occupying fully ninety minutes, the act was performed as an unbroken adagio, but an adagio of extraordinarily fine texture, the string opening being grey and extended yet almost weightless. Nor at any subsequent point were there any histrionics: the calamitous moment later in the prelude, where the Dresden Amen falters in its ascent, was quite unforced, contributing to the tragic aura on a much longer span. Quite how Goodall achieves his long-range conception remains a mystery. On the podium he does almost nothing: at some of the most tremendous moments he would be found moving one arm as if stirring a hollandaise at a particularly delicate stage, and only very rarely did he lift both hands above the level of his shoulders. The music went on with what seemed its own slow majesty.

The soloists were those of last year's ENO production, with the dominant role of Gurnemanz taken marvellously by Gwynne Howell. Goodall's tempo caused problems for all the singers, not least the ENO Chorus, but Howell maintained a wonderfully appropriate blend of fervour and gentleness. Warren Ellsworth as Parsifal was in much less secure form, the weak top not matching the richness of his lower register. Given the warmth and lightness of Howell's singing, the music almost sounded as if designed for three baritones, with Neil Howlett beautifully providing a rounded, undemonstrative Amfortas. Shelagh Squires could not be faulted for her delivery of the four notes remaining for Kundry, but of course the evening belonged to the long-matured, unselfconscious gravity of Goodall, and thereby to Wagner. (*Times*, 10 August 1987)

Covent Garden 1988

What Bernard Haitink and Bill Bryden are together attempting in the Royal Opera's new *Parsifal* is nothing less than the redemption of the redemption, the acceptance within the work of a straightforward religious design that needs no processions or ultramontane healing, nor any mystic gloom in the orchestra. One may feel that a saved *Parsifal* is less interesting than the fallen triumphs of other interpretations, but this is a totally clear, honest and remarkable answer to the charge that the work's sacredness is all decadence and self-delusion.

As before with *The Mysteries* for the National Theatre, Bryden validates the religious meaning as a communal act of storytelling, something that people put on naively rather than engage in liturgically—something that, too, is happening almost here, almost now. The stage becomes illuminated halfway through the prelude to show people gathering within the toppling Gothic arches of a church grown strange and ruinous (the set is by Hayden Griffin). Searchlights, costumes and ARP wardens suggest that the time is the early 1940s, though that is not insisted upon: altogether the production is never insistent. Gurnemanz comes forward and dons a cope to start the play, while most of those onstage simply watch, and in their concentration make the long passages of narration powerfully dramatic. It helps that the storyteller is sung and acted by Robert Lloyd with unparallelled ease and naturalness: every word is strikingly audible, besides being moulded with self-effacing artistry. The effect is of simplicity, gentleness and amiability, of important things being related with no false reverence but with quiet concern.

When the opera turns from narration to ceremonial and action, in the grail scenes and throughout Act 2, the stage audience appropriately withdraws, though they leave behind them the atmosphere of plain seriousness they have engendered, partly because this is the manner of the performing (in which, as grail knights, they take part), and partly because everything important is placed well at the front of the stage and candidly lit. The low-church unfussiness of the first grail scene, in particular is deeply impressive. The men have simply put on faintly Masonic sashes to become knights, and they sit at long tables to receive communion soberly. In going they honour the grail not with nods, crossings and genuflections but rather by walking towards it, one or two at a time, and standing for a moment looking straight ahead. This is the pride of the humble, which the production does so much to exalt.

The middle act is not quite so steadfast. Willard White is a sonorous Klingsor, his summonses richly booming, but the production's abstinence from magic and mystery leaves the flower maidens as a gaggle of garlanded ladies in nightdresses. Fortunately Waltraud Meier overcomes this handicap of costuming (she is much better served by a sensuous pink and cream creation in which to leap and slither in the first act). For one thing, she takes possession of the stage without a shred of embarrassment or inhibition; she also acts brilliantly with her voice. As a hysteric she is exultant, harsh or wild as occasion demands, though, astonishingly, she is always in full control of her voice. Then as a temptress she manages to convey at once warm, inviting liquidness and calculation; she is both beguiling and canny, and stil more intensely beguiling when she becomes desperate. Her long dialogue with Parsifal, where Peter Seiffert rises to her challenge to produce his most pointed singing, is lucidly acted. Parsifal stretches out his arms in the posture of crucifixion, and she interlaces hers with his to make her proposal of an erotic salvation. Then, singing still with furious seductiveness, she lies back before him to repeat her entreaty: the alternative to renunciation is presented absolutely directly.

After this, the fumbled handling of the spear at the end of the act is pure bathos. But the third act, mirroring the first, restores the production's credit. This is also where Haitink's calm and cool unfolding of the score is specially valuable: one might want more agony (with Simon Estes as Amfortas singing below his best, the wounded, death-seeking voice in the work is further weakened), but the lack of pretension in the pit suits what is happening onstage, and for the same reason it is right the music should sound so open-textured and pastel-shaded, so unpressured and unaffectedly eloquent. Haitink effectively places the woodwind at the centre of the musical drama, and gains excellent support from his players. On either side of his confrontation with Kundry, Seiffert offers a puppyish Parsifal who moves towards solemnity but remains lax in phrasing and monochrome in the hearty benevolence of his singing. John Connell's Titurel is a sepulchral as could be wished. (*Times*, 30 January 1988)

Bayreuth 1989

The specialness of *Parsifal* at Bayreuth is of course the specialness of a piece made for the building in which it is being heard: here, the place becomes the work. And there is the added glory of hearing the score played not only by the orchestra which knows it best but also under the conductor who must have performed it more often than anyone else now living: James Levine. Levine's *Parsifal* is slow: so slow that one hears almost every note or chord individually, even while the phrases extend in long placid lines; so slow that one hears the ache and the agony and the interrupted benedictions. But if there was anything tedious in the orchestral contribution to Tuesday's opening performance of the festival, it came rather in the faster music, espcially that for the Flower Maidens. Levine clearly is not seduced by seduction at all so much as by a yearning in the score that, in his performance, is as much erotic as spiritual, partly because everything—except the ostensibly erotic music—sounds so captivating. There is a soft, glowing texture to much of what Levine does, a translucence that lets one hear at once the blend and make-up of the instrumentation, a gauzy beauty recalling Debussy's remark about this score. The yearning is also musical: the yearning for the high treble of heaven, of course, but also the yearning of melody for liberation from harmonic responisbility, the wish for a state of musical grace unknown in western culture since plainsong. This Levine brought out most intensely in the third-act prelude where melody and bass begin to part company (they seemed extraordinarily to be in different tempos at the same time) until the melody is brought crashing to earth. But this was only one moment among many where Levine's experience of this score, this orchestra and this theatre produced illumination.

The negative side is that, by all accounts, the price of Levine's continued appearance at Bayreuth was the scrapping of the powerful, strange and imaginative Götz Friedrich production in favour of something very much more straightforward, not to say staid, contrived by Wolfgang Wagner. Obdurately ignoring any innovation in stage design during the last thirty years, Wagner offers a simple platform bounded by half a dozen fat, tapering pillars. For the forest scenes they look like dusty columns of raw rock crystal, or more like giant strips of crumpled cellophane; for the interiors, whether the grail temple or Klingsor's castle, they turn to become steep-sided ziggurats (although, in a piece of decorative ineptitude, one can still see the quartz shapes, jutting around the edges). The production is generally faithful to the stage directions, in that it has so little dramatic life one seems to see the stage directions leaping about in the persons on the platfom, so that the Knights' revulsion at Amfortas's wound, or their threatening of him in the last act, come out of nowhere. The Flower Maidens are houris in ponytails and the principals are left to stay still or drift.

William Pell as Parsifal tries some primitive jumpiness in the first act but looks awkward and soon drops it. Nobody else can be said to act at all. Except, that is, Waltraud Meier with her voice. She is, as always, totally wonderful as Kundry, managing to sing everything, even the shrieks and the laughter, while making every word audible and registering a vast range of colour. In her alluring of Parsifal she is gorgeous but always perfectly in control, watching herself and him at every instant: the sound is thick cream, but it is being carved with a scalpel. Hans Sotin, though not in best voice, produces a splendid timbre for Gurnemanz: dark and soft, like the rather rabbinical gaberdine coat he wears in the final act. Bernd Weikl's Amfortas came through vocal problems to a sure and searing despair, and Franz Mazura, despite a costume of shiny red, purple and black stripes that made him look like a chocolate, presented an unusually sung, rather than scowled, Klingsor. The new US Parsifal was disappointing. There is real strength in his voice, as he showed in an almost reckless outburst of 'Amfortas! Die Wunde!'; there is also lyrical ardour and youthfulness. But the unconstrained vibrato—and even more the slippery intonation—suggested he is doing too much too soon. He cuts, though, a tall figure, and when he lifted the Grail, rotating it in brilliant crimson light around the audience who completed the circle of knights, the magic onstage for one minute equalled that in the pit. (*Times*, 29 July 1989)

Amsterdam 1990

There is a strong *Parsifal* tradition in Amsterdam, going back to 1905 when this was the first city in Europe to break the Bayreuth monopoly on Wagner's last work. Fittingly the piece is now being revived to open a new chapter in the history of the Netherlands Opera, the first season for which Pierre Audi is responsible as artistic director. The producer is Klaus Michael Gruber, whose operatic experience includes the abandoned Paris *Ring* of the mid-1970s. His ambition here seems to have been to render this most static of operas almost stationary, to efface the Christian symbolism, and to leave only a few key events to focus the sustained uncertainty.

The production's great success is its reappraisal of the hero as a man who ends the opera as ignorant as he began it. There is no grail in the final scene, no assumption by Parsifal of the role of priest-king: instead he stands alone at the front of the stage throughout the apotheosis, his head tilted to one side as it has been for most of the time, listening and not understanding. The shooting of the swan is signalled feebly by the falling of a white cloth, and the end of the second act looks deliberately fumbled: Klingsor does not launch his spear; instead stage lightning flashes from it, and what Parsifal picks up is a curlicue of a bolt. Inevitably the audience laughed. There are, however, a few striking pictures. Amfortas arrives with just one retainer, or perhaps controller, pacing behind him with an arm outstretched. Klingsor's garden is a collection of faintly erotic balloons with their ancestry in Bosch and Miró, while the flower maidens lie supine in a circle to sing their seductions.

Hartmut Haenchen conducts an energetic performance, even if the lack of control sometimes shows up the orchestra's weaknesses. The austerity of this production requires from the cast intense dedication and conviction, which no doubt will increase. Already it is clear that Jan-Hendrik Rootering is an outstanding Gurnemanz, baritonal in quality, using his lyricism and marvellous control of colour to suggest a man of more poetry than authority. Barry McCauley is a jerkier artist as Parsifal, with some rough tone and a generally ejaculated mode of delivery, but perhaps these are intentional notes of wildness to complement his physical stillness. Nadine Denize displayed formidable strength as Kundry; Henk Smit is a grave Klingsor with his hands in the pockets of a red dressing-gown; Wolfgang Schöne presents an unforgettable image of the crowned, wounded king. (*Times*, 8 September 1990)

Houston 1992

Robert Wilson spent a decade planning his production of *Parsifal*, which was first staged in Hamburg last year—not happily, by all accounts. Now his concept has finally been realized in his home state of Texas, where it is the highlight of David Gockley's twentieth season as general director of Houston Grand Opera. It has been a long wait, and it goes on being a long wait, not only because short intervals barely interrupt the opera's slow continuity, but also because the whole feel of the production is of waiting, of attendance, of attention. As such it is a very Wilsonian evening, empty of narrative but alert in atmosphere. It is also a very Wagnerian evening, for the whole way the production looks and moves is in deep submarine echo to the music. Almost nothing happens. From an opera not exactly spinning with incident, Wilson removes even the events one would have thought indispensable. There is no grail ceremony. The chorus sings from the auditorium balconies, to marvellous effect, making the entire theatre, not just the stage, a temple. In the absence of a communion service Amfortas's attendant youth simply reaches into a crystal rock for an undefined object, thus intensifying and amplifying the sense of the numinous by divesting it of imitation. Instead of copying Christianity's sacred act, the production strains to convey a mystery of its own, for as the music moves through time and space towards the grail castle of Montsalvat, so a giant disc of white light descends, a wonder in itself and a greater wonder in pointing—through the evident manufacturedness of plexiglass, cables and fluorescent tubes—to some imaginable floating halo beyond the powers even of Wilson's stagecraft and the combined technical expertise of Houston and Hamburg. Another central action withdrawn is Kundry's kiss, and again the moment is powerfully charged. A kiss we cannot see must be happening on some cosmic plane. It is the unseen characters who touch here, not the singers who have to give them voice and some representation onstage.

More generally the manner of that representation is also marked by withdrawal. The singers move like sleepwalkers, or like noh actors (monochrome costumes and make-up), or like people with this music in their motor systems. Posture is steady and erect; arms are held stiff, or choreographed into twists and swoops, but never used to explain or accredit what is sung. This places the singers under a naked glare. Since movement here exists only for and of itelf, one notices any flicker, and since the singers have no other means at their disposal, they have to convey everything in the music only with their voices. They come across with an intense presence. They are beings of another kind. Nor is there any stage architecture to give them a habitation. Attention is focused not only on the singers and the music, but also on the few magic acts that remain, such as the descent of the glowing torus. The whole drama is begun and ended by a little boy in a loincloth walking slowly across the stage: Parsifal's double or spirit. Halfway through the first act a huge stylised wing, as if made from paper, falls in slow motion through the rectangle: it could be the swan passing over to meet Parsifal's arrow, but Gurnemanz is singing of angels, and it could also be the wing of the dove. Then the spear, a slender shaft of light, floats without visible means of support into Parsifal's grasp. Of course not everything quite sustains the miracle. One could wish Wilson had made the flower maidens invisible as well as the grail knights. Even here, though, the production is level and cool, not so much other-worldly as simply and very beautifully other.

It has splendid support from Christoph Eschenbach, conducting a performance of passion and fluid speed, though a decent forte is hard to attain in this company's large theatre. The central performances, too, respond magnificently to the demands of Wilson and Wagner's music. John Keyes displays a voice of baritonal fullness and sure length of phrase. At the end he shows commanding authority, grandly preferring vocal strength to ring. Harry Peeters is a wonderful Gurnemanz, looking as impassive as a statue, but his young man's voice flooding with richness and nuance. Richard Paul Fink sings a happily direct and strong Klingsor. There is no need for him to croak his wizardry when he can prove it by delivering most of his part perched without safeguard on his high tower. Dunja Vejzovic is a strikingly powerful Kundry and fully takes on the spirit of the production. (*Times*, 21 February 1992)

Carter

Elliott Carter drove on through all the 'Stop' signs put up by age. In his mid-sixties, after two decades devoted to just half a dozen big chamber and orchestral scores, he began writing songs. In his mid-seventies, when he seemed to be winding down with pieces for smaller formations, he starting producing orchestral works again. He composed his Oboe Concerto for concerts to mark his eightieth birthday, and still there was more, including his *Symphonia* for orchestra, a work in three parts, of which the first were *Partita* (1993) and *Adagio tenebroso* (1995).

Oboe Concerto

On Monday evening, during a pause in a procession of Messiaen events, it was time for the South Bank to salute Elliott Carter, a man born the day after Messiaen but in so many respects musically his antithesis: secular, continuously progressive, contrapuntal, atonal, unrepeating, constantly on the alert for change. Where Messiaen's latest pieces belong to a musical personality that had been formed in its essentials by 1930, Carter's exist in a world then unimaginable, and his astonishing late creative energy was proved at this Queen Elizabeth Hall celebration in performances of three big, unceasing works written within the last four years: his Fourth Quartet, *Penthode* for five mixed quartets, and the Oboe Concerto that had its first performance in Zurich six months ago.

This last is an achievement to amaze. The form of the work suggests the composer listening with intense concentration and acuity to his solo instrument—or more precisely to the sound of it as played by his intended soloist Heinz Holliger—and responding with music in which not only the almost continuous solo line but also the entire orchestral score springs out of oboeness. At first one is struck by the brilliant, surprising and yet exact ways in which the oboe's melodies and motifs are spread, bounced and extended by a chamber orchestra of single wind (but without oboe or bassoon), strings and two highly active percussion players. But then the piece starts to reveal ever more virtuosity in the matching of sound as well as material: the imitations of oboe multiphonics by a concertino quartet of violas, or by a duo of piccolo and clarinet, are quite extraordinary. They show Carter fully abreast of the concerns of many composers half a century younger than himself, and technically equipped to surpass them all. Perhaps because it is infected by likenesses more than contrarieties, the concerto has a formal simplicity and a generosity of slow music unusual for Carter: if too brilliant to be called relaxed, the work has reached a new and happy balance. It was zestfully performed by Holliger with the Ensemble InterContemporain under Pierre Boulez. (*Times*, 14 December 1988)

Partita

You do not have to be eighty-five years old to feel marooned in the past while time races on, but you probably do have to be that age—and, specifically, to be Elliott Carter—to have the reverse feeling of desertion by time's skidding hurriedly backwards from a point you thought was not only yours but everyone's. At a public interview before the world premiere in Chicago of his newest orchestral work, *Partita*, Carter reacted passionately to a question about the future. How could he have any certain hope for his music, he said, when the last decade had seen a rush of young composers—by whom he probably meant anyone under seventy or so—'writing like Brahms, and doing it badly'? His tone was regretful, bewildered, but not bitter: he has too much gaiety of mind ever to turn sour—or, indeed, ever to write like Brahms. We therefore have the paradox of an aged composer producing some of the most exhilarating music around, and doing so with majestic accomplishment (if that does not seem too settled a term for this athlete of the mind) in his new piece, which goes straight up among his finest.

But perhaps the youthfulness is not so paradoxical; maybe only the old, in these jaded times, have their innocence intact, and stay able to be surprised by immediate sensory impressions, as Carter is evidently surprised and delighted by sounds. Simplicity and directness have always been as much his blessings as the vaunted 'complexity'. (Why should this always be introduced as a problem? Who complains of the complexity of a forest?) Indeed, the abundance, to give it an apter name, comes out of a simple certainty about the nature of a composer's task, at least in the way Carter has expressed that task in words. Questions of language and style do not arise; history is only what was. The contemporary composer will do things differently by virtue of being a different person in a different age. 'My musical intention', he said in a short note on the new work, 'was to present the many changes and oppositions of mood that make up our experience of life. In general, my music seeks the awareness of motion we have in flying or driving a car and not the plodding of horses or the marching of soldiers that pervades the motion pattern of older music.' Hence the view he stated in another pre-concert discussion, quite without any desire to be provocative, that the music of our own time (a period which in his case comfortably includes Stravinsky's *Rite of Spring* and Symphony of Psalms, the works at issue) is inevitably more vivid to us than the music of the past.

This unreconstructed, undeconstructed modernism might seem quaint were it not robustly supported by creative practice, and in particular by that practice as exhibited in *Partita*, even if the score has more in common with 'older music' than Carter is inclined to allow in his verbal pronouncements. The title is one connection, though not in the most obvious way: the Baroque synonym for 'suite' is used here, Carter said, for its modern everyday meaning of 'game' or 'play', as in (this was his example) *partita di calcio*, or 'football match'. The music lives up to this: it is bright; it is often fast; its parries are volatile; it sometimes has to do with rival teams of players (or with one against a pack); and it proceeds, as the composer took some pains to point out, according to rules. At the same time the suite idea seems to be somewhere in the background of this continuous eighteen-minute sports event. Much of the music dances, partly by virtue of the fact that the exuberant swirls and flourishes, and the statelier measures, are generally defined by a metre—often a triple or compound metre. Given the prominence, too, of the piano in the orchestra, the dancing rhythms occasionally suggest splinters of *Petrushka*.

Stravinsky and the Baroque: the references in Carter's music of the 1990s are pretty much what they were in the 1930s and 40s, and *Partita* reinforces the impression, created by the Oboe Concerto of 1986–7, that the late works will in time make us see the output as whole, not broken between an early phase of neoclassicism and a long modernist celebration. The only problem is that the old bipartite view has always been the one Carter put forward. As he explained it on this occasion, his first enthusiasm was for the iconoclastic music he heard as a boy in New York in the 1920s: the music of Varèse, Ives and others. But he decided he could not join that band without learning how to write, which was why he went to Nadia Boulanger and got himself fixed up as a Stravinskian. Only in the late 1940s did he realize this was not why he had become a composer, after which awakening he threw away the baggage of traditional forms, styles, and gestures.

It is a good story, and since it is the composer's own, one has to give it some credence. But it is not the whole truth. For one thing, even Carter's most resolutely neoclassical scores seem to know there is more to life than keeping your counterpoint clean. For another, even his most recklessly adventurous pieces—of which *Partita* must count as one—are precision-engineered. Control is absolute. Certainly the music is impatient with the old constancies: Carter finds analogues for it in literary treatments of sweeping change and movement, whether Lucretius's telling of the formation of the universe, in the Double Concerto; Saint-John Perse's vision of great winds across North America, in the Concerto for Orchestra; or now, apropos of *Partita*, a Latin poem by Richard Crashaw, in which a floating bubble tells of its transitory existence in trimeters. 'Sum fluxae pretium spei' (I am the prize of flowing hope), it sings, in a line the composer thought of using as his title, but happily decided against. For it is not only hope that flows in Carter's music but intelligence—an intelligence that appears to reside in the notes themselves as they pursue their courses, perhaps because all movement is motivated by tensions contained within and between the notes: tensions of pulse and metre, of harmony, of attraction towards some point in registral space. The neoclassical dream was a dream of objectivity, a dream of music as self-propelling mechanism. It is a dream Carter still cherishes. Only the speeds of his music's movement are altered, and the consistently forward direction. Neoclassicism was also an attempt to repeat the past—in the sense not just of Stravinsky repeating Bach, but of musical ideas forever repeating themselves. (Modern neoclassicism is no different.) Carter's music since the end of the 1940s achieves its modernism not by sounding like Ives or Varèse but by never looking back, by creating form out of movement—by, as he put it in Chicago, 'rolling on like plainsong'.

Quite how it rolls on is less easy to say. Carter suggested in his spoken commentaries some kind of process leading from the two opening chords—a wham from the bottommost instruments followed by a high treble trill—to the two in the middle register that end the piece: a gradual closure of bounds. But some of the most soaring music comes near the end, as does some of the most thudding, and the drifts of musical thought, generally over in a few seconds, are surely directed by far more local conditions. Just how local—and just how critical it is to get them right—was demonstrated at one point in the final rehearsal, when Carter got up from his seat and walked forward to ask his conductor, Daniel Barenboim, for 'more A flat'. This was one rare moment when his age told, for by the time he reached the podium Barenboim was worrying about another A flat. (There must be several thousand of the things in this extraordinarily detailed score, most of them, like their companions, decisive in one way or another.) But once the confusion had been resolved, it quickly appeared the composer was right to ask for more than he had written, and right for reasons having to do with the way a particular passage reaches its goal. A rather tumultuous orchestral rampage, in the struggling rhythm of threes against fours, finds its destination in a single note—the A flat—struck simultaneously on glockenspiel and harp. As originally played, the conclusion was limp, even a joke: the mouse emerging from the mountains. Given full force, it suddenly clinched the entire gesture.

But not everything that moves through this score is so massive or so fast. Right after the glockenspiel-harp A flat there is a sequence of sustained notes (in Carter's usage they sound more stretched or restrained than merely held, as if stationariness could be attained only as a product of motions in conflict), with star points in the high treble. Another moment of slow beauty comes near the start, when a melody seems to grow out of the delicate worry between two flutes, and then to ripple out from them into muted violas, violins and trumpets: here, at least, the composer's allusion to plainsong did not appear far-fetched. Or to give an example from close to the finish, there is a point where all the violins in unison suddenly surge forward, and a whole Tchaikovsky slow movement (the marking is 'appassionato, legato') is encapsulated in three bars. For of course *Partita* is not all flight from the past: it is also a rejoicing survey, one in which echoes do not entomb the music but are fleetingly saluted.

Asked before the performance what music he had been listening to lately, Carter replied that he had been absorbed in Berlioz, and possibly one can hear another echo, of that composer, in the cor anglais solo of *Partita*. Carter had said he thought of *Partita* as a work of 'long lines but fragmented lines', following an idea of interrupted, jostled lyricism he had been exploring since his violin solo *Riconoscenza* of 1984. At the end of the third movement of the *Symphonie fantastique* the cor anglais provides a foretaste of Carterian bravely-continuing melody when, repeatedly put off course by the timpani, it keeps recommencing its eclogue; in *Partita* the same instrument—more comically, like a bore in a bar—goes on laboriously trying to tell its simple story, undeterred by the liveliness all around. Other solos in the work are more exuberant, and speak more of the US in what they call to mind—especially the wild breaks for E flat and bass clarinets. After a period when Carter's orchestral pieces were either splendid epigrams (*Three Occasions*) or concertos, here at last is a return to the scale and the limitlessness on which his imagination most thrives. And *Partita* is only the beginning. Two more works—independent, but also joinable with *Partita* to form a triptych—are planned.

Carter's last big piece for big orchestra was his Bicentennial offering, *A Symphony of Three Orchestras*. Since then constraints on rehearsal schedules in the US have meant that, as he put it in Chicago, 'most of my works can't really be played now by American orchestras', and so perhaps there seemed no point in adding to the list. In the case of the new piece, there was the promise of adequate rehearsal time, made possible by an imaginative fund set up by Hope Abelson, and the result was a beautifully smooth-running first performance by Barenboim and the Chicago Symphony—smooth-running, that is, until all the lights went out a couple of minutes before the end—with spectacular work from flutes and clarinets in their respectively mellifluous and extravagant threads through the aerial tapestry. No doubt many more of the players will be able to enjoy themselves—and Carter's music is all about performers enjoying themselves in extremes of skill—once the piece is thoroughly played in through performances in May and next season. Maybe time is now swerving around, like a returning wave, to catch up with Carter before he hits his tenth decade. (*New Yorker*, 2 May 1994)

Adagio tenebroso

Elliott Carter is perhaps beginning to show certain physical signs of age, but signs that might be associated with a man entering his seventies rather than one who will soon be eighty-seven. 'People tell me I'm an old man, but I don't feel old.' Nor does he sound old: not in conversation, and not in how his music goes on behaving.

Both in his music and in his life he remains an optimist and a humorist. He tells the story of how last year, when he was working with Daniel Barenboim on the first performance of his *Partita*, Barenboim half-jokingly suggested he ought to write a comic opera next, and he half-jokingly said he would set Ionesco's *Bald Prima Donna*—if Barenboim could get him a commissioning fee of a million dollars. A little later, Barenboim came back from Europe to report success: Berlin would pay the required sum. 'They didn't like the subject, though. They thought an American opera ought to have an American libretto. What about if I were to set something by Woody Allen?'

Adagio tenebroso, his new work commissioned for tomorrow's Prom, is a big, bold score that follows on from the exuberant *Partita*, but turns to darker colours and generally slower speeds. 'There are many changes of character', he says. 'The piece begins *tranquillo* and becomes progressively more dramatic—and with greater use of silence—attending to many different feelings subsumed under a sombre view of life. *Partita*, had mostly woodwind solos; this work has mostly brass solos; and the last piece will have mostly string solos. It'll be a great gust of wind, with the orchestra flying around. . .if I can manage it.'

This flicker of self-doubt is not just an instance of Carter's gentlemanly modesty; it bears witness, rather, to his habit of creating at the limits of what is possible, for orchestras and for himself. 'I have to interest myself continuously', he says, in partial explanation of why his music has normally been so mercurial. 'And the uneven rhythms have to do with the time when I was a young man, when we admired crafts rather than machinery.'

In that connection, *Adagio tenebroso* is distinctly unusual for him, not so much in its slowness (for its slowness is still irregular and abruptly broken) as in its repetition, near the start, of a rising sixth that becomes for a while an idée fixe. 'One of the things that I've been concerned with has been the constant fluctuation of material, because it seemed to me to be a good idea. Now I don't know. Maybe I've avoided thematicism too much.' Yet he says this without any sense of real regret: the point is, rather, not to be bound by what one has achieved, but to retain the possibility of sparking off in a new direction, as the new piece does in approaching the thematic principle. And he remains as insistent as ever that there is no going back to nineteenth-century ways of thinking. 'One wants to catch the lived present and the presence of the present—which immediately eliminates the weepy side of Brahms.'

He is also disinclined to agree that the ubiquitous fifths of *Adagio tenebroso* suggest a rapprochement with his music of fifty or sixty years ago. 'All my past is my past: even those neoclassical pieces are still part of me. As for the fifths, there are a number of pieces that do this. There's a little piano piece by Carl Ruggles. And then that song of Ravel—a setting of Ronsard that has the piano just in fifths. Or the opening of Beethoven's Ninth: the sound there of the perfect fifth. Or Stravinsky's *Les Noces*. Also, fifths make a big orchestral effect.'

For him the new work belongs firmly with, in and of the present. 'In recent years I've gotten involved in a particular kind of harmonic system, a system I built up pragmatically. I found a hexachord that includes all the possible three-note chords, and all my works have been completely based on that since the first number of *A Mirror on Which to Dwell*. It's a matter of internal coherence. I begin with a large-scale rhythmic diagram, which is not evident and not really meant to be heard; it has three or four different levels of rhythmic activity tucked away.'

Whether this tussle of speeds and rhythms is meant to be heard or not, it surely contributes to the complexity of movement in Carter's music, and in particular to the absence of a single guiding line or voice. Like *Partita*, *Adagio tenebroso* was stimulated by Richard Crashaw's bubble's eye view of human existence in a poem which is in tune with both the high classicism and the mutability of his music. 'I imagined a kind of shadowy world in which things change. The bubble now is flying over the sadder parts of life. (Boosey & Hawkes are concerned that I don't call this my Bubble Symphony.) I read the poem, and I thought, well, it would be interesting to write a series of pieces that gave a picture of life. And I began to think of paintings, such as Chardin's boy blowing bubbles. The fragility of life as symbolized by the bubble. . .' He pauses for a moment, and then adds with a habitual twinkle: 'That's what an old man should be thinking about.' (*Times*, 12 September 1995)

da lontano

The marking appears quite often on musical scores: *da lontano*, 'from the distance'. But all distances now are near, with non-western music so readily available in western concert halls and record stores.

here and there

The South Bank/Radio Three festival of Asian and African music is proving immensely successful as well as revelatory, with large audiences to welcome music that is, after all, not so very alien. Hearing a Turkish ensemble play pieces from the Ottoman court is to recognize the Islamic strain in the monodic song of medieval Europe, while the north Indian singer Mohammed Sayeed Khan is clearly engaged in the same business as virtuosos of a more familiar sort, that of pushing a given form to the borders of technical possibility and artistic licence.

Sayeed, practising the art of *khyal*, or 'fantasy', offered an hour-long improvisation in the common slow-fast pattern of Indian musicians, choosing a rag from the court of Akbar, and recycling it with ever-changing embellishment, which his hands seemed to echo as they moved with the grace, linked independence and suddenness of a pair of fish. Extraordinary precise lip control produced a great variety of tone within the thin nasal colour that matched the sarangi playing of Asif Ali Khan, who shadowed his master exquisitely, and occasionally was rewarded with a solo break as, most deservedly, was the tabla player Latif Ahmed Khan. The climax of the performance came with the tabla bounding through intricate contortions of the twelve-beat formula.

The Turkish group appeared, by contrast, rather modestly equipped for their task. Two recorder-like instruments, a lute and a fiddle accompanied a duo of elderly gentlemen singers, all the musicians peering rather nervously at their notation, and conveying none of the charm and enjoyment so freely communicated by the royal musicians of Bangkok and by an ensemble from the western Chinese province of Xinjiang. Thai music is still essentially ceremonial and religious: the performance began with a drum blessing, involving the lighting of fragrant joss sticks, and featured slow chanting for voice or oboe with the accompainment of drums, gongs and finger cymbals, as well as faster music led by a pair of xylophones on boat-shaped frames of vermilion and gold. The elements of solo exhibitionism in the last of the group's selections seemed against the nature of the art—but then the programme reminds one that this was a work by the early twentieth-century musician Luang Pradit Pairoh 'generally considered to be the greatest Thai composer'.

Criteria for understanding the Uighur musicians of Xinjiang were perhaps easier to find. Disporting themselves in vibrant silks and velvets with metallic embroidery, they were the very image of a state folklore troupe. (*Times*, 14 July 1987)

'Turkish' and Turkish

One of the problems presented by Mozart's *Abduction from the Seraglio* is that the noblest character, Bassa Selim, never gets to sing. As a result, it can easily seem that music is able to serve only the weak: the four Europeans who, caught in the act of abduction, are shamed by Selim's benevolence and, beside them, the comically absurd slave Osmin. Selim is shown as the pattern of magnanimity, which was, from Mozart's point of view, one of the chief virtues in a ruler. Yet his realm is musically defined only by a caricature of Turkish military music: the insistent piccolo and quick crashing cymbals of the overture and of Osmin's numbers. While the libretto finds sagacity and enlightenment at home in the Orient, the music can discover nothing but strangeness and barbarism.

The current Salzburg Festival production offers a fascinating new perspective, wonderfully achieved. In the hands of a director from the Islamic world, François Abou Salem, the work gains not just a rich dramatic texture but also a deeper musical expression of the Levantine port and palace harem where the action takes place, for Abou Salem takes the bold step of adding to Mozart's score a pair of players on Turkish instruments. A drummer (Pierre Rigopoulos) joins in the opera's 'Turkish' music, disinfecting the crudity by concurring in it. And Kudsi Erguner, on the ney, a long end-blown flute, wanders through from time to time, quietly introducing a much more sophisticated voice from the musical East. His interventions are very beautiful and sensitive. The most important of them come before the start of the third act, whose music his contemplative solo seems to introduce, and in the finale, which is interrupted for a cadenza from him. The Europeans, having gained their liberty, sing of their joy and gratitude. Then the music stops on a dominant chord, and, as Erguner starts to play, attention shifts back to Selim. With two other figures, he starts to whirl and slowly to retreat into the back of the set, to the serenely exhilarating music of the ney and drum. Selim, after the adventure of the opera, is going back to a civilization that Mozart's music cannot comprehend but only stop and listen to. When Mozart's music picks up again, for the concluding chorus, the Europeans look as if they might have made a poor choice in turning their backs on Selim's world.

The dramatic realization of that world is full of life. Francine Gaspar's set is a world in itself, opening out to the back (through the arcade of the courtyard in the archbishop's palace, where performances take place), to the sides, where trellised embrasures can slide up or down to be windows or doorways, and to the underneath, through an elaborate system of traps. Drifting in and out of this world come servants, soldiers, children and ladies of the harem. The ladies are softly supportive of Konstanze, while the soldiers are dressed to suggest a modern Middle East, though the updating is no more insisted on than the crosscultural aspects. Marc Minkowski's conducting is generally quick, always colourful and highly musical: a consistent delight and revelation. Elzbieta Szmytka plays sympathetically against the generous but intense and alert Selim of Akram Tillawi. Paul Groves produces an appealing sound as Belmonte, and his ability to sustain a long note is astonishing. Malin Hartelius and Andreas Conrad are an effective pair as Blonde and Pedrillo, and Franz Hawlata is an excellent Osmin. This character at the end makes the right decision, wresting his eyes from Blonde to rush back to the entranced Selim. (*New York Times*, 31 August 1998)

yes and noh

In 1930, right after *Mahagonny* and *The Threepenny Opera*, Bertolt Brecht and Kurt Weill created a young people's show based on a noh play. At the Japan Society on Wednesday the two pieces were presented as a double bill: *Taniko* (The Valley Rite) performed by the Nohgaku-za of Tokyo and *Der Jasager* (The Consenter) in English by US singers.

Resemblances abound. Except for sententious choruses added by Brecht, religious references omitted by him and lengthy cuts made by his source, Arthur Waley, *Der Jasager* has virtually the same text as

Taniko. And Weill's music for the boy hero even recalls the chanting of the child noh actor, fixing on one note that is often approached by one or two upward steps. This cannot have been deliberate imitation, though, for all Brecht and Weill knew of their original was the script, which appealed to them as a lesson in how individuals should, for the good of the group, be ready to accept even death. The boy at the centre goes with others into the mountains, in the hopes of gaining help for his sick mother. He falls ill and is given a choice. Either he must agree to being hurled down into the valley so that the expedition can proceed unhindered or they will all have to go back. He agrees to the plunge.

In the noh play a god arrives to restore him to his companions. In the Brecht-Weill version, his death is the end, which is perfectly all right, because *Der Jasager* is one of Brecht's most absolute achievements in avoiding the audience's sympathy with the characters. What he and Weill offer instead is an austere moral lesson.

One may think this a poor exchange for the pathos, intensity, grace, wisdom and humanity of *Taniko*, which, in a highly stylized form, presents the situation starkly. In this performance, once the boy had made his decision, his supine body was lifted swiftly by two companions, who then ran with him to a little square platform that stood for the mountain ridge and put him down to be covered with a brown cloth by his teacher. All this took about ten seconds, used no emotion from the performers, and was frightening. The boy's covered body remained a scar on the stage. Divine intervention was desperately needed.

At the parallel place in *Der Jasager* the three students who carry the boy sing a march-lament and one could not care less. (*New York Times*, 11 April 2000)

sarod

Ustad Amjad Ali Khan's concert at Carnegie Hall on Tuesday evening was a marvellous demonstration of the art of the sarod, an instrument that three centuries of tradition in India have contrived to make sound rather like an electric guitar, at least when amplification is used, as here it inevitably was. Like the electric guitar, the sarod is capable of imitating all the subtlety of the human voice: it can be a stalwart baritone or a keening soprano. Again like the electric guitar, it can go way beyond the voice in terms of register and speed. The instruments are also similar in that both can produce a wide variety of colours and glissando effects, obtained by moving the fingers of one hand on the strings during the precious decay time after the other hand has done the plucking.

Khan's were the right hands to be doing these things. In the two ragas he performed in the first half, his playing in the early slow sections had sounds wafting in the air, beautifully tuned and often leaving delectable trails of glissando behind them. The note might skid up, down and back again all in half a second, everything achieved with perfect control and judgement.

Accompaniment in the fast metrical continuations came from two different percussion instruments. In the first raga Tanmoy Bose played the relatively familiar tabla, or small pair of drums, with exquisite gentleness and hands flickering on the skins. Khan agreeably allowed him his solo opportunities. But in the second raga his partnership with Fateh Singh Gangani on the less usual pakhawaj—a hollow log drum with a skin at each end—was more one of two travellers journeying together, or dancing together, the sound of the sarod folding into that of its sonorous companion.

In the second half, Khan was joined by his two sons, Amaan Ali Bangash and Ayaan Ali Bangash, both also playing the sarod as coming masters of at least the fifth generation. This was a chance to watch the handing down of skills from teacher to apprentice. Khan would play something and have one of the young men imitate him. If they seemed hesitant, he would repeat the difficult interval. But he was also obviously pleased when they took off on their own; the performance ended in a jam session, with both percussionists also involved in exciting and humorous dialogue. (*New York Times*, 25 May 2000)

Gubaidulina

One of the first Soviet composers to benefit from *glasnost*, Sofia Gubaidulina became known in the west in the mid-1980s, especially for her violin concerto *Offertorium* and her female-male dialogue *Perception*, for soprano, baritone and string septet.

Tanglewood

Sofia Gubaidulina is a small, trim woman in her mid-sixties with a wide bowl of black hair (the gift of her Tatar ancestors) and a candid smile she repeated after each of the five performances in Wednesday's Tanglewood concert entirely devoted to her. Her appearance accords with the simplicity of her music, which is not the simplicity of old modes, few notes and repetitive forms but rather that of creative spontaneity. It is as if, when she composes, she has nothing in her head but the idea of certain musicians in a room. What will they do? What will happen? The process of composition is a way of finding out.

Take the four flutes of her 1977 Quartet. They start to talk to each other, at first with single notes and pairs, and gentle music begins to unfold. But this is not it. They start again, exactly as before, and a different musical path is taken. Eventually, after other stops, we arrive at what seems to have been the point: a blinding shriek such as one had not expected these instruments capable of.

Music like this needs patience. You have to be prepared to follow its fanciful, probably rather uneventful course in order to be there when the shock comes. Flutes turn angry. The players of the Third String Quartet suddenly pick up their bows, after several minutes of quiet pizzicatos. Four timpanists, in the percussion septet *In the Beginning there was Rhythm*, thwack their instruments as loudly as possible and then turn the resonances into glissandos, like curling smoke, by means of the pedals.

Some works seem pure play. *Quattro* was one in this concert, a comedy of threats and alliances played out by two trombonists and two trumpeters, squaring up to each other like bristling animals in a cage. But elsewhere in Gubaidulina's music the games can imply much more, for it is in the nature of her simplicity that she can keep up high spirits when considering the spirit.

Some works, too, do not arrive at a moment of transformation but are intense all through, the example here being *Rubaiyat* for baritone and ensemble, well placed at the end of the concert. This setting of Persian poetry in Russian translation—quite without musical orientalism, for Gubaidulina in her frankness sees through codes and conventions—was strongly projected by a group of Tanglewood students under Reinbert de Leeuw, and the challenging solo part, covering the whole range of a countertenor's voice as well as a baritone's, was delivered by Brian Nickel with gripping authority and an excellent command of the language. A note in the programme suggested that the catalogue of personal griefs in the text could have had, in 1969, an autobiographical weight, since at that time Gubaidulina was battling official disapproval in the Soviet Union. But the work is more likely to have been meant as a portrait of the sorrowing Jesus, given a Persian disguise so as not to be recognized by the apparatchiks. (*New York Times*, 18 August 1997)

Second Quartet/String Trio

Sofia Gubaidulina is seventy this year, and eternally a child. At the Kosciuszko Foundation on Tuesday evening for the Lyric Chamber Music Society's tribute to her, she looked at once determined and vulnerable. Over her compact face, with eyes staring warily or piercingly or gleefully out of deep shadow, the Muscovite crown of her hair is still black. She smiles openly and easily, with a child's delight. When the musicians played Mozart, she sat back and listened, intently. When they performed her works, she leaned forward to watch, intently.

Her music is child's play: very simple, deeply engrossed, quite unselfconscious and rather remote from adult concerns. Speaking before the concert about her Second Quartet, she described how it represented earthly things in expressive playing, with full vibrato, and heaven in harmonics. Nothing could be simpler or more immediate. And it worked. The Moscow Quartet, performing strongly and with total conviction, had reached at least another planet by the time it got to the melody in harmonics at the close, having come from an earthbound unison.

The String Trio, written for this group, starts in a similar way—not with a seamless single note, though, but an abrupt chord passed to and fro. The effect is slightly funny: a quarrel in which three people are disagreeing by saying the same thing. Though humour is surely intended, there is no warm collusion with the audience here. Gubaidulina stays alone with the universe, conveying the divine foolishness that is part of the universe. She may be unaware of what her music means, being so absorbed in what it is.

Like the Second Quartet in its progress as well, the trio ends with the particularized ineffable: tragic slow, low melody in the cello under mechanical reiterations in the other instruments. In this performance it was another moment powerfully achieved. (*New York Times*, 13 April 2001)

a handful of pianists

Vladimir Horowitz

In all his long career Horowitz has probably never before had to play against competition from the Pope, but of course the Festival Hall was packed for the second of his Saturday tea-time recitals, and no doubt it would be so if he appeared every week in London, not just twice in a generation.

Surely his only reason for keeping himself scarce must be that more standing ovations would embarrass him, for at his recitals they are de rigueur. His showmanship demands a similarly spectacular response, and all is thoroughly justified by his confident ability to delight his audience in his unique manner. Where others play piano music he simply plays piano, and it seemed almost an irrelevance that here he was choosing sonatas by Scarlatti, some Chopin, some Liszt and two Rachmaninoff preludes, for what he was really performing was Horowitz.

An attempt to follow his performance of the Chopin F minor ballade in the score was foiled, for the notes on paper seemed quite alien and confusing behind the dazzling clarity and personality of the sounds. And though in this and other performances there were accidents that betrayed age, everywhere there was the special distinction of melody so vivid, alive and fundamental that it would be a discourtesy to call it song-like: rather this was a model that no singer could match.

Perhaps Horowitz's secret lies in how each note blooms after the attack, so that its weight is shifted into the resonance. But it is impossible to explain the subtler effects: the tentative fragility on the very edge of being awkward, the rampant power that never sounds forced or obliges the instrument to be less than beautiful, the layers of pearl screen and silk that Horowitz can draw and disclose to change and charm his sound, or the ironies that can steal in to reveal him not only as angel but as divine clown. (*Times*, 31 May 1982)

Sviatoslav Richter

Returning to London after an absence of nearly a decade, Sviatoslav Richter was welcomed back to the Festival Hall last night with flowers, ovations, maximum applause and maximum concentration. Very possibly absorption was helped by his idiosyncratic lighting: on a darkened stage, in the glare of a little lamp he himself operated, one saw only his hands kneading the keys and his head in profile, an object so high and massy there is as much of it above the line of his spectacle frames as below. The effect was at once business-like and intimate, private without being confessional. This was the quality too of Richter's musicianship. He does nothing for his audience: even the fiercely virtuoso Bartók encores were skimmed without any sense of show, and one had the impression that the entire recital could have happened in exactly the same way, encores included, if there had been not a soul in the hall but the pianist and his page-turner.

To say this, though, is to risk a merely sentimental image of the 'serious' musician. In his seriousness Richter lives dangerously, taking immense risks in terms of dynamic contrast, of quasi-orchestral display (the first of Schumann's *Nachtstücke*), of deep senority in a tidal rush (the third of the same set), and especially of phrasing, so that the pattern never seems quite set until it is complete (an exception here was the trio in Schubert's G major sonata, where there was the relief of fixed form and supreme polish in an area somewhere near a Tchaikovsky waltz).

The Schubert performance, with full repeats and totally unhurried tempos, dominated the recital not merely by its length. Richter's apparent openness to the moment proved to have long-term justification in, for example, the way the opening sequence—at first utterly quiet and cold, like something long unused—gained in colour and clarity in the exposition's repeat and then further in the recapitulation, or in how the ambling tempos of the first three movements were complemented by the finale, bright and splashy like a mountain stream, yet still oppressed, like a stream compelled to run in circuit. All that tarnished the brilliance and precision of ornaments in this movement was the clattery upper treble of the Yamaha instrument, which was better tuned to the combination of edge and commanding power Richter brought to Prokofiev's Fourth Sonata. (*Times*, 21 March 1989)

◆

For his second big public recital here, in the Barbican Hall, Richter had announced a tantalizing programme of music from the first half of the century, ranging from Szymanowski to Webern by way of Bartók and Hindemith. These rare treats were, though, reserved in the event for a private audience at the National Gallery, and what we heard last night was an altogether more ordinary sequence of Mozart sonatas and Chopin études.

But of course it was not ordinary in the playing. As in his Festival Hall recital, Richter took advantage of full repeats in the Mozart (even including the reptition of the second halves of sonata allegros) to explore different possibilities in the same music, an improvisatory fantasy prising nuances out of his studied calm. Right at the start, the opening of the E flat sonata K.282 was an easing, a settling into the evening first time round; then it returned with firmer rhythm and substance. On the other hand, the beginning of the A minor sonata K.310 came initially with sharp, stinging attacks, which were progressively modified at each return. The other sonata, the 'easy' C major K.545, showed in its fast movement Richter's ability to make the blithest melody seem earnest, important, totally unsentimental, and yet graceful. He is a musician who refuses to charm, and who seems detached from his power to amaze, exerted here in fast readings of all the finales. It is almost as if he were simply watching his hands at work, flickering over the keys as separate creatures.

This was very much the impression in the Chopin studies, several of which were taken at bewildering speed, with an effect of hectic urgency (the C sharp minor from Op.10) or skimming weightlessness (the D flat from Op.25). Chopin's melody (notably of course in the big tune of the E major) was as restless as Mozart's, and the assaults of the 'Revolutionary' or the A minor from Op.25 were intense, granitic. The latter work brought roaring applause that took fully five minutes to dwindle as realization dawned that Richter so suddenly, without giving an encore, was gone. (*Times*, 30 March 1989)

Maurizio Pollini

The formidable programme was characteristic—two Himalayan peaks of the piano literature, Boulez's Second Sonata and Beethoven's Diabelli Variations, with the Alp of Webern's Variations as a warm-up—but Pollini was unusually gentle in the first half of this Festival Hall programme, which gave his Boulez performance, in particular, a fascinating new light and clarity. The violent interjections of the first and last movements had been drained of the rampaging human voice they gain in most performances, and had instead an unnervingly precise mechanical identity, while in the slower music Pollini showed what an artist of colour and resonance, and indeed harmony, Boulez was in the late 1940s. Another lesson of this performance was the central importance of tempo, which in Boulez defines shape and direction, and which needs therefore to be fluid yet always under control. Pollini made the work a symphony of tempos, sometimes so that one felt the speed and movement to be primary, the actual notes almost an arbitrary in-fill to support a musical energy that had its own existence. Equally remarkable was the stone-dead coldness of episodes where the tempo is slow and unchanging, notably the beginning of the second movement and the very end of the work, both echoing the closing bars of the Webern.

In the Beethoven Pollini was in more typical form, especially in the acute force of his high trills (often with the effort towards them expressed in a lunging groan), the solid bass lines, the absolutely clear counterpoint, and the astonishing high speeds, right to the point of danger in the first presto variation. One effect was to emphasize how so many of the variations are variations on a small motif as well as on the Diabelli waltz: a bridge was thus thrown across to Webern, especially in the mirror patterns of the eighteenth variation. But Pollini's penetrating, unillusioned view also suggested a strong element of parody and despair in almost everything: even the slow movement before the fugue seemed a coldly imagined imitation and disparagement of the new bel canto. (*Times*, 26 October 1990)

◆

Pollini has denied that his performance of a work will or should be influenced by its context in a programme, but the Debussy Etudes in the first half of his concert at Carnegie Hall on Monday night seemed to be looking forward in terms of density and sheer speed to the work that was to come after intermission: Boulez's Second Sonata. True, Pollini's Debussy is always dynamic. There will be colour in abundance, but first is action. Here, though, each of the Etudes was set to an intensive pulse, keeping movement alive—with extraordinary virtuosity and control—through undulations of tempo. With the most disembodied pieces, like the study in fourths, Pollini was reluctant to linger and open up. The virtues of his performance were the virtues of strength, as exemplified by the equality of his hands in the study in sixths or the deep, full, but crisp-edged sounds of the study in chords at the end.

Boulez's sonata gained a lot from similar agility and sturdy force. Lacking both tonal harmony and recurrent themes, this is a sonata that is, as it were, mimed. The words are missing, but the message gets across by means of contrasting textures, intensities, speeds, styles of presentation. In the finale, even the appearance of a fugue is maintained.

The achievement has often been seen, not least by Boulez himself, as creation by destruction: a wild and brilliant young man's rebuttal of standard ways of doing things. Pollini's approach, though—in a performance played most impressively from memory—was much more positive. The drive was consistent. Passages of polyphony, mounting in energy and wonder till near the end of the finale, were made to sound orderly, if bewildering at the same time. There was no harshness, but rather strength. Long chordal sequences were musical boulders, and the big four-attack shape in the first movement was more majestic than violent. Projecting the music principally from the bass-baritone register (sometimes with vocal support), Pollini made it urgent and robust, not inflicting indignities on Beethoven but shouldering into his company.

Having completed his journey, Pollini was able to return to Debussy with seemingly more tolerance for sensuous magic. The three preludes he gave as encores showed a resolute determination (*Des Pas sur la neige*), a tempest of storming fingers and snapped rhythms (*Ce qu'a vu le vent de l'ouest*) and magnificent, glowing resonances arising slightly after the hammer strokes (*La Cathédrale engloutie*). (*New York Times*, 25 March 2000)

Murray Perahia

Murray Perahia began his recital at Avery Fisher Hall on Sunday afternoon with a group of Bach chorale preludes as transcribed by Busoni. *Nun komm, der Heiden Heiland* was a gem of counterpoint in which the voices were equally clear, equally melodious and equally distinct in colour. There was a beautifully soft bass line—a special characteristic of Perahia's, freely and wonderfully used throughout the recital—and a firm sounding of the chorale tune. In *Nun freut euch, lieben Christen*, the rushing right hand was all joy. In *Ich ruf' zu Dir, Herr Jesu Christ*, what mattered was the slow melody, and the want that it created for a much larger musical span.

That want was duly satisfied—and how—by the Goldberg Variations. Perahia not only obliged his piano to sing the opening Aria, he had it sing in three subtly different voices one after the other, voices arising from the different registers of the melody and all concurring in phrasing and feeling. Singing tone remained of paramount importance—not just singing melody but also, as in the chorale preludes, singing polyphony. Sometimes the song in a movement would not finish until the last few notes of the final harmony had been sung into place, giving musical life to a gesture which could seem merely functional, a matter of routine. In Perahia's view, nothing in the piece is routine.

But song is not the whole story. He responded to Bach's humour, especially in movements where some bumptious little figure goes leap-frogging down the octaves. The gigue-style variation provided an example, with laughter in the running figuration, and the comedy was given a reprise in the next movement. As the performance went on, so the connections began to broaden and deepen, and what had opened as a suite of character variations started to come into view as one whole body of music. After the Adagio—where the climax in the second half was prepared and executed with a purely musical poignancy, acutely to the point—all the variations seemed to flow on from one another, the relationships of motif and harmony effortlessly revealing themselves, the lines singing still and now also gambolling. The last variation, the Quodlibet, was part of this flow of song, humour and athleticism, and at the same time it referred back to the comic pomposity of the French overture at the start of the work's second half.

After this, the repeat of the Aria came just as it should. Simplicity was being recovered, but it was both the same and not the same. The notes were, yes, identical to those that had been heard an hour before. But what one might hazily have recognized as implications in that first playing were now returning as full, solid memories, Bach's memories and, installed with Bach's, Perahia's: memories not to be forgotten. (*New York Times*, 24 October 2000)

Kathleen Supové

Sometimes the difference between downtown music and uptown music is all in a foot or two of skirt length. For example, the programme that the pianist Kathleen Supové gave at the Flea Theater in TriBeCa on Tuesday evening, built around big ostinato pieces by Frederic Rzewski, John Adams and Alvin Curran, could easily have been played by, say, Ursula Oppens at Weill Hall. Oppens, though, would probably not have performed it in fishnet stockings and a hand's breadth of leopard-skin print below tuxedo jacket and evening shirt. On Supové, this costume was appropriate, she being half concert artist, half nightclub hostess. She presents herself with boldness and swagger, but her effrontery seems, like most people's, to conceal a kind of naivety, which comes out both in the rawness of her playing and in the small, unselfconscious charm of her spoken interventions. Among the latter, in her Flea concert, were a fantasy about meeting Tina Turner and Rzewski in a music store, a Chinese fable and a rant against tunes one cannot get out of one's head (as if there were nothing in the world more important to protest about).

Supové's musical performances were, in a similar way, brave and to a degree misdirected. Her generally loud playing allowed little possibility of nuance, and she would often go for an extreme of speed, putting her energy out of focus. Adams's *Phrygian Gates*, which in other hands can ripple out in widening circles of blissful harmony, was here rampageous, chugging and fuming from moment to moment. Supové was pushing the car when she could have got into the driving seat. Her style was better suited to Rzewski's *Winnsboro Cotton Mill Blues*, whereas the humour of Aaron Jay Kernis's *Superstar Etude* No.1 she missed. Kernis writes for the ironic virtuoso. Part of Supové's value is that she is absolutely in earnest and up front.

On this occasion her most intriguing venture was Randall Woolf's mysteriously titled *Adrenaline Revival*, in which each note sparked off an electronic sound, recreating the effect of Cage's prepared piano without the need to litter the piano's strings with bolts and bits of rubber. The piece was simple in design: a chain of dance-like sequences, each within a restricted register. Its poetry was in its deft electric janglings and echoes. (*New York Times*, 24 September 1999)

Postcript: the Van Cliburn Competition

The eighth Van Cliburn International Piano Competition behaved as such competitions should. It generated dissension within the jury, especially concerning the Korean pianist Ju Hee Suh, very publicly supported by John Lill and others against the majority decision of their fellow jurors. It produced an audience favourite in the English entrant Andrew Wilde, who made the finals last time but here was eliminated at an early stage, only to find an ad hoc movement enthusiastically championing him on to a New York debut in the near future. And of course it encouraged all the usual discussions about the purpose and morality of competitive music-making. At the final ceremony, Van Cliburn himself asked that we should think of the event not as a contest but rather as a festival of pianism. That could only be a pious wish: the audience had come to cheer a conqueror, to preside at the Olympics of the piano, to watch the birth of a star. Under those circumstances, a sensitive jury will select not the 'best' musician (in any case an idea whose grotesqueness needs no emphasizing) but the one who will best cope with the sudden elevation, the interviews, the recordings, the string of more than a hundred international concert engagements within a year, and the jet-lag.

The choice of the Tashkent-born Alexei Sultanov, though at nineteen he was the youngest of the six finalists, looks judicious. Sultanov is a young man of exceptional dynamism and strength of will, massively in control of a formidable technique, seizing the piano in his grip and using it to reshape whatever music lies in his way. In the final round, for which two concertos were required, he powered a path through the Chopin F minor and the Rachmaninoff No.2, ignoring all opportunities for interest, giving a ruthless competition display of big tone and high speed. His victory lap through Chopin's *Grande valse brillante* was taken about fifty-per-cent too fast and brought the house down. There is quite definitely no danger of this boy being spoiled by the attention and the engagements that will now be his.

The silver-medal winner, the Brazilian José Carlos Cocarelli, was a less obvious choice, except as the safe middle-ranker any jury of fifteen is likely to come up with. He is a fluent player, but inclined to urge and strive and press the point beyond what he delivers: his Chopin F minor Concerto would have been better for not being so insistently dramatized, and in the Brahms D minor he was just out of his musical depth. It is, of course, an absurdity for anyone to have to play these two concertos in a single evening.

Benedetto Lupo, coming from Bari to take the bronze medal, was the highest-placed performer with an evident musical mind. Having a strong left hand and an individual sense of phrasing and movement, he seemed always on the point of mature interpretations of his concertos (his choice was the same as Sultanov's), but he was let down by frequent slips. So was Elisso Bolkvadze, whose pure dexterity in high treble runs, was a pleasure in the second Saint-Saëns concerto, as much as her Brahmsian spread of tone in her Mozart concerto was a curious surprise. Here too, is a musician in the making.

The other finalists were Alexander Shtarkman and Tian Ying. The former gave clipped, strict-rhythmed performances of his concertos, his manner suiting Prokofiev No.3 rather better than Mozart, but his display piece on the final evening, the Bach-Busoni G minor Prelude, suggested a much more acute, quiet, searching musical intelligence:

here was proof that catching a competition in its last stages is like joining a meal for the port and nuts.

Ying's Chopin—yet again the F minor Concerto—was the most fascinating experience of the finals, and predictably earned him fifth place. His quality of sound is intensely imaginative, achieved and beautiful, with the capacity for largeness and fullness, and he showed in his phrasing a courtesy towards the music, inviting it rather than applying force, that was rare. This is an undemonstrative and unpretentious musician, a young man who perhaps needs a competition to bring him notice, but who has nothing to do with the piano as sports equipment: his Beethoven Fourth Concerto was also full of wonderful ideas. It is to the credit of the Van Cliburn that such a one was advanced to the finals, even if talents of a different kind inevitably took the medals. (*Times*, 23 June 1989)

Purcell 1995

The tercentenary of Purcell's death, coming as the 'early music' movement reached its peak, was celebrated in triumphant style, onstage and in print.

the forgèd feature

Now more than ever we are listening for what Gerard Manley Hopkins found—or, rather, for what famously found him.

> It is the forgèd feature finds me; it is the rehearsal
> Of own, of abrupt self there so thrusts on, so throngs the ear.

'So that'—to continue the poem in the poet's gloss—'while he [Purcell] is aiming only at impressing me his hearer with the meaning in hand I am looking out meanwhile for his specific, his individual markings and mottlings, "the sakes of him".'

We might think we are better placed to find these 'markings and mottlings', these 'sakes of him', now that Purcell's music is vastly more available than it was to a young priest in Oxford in April 1879, when the Purcell Society had only just set out on a complete edition, and when the 'forgèd feature' cannot have been finding anyone from out of its ensconcement in much more than those relatively few anthems, sonatas and songs that had been in regular performance since the composer's death. What 'throngs the ear' in this tercentenary year includes the overtures, songs and act tunes he wrote in abundance for the London stage in the 1690s, the two dozen ceremonial odes he produced for royal birthdays and other celebrations, odd keyboard pieces recently rediscovered, new formats for music we thought we knew (such as the compositions for the funeral of Mary II), the whole wild miscellany of anthems and songs, and even the semi-operas, which were for so long either despised or regretted. An anniversary has forced us to pay attention to these strange and perhaps unwelcome signals from the past: to *King Arthur* at Covent Garden, to *The Fairy Queen* at the London Coliseum. But more than an anniversary—a rolling enthusiasm for musical resurrection that surely has deeper springs than in record-company accountancy—has been responsible for restoring works, such as some of the odes, which had perhaps almost never been performed during the two centuries before Robert King began his complete set of recordings in the 1980s. 'Would that I had Purcell's music here': so Hopkins concluded to Bridges his remarks on the sonnet. He should have been born in the age of the compact disc.

Whether he would then have had Purcell's 'abrupt self' finding him is another matter. That word 'abrupt' might suggest that what was impressing itself on him was Purcell's quirkiness from the viewpoint (or hearpoint) of one for whom Bach and Handel represented a norm. As his contemporary Hubert Parry put it: Purcell's 'circumstances put him completely out of touch with the choral methods of the great period; and the standards and models for the new style, and the examples of what could and what could not be done, were so deficient that his judgement went constantly astray.' Now, of course, we know better—or at least we have come to rather like music which goes 'constantly astray' by established standards—though we must wonder whether we also hear better. Understood against the background of subsequent Baroque practice—a background which the music of the late seventeenth century, however anachronistically, conjures up for us by its similarities of tonality, texture and genre—Purcell's momentary dissonances, especially in earlier works, can be intensely grating, and if we recoil from Parry's explanation that the poor composer needed only exposure to some thorough Germans and a decent textbook, we may yet find our ears jumping to their own unwarranted conclusions in interpreting the harmonic spice as expressive of intense feeling, and perhaps thereby of 'abrupt self'.

Take the introduction to the anthem *Behold now, praise the Lord*, a work Purcell wrote at around the age of twenty for the Chapel Royal of Charles II. For Robert King, in his biography of the composer: 'The opening of the string symphony is ravishing in its daring harmonic and melodic lines, highly attractive in its desolate beauty.' This is fine as a description of the effect the music has on us if we hear it with ears trained by later and more orderly harmony, but if we try to temper our response with some historical consciousness, we may find that what first sounded 'daring' is reversion. Jack Westrup, in a pioneer study reprinted nearly sixty years after its first appearance, finds in this same piece that 'the old harmonic traditions still linger, giving to the music what seems to the modern listener a pleasant suggestion of antiquity'. More recent authors—profiting from, as well as contributing to, the great boom in Purcell scholarship during the last fifteen years—are able to go further. According to Martin Adams, in *Henry Purcell: The Origins and Development of his Musical Style*, this early anthem 'seems indebted to the sinuous chromatic lines of Locke and. . .proudly displays its contrapuntal virtuosity'. Peter Holman, in his monograph on the composer, agrees about the Locke connection, and adds the suggestion that the particular dissonances ('six 6–4–2 chords in the first section') suggest Purcell was acquainted with some overtures by Lully. We are now some way from King: 'desolate beauty' has become antiquarianism, imitation and proud display.

Two points emerge from this. One is that precisely when Purcell sounds most individual—most wayward, most shocking, indeed most abrupt—he may in fact be depending on his predecessors (on Matthew Locke, on Lully and on English traditions of choral and consort music reaching back more than a century to Tallis and Taverner) and may also be, in that dependence, sharing elements of style with his contemporaries, such as John Blow and Pelham Humfrey. The second is that his music's ostensibly extreme emotion can be differently understood.

A striking instance of Purcell's seeming modernism comes at the end of his second three-part fantasia, whose cadence, left open in the manuscript, was fulfilled two hundred years later by *Parsifal*. But of course artists well separated in time can arrive at similar results for quite diverse reasons—one in this case tugging against the growing force of the new major-minor harmony, the other pulling away from its diminishing grasp—and it is hard to imagine that Purcell, even in what appear to have been unusually private compositions, was dealing with spiritual grief of a Wagnerian order. This is not to say that his language of emotional reference was fundamentally different. We lack a theory of musical meaning from this period, but in another sense we have the most complete possible dictionary of music's affects in the corpus of Purcell's settings of English words. We know quite specifically what sort of music he felt to be joyful or prayerful, lamenting or refusing, commanding or inviting, anguished or perplexed, stormy or calm, and his vocabulary does not surprise us. He is not singing some alien language. On the contrary, it is the exactness and resolve of his word setting that has always excited the keenest admiration, and been taken as a model by composers from Handel down to George Benjamin. However, there are many ways in which the same expressive motif—say, dolefulness—can be presented by a composer and interpreted by a listener, and the resulting manifoldness of musical expression is perhaps what Hopkins had in mind when he distinguished between the 'meaning in hand' and the 'individual markings and mottlings'.

To be ravished, as King is, by the 'desolate beauty' of the symphony before *Behold now, praise the Lord* is perhaps to stand in lonely isolation with the music, all awareness of paradigms, prototypes and progeny swept away. To think of the transition into the last scene of *Parsifal* at the end of the three-part fantasia in F is to indulge in a historical false relation. Such delights and correspondences may contribute to our musical experience, but they cannot be means by which the forgèd feature finds us, if find us it will. Adams's diagnosis of Purcell's harmonic venturesomeness as display—as the accumulation of dissonances and modulations, so that figments of fright and mourning come to make up a brave parade—is much nearer the heart of the matter, and other writers, notably Jonathan Keates, support Adams in defining Purcell's art as selfconscious. But if selfconsciousness and display were all (as emphatically for Adams they are not), we should have to admire Humfrey as much as Purcell, and Locke more.

This is an option we would perhaps rather avoid. There are, to be sure, pieces by Purcell that are as short-winded as Humfrey's, as plain as Blow's and as uncontrolled as Locke's. It is quite clear, too, that Purcell learned a lot from all these elder masters. But it is equally clear how far he differed from them—how far he (for let us not in Purcell Year be mealy mouthed) exceeded them. Those he left behind in 1695 were aware of this: Dryden expressed it in his beautiful elegy, which is beautiful partly because its rhetoric rings with the charm of knowledge and the knowledge of loss. Andrew Pinnock, in *The Purcell Companion*, is right to warn us that we might be maintaining Purcell's pre-eminence 'in ignorance of much of the best music by composers he himself admired', but in the same volume Bruce Wood shows how, time and again in the odes, what Purcell took from Blow he improved. No doubt Purcell's contemporaries have been standing too long in his shade: most of Wood's samples of Blow come from unpublished works, and Adams, who also quotes much from the older composer, whets our curiosity by taking a more sanguine view of Blow's relationship with Purcell as 'mutually beneficial in the same sort of way as the much more famous one between Haydn and Mozart'. But the Blow revival, when it comes, looks likely to enhance rather than diminish our admiration for Purcell.

If we want to come closer to the composer by finding a ground for that admiration in some acquaintance with the man, we may be unlucky. The documents that survive, other than musical prints and autographs, are terribly few: one letter, one will, a few definitions of terms, probably a couple of pages about counterpoint and keyboard playing, probably not the preface to the *Sonnata's of III Parts*, which is so much more polished, and certainly not the preface to the other major work published during the composer's lifetime, *Dioclesian*, for which Dryden lent his services. (All these texts—together with many other contemporary and later writings impinging on Purcell and his music, including those quoted above from Parry and Hopkins—are included in *Purcell Remembered*, edited, like the *Purcell Companion*, by Michael Burden.) Reliable references to the composer in other records are also sparse, and often characterless. As Westrup put it at the start of his book: 'A life of Henry Purcell is of necessity a slender record.' Newer research has not made it very much fatter. The kind of thing we now know, and that Westrup did not, is that when Purcell was fourteen or fifteen he authorized the supply of two new violins for the Chapel Royal.

That detail is included by King, who generally is more zealous than the composer's other three recent biographers—Jonathan Keates, Maureen Duffy and Margaret Campbell—in tracing through Andrew Ashbee's *Records of English Court Music*. However, the essential facts remain scant, and the twenty-two pages on the life that make up Peter Holman's first chapter, in a book otherwise devoted to the works, are enough to contain pretty much all that is known. The biographers therefore have to find other things. Campbell, in her admirably straightforward book, fills in the framework of British political, courtly and theatrical life most thoroughly, and when she comes to the music modestly defers to other Purcellians, especially Curtis Price, from whom she quotes frequently.

Keates covers similar ground in a much more swashbuckling manner: his book, of all those under review, is certainly the most enjoyable read. Almost every page has some ripe anecdote, or else some juicy passage of commentary on this work or that, for, unlike Campbell, he plunges boldly into musical (and literary) criticism under his own ensign. Those seeking a view on the court ode, on seventeenth-century Anglican spirituality, on the comedies of Shadwell, or on the difference between Purcell's trio sonatas and those of 'composers like Telemann, Quantz and Fasch' will find themselves amply supplied. Keates is vigorous, entertaining, flamboyant, proud: in a word, Purcellian, if at the expense of becoming himself, more than his cherished composer, the book's subject. There is something splendid about how his guesses turn into certainties, and about his sublime disregard of irritating facts. Nicholas Staggins is suddenly lambasted as 'a totally undistinguished figure whose indestructibility as a talentless official *apparatchik* makes him a late seventeenth-century equivalent of the egregious Tikhon Khrennikov', when we know almost nothing of Staggins's music, and less of the poor fellow's personality.

King and Duffy are both closer to the evidence, though in different ways. King's book profits, as already suggested, from his conscientious relaying of references in the court annals and also from his intimacy with the music, even if that intimacy is sometimes rather swooning. He talks about more pieces than do any of the other biographers (though Keates runs him close); the one curiosity here is that he should have so little to say about the instrumental music. What puts his book into a category of its own is the lavishness of its illustrations, which feature manuscript and printed music, title pages, portraits, maps and scenes from Purcell's London.

Duffy is also a digger in the archives, but she characteristically ploughs her own furrow, and comes up with a good deal of new information about Purcell's non-musical brothers (Charles and Joseph, both navy men, and Edward, a soldier) and about his wife's family. She also has a nice anecdote—missing from Keates's festooned collection—concerning an encounter between Charles Seymour, Duke of Somerset, the dedicatee of *Dioclesian*, and a farmer instructed to make himself scarce because the duke's carriage was coming along the lane: 'But the farmer refused to stand aside, saying, "I will look on him and so shall my pig", and he held the animal up by the ears until the coach had passed'.

Also, what is more germane to the composer, Duffy shows tact and understanding in her consideration of the few events in his life we know about, or are almost certain we know about. One of the most significant of those events must have been the death of his father (or of the man who is by far the most probable candidate for that responsibility: Westrup supported the alternative claims of Thomas Purcell, now generally regarded as the composer's uncle and later protector) when he was four or five years old (the precise date of his birth being one of the many facts we do not know). Keates declines to speculate on what effect this might have had on the boy; King becomes a bit modern ('traumatized') and soppy ('The wistfulness that is so prevalent in Purcell's music could therefore be seen as the manifestation of a little boy crying for his lost father'). Campbell suggests 'he would have suffered not only the grief of losing a parent, but probably missed hearing the sound of music about the house'; but Duffy carries this further. The family's subsequent move away from the court singers' quarters 'must have seemed like a kind of exile from music itself'. She also invites us to see the composer's 'commendable ambition of exceeding every one of his time', to quote from the recollections of Thomas Tudway, who could well have been a fellow chorister with him in the Chapel Royal, as rooted in 'his position as Henry Purcell II, son of a revered and lost father whom he should, and would, try to excel.' This fits, and adds a colour to our sense of Purcell's showiness.

The biographers also demonstrate their different priorities, sympathies and limitations in considering the works, as one finds in going to them for enlightenment about, for example, the 1692 birthday ode for Queen Mary, *Love's goddess sure was blind*. Everybody repeats the old story—one of the handful of tales from the composer's life—that Purcell included a folk tune, 'Cold and Raw', in the bass of the ode's soprano air because Mary had once asked for this song in preference to his own, though Duffy and King rightly show some caution in interpreting this bit of hearsay not written down until nearly a century later. They and Keates (Campbell offers no musical commentary here) also agree about the excellence of the ground-bass duet 'Many, many such days may she behold', draw attention to the pair of recorders accompanying the earlier duet 'Sweetness of nature', and remark on how the ode ends with a 'meditative quartet' (Duffy), a 'pathos-laden quartet' (King), a quartet where 'soloists move meltingly into the minor, among heart-stabbing dissonances' (Keates).

If we turn now to the musicologists, we are in for some surprises. 'Sweetness of nature' has violins, not recorders, in tow, and needs to be considered alongside Italian songs from a volume published in London some years before (Holman); the 'Cold and Raw' song is for countertenor, not soprano (Wood); and the final quartet bears comparison not with the ending of *Dido and Aeneas*, as Keates and Westrup propose, but with 'the early funeral sentence *In the Midst of Life* and with Fantasia No.7' (Adams). One problem for the biographers is the sheer pace of Purcell research: the corrected edition of *Love's goddess* appeared just last year, and the atlas of connections, within the composer's output and between his works and those of others, is only beginning to be drawn. Another problem is that impressions of affective meaning, as concerning the *Love's goddess* finale, are rendered unnecessary by the ready availability of recordings (by King and by David Munrow)—and especially unnecessary when they fail to address the textual deficiencies of those recordings. Even were the impressions less redundant and better informed, they would have to be tempered by our estimate of Purcell's selfconsciousness (Keates, aware of this in the composer, does not let it stop him telling us what we should be feeling, and on occasion what Purcell at the time was feeling) and backed by something more than the authors' implicit assertion of their own cultivation and sensitivity.

The great value of Adams's book lies in this, that it takes the trouble (and requires from us the effort) to ponder questions of how expressive purposes are served by notes. On the close of *Love's goddess*, he agrees with his biographical colleagues about the music's emotion, saying how 'a remarkable lamenting verse' goes into a chorus 'shot through with the sorrow of those left on earth after the Queen's death'. But this judgement is supported by analysis. In the short version (his book, oddly but usefully, presents its findings first in simple form, without the Roman numerals, diagrams and other arcana of harmonic analysis that are later introduced), he explains how the quartet's relationship with the two earlier works he mentions is based on 'distinctive sonorities in common, produced by motivic concentration within an intensely line-driven texture', and then indicates how it goes beyond its precedents, in that 'harmonic tension has a much more prominent long-term role, deeply dependent on local repetition to articulate harmonic prolongation and specific-pitch connection'.

Here one might want to pause to consider how different such language is from Purcell's own—'Composing upon a *Ground*. . .[is] generally used in *Chacones*, where they regard only good Air in the *Treble*, and often the *Ground* is four Notes gradually descending'—and to wonder what musicological discourse will be sounding like after another three hundred years. Adams is, of course, writing for a professional audience, not for the general reader so well served by Holman, who provides not only as full a biography as can be written, but also a biography responsive to the period. From his knowledge of mid-seventeenth-century teaching materials, for example, he draws conclusions concerning not just how Purcell was instructed but how his apprenticeship would have marked enduring aspects of style (modal melody in conflict with diatonic harmony) and how the condition of music at the time was like the condition of the natural sciences (scholastic authority in conflict with rationalization from experience). This is highly stimulating, and prompts the wish for a book on Purcell which would set him in his intellectual climate, for he surely had more in common with such contemporaries as Isaac Newton, Christopher Wren, Robert Boyle and John Locke than he had with the mistresses of Charles II blowzing in the pages of the biographies. Can we hear, as the king in the Chapel Royal stamps his foot in time with Purcell's Frenchified anthems, the sound of Locke reading Descartes? Can we see, in the sonatas' 'just imitation of the most fam'd Italian Masters', the outline of St. Paul's?

Holman further provides essential information, missing elsewhere, about how Purcell's music was performed: the dimensions, layout and liturgy of the Chapel Royal, the evidence for dancing in the odes. His chapters on the music, considered genre by genre, are also clear, bang up-to-date and full of insight. And he includes the best bibliography. *The Purcell Companion*, to which he contributes on the consort music, is also thoroughly worthwhile. Besides Wood's essay on the odes and Pinnock's on 'The Purcell Phenomenon' it includes the editor's introduction to Purcell's fellow musicians, both composers and singers, Roger Savage's typically witty and erudite survey of the theatre music, and Andrew Parrott's piece on 'Performing Purcell', which thoroughly marshals the forces of learning (233 footnotes in forty-eight pages) to support controversial positions. Of the biographies, Duffy's has the most pregnant things to say, for all that it sometimes skims through the music and has strange locutions ('Pelham Humphreys', perhaps in solidarity with Pepys).

'Purcell', she says, 'remains supremely the musical exponent of desire', and one thinks of an exponent in arithmetic, raising something to a higher power. In this conclusion she is at one with Adams, whose project is to show how Purcell's music accommodates a jostling of many pasts—many English pasts, the 'fam'd Italian Masters', Lully—to create a new present, whose individuality is secured precisely by the accommodation and the jostling: the accommodation of long-range harmonic planning, the jostling of detail that flows with or frustrates the plan. Ends are sighted, and kept in sight, though events may run counter to them. 'The uneasiness a man finds in himself upon the absence of anything whose present enjoyment [would carry] the idea of delight with it', writes Locke (John, to be sure), 'is that we call *desire*.' This is the sound of the forgèd feature. (*Times Literary Supplement*, 15 September 1995)

King Arthur

After a couple of minutes of music—a short overture followed by an orchestral air—the stage is taken by actors, and then almost half an hour passes before anything is sung. This is semi-opera. In modern times *King Arthur*, the most prestigious example of the genre in having Dryden's words and Purcell's music, has always been adapted, either by condensing the long passages of dialogue into narration, or by largely replacing them with songs from elswhere in Purcell's copious output, as Colin Graham did in his English Music Theatre production of 1971. Dryden's text, everyone has said, could never again hold the stage; besides which, we expect the characters in opera to sing, whereas in *King Arthur*, as it was conceived, the main ones never do. However, during the years since the Graham version, and in company with the early-music revival, opinion has been growing that semi-opera would have to be presented with the full intended resources of actors, dancers and musicians, and at full, Wagnerian length—though it has taken the circumstances of a tercentenary, and of a generously funded French ensemble, to let that happen.

When the wait has been so long—three hundred and four years since the first production, and perhaps hardly less since the last that preserved anything like the original form—the simple presence of the piece in the theatre, happening here and now, was almost satisfaction enough. When the effect was so excellent—thanks to the musical ease and pleasure of Les Arts Florissants under William Christie, to the brilliant stagecraft of Graham Vick and his designer Paul Brown, and to the experience gained by everyone through a run of performances in France before the three at Covent Garden—satisfaction turned to triumph. Christie's lightness on first beats and his generally slow tempos gave us often a gentled Purcell: hardier rhythms are possible, but probably not if the music is to show such a combination of sophistication and sensuous relish in its colouring, in everything from the splash of theorbos and the rusticity of oboes and flutes to the icicles of detached, non vibrato string chords in the Frost Scene. The singers, including many regular members of Christie's troupe, were also at once fresh and elegant. Claron McFadden and Sandrine Piau were a luscious pair of river sirens, calling to Arthur to:

> Come bathe with us an hour or two
> Come naked in for we are so

— as indeed they were, at least from the breasts up. Susannah Waters sang a silver-bright Cupid, flew in ice-blue babygro, and disdained the strategem of the first interpreter of this role, the noted beauty Mrs Charlotte Butler, who, according to Roger North, turned her back because she did not want to show her face 'contorted as it is necessary to sound well, before her gallants, or at least her envious sex'. Petteri Salomaa was eloquent in various bass roles.

Splendid as the music was, Vick's and Brown's achievement was even more remarkable, because it had to be made out of nothing, and because so much depended on it. Heroic drama is heroic not so much because of what the characters are as of what they say—and, even more so, how they say it. This is drama by posturing, and Vick found ways to make his people posture superbly. The potential bathos of entrance—when, in walking on to the stage, heroes may show themselves as not yet heroic—was banished by having the characters arrive suddenly, on trolleys, to take their places fully fledged on the raised rectangular acting area. Doubts about the genuineness of so much high rhetoric were cleared away by a relentlessly rhetorical mode of delivery, even in what might have been intimate scenes, with each monster of speechifying shouting bold intentions and no argument brooked. (No argument exists to be brooked in a drama that unfolds with a calendrical stateliness.) And the visual vocabulary, to give these people a look as emphatic as their declamation, came from widespread traditions of pomp and heraldry: kabuki for the Britons (but with wide woollen leggings and profuse Celtic ornament), fifteenth-century manuscript illustration for the armour of the Saxons. The scene of Arthur's single combat with the Saxon leader Oswald—a 'hieroglyphic', Walter Scott called it—had the two heroes calling to one another from atop magnificent hobby-horses, and in more mobile sequences the pictures were equally spectacular, gaining the miraculousness of Baroque machinery by other means. Lines of poppies, lilies, sunflowers, trees grew up from the floor. A semicircular back panel turned to change colour from British gold to Saxon red. Merlin descended like God the Father in a ring of rainbows. And in the final masque of Albion, wonder followed wonder: a white cliff, like the sliced half of a huge plum pudding, rotated to show shepherds and sheep on the greensward, Aeolus (with wildly blown wig) and Honour (in a flutter of Union Jack) flew, and Venus strode forward in a white trouser suit decorated with flowers.

It could not have been better done. As to whether it was worth doing, certainly yes, to provide an exploration and a special occasion. But one has to doubt that the world has rediscovered a masterpiece—still less a new vein of masterpieces. Curtis Price, writing in the programme, would have *King Arthur* 'in the repertory of any opera house that is prepared to mount other works in which music is combined with spoken dialogue—*Die Zauberflöte* and *Fidelio*, for example'. But the Dryden-Purcell piece is surely removed from that exalted company by the lesser place it finds for music, in terms both of time and of dramatic scope. The musical items account for well under half the work's duration, and though two principal characters—the spirits Philidel and Grimbald—sing as well as speak, they do so only in one short scene in the second act. Otherwise they are—like Arthur, Oswald, Merlin and the rest—speakers and, where music is concerned, listeners.

The much-vaunted 'integration' of the score into the drama of *King Arthur* rests on this presenting of music as something heard. In opera generally—and certainly in *Die Zauberflöte* and *Fidelio*—music is voiced to us; in *King Arthur* we watch and listen as music is voiced to other people. We hear at second hand. In the scene where Philidel and Grimbald sing, they do so in order to lead and mislead, respectively, the British army through the night. The Frost Scene is an apparition called up by the Saxon magician Osmond in order to show Arthur's wife Emmeline, who has been abducted to the enemy camp, that even the coldest folk can be thawed by love. There is also a more benign entertainment for Emmeline in the British camp, a loop of songs and dances (including the sirens' duet) meant to ensnare Arthur, and a pagan invocation scene, of the sort put into many plays of the period for the sake of music. It is a feature of Dryden's dramatic rationalism that the people onstage normally encounter music only when people off stage would encounter it: at religious ceremonies and at divertissements. Heard under any other conditions, music has to be a warning that the hearer is in contact with irrational forces. Sung drama, Dryden wrote, allowed 'that sort of marvellous and surprising conduct, which is rejected in other plays'. But, evidently, things were not to be marvellous and surprising all through, or even for too very long.

Dryden's song texts often short-circuit music's power by making that power their subject: through ostentatious celebration they emasculate. The Britons' victory song at the end of the first act, echoing the 1687 St Cecilia ode, exclaims on 'the double, double, double beat of the thundring Drum', and elsewhere there is play, as in that ode, with the implicit visual pun that makes pipes and flutes instruments of dalliance. When music keeps its potency secret from the words, as it does in the sirens' song and the passacaglia of nymphs and sylvans that comes next to lead Arthur from his path, this can only be a sign of sinister purpose. The whole play—indeed, the whole genre of semi-opera—reeks of a mistrust of music, and though Dryden had come on since his preface to the 1685 *Albion and Albanius* (''Tis my part to invent, and the musician's to humour this invention'), in introducing *King Arthur* he could still speak of the necessities of music as disadvantages to the poet. It is not hard to imagine how he might have reacted to the knowledge that, on account of its music, *King Arthur* would go on being performed for a century and more, and that it would now be played in a theatre consecrated to music as a piece by 'Henry Purcell and John Dryden'.

Yet there is the unusual candour in the text of *King Arthur* that it seems to acknowledge its deafness to music by finding a dramatic figure for that disability in the blindness of Emmeline. She, at least while she stays blind (she rather goes off afterwards), has the most startling lines as she tries to transcribe what she cannot experience into terms she can understand. Of a trumpet, for instance, she says: 'And I can tell you how the sound on't looks. It looks as if it had an angry fighting Face.' Emmeline, blind, talks about seeing. Dryden's text, deaf perhaps from wilfulness or pride, talks about hearing, outside those moments where it places itself in the mouths of spirits, sirens, nymphs and sylvans.

The scene in which Emmeline regains her sight ought to be crucial, and it is a great pity that Purcell's music for this passage is lost, if it ever existed. Dryden's text has Philidel using a Puckish technique to perform what must be the earliest cataract operation:

> Thus, thus I infuse
> These Soveraign Dews.
> Fly back, ye Films, that Cloud her sight

He then delightfully invites Emmeline to:

> Now cast your Eyes abroad, and see
> All but me.

After this, 'Airy Spirits appear in the Shapes of Men and Women' to sing to her that love is intensified when lovers can see. The music, of course, would have completed the equation of blindness with deafness as it displayed how the expression of love is intensified when those expressing it can sing. (Christie played instrumental music for the sight restoration; a better solution might have been to have had the whole scene newly composed, into music that would fit with Purcell, not parody him.)

If semi-opera demanded supernatural beings, its outstanding model was—even above *A Midsummer Night's Dream*—*The Tempest*, which was indeed the instance of one of the first examples of the genre, given in 1674 with music by Locke and textual amendment by Dryden and Davenant. *King Arthur* unashamedly steals a lot from that source: Philidel and Grimbald are Ariel and Caliban, Merlin is Prospero, and Emmeline is Miranda (or Dorinda as she became in the Davenant-Dryden reworking). Indeed, wipe off the seaspray from *The Tempest*, quieten other echoes from Shakespeare and from Spenser, and not much is left of *King Arthur* but national pageantry. And yet that little is not without interest. *King Arthur* is a drama of reconciliation, in which Britons and Saxons go beyond walloping each other to join in a vision of future peace and union. The victory song was in Act 1; Act 5 is more about the pleasures of peace, and as the spoken play falls silent and the masque takes over, so the gaze turns from the heroes to the common people: shepherds, harvestmakers, lovers.

Coinciding with the run-up to the VE Day jamboree, these performances of *King Arthur* spoke to a national pride that has less to do with bombers, tanks and Montogmery than with gas masks, ration books and Vera Lynn, and that homeliness of British patriotism was touchingly honoured in the production. According to Dryden's stage direction: 'The scene opens above, and discovers the Order of the Garter.' Not here. What we had was a stage filling with British worthies—the guardsman, the bobby, the boy scout—a vision certainly more charming and perhaps more true. (*Times Literary Supplement*, 19 May 1995)

around New York

Diverse in its streams and destinations, the city becomes, at a moment of crisis, home to a vast 'we'.

the Pierpont Morgan Library

Pierrot lunaire always sounds strange. Its voice—the voice of the soloist who declaims elegantly crafted nightmare poems in a manner between speech and song—comes from somewhere unfamiliar, a place known only to this piece. The voice speaks of sexual obsession, cruelty and blasphemy, of lurid visions and black practical jokes. It does not seem to have heard of normal behaviour, nor does it take the bizarre events and feelings it describes entirely seriously. A psychiatrist might want to describe it as the voice of a paranoid.

If this is madness, though, there is method in it. On Tuesday evening at the Pierpont Morgan Library, in a performance conducted by James Levine, the accompanying music for mixed quintet sounded as weird as it has to, but also lustrous and suave a lot of the time. Schoenberg's sense of instrumental character and colour was very much in evidence, whether in Rafael Figueroa's grand phrases on the cello or Mike Parloff's cool flute tones and spiky piccolo. The performance also had the special benefit of Peter Serkin at the piano, crisp and crystalline in the high register to which Schoenberg often resorts at the mention of moonlight or glass in the poems, rock hard, enclosed and solid in the bass.

Serkin's playing also helped bring out how much method Schoenberg displayed in filling the music with cross-references of theme and motif, quite outside the couple of movements written in strict polyphonic forms. Levine was with him in this. Because the movements were made to flow together, with barely a beat of a pause from one to the next, they bounced off each other. Without intermittent completions, the music stayed alive. And its textures were alive as well as beautiful.

The voice above and within them was that of Christine Schäfer, the outstanding Pierrotiste of the moment. She did not have much need of the score in front of her. Sometimes she seemed to be making it up as she went along, thinking a phrase before uttering it. There was immediacy, too, in her use of a huge range of vocal timbres, from barely tuned speaking to almost song. Yet she was true to the music throughout, and true to this performance of it, to the delicacy and the rococo flourishes Levine had his players discover.

The performance was given as part of the imaginative series 'The Collection in Concert', with which scores from the library's holdings are brought to life. And this was the strangest moment of all, to walk out of the recital room and see Schoenberg's manuscript, very neatly laid out and with the markings he made as conductor of the first run of performances, the pages looking so ordinary. (*New York Times*, 29 May 1998)

St Mark's Church (East Tenth Street)

Anyone who has seen the new *Star Trek* movie will have no trouble recognizing Meredith Monk and her fellow performers as they appear in her *Celebration Service* at St Mark's Church in the East Village. They clearly are the Ba'ku, a peace-loving people who have gained the secret of eternal youth and rejected technology, even though their earth-tone clothing looks suspiciously machine woven.

The religion of the Ba'ku is unstated in *Star Trek: Insurrection*, but it must surely be much as Monk imagines it in her hourlong ceremony of song, recitation and gentle calisthenics. Happiness is all. Happy texts come from everywhere: a twentieth-century Osage woman, Martin Buber, poets of ancient India, Afghanistan, Japan and China, the ubiquitous Hildegard von Bingen. Happy music comes from the throats of the performers in Monk's habitual style, which abstracts from Appalachian folksong and Gregorian chant the lowest common denominator. Happy people sing and smile.

Their happiness is engaging, but disquieting. For a long time Monk has calmly gone about breaking the normal contract of performance, whereby performers do something excellent. She is not in the business of excellence. She prefers pleasantness. There are some nice moments in *A Celebration Service*, including a bit of organum near the start and a twelve-part canon excerpted from *Atlas*. (Several additional numbers, too, come from other works by Monk.) But the most complicated melody is one the audience is invited to sing, 'Processional'.

With nothing happening on Friday that demanded expertise (happiness being the most undemanding emotional state), one felt present at something like a grade-school show. The point was not to be moved, stirred or struck, but to condone, and perhaps this is asking too much when the show is being put on by grown-ups. So sweet, so tender and so unassuming, *A Celebration Service* was distinctly aggressive in its demands for a sympathy it refused to earn. (*New York Times*, 11 January 1999)

St Paul's Chapel (Columbia University)

You might think you are hearing wind across an empty plain, or the ringing of railroad tracks as a train approaches, or a choir performing somewhere high above, or the reverberations of a great bell, but in fact you will be in St Paul's Chapel at Columbia University, where every day until Monday Jeff Talman's electronic piece *Vanishing Point 1.1* is being played repeatedly.

Talman created his soundscape to match the echo-rich acoustics of the Byzantine-inspired chapel. As he explained in his introductory remarks on Wednesday evening, he began with a recording, made in the chapel in 1987, of one of his more conventional pieces. Listening carefully, he identified a section of just 1.1 seconds of absolute silence—or rather of human silence, for though no musician was performing or audience member rattling a programme, the chapel was singing its own song. There was the sound of an acoustic space, as there is when one walks into an empty church. Computer analysis revealed the frequencies and bunches of frequencies contained in the chapel's thrumming, and Talman then worked with these to compose his piece. Pure tones, generally lasting several seconds, suggest bell-like or other metallic resonances; groups of tones produce the effect of wind or voices, and in the extreme treble there is sometimes a fizz or crinkling. Because everything is derived from the building's particular acoustics, everything feels at home. There is a perfect fit. You sit or stand or walk in an ambience that is alive, interesting, but also essentially at rest. Although *Vanishing Point 1.1* loops back every twenty minutes, you will probably want to stay longer, placing yourself differently in relation to the sounds.

When you leave, you may find that your ears have woken up a bit. You failed to notice this before: the noises of paper and cans blowing across the terrace of nearby Low Library and their echoes from the buildings around. Another space is singing. (*New York Times*, 24 September 1999)

Central Park (and Carnegie Hall)

Anyone walking through Central Park to Carnegie Hall on Monday evening would have heard a tumult of bird songs, all gloriously out of time with one another or with the tempos of falling petals and shivering leaves. The 'pulse of nature' belongs to the world of metaphor, but it was a metaphor vividly evoked inside the hall, when Wolfgang Sawallisch conducted the Philadelphia Orchestra in Sibelius's Seventh Symphony. What helped was the resilience of the sounds: the splendour and sway of the strings, moving as one body, or the grandeur of the brass, rising to motivate change from behind the scenes, or the fullness, beauty and sometimes strangeness of the woodwind colours. But just as important was the steering of sounds to present the symphony as a single thing, developing in response to forces inherent within it. Nobody was making it happen. Just as nobody manoeuvres the clouds to let the sun burst through, so the opening of the symphony, for example, seemed merely—but magnificently—to unfold, through dark sounds and opaque harmonic progressions that were moving themselves around to create an opening for sudden woodwind brightness. The work went on like this, travelling toward its biggest climax—a real yelp here—and away. (*New York Times*, 4 May 2000)

Cami Hall

Nothing is normal now. Friday's concert by the Friends and Enemies of New Music—one of the first concerts to take place in New York City since the events of Tuesday morning—went on sombrely. The audience at CAMI Hall, across the street from Carnegie Hall, was subdued. Those present who had arrived on foot, whether through the streets or across the park, would have passed groups of people gathered in the darkening light with candles: standing outside firehouses, on the steps of the Metropolitan Museum or seated around the Bethesda Fountain. Some of these groups were silent, others were singing patriotic songs, not with gusto as on other occasions, but with quiet fervour, making those songs into prayers.

The sight would have been impressive even without the collectively murmured tunes and the candles, for this is normally a city of people moving through the streets singly and in twos and threes. A cluster, still and composed, is an anomaly. Just by being together, people were saying something new and unusual.

Inside the hall it was hard not to hear candles and prayers in some of the performances. Andrew Violette played his Piano Sonata

No.1 with hard-edged brilliance and attack, as if shocked into defiance. John Link, in his solo Sonata for electric bass guitar, made murky music that seemed to be trying not to think of other things.

These were messages from earlier times. Violette's piece was a youthful composition from more than twenty years ago, perhaps fired by an admiration for the music Pierre Boulez and Olivier Messiaen were writing thirty years before that, but more symmetrically phrased, with its own harmonic character and also with its own daring, not least in landing unashamedly at the very end on a tonal chord. Link's was an effort to have the instrument not do what it wanted to do: hum rock basses. But both works suited this moment.

Ben Yarmolinsky's Sonata for violin and piano had a strong performance from Renée Jolles and Christopher Oldfather, Jolles playing with tremendous energy and sureness, determined to make a rather circuitous and hazy composition speak. Oldfather was excellent again when he had the chance to shine alone, in beautiful and wistful pieces by David Chaitkin.

In a way, though, all this was prelude. The purpose of the evening was to pay homage to Francis Thorne, a little in advance of his eightieth birthday, and his Rhapsodic Variations No.5 concluded the evening, again with Jolles and Oldfather performing. Here was music that wheeled on boundlessly through diverse musical moods—extravagant, firm, pensive—while honouring its roots and maintaining its composure. It was superbly played, and, again, it touched the temper of the time. (*New York Times*, 17 September 2001)

Tippett

Creative into his late eighties, Michael Tippett was a heartening and colourful figure at performances and premieres, including those of his last opera, *New Year* (1986–8), and his setting of Yeats's *Byzantium* (1989–90). Farewells, when he died at the age of ninety-three, had to be celebratory.

New Year

Tippett keeps on getting younger. Just ten weeks from his eighty-fifth birthday, here he is in Texas, sportively bejeaned, taking a gentle bow after a work which, but for the modesty of the amplification and also of the scenic resources, would have to be called a rock opera. Saxophones wail, a large percussion group batters and jangles in urban syncopation, electric guitars squelch out disgust. A male vocalist, couched in an armchair with Budweiser and cigarettes, cynically leads and misleads us as master of these ceremonies. A chorus of louche modern types judders. At Houston Grand Opera it is *New Year*.

But it is also old Tippett, in that what we are probably to see as a black, bleak vision of the contemporary city is cracked by what we are probably to see as hope and love. It is the same story: it is most particularly the same story as *The Midsummer Marriage*, for though we are now at the opposite time of year, this is again the moment of collective celebration (so important to Tippett, this Greek ideal of the artist enjoining a public forum), out of which a young woman is kept by her anxieties and tightnesses. Rather in the same way, the situation of that first opera is here encased and problematized by the contemporary images of rock music, robotic dance and science fantasy.

The problems, but also the fascinations, arise because while Tippett wants to use these things as markers of modern alienation (we are in 'Terror Town'), he himself is not alienated at all: indeed the youthfulness of *New Year* is very largely the youthfulness of an exuberant embrace, an old man's naked rush into the sea of new sensation, flinging off the clothes of habit and experience. Four decades ago in *The Midsummer Marriage* he found a unified world for thoughts of Jung and Yeats and Blake, of Mozart and the English madrigalists and the musical twentieth century. Now the thoughts are the same, but they have become wild and scattered, not the steady light but sparks in the dark.

Perhaps in a way this is more honest, but it is certainly less entrancing, especially when, as usual with Tippett, the drama is a play of emblems rather than characters. The first act introduces us to the chorus of the anonymous Presenter and his Terror Town gang; to Jo Ann, the child psychologist frightened into isolation in her room; to her black brother Donny, in every way her shadow as he dances the streets with pride; to their adoptive mother Nan; and to another, future world populated by the computer wizard Merlin, the space pilot Pelegrin and their bizarre queen Regan, who is too much a whistling kettle of rage to have much force as a symbol of power, still less as a satire. Nor do the troubles of this act end there. The exposition is abrupt, enigmatic, slantwise, but also long drawn out, and patches of the score sound under-composed (a duet for Jo Ann and Nan accompanied only by dabs of percussion and string tone) or else cobbled from clichés (Donny's bird dance, which ought to be an exhilarating break, is kept on the ground by a conventional fanfaring trumpet and jazz-skirling clarinet).

Of course there are startling moments—notably Pelegrin's aria beginning with a long melisma over parallel string chords that reflect Indonesia and medieval organum from their glistening surfaces. But such things do not begin to energize the box of tricks until the two later and shorter acts, and then only in the magic scenes: the ritual dances of the second act, and the *Magic Flute* trials of the third, where Jo Ann, led by Pelegrin, drinks from a lake of tears summoned by oboe-led lamenting and then spins in an airy dance for three flutes. Things like this show Tippett's creativity is still fresh, if not fresher, and of course his naivety is only the down side of his freshness: the naivety of electronic clusters for the space ship, the naivety of so much in this loose, forced plot.

But what is most astonishingly inexperienced in *New Year* is the uncertainty of tone, the weak self-mockery that flaps around the figures of Merlin and Regan particularly. The piece is not helped by a production (by Sir Peter Hall) still some way off being smooth and sharp, nor by cumbersome and noisy stage machinery, nor yet by an orchestral performance (under John DeMain) that only gathers confidence as it goes along. There is, though, a fine, hard-working cast.

Helen Field is a Jo Ann who is intense and plaintive in everything she does, Krister St Hill a vocally firm and physically live Donny, Jane Shaulis a warm Nan. Representing the future, Peter Kazaras releases Pelegrin's rhapsodies in silver, James Maddalena wins some belief for Merlin's manic fuss and fervour, and Richetta Manager offers a Regan brilliantly thrusting out her scolds. Next summer most of them will be in Glyndebourne for another New Year. (*Times*, 30 October 1989)

Byzantium

Sing it like a bird; sing it like a flame. Tippett's setting of Yeats's 'Byzantium', heard at the Proms, takes these images of bird and flame and fuses them into sound, into a singing soprano line of rhapsodic agility and brilliance, a line igniting new, wordless images in a supporting orchestra that is a cascade of overlapping ensembles. The words, which seem to have pressed themselves forward to be sung, burn themselves up in the process: hence the flame of verbal sense that yields to leap and yelp and high melisma in twenty-five minutes of mostly fast-moving music, moving fast to embody those other Yeatsian images of dance and fury. The poem becomes, in Boulez's terms, a central absence, disappearing from the music it has given rise to, and perhaps one has to look to Boulez's Mallarmé portrait, *Pli selon pli*, for a comparable case of music in ecstatic concurrence with poetry, of poetry not being set to music but, rather, engendering a whole new sounding world. It is a case of that rebirthing which Yeats's poem already inside itself displays in its tidal replacements, stanza by stanza, of a few drumming words and ideas, and which at the end it consciously identifies, in the couplet:

> Those images that yet
> Fresh images beget.

Tippett's response to these lines is extraordinary. The voice multiplies Yeats's repetition into an obsession with the word 'images', given always the quick rhythm it had in the opening line of the song, and eventually summoning the musical images which had come before any words, in the orchestral introduction, but which the singing voice, present now, can find words for: 'dolphin' for the brilliant fanfaring trumpets, 'gong-tormented sea' for the chugging bass-register toccata of percussion and electric organ. In the cycle of image begetting image, it seems finally to be the words that have been begotten by the music. Elsewhere, in the traditional way, musical images are named by the voice as or before they occur. But music is not subservient to poetry here: it can enforce its privileges by interpolating into the text ululations and Tippettian cockcrows, or even by breaking words apart to let loose new ones. This happens most remarkably on 'recede', whose second syllable is freed to become another image of renewal.

The spirit of renewal within the music is conveyed tirelessly by the vocal line, taken by Faye Robinson at this European premiere, as in the United States in April: her performance was one of astonishing energy and stamina, moving the power lightly, keeping up with the dance, the wide-eyed wonder and the radiance in Tippett's vision. The orchestra seemed to flag a bit in the middle, despite so many outbursts of brilliance from the BBC Symphony under Andrew Davis. Maybe there is some lack of underlying muscle in the music; maybe it just seems that way when one sees so many players spending so much time waiting: the piece could well have given a quite different impression over the radio. The surface sound is consistently of bounce, brightness and life. Tippett could not lose his youthful vitality without losing himself. Here he was, on the platform after the performance, spry in vermilion windcheater, lemon T-shirt and trousers festooned with singing circles of clashing colour. The music—audacious, fantastical, a touch gawky—is made to match. (*Times*, 9 September 1991)

The Judgement of Tippett

The first act of Tippett's second opera, *King Priam*, ends with a scene familiar from fable and painting but perhaps never before sung. Paris, the young Trojan prince, is being asked to choose. Will he honour war and the city's safety, in the shape of Athene? Will he elect for marriage and home, represented by Hera? Or will he give the golden apple to love and to Aphrodite?

Tippett was well aware of his obligations to the first two goddesses. War he refused to support, by his action as a conscientious objector, but he did not decline public duty: indeed, refusal of war was part of that duty, though the larger part was art. Opera, for him, was music in the public domain. Whatever the mean practicalities of the opera house, he shared Wagner's sense of opera as the Greek theatre of the modern age—the artist's forum, as important as the politician's. Throughout the half century from the start of the 1940s to the end of the 1980s he was always working towards, on or away from an operatic project, and the result was a sequence of five operas, of which the first four were all introduced by the Covent Garden company: *The Midsummer Marriage* in 1955, *King Priam* in 1962, *The Knot Garden* in 1970 and *The Ice Break* in 1977. *New Year* followed at Houston, Texas, in 1989. Athene had her due.

As for Hera, if music can be described as the marriage partner of Tippett's life, he was consistently faithful, from the time when, as a young man struggling to find a voice, he could easily have felt he had picked the wrong mate. No composer had to work so hard as a student. Few had to wait so long for their industry to be rewarded: Tippett was past thirty before he was writing music he felt had permanent value, and fifty when he had his first opera staged. Home, too, he valued all through his life, though his sense of home changed. His began as, and remained, essentially English music. It reawakened in the twentieth century the boisterous word-setting of Purcell and the bounce of the madrigalists, and its roots were in folksong. From *The Midsummer Marriage* onwards, it evoked, in some of its most characteristic sounds, the landscape of southern England, where Tippett spent all his life: the roll of downland hills in slow, warm melodies associated with cellos, horns or the low mezzo-soprano voice, and dappled sunlight through spring trees in the hocketings of flutes or violins. Latterly, as television joined the view out of his window, Tippett's idea of home broadened, to embrace the United States, in particular. The seeds had always been there. The off-the-beat drive and lilt of his rhythm came not just from English madrigals and poetry but from jazz, which is one reason why his earliest works, for all their Englishness, seem close kin to what was being written at the same time by such US composers as Copland and Carter. But in the 1970s and 1980s his identification with the United States became intense. *The Knot Garden* takes place in England, almost certainly in the home counties. It belongs in an English tradition of domestic dramas. *The Ice Break*, though, is US. Its locations and its themes—conflict between the middle-aged and the young, between holding on to the values of the old country and integrating oneself into the new, between black and white, between the individual and the crowd, between athlete and intellectual—are those of the USA and of television. Huge in scope but tiny in dimensions (like television), it is happening at home, as much as *The Knot Garden* and *The Midsummer Marriage* were dramas of home in more specific and picturesque senses.

So much for Hera and the hearth. However, there can be little doubt which goddess claimed Tippett's first allegiance. He was, like Paris, for love. Music generally is. But in Tippett's case, the virtues of love are heard as boundless. Love is hope. With the composer's sense of his calling to speak on public issues growing ever keener, in *The Ice Break* and *New Year*, love becomes, more and more, the only hope. But love, in the brilliant score for *King Priam*, keeps trying to reach through to characters who are imprisoned by wilfulness, compulsion or duty. And love is the motive for reconciliation and renewal in the more private dramas of *The Midsummer Marriage* and *The Knot Garden*. To love is to discover the possibility of rebirth, and rebirth is what all of Tippett is about. He may have put it slightly differently. The only truth of his work, he said, was that of the need for each of us to recognize within ourselves the darkness and the light: the evil and the good, the strange and the familiar, the assertive and the passive, the female and the male. But we do that, in Tippett's world, not under the serene illumination of self-contemplation but by the blazing torch of Eros: 'Love such as this', Helen/Aphrodite sings in *King Priam*, 'stretches up to heaven, for it reaches down to hell.' Each of the operas has at least one encounter with such erotic abandonment: Tippett, whose indifference to convention can be overstated, was canny enough not to leave out the love scene. But much more continuously present is the sound of love in the exuberant rhythm, forcing or flickering melody and rapturous colour of his music. This is love being expressed not by one of the characters onstage—or, as it might more usually be, by two—but by the composer himself. And it comes in the music, not in the text, even though he wrote his own librettos.

These are by no means so bad as is often claimed. That for *King Priam* is a sharp piece of theatre, clearly indebted to Brecht, but creating its own world and full of strong scenes. The others, all set more or less in contemporary times, are all of them less urgently paced and less disciplined in diction, though their mixture of slang with high-flown phrase-making and quotation is not so distant from the speech of some people in actuality (including the composer himself) and has a distinguished history in twentieth-century poetry and poetic drama as a way of conveying a discordancy of voices within one character. Even so, the point of the words in a Tippett opera is not so much to provide a sketch of the action, which music will fill out, as to offer a screen, through which music will burst. When we recall the music of one of his operas, what we remember is probably less likely to be a moment where the music reinforces the words than one of a more purely musical character, where the words are virtually meaningless (Sosostris's oracle in the last act of *The Midsummer Marriage*), actually meaningless (Achilles' war cry in the second act of *King Priam*), rendered meaningless by musical elaboration (much of Jenifer's role in *The Midsummer Marriage*, or the choral music of that opera and *King Priam*) or—most likely—totally absent. There can be few other operas, outside those of Wagner and Birtwistle, where the orchestra is so much the most voluble character. *The Midsummer Marriage* is largely defined by its luscious, lustrous choral-orchestral textures, and much of its second act is played by the orchestra without voices at all. In *King Priam*, *The Knot Garden* and *The Ice Break* the drama is one of instrumental soloists and groupings, and what provokes that drama—the libretto—we may well feel to be less interesting.

What is enacted on the stage may be enigmatic and even vaporous, but what sounds from the pit is not only exultant but sure. Take *The Midsummer Marriage*. For all its much-noted echoes of Mozart (of *The Magic Flute* in the magic-ancient setting and the subjection of a young couple to trials before marriage; of Figaro and Susanna in the figures of Jack and Bella) and Wagner (King Fisher = Wotan), it has more in common with the operas of Schubert, Weber and Stockhausen—operas more lyrical than epic, operas where flights of brilliance and points of charm are placed in a ramshackle holding. Its invitation is less to weigh the great questions of existence than to engage, in sympathy with the chorus and dancers onstage, in sheer abounding pagan pleasure. The drama of spiritual combat and maturing is not so much empowered by the score as excitably followed and rejoiced about. And to the music's purpose of flown, gleeful witness, a magpie libretto—one full of opportunities to rush and wonder—is much more use than a soberly sustained myth. The renewal that is being prepared in the stage action is vitally present in the music all along. Love does not have to be discovered by means of journeyings up to heaven and into the bowels of the earth. It is here, in the score. As for its object, it looks not to the words, not to the audience, but to the future. It is thus, by projecting its gaze into the future, that love becomes hope. When the score reaches its settling into A major, as Mark and Jenifer open their eyes to each other, what we hear is not the joining of animus and anima but rather the slow exhalation of a desire that such a blessing could be. (*The Opera House*, No.15, Summer 1998)

being in Assisi

Messiaen's opera *Saint François d'Assise*, first performed at the Paris Opera on 28 November 1983, steadily grew. But the composer's view was always sure and the same.

Paris 1983

God does not choose his saints for their learning or his composers for their theatrical flair. It never seemed likely that Messiaen would write an opera, nor did he himself ever entertain such pretensions. When Rolf Liebermann first asked him, in 1974, he sagely replied that he had no gift for the theatre. But Liebermann persisted, Messiaen yielded, and now, after much delay, we have the result: an evening of Wagnerian length in which holy mysteries are celebrated with much splendour and strangeness.

Messiaen has described his opera as showing 'different aspects of grace in the soul of St Francis'. This is not a particularly dramatic subject. It is, however, an apt one for a composer who has always concerned himself with presenting the intervention of the divine in the human as an exposition of unquestioned and unquestionable fact. Eight scenes are iconically displayed, all boldly setting forth and repeating symbols in whose composition Messiaen has drawn on the resources of a creative life spanning five decades. One recognizes sounds from throughout his output: a mystic harmony from *Le Banquet céleste*, his opus one, or the eerie noise of a wind machine or brass mouthpiece from his otherwise most recent score, *Des Canyons aux étoiles*. . . No synthesis is attempted, for synthesis would require development, which remains wholly alien to Messaien's art. Instead the knowledge of a lifetime is placed at the disposal of eight scenes, that each may be as astonishing as possible.

The first, 'The Cross', has St Francis discoursing to his disciple Brother Leo on the 'perfect joy' (strings and ondes martenot in toothsome concord) to be found in sharing Christ's suffering. In the second, 'Lauds', he sings part of his *Cantico delle creature* while the community recites matins, and in the third, 'The Kissing of the Leper', he overcomes his remaining self-love in curing one of the most deformed of outcasts. This is perhaps the most remarkable scene, going back to Messiaen's earliest orchestral music to portray the broken horror of the leper's spiritual desolation and then the wild abandon of his post-miracle dance. Powerfully it ends the first act.

The second is similarly in three scenes but much longer: a full two hours. It also leans most heavily on its audience's generosity in bringing an angel to the stage, for though Messiaen's music might possibly summon spectacular visions to mind, the theatrical reality is something else: an all-too-corporeal lady dressed up in a shell-pink nightdress with awful garish wings of red, yellow, blue and black. One cannot blame the designer, Giuseppe Crisolini Malatesta, who has done his best to follow Messiaen's own directions. Rather the problem is one central to the work, that for the first time we are seeing the images that Messiaen's music has always worked towards, and where the theatre of the imagination can be grandiose and marvellous, the real thing is likely to be absurd and comical. So it turns out in the fourth scene, 'The Angel Traveller', where the heavenly visitor catechizes the Franciscan brethren, and one has to suspend disbelief more than somewhat, too, in scene five, 'The Angel Musician'. Here, though, Messiaen goes a long way towards fulfilling his aim for music 'so lovely that St Francis faints' when the angel's treble viol solo in fact sounds out from the three ondes martenot. The act ends with the sixth and longest scene of the opera, 'The Sermon to the Birds'.

The final act is of more modest proportions, having two scenes of about half an hour each. The first is 'The Stigmata', a dialogue for Francis and the voice of Christ in vast choral harmony, the second 'Death and the New Life', where grave litanies give way to a ferociously exultant affirmation of the bliss to come, shouted out by an orchestra of a hundred.

So enormous an apparatus—still less than Messiaen would have liked—creates problems of housing, which Sandro Sequi's production disarmingly solves by filling most of the stage space with non-active participants: woodwind to the left, percussion to the right, brass and ondes martenot in boxes, chorus in stepped ranks on the main stage.

Sublimely incautious and thoroughly magnificent is the orchestral performance under Seiji Ozawa, an intoxicating vindication of Messaien's sureness in this area at least. Another to triumph is José van Dam in the long central role, which he sings throughout with the simplicity of unforced authority. Christiane Eda-Pierre is properly composed and pure yet still womanly as the Angel, and Kenneth Riegel sings and dances an unabashed Leper. The brothers include a fine young baritone (Philippe Duminy). (*Times*, 1 December 1983)

the composer's view 1

It is hard to write about Olivier Messiaen without making him sound like a plaster saint, but his sweetness of temperament, his composure and his modesty are sublimely untouched by anything of modern doubt or self-promotion. If anybody else were to mention Monteverdi, Rameau, Mozart, Wagner, Mussorgsky, Debussy and Berg as the only operatic composers to merit consideration beside his own work, the effect would be one of unpardonable arrogance, but Messiaen speaks with such open sincerity that objection is silenced.

During the course of our conversation I suggested he had made things difficult for himself in *Saint Francois d'Assise* in bringing an angel on to the stage, since no soprano of flesh and blood could live up to his own description of the heavenly visitor as 'a beautiful, enigmatic butterfly'. But his response was more puzzled than reproving. He had gone to the Uffizi, seen an excellent angel in an Annunciation by Fra Angelico, and made that the pattern for his costume design. What could be more obvious?

Everything about his work he describes as if it were similarly self-evident. When he was asked by Rolf Liebermann to write a work for the Paris Opera, the subject had of course to be religious. 'My dream was to make a Passion and Resurrection, but I think it is impossible to put Christ on the stage: that is something *trop beau*. So I chose a man who was not God, but who most resembled Christ in being chaste, poor and humble, and in receiving Christ's wounds. Also, St Francis is dear to me because I am an ornithologist, and he loved and preached to the birds. Having made that choice, I left out everything that was secondary to the progress of grace in his soul. I left out the dispute between father and son, on account of its being too psychoanalytical, and I left out St Clare, the interviews with the Pope and the voyage to Egypt.

'The first of the three scenes to be performed in tonight's concert is "The Kissing of the Leper". One sees a leper who is not only horribly disfigured but also wicked. St Francis, despite his revulsion, approaches and talks to him, and gradually he is inwardly transformed. St Francis also is transformed, and embraces the leper. Double miracle: the leper is cured, and Francis becomes St Francis from that moment.

'One then passes in this concert selection to the last act. St Francis is alone in a cave, and he asks to understand the sufferings of Christ. There is a choir which is the voice of Christ, and which grants him the same wounds to be reproduced in his body. The scene is a terrible one, because the whole first part expresses a sensation of extreme anguish, but then that suffering is transformed into an extraordinary celestial joy, because St Francis is profoundly happy at this sign that he has been chosen by God.

'Then in the last scene St Francis is exhausted by penitence, by privations and also by the stigmata. He bids farewell to his brothers and to the birds, and the angel and the leper reappear to lead him into Paradise. The choir sings of the Resurrection, transforming St Francis's theme into a chorale of glory.'

For Messiaen, charmingly touched as he is by the present run of concert performances, the work remains essentially one for the theatre. 'It is a work I imagined with decors, people onstage, costumes—and also an individual who is very important: the orchestra, which is part of the action, because one sees some of the instruments on the stage.'

That at least was how the work was presented in Paris, in a production with which Messiaen professes himself happy, except for the lack of birds for St Francis's sermon to them. I suggested that the work might profit from a more stylized treatment, looking towards Japanese theatre. 'That is possible: I would not say no. In Tokyo the three scenes were performed in a semi-scenic version in the Catholic cathedral, with the singers in costume and the angel high in the organ-loft. That was better than a concert performance, but I would prefer to see it in a theatre.'

Might his experience in the theatre now lead him to a second opera? 'You know, I worked on *Saint François* for eight years. I am now seventy-seven: I have to think of smaller works.' As to what those smaller works might be, he is unforthcoming: 'I never speak of things until they are finished.'

We turned to works of the past, and to Messiaen's often misunderstood statements about transcribing colours and birdsongs into his music. 'When I read or listen to music I see colours inwardly, not with my eyes but in my head. Every sound-complex has a corresponding colour.' For everyone, or just for him? 'For me. I think the correspondences exist for everyone, but they will vary from person to person.' I point out that blue is associated with A major in his music, but with F sharp major in Scriabin's. 'Oh yes? But then I am by no means a disciple of Scriabin.'

As for the birds: 'I take down the songs with pencil and paper, quite simply as musical dictation, but afterwards I transform them into my music. Of course, I always arrange them in some way: I am not a tape-recorder.'

I asked finally which works he now feels closest to. 'Those that I think are most representative, because they contain colours, because they contain birds, and because they contain my religious faith too, are *La Transfiguration*, *Des Canyons aux étoiles*. . . and *Saint François*. I also love the *Vingt Regards* and the *Méditations sur le mystère de la Sainte Trinité*. Some works may be better, some worse, but whatever I have done is sincere.' (*Times*, 26 March 1986)

London 1986

Whatever else may be said of Messiaen's opera *Saint François d'Assise*, the scale of its daring takes the breath away, not only because it requires colossal forces and lasts as long as *Götterdämmerung* but perhaps more particularly because it takes on, if only implicitly, a problem central to Messiaen's art: that of the relation between religious revelation and everyday experience.

Most of his previous works had been granted the holy gift of indifference to the world. They are musical stained-glass windows, using all the resources of music to paint pictures of the most marvellous stories and promises of the New Testament: the splendour of resurrected existence, the brilliant glory of the Transfigured Christ, the preciousness of the Incarnation. They do not ask questions. In turning to the story of St Francis, however, Messiaen faces himself with a man who did ask questions. Born in an age when new ideas of individual responsibility were surfacing and requiring people to do something about God, Francis took the simple but severe and absolute step of just following His example.

It is true that Messiaen treats the subject as a miracle story and shows no interest in Francis as a person. The three scenes given in Wednesday's Royal Philharmonic Society concert write the wonders of the saint's reported life across the marvels of the composer's musical inventory, so that, for instance, a huge chorus jabs out Christ's words 'I am the Alpha and the Omega' to a bird-shriek last heard in *Oiseaux exotiques*, or a healed leper dances to a movement that could have come from the *Turangalîla* symphony, or characters sing in the modal chant of the early songs.

Nevertheless, there is the temptation to understand *Saint François* as the story of a real man, and to wonder what the thing means; for only in comparatively rare passages, notably in the hugely scored C major crescendo of the close, does Messiaen dazzle the senses and silence doubt. The more normal method of the opera is to proceed slowly, illustrating each phrase with swoops of colour-harmony and fantastic bird-calls, immense chords and some new effects, such as the weird low rattling tones of the ondes martenot. If the opera is to work as hagiography, then it would need to be seen, and preferably in a manner that took it as far as possible from naturalism. Anything less is bound to raise a question of how one may accept so vast and undoubting an affirmation of spiritual truth—though at least there was no worry about the musical truth of a positive, large and brilliant performance at the Festival Hall, the BBC Symphony Orchestra conducted by Seiji Ozawa without a score. Dietrich Fischer-Dieskau was a giant of solemn authority as St Francis and Maria Fausta Gallamini sang out clearly and purely as the angel; Kenneth Riegel repeated his anguished leper from the Paris premiere of two years ago. (*Times*, 28 March 1986)

the composer's view 2

In a practice studio in a former warehouse in Bermondsey, in a swirl of noise and clatter from musicians taking a break between rehearsals for *Saint François d'Assise*, there is a centre of stillness: Olivier Messiaen sits talking, his hands at rest in his lap, or else he stays waiting for the next question to come in stumbling schoolboy French; his smile is one of complete peace and candour, his face and eyes open, translucent, so that he seems young beneath the wispy white hair, still a child. There ought to be angels who look like this.

Serenity, humility and purity are the whole story, but they are also only part of the story, because Messiaen speaks rapidly and confidently of his works, his views, his plans: the angel has a sharp, clear mind, and it is good to have evidence of this when his appearance at recent concerts has been that of a man shuffling in tiny steps, watched and fussed over with a new needfulness by his wife, Yvonne Loriod, her own eyes and movements as quick and bright as her pianism, or as the birds she emulates when playing Messiaen's music.

I asked him first if, like Stravinsky at the same period of life, he was finding new musical enthusiasms. 'I have never changed. I have always loved the birds, and as far as human music is concerned, I had wonderful teachers: Jean and Noël Gallon, Maurice Emmanuel, Marcel Dupré, and Paul Dukas, who was a great composer and a sage, a philosopher, a sort of Buddha. Nowadays I still listen to discs and go to concerts: I even go regularly to the L'Itinéraire concerts, which are the most avantgarde in Paris.' But his opinions have not altered about what is important for the next generation or two. 'In France there is a very great musician who has made himself above music: Pierre Boulez. And then there is electronic music, which has changed the ways of thinking and orchestrating of every composer today, even those who haven't composed electronic music, like me. And finally in England you have a great musician who is a marvellously gifted young man: George Benjamin.'

Messiaen's life in other respects, too, proceeds without essential change. When he is not travelling, he still plays regularly for the 10 o'clock and 11.30 masses at La Trinité: 'It's not a very beautiful church, but it has a very beautiful organ, one of the best in France. I've been playing it now for fifty-seven years: I'm a very old organist!'

He also continues, of course, to compose. A new piece for piano and ensemble, *Un Vitrail et des oiseaux*, will have its first British performance tomorrow, and another new work, for piano and orchestra, is scheduled for performance next November by the BBC Symphony Orchestra under Boulez. Yet another new large orchestral piece is his current project. Does he keep particular times or places for composition? 'I like to work in the country, in the mountains: I have a house in the country, in a place where there are four lakes and a circle of mountains.' He composed his big piano piece *La Fauvette des jardins* (The Garden Warbler) there. 'I had listened to the birds and walked there for years, and wrote a piece which recalls for me my own landscape. There are personages which are like leitmotifs: there's the personage of the mountain, the personage of the lake: these are individuals, and though of course they're immobile, they still stir, and they sing. And for the birdsong I heard and notated three hundred garden warblers, and out of those I made an ideal, choosing from the best.'

If the sounds and sights of nature were written into his music, could he work in Paris? 'Yes, sometimes. A musician always has music in his head, day and night, in the street, at home, everywhere.' So a piano is not necessary to him when he is composing? 'I can work without it, yes, but I like to place myself at the piano. Works for piano, clearly, I write at the piano. But for orchestral works I write a first version which is not a piano reduction but something more: there may even be pages which I write directly in score, like the bird concert in *Saint François d'Assise*, which would be impossible to write in reduction.'

Does he make sketches? 'I think a lot. I think for years. Then, when I begin, it's essentially a definitive version, which I don't change. I couldn't, for instance, take up an old work again, because I don't have the same aspirations, the same wishes.' Has he ever abandoned a work? 'Oh no, I keep everything: they are all my children.'

Had there ever been a work that he had not completed? 'No. I'll give you an example: *Les Corps glorieux* for organ, which I wrote in 1939, just before the war. I was called up at the point where I was thinking about a fortissimo finale. Then when I came back from the war, three or four years later, I decided to leave the work as it was. It's better.'

Even so, there are works which he has not published, like his Mass for soprano and violins. 'It's not a good piece. . . . If they haven't been published, it's because they're very bad. It's better that the good works should be published. *Saint François d'Assise* has taken a long time to engrave: so far only the third scene has appeared, but I hope the sixth will be out by Christmas, then the seventh in six months' time, and so on.'

I asked which of all his works was the most important to him. 'Personally, the one I prefer is perhaps *La Transfiguration* for choir and orchestra. It has the most of faith, of religious meditation. It's a resumé of all my work.'

Returning to *Saint François*, I asked if he had written the work beginning at the beginning and going through to the end. 'No, I never write anything from beginning to end! First of all I wrote the text, keeping from all the stories only what concerned the progress of grace in the soul of St Francis. For instance, I eliminated his struggle against his father, because that would have introduced questions of psychology, of the Oedipus complex, which would have been awful.

'I wrote the words myself, since that allowed me to make adaptations when it came to the setting, most of all in order to place good vowels for the singers at the high notes, where you have to have "O", "A" or "E". Then I wrote the music, and finally I did the orchestration, but not in the order of the drama. I spent a lot of time on the sixth scene, almost a year and a half, because it was so difficult. Then I did the fifth scene, and at the end the first scene: that was orchestrated only about a month before the performance.'

Had Messiaen ever experienced doubts about matters of music or theology? 'No. I am very lucky. My parents were not believers, but I was born with the faith, without doing anything: it's just a marvellous gift. If I have doubts, I fortify my faith by reading theology. I read the Gospels, the Psalms, the Apocalypse, the Epistles of St Paul, but I also read the great theologians—St Thomas Aquinas, and also modern theologians: Guardini, Thomas Merton and von Balthasar, the greatest theologian of the twentieth century. As for music, no, I've always had confidence in myself, which is very lucky, because most musicians today have anxieties. And essentially I haven't changed.' (*Times*, 10 December 1988)

London 1988

Despite the vast lesson in glorious humility that Messiaen's opera provides, we cannot but be proud that the most distinguished composer alive should have chosen to spend his eightieth birthday in London, and that London should have been able to present him with such a magnificent performance of what is in every way his largest work. Its first production at the Paris Opera five years ago displayed its problems at least as much as its triumphs; here the latter were in the ascendant, partly because the stage movement was placed within, and sometimes overwhelmed by, the action of the orchestra. Spreading over an enlarged platform, the hundred and twenty or so musicians were a sea of instruments around the cruciform acting platform, this set at an angle so that banks of bells and other percussion played around the 'head' end of the cross shape at the rear left, with violins at the front left and a great wedge at the right for the rest of the orchestra. The oddities of Messiaen's scoring—the huge wind ensemble, with such rarities as contrabass clarinet and big bass tuba, and the three electronic ondes martenot as well as all the percussion—were thus clearly on view, as was the work's important relation to *Chronochromie* as a gigantic stained-glass window of stylized birdsongs.

Of course there were some patchy moments in a performance that lasted for five hours with two short intervals (the strings became dangerously ragged at one difficult point in the second act), but there was an awful lot that came out blazingly right from the London Philharmonic Orchestra under Kent Nagano's dynamic, authoritative and confident direction. The woodwind and percussion, who have so much of the swirling, nattering birdsong, were full of spirit, and the weird noises of the ondes martenot were offered without apology. Splendid too was the singing of the London Philharmonic Choir, whether in staccato incantations, ominous grey brush-strokes or resplendent chorales, the very end of the work being carried to a dazzling pitch of intensity and volume. Their contribution was helped by the screening, which gave them a strong audible presence while keeping them visually in the shadows: the words of Christ thus came appropriately from the unseen, and attention was held on the instrumentalists and solo singers.

Among the latter, David Wilson-Johnson sang with unfailing nobility and ease as the saint. Given the length of the part, and the frequency of musical repetition that must make it hard to remember where one is, he could be forgiven for singing most of the first two acts from the book, though his added power in the last act gave some hint of what we had been missing. Maria Oran was the Angel, sounding aptly clear and bright like a stroked glass, and Kenneth Riegel repeated his sympathetic Leper from the Paris production, grazed and warped with hurt, then bravely simple in his joy. There was also simple, beautiful and eloquent singing from John Graham-Hall as Brother Masseo and Nicholas Isherwood as Brother Leo.

The essential problems of the piece have to do with its disconcerting range of tone. In his music for the Angel's entries, as in his wildly fortissimo extensions of birdsong, Messiaen represents the gift of grace as a shock, shaking the senses, and yet his images of grace itself are often sweetly pious: in the stigmata scene, for instance, the climactic prolongation of the Angel's summons, here done wonderfully as a kind of unstoppable bark for chorus and orchestra, immediately gives way to soft calls of 'François' haloed by ondes martenot. Perhaps a universal spirituality has to have a place for Lourdes as well as Chartres, Lhasa, Bali and Nara, but this does present difficulties in the staging. Michael Rennison's production boldly presented both aspects at once: the ritualized, flamboyant and unpredictable in the hint of kabuki in Mark Wheeler's set, and the religiose in the gentle tread of the monks and the awful Fra Angelico costume Messiaen requires for the Angel. Climactic moments were variable: Francis's embrace of the Leper surely requires a little more than hands placed on shoulders, but the granting of the stigmata, to a saint clasping himself onto a large bare cross, was powerfully done. It still seems possible, though, that something more wholly formalized—perhaps with masks, brilliantly coloured costumes and stiff, vivid gestures—would find the right dramatic echo to this thoroughly extraordinary work, a work which, though so far from the temper of the time, was cheered and cheered and cheered on this occasion. (*Times*, 12 December 1988)

Salzburg 1992

Shortly before his death, in April, Messiaen was looking forward to two big performances this year: the premiere, in November, of the immense piece he had recently finished for the New York Philharmonic, *Eclairs sur l'Au-delà*, and the Salzburg production, in August, of his opera *Saint François d'Assise*, the work's first full staging since it was introduced at the Paris Opera in 1983. As it was, this Salzburg performance had to go forward at a delicate moment: too late for the composer's participation, too soon to have been freed from his expectations, or at least from other people's expectations of his expectations. Messiaen, who understood resurrection, would perhaps have recognized how death bestows a liberation on any artist's works. Until that time they exist in a chrysalid state, while the creator sets the terms for performance and interpretation. Only afterwards can they take wing.

The present betwixt-and-between condition, where *Saint François* is concerned, may account for the unsettling mixture of glory and gaucheness in this production. Its hardware must have been in preparation well before Messiaen's death, since José van Dam, the singer of the central role, mentioned in the Salzburg programme book how his first contacts with Peter Sellars, the director, had given him the impression of a 'St Francis at the centre of projections', and Messiaen himself, in another programme-book interview, spoke of his intention to be in Salzburg in order to 'prevent wrong notes in the music but also. . .in the lighting'. One can infer that he gave his blessing to the presenting of his opera as a sophisticated light show, as well he might, since he often talked about experiencing colours when he heard or imagined music. Besides, James Ingalls's lighting machinery, the production's most startling near-success, surely needed more than the four months since the composer's death to design and assemble.

It dominated the set: slightly tilted to the right, a great square frame of fluorescent tubes, a grid of parallels, perpendiculars and diagonals capable of signalling in white or in rainbow colours. Harmonies of blue and red stripes, sometimes with cyan or magenta, realized the colour scheme that Messiaen associated with his most characteristic mode, the scale alternating whole tones with semitones. At the same time these harmonies vividly recalled what the composer probably admired before all other human artifacts, the stained-glass windows of Chartres and the Sainte-Chapelle. But these were only some of the possibilities. Slants of blue, green and yellow suggested an abstract summertime outdoors, a landscape for those birds whose songs resound—discreetly or with grand, affirmative amplification—throughout the orchestral score. A huge gold cross could shine out, or the apparatus could become a chequerboard of white lines, making the eye blink and jump, or else, for the scene of the saint's stigmatization, there could be just five rays of sore red.

Many of these effects were breathtaking. And yet they were not quite breathtaking enough. Whenever Messiaen spoke about his synaesthetic experience of light alongside sound, the impression he conveyed was a kinetic one, of colours swirling, bulging, rolling. Even his beloved stained-glass windows have their dynamism, since the repartitioning of the same few colours, as the eye moves down or across the field, shakes on the retina to create a visual fizz, a stationary blaze. The Salzburg square, almost throughout, produced its effects symmetrically and slowly and carefully, though when the end came one understood why Sellars and Ingalls had reserved their dazzling flurry of illuminations for this gigantic C major of joy as the saint's soul reaches its home in heaven. For the four hours up to then it was all too clear what was going on. The colours could not match the music in speed of movement, and the effect was ponderously mechanical as one bar after another switched into life. It might help if the technology could be screened, or some other way found to lessen the obviousness of the means, unloose the light beams from the dead weight of their scaffolding. This is worth wishing for, since the production is to be seen again in Paris in December (but not now in Los Angeles, though it was the Los Angeles Philharmonic, under Esa-Pekka Salonen, that was giving the colours of the score their stupendous recreation).

Possibly because he was aware of himself as writing an opera, Messiaen was open to influences to a degree unusual in his mature music: he himself pointed to Pamina as the prototype of his Angel, though the atmosphere that wafts around the role is more Mélisande's, and the 'theme of decision' comes from the end of the first act of *Götterdämmerung*. But in its nature *Saint François* is apart. This is not a drama that music accompanies, enhances, embraces or enlarges; it is music within which some compartments of a drama are being manifested.

Dwarfed by the orchestral score, how are the characters to behave towards it? Sellars's solution is ingenious. As in his recent productions of *The Magic Flute* and *The Death of Klinghoffer*, he has the singers use their hands and arms a great deal in formal movement. He steers clear of the body language of Christian tradition—the crossings, benedictions and genuflections—but establishes gestures and postures that intimate the sacred and, even more usefully, suggest people being acted upon by, rather than themselves acting, what they sing and hear. When Francis tries to calm Leo by explaining that pain and sacrifice are paths to 'perfect joy', his hands come together and make a slow dive down in front of his body, betokening a bliss that includes and surpasses the erotic (very true to Messiaen, this spirituality that rejoices in the flesh, though perhaps not so true to the historical Francis). When the Angel comes onstage he accompanies his musical signature—an upward rush for strings and ondes, followed by a shrill twirl for oboe and clarinets—by an urgent motion of the hands, separating as they sweep up from the chest to above the head. He seems shocked by sound, possessed by it.

Other aspects of the staging pull against the fabric. Sellars and his set designer, George Tsypin, scatter the scene with video monitors, half of them flying, half of them built into blocky rows, columns or arches on the platform. Not only were the flickering images—a poinsettia bush (for a line in the libretto), birds, a young monk suffering agony or ecstasy in a wilderness—irritating in just being there, they were also crude in colour, superfluous and banal. The birdsongs that Messiaen creates with his wind instruments, ondes and percussion are a salute to nature, but from a new world: they have very little still to do with the pecking, staring, puzzled creatures being shown on screen. Even worse—not just irrelevant but shockingly out of tune—was Sellars's introduction of an elfin young woman with crimson wings and costume to execute the Leper's dance and reappear later. The apparition was all the more lamentable when the singing Angel had arrived with such ease. Dawn Upshaw, dressed in quiet grey and blessedly wingless, had simply loomed up from behind a bank of the monitors: the supernatural slid into the proceedings without fuss, like an animal into water, and revealed itself far more persuasively thus than as the mauve-draped, polychrome-winged figure of the Paris premiere.

That original Angel was an embarrassment: much better—finer and stronger—this entry of the divine messenger as a hushed secretary. Nor was this just an achievement of costume design (by Dunya Ramicova) and stagecraft, for Upshaw was singing the music with unalterable poise and accuracy and simplicity—indeed with grace, with a tone so light and pure it seemed a glance from the mind, engaging nothing physical. And yet this large theatre was filled—and at the same time stilled—by her dramatic presence. So successful was this grey Angel one could wish Sellars and his team had gone further and found some alternative to monkish dress for Francis and his community. The work's value—and one might even say its sacredness—lies not in its borrowings from Christian history and ritual but in what it declares and embodies about human experience of time.

But the musical performances were in another realm. Van Dam—darker, graver than in Paris nine years ago—was again majestic and selfless, letting the grand phrases roll. His distinction is not to have made this opera his own but to have devoted himself, wholly, to this opera, and thereby to have entered into its strange spirit. Messiaen suggested Musorgsky's Boris and Debussy's Golaud as kindred roles to his St Francis, both these antecedents being men harried by doubt. Van Dam's performance similarly projects a troubled mind, a worriedness at the edge of exhaustion and disbelief—a saint before sanctity. (Messiaen's choice of a low baritone is already anti-historical: the real St Francis is said to have had a light tenor voice, though he did indeed sing in French.)

The other heroes of the production were Upshaw and the orchestra, the latter fulfilling all the score's demands for beauty, oddity and supreme fullness of sound, while Salonen maintained an extraordinary clarity of rhythm from players disposed over a large area. The young-voiced Arnold Schoenberg Choir also made a strong effect, though not placed to best advantage: a large wooden construction, visually balancing the light box a little and evoking a semi-built cathedral, was barely used, and even when it was, at the climactic end, it failed to thrust the choral sound forward as one had hoped. Smaller parts were excellently done. Ronald Hamilton was the Leper, spitting blood in his long vituperation. Two other tenors, Thomas Young and John Aler, were caustic and consolatory. The young baritone Urban Malmberg offered a beautiful performance as Brother Leo, well serving and well served by Sellars's extension of the role, so that the relationship between master and pupil, in an opera generally lacking human connections, became a strand of warmth and affection. Here was a becoming obeisance to a composer who was himself revered and loved as a teacher. (*New Yorker*, 14 September 1992)

Salzburg 1998

Selflessness was one of Messiaen's fundamental qualities as a man and as an artist, and in his opera *Saint François d'Assise* he was selfless enough to have nearly three hundred musicians exerting themselves for more than four hours (discounting intermissions) to tell the story of abnegation. The hugeness of the score is a measure of its humility. In giving everything away, Francis of Assisi gained the world: the wind, the flowers and the birds he praised in his *Cantico delle creature*. Similarly Messiaen—though he would have refused the comparison—set aside all claims of self-expression and so could receive into his music the whole world of sound: from colossal consonances for the entire chorus and orchestra to weird nighttime sonorities made by three ondes martenots, or from calm chant, which is the manner of most of the solo vocal writing, to delirious exultations of birdsong. Because of its scale *Saint François* will always be a rare work, and this is right: it needs to be a special occasion. But it also needs to be available. For the moment, its future lies with the 1992 Salzburg Festival production, which has been brought back this year and may now appear again in Paris and Berlin. Sooner or later the work must also be done in the United States.

Coming to the virtues of the present revival, it is hard to know where to start. Triumph is general: for José van Dam in the title role; for all the other soloists; for Kent Nagano, the conductor; for his magnificent British orchestra, the Hallé of Manchester, and for the Arnold Schoenberg Choir from Vienna. Van Dam, who has been St Francis in every staged performance so far, sings with unswerving force. He sounds like a dark, low trumpet, always there to the full, always secure, and at first his certainty is forbidding. But this is surely how Messiaen wanted it. The opening scene is there to show that Francis's feelings are not earthly but divine: he exhibits compassion for an anxious young monk not by lending comfort but by demanding more suffering. As the performance goes on, Van Dam's hardy strength, formidably sustained throughout this long role, proves itself. Sentiment can be done without. Power counts.

Dawn Upshaw just is, simply and purely, the voice of the Angel. Chris Merritt writhes with vocal fury as the Leper. Urban Malmberg gives a fine, appealing performance as Brother Leo, his youthful baritone seeming to pick up resilience from Van Dam. Contrasted tenors, Guy Renard and John Aler, enact the distemperate Brother Elia and the head-in-the-clouds Brother Masseo. Upshaw, Malmberg and Aler were all there with Van Dam when this production was first done, and their performances have grown with his. It is not a question of finding more in the music, but of trying less. There is serenity and acceptance in what they do.

Perhaps we are beginning to understand what we have got in this work—or at least to understand what a puzzle and a challenge we have got. Besides being huge and humble, the score is as ancient as plainsong and as new as yesterday in its musical resources. Most paradoxically of all, it is, in a godless century, as bold as an icon.

Any staging is bound to be measured by its failures, and Peter Sellars has defiantly kept his most extravagant ones from 1992: the video monitors that litter the stage, flickering with unwanted images. But he is responsible, too, for visual wonder, in the workings of a huge array of fluorescent tubes responding to the light and colour in the music. And there is appropriateness in the quiet care with which the principals onstage handle one another and comport themselves. Meanwhile, Nagano and his orchestra perform with alacrity and vividness, and with almost overwhelming glory in company with the chorus in the closing moments. If music could make us good, this music would. In the silence after the last ecstatic chord you thought you heard the Devil screaming. (*New York Times*, 27 August 1998)

Salzburg 1998 recording

Much of the orchestral material, as in most of the works Messiaen wrote from the early fifties onward, consists of imitations of birdsongs, most of them notated by the composer in the wild. Woodwind groups and percussion ensembles evoke the brilliant chirpings of robins and warblers, the cooings of doves and owls, the harsher tones of hawks or the vibrant calls of birds from New Caledonia. Meanwhile, the human voices comport themselves with Franciscan humility. The characters do not sing: they chant. And for each of them, the chant moves through a small number of formulae. In the extreme case of Brother Leo, the youngster among St Francis's companions, the chant is fixed to the same words as well as to the same melodic shapes in three of the four scenes in which he appears, so that he comes on each time singing the same thing. More usually, the formulae are adapted to different verbal phrases, just as, in the plainsong chanting of a psalm or a hymn, melodic figures are repeated through different verses.

This effectively inhibits, of course, the use of the singing voice to intensify the expressive meaning of the words, since the melody at any point will be taken from the character's pattern book, and the pattern, once started, has to be followed through to the end. But this is not a disadvantage, because Messiaen was not normally concerned with singing as a way of enriching verbal sense or revealing states of mind. St Francis, who sings in all but one of the opera's eight scenes, is shown in various attitudes: giving lessons to his brothers in the spiritual life (ornithology included as an appreciation of the created real), praying, discoursing with a leper and with an angel, preaching to the birds, dying. But in his music he is always the same: steady, resolute, moving through the strong contours of his melodic repertory. The music is there not to portray him but to present him. Where, in a stained-glass window or an early painting, Francis might be shown looking virtually the same in different scenes from his life, so here he sounds virtually the same. His melodic sequences are his distinguishing features, equivalent to the tonsure, the habit and the short beard. In this iconic world of representation, the more conventional the depiction, the more vivid the presence of the character in the image. Lacking musical conventions, Messiaen has to invent his own, in the form of melodic motifs, but having invented them, he sticks with them.

Hence, in large measure, the unusualness of *Saint François* as an opera. What the characters sing is not sprung out of them by the dramatic moment: it is, rather, what they have sung many times before.

Even at the start an awareness of repetition is imposed, for the opening scene is a straightforward procession of verses and refrains. There is the feeling of experiences being remembered, and of a link being drawn between events in the performance and events in thirteenth-century Umbria, as if both were part of the same thick present, an eight-century fleck of eternity. Dense in reiteration and with liturgical verse-refrain forms continuing central to the structure, the work is a commemoration, like the church dramas of medieval cathedral worship, in which a story from the past is held up to view, and in which—because the effort is all of memory, not interpretation—it reachieves the immediacy of happening now. And though St Francis does not change we do, through living for a while in a shared present with a man of the middle ages.

Whether the change is a benediction must be for individual listeners to know. Acts of grace, as presented in the opera, are violent. Grace is slammed into people. When an angel comes knocking at the monastery door, a spirit hand's gentle taps are heard from the orchestra as tremendous chords, repeated in an emphatic rhythm. The same image recurs when St Francis is granted the ultimate request he has for his mortal life, and the five wounds of Christ on the Cross are repeated in his body. In the following scene, at the moment when St Francis dies, the huge choir calls on God with a fierce yell. Here is another reason for the work's personnel to be so numerous: to make a divine din.

Messiaen himself would undoubtedly have dismissed the notion that his work could offer a religious experience. His dismissal is even present inside the piece, in words his libretto adapts from St Thomas Aquinas: 'God dazzles us by excess of truth. Music carries us to God by want of truth.' Music is preparatory, giving us not knowledge but an awareness of the knowledge we need. Yet Messiaen was explicit about his wish to create his own dazzlement, for instance by the explosions of colour and clamour that happen in *Saint François* or by the slow, sweet melody the angel plays to the saint in the fifth scene, a melody carried on the unearthly breeze of electronic sound, from three ondes martenot, across a blue sky of concords from orchestra and wordless ('worldless', one might say) chorus. But the object of the dazzlement, for him, was to convince his audience of the truth behind—not within—the moment of expression.

Saint François is amazingly unlikely. A major religious work coming at the end of the twentieth century. A work in which the goal of spiritual music is not a cover for false naivety and nostalgia but instead a challenge the composer accepts to accommodate as broad and various a range of sounds as possible, and, above all, to imagine the previously unheard. A work in which extreme sophistication, in the handling of instruments and the composition of harmonies, goes hand in hand with extreme simplicity, in the repetitive forms. A work possessing the rarest quality: certainty.

Everything in *Saint François* speaks of certainty, but most of all its continuous present, its absence of development—musically as well as in the treatment of character. Exactly as the sung melodies keep returning, so do the themes and birdsongs of the orchestral fabric. What Messiaen calls themes are not subjects such as appear in Bach, Beethoven or Wagner—least of all those that signal characters. St Francis's pronouncements, for example, are nearly always introduced and punctuated by a short, robust melody (a melody he takes over into his voice just once, in the first scene, where he quotes St Paul), by a 'theme of decision' (an affirmative dive of chords) and by the cry of a kestrel. Beyond this elementary function, repetition is crucial for itself. There are, to be sure, things that occur just once, including some fine set pieces: the ebullient dance for the leper, after he has been embraced and cured by the saint, or the concert the birds make after they have listened in silence to St Francis's sermon. There are these single images. But like figures in a stained-glass window, they are overwhelmed by the background of repeating elements. *Saint François* has this in common with stained-glass windows, too, that it awes one by its resonant colours and that the narrative is less important than the design: the repetition from panel to panel of the same elements, and the presence in all those elements of lustre.

Repetition also keeps the music in a continuous present, where time is not long but deep. We are not carried forward, as in most western music, but held stationary. The time is not that of our lives but time that has not been touched yet by human beings, time within which every instant lasts forever. In giving us this time—in presenting us with the fresh present—*Saint François* exceeds the boundaries of its particular denomination. It is about eternity before holiness. But eternity and holiness may be the same thing. (2000)

Boulez

Pierre Boulez's most startling creative work came early, climaxing in the violent beauty of *Le Marteau sans maître* (1952–4), for a septet of dissimilar instruments including the contralto voice. Many later works he left unfinished (e.g. his Third Piano Sonata, 1955–7), disclaimed or recomposed: *Pli selon pli*, for soprano with an orchestra rich in chiming percussion, he began in 1957, first presented whole in 1960 and went on revising until the end of the 1980s. Meanwhile he gained and maintained acclaim as a conductor and forthright musical presence.

at sixty

Modern music grows old alarmingly. Pierre Boulez now is sixty, and the opportunity was taken to celebrate with a long weekend of concerts and an exhibition in Baden-Baden, which has been his home town since 1959. This solidly respectable spa, this German Cheltenham, survived having Berlioz and Brahms as summer visitors in the 1860s, but perhaps has never quite got used to housing a master of the avantgarde. After one lady had patiently explained to her elderly husband about this 'Hommage à Pierre Boulez' he turned swiftly to her: 'Er ist tot oder?'

In truth there were moments when it was a bit like that. The nature of exhibitions is to seem commemorative rather than jubilant, and the long glass cases in the Kunsthalle, containing scores, sketches, letters, postcards and photographs, did convey a funereal solemnity not altogether alleviated by the reverberating sound of the *Ring* being eternally replayed in some part of the building.

On closer inspection, though, the whole thing came to life. Word of mouth had always had it that Boulez's teenage counterpoint exercises were enough to make one's hair stand on end: here was a page of seven-part essays to prove not only that he could rival Obrecht but also that his neatly minuscule handwriting has not changed in more than forty years. There was also a stylistic exercise, a setting of Psalm 97 in four-part canon after the Bartók of the first movement of the Music for Strings, and from the same period a copy of the first movement of Webern's Concerto done on two staves.

To see this in Boulez's manuscript was to be reminded of how much he owed to Webern, especially when on opposite walls one could inspect the long-withdrawn score of his *Polyphonie X* of 1950–51 and then in another chamber hear on tape this extraordinary Utopian fantasy of what orchestral music might be: a cross-current of solo phrases and sentences in limbo, conducted with remarkable authority by Hans Rosbaud, but causing increasing restlessness in its audience.

Tantalizing glimpses of letters from Cage, dating from this same period, bore witness to their friendship. Cage in 1950, having recently returned to New York from Paris, was quite the modernist, scoffing at composers of pentatonic music and looking forward to meeting Milton Babbitt. By 1952 he was suggesting that his next work would be long and forever unfinished: perhaps it has been so.

A more durable friend was Stockhausen, whom one found in a moving letter of February 1960 responding to criticism Boulez must have voiced about his recent *Zyklus* for solo percussionist. He obviously wanted to write off Boulez's misgivings but could not bring himself to do so, feeling that Boulez 'gave the measure' to what he composed.

Though it is doubtful Stockhausen still feels the same way, his was the most touching contribution to a concert of tributes from contemporaries and disciples. The piece was his *Klavierstück XIV*, very much in the style of its two predecessors but shorter, performed here by Pierre-Laurent Aimard, complete with its kisses blown towards the dedicatee.

Other homages may have been more straightlaced, but testified to the respect and affection Boulez enjoys from his most eminent colleagues. Carter provided a witty flute-clarinet duet with the apt title of *Esprit rude/esprit doux*. From Berio there was a jittery little wind quintet, from Nono a bit of heavy breathing for bass flute, contrabass clarinet and electronics, from Bussotti an impassioned fragment of viola concerto, from Holliger a straining from nine instruments towards the upper limits of audibility (rendered excruciatingly on tape), from Denisov a coolly Romantic adagio for horn and ensemble, from Höller an impeccably professional *Improvisation sur le nom Pierre Boulez*.

One begins to sound like the registrar of gifts at a wedding, but the real essence of this festival was to offer a little retrospective of Boulez's own works—one offering surprises at every turn. *Le Marteau sans maître*, for instance, has probably not often been played with such a taut combination of loveliness and attack as Boulez himself here obtained from members of the Ensemble InterContemporain with Elizabeth Laurence. The pace was generous, the phrasing ample as Boulez now likes it, but the feeling was electric, the xylophone player and percussionist pouncing on their parts. It is time Boulez made another recording of the work, preferably with these musicians, for Laurence has the rare ability to execute the sprechgesang without sounding venomous: she has a gloriously full yet fresh tone.

Other discoveries included the Arditti Quartet playing the whole forty minutes of the published *Livre pour quatuor* (1948–9), whose highly elaborate crystal castles are made only to be left uninhabited, and Pi-Hsien Chen presenting the intemperate early *Notations* for piano. The ninth of these twelve pieces, which keeps insisting on a note in the extreme bass, is in its miniature terms a rage against annihilation comparable with the finale of Mahler's Sixth Symphony, and one hopes Boulez will allow the set to be published, even though he is working on orchestral developments of his teenage sketches. Bernhard Wambach's beautiful resonances and alacritous rhythms in the Third Piano Sonata ought to have been a stimulus towards getting that work completed.

Meanwhile Boulez's hottest work in progress is *Répons* for six electronically modulated tuned percussion and small orchestra. Since the performance at the 1982 Proms the work has grown again to forty-five minutes, at which length it begins to seem more at ease, more equal to the space it occupies. Boulez has added a sequence of fantastic dances, led by the main ensemble and excellently conducted here by Peter Eötvös, who was overseeing this complex score for the first time. There follows a quiescent cadenza for the percussion soloists alone: a coda in the present context, but surely to become no more than a lull before battle is re-engaged.

One may not share the view recently expressed by Jean-Jacques Nattiez, the guru of musical semiology, that *Répons* is a modern masterpiece on the level of *Pelléas et Mélisande* or *The Rite of Spring*, but it certainly is a marvel. Boulez at sixty remains the most awesomely gifted of composers. (*Times*, 11 April 1985)

London 1989

For a composer who spends so much of his time thinking about the future, a retrospective may evoke as much dismay as pleasure: having disposed of the history of music, Boulez now finds he is encumbered with the history of himself. However, for the rest of us the BBC's festival at the Barbican, which opened last night, will provide a rare feast of musical splendours and challenges. Never before, anywhere in the world, have so many of his works been presented together.

The first concert began appropriately with the massive gauntlet he threw down right at the beginning of his creative life, when he was twenty-two: his Second Piano Sonata. This is a work that has usually been considered, not least by its composer, as fundamentally negative: an assault of Beethovenian weight which hammers at received notions of sonata form, and watches what happens when the lessons of Schoenberg and Messiaen are set to annihilate one another. Here, though, Pierre-Laurent Aimard showed it in an altogether more positive light, picking out from the onslaught gestures of electric invention. One may have missed the sheer seriousness that Pollini, above all, has found in this score, but Aimard's handling of the slow movement was immensely impressive for its achievement of objective contemplation and its grasp of a continuity extending through all the asides. Perhaps, too, the violence of the work does not need to be pressed in every performance: there is room for an account that reaches luminous tranquility, rather than exhausted despair, on the last page.

Aimard's performance also had the advantage of making the sonata a prelude to the work performed after the interval, *Pli selon pli*, rather than a severe contrast. Unfortunately, owing to lack of rehearsal time, the final fold of this five-part portrait of Mallarmé could not be revealed, but that may have had some beneficial effect in throwing attention on the fourth movement, the work's great opening into vastness. When the new version of this movement was done by itself, at a BBC concert three or four years ago, it seemed a slightly fussy elaboration of the stark original, but here, thanks partly to intense contributions from the cellos and a clear ensemble of flutes, the impression was of an echo-bound amplification of the music, as well as of an exact response, in imagery and function, to the poet's vision of foam and flotsam after the spectacular natural catastrophe of death. It helped this movement, too, that the new soloist, Christine Whittlesey, should bring to the music an open, fresh tone, the voice of a Mélisande. She was sometimes withdrawn, but she brought an edge of danger and daring to go with the spaciousness and fine instrumental detail of the orchestral performance. (*Times*, 16 January 1989)

◆

If the BBC/Barbican Boulez festival leaves a rather melancholy wake behind it, that is perhaps less the fault of the sometimes disappointing attendance than of the nature of Boulez's career. Built into the notion of the retrospective is an expectation of achievement to be glimpsed in early works and then mountingly revealed in what has followed; but Boulez's life has not gone that way. Of the twenty works in these programmes, all but seven had been at least begun thirty years ago. Perhaps inevitably, the festival has violently reinforced the impression of a prolonged stalemate. It has done so partly by inviting us to judge such relatively recent miniatures as *Messagesquisse* by the standards of the Third Piano Sonata. It has done so also, and less predictably, by allowing us to renew visual contact with Boulez's single major work of the 1970s, the orchestral *Rituel*, for here in dramatic terms the composer-conductor is shown as a passive bystander at his own machinery.

There is another, even more striking and sombre stage display of impasse in his most recent piece, *Dialogue de l'ombre double*, where a clarinettist is trapped in a hexagon of music stands, all filled with lines that bounce around restricted groups of notes, all due to be executed before the shadow clarinet on tape—which has summoned the soloist and, pitiless, leads him from one page to the next—allows the player to leave. With artificial reverberation to intensify the sense of enclosure, the piece is as obsessive, impelled, grey and trivia-worn as a Beckett monologue, which is perhaps to suggest that it faces the consequences of a post-catastrophe creativity more starkly than did its parent work, *Domaines*, where the clarinettist's circumscribed ideas are interpreted as invitations to high-style virtuosity by a sextet of answering groups. Alain Damiens was the fluent, responsive soloist in *Dialogue*; Andre Trouttet worked soft, smooth multiple tones into *Domaines*.

Here the reworking is positive, pessimistic, but more often Boulez's urge to revise seems yet another symptom of a cauterized imagination, a case in point being the brand new version of the first movement of *Livre pour cordes*. This began life forty years ago as the opening of a quartet, which Boulez then echoed and refracted in his arrangement for string orchestra, two decades later. Now he has spliced together the two parts of the movement, added a coda and simplified the texture. His own explanation is that the new version has allowed him to achieve the 'clarity of contrast' he wanted in the first place: but can that really have been the aim of the original nervy, intense, restless quartet movement? One might feel rather that a dense engraving, having been covered with colour washes in the 1968 version, has been spirited away, leaving only its glamorous echo.

To end the last concert, the composer conducted the BBC Symphony Orchestra in a splendid performance of the *Notations* derived in the late 1970s from piano pieces of 1945. Other performances of works from this period turned up the challenging light that the music of Boulez's twenties and early thirties cast on what has followed. The Ensemble InterContemporain under Peter Eötvös, with Elizabeth Laurence as soloist, gave a lucid performance of *Le Marteau sans maître*, and Pi-Hsien Chen and Pierre-Laurent Aimaird argued persuasively that *Structures Ib*, duly slowed down, is as rich in incident and dialogue as *Structures II*. If these still seem to be the works that count, one has to recognize that Boulez's subsequent block is not a personal problem, but rather a block in the development of music. In bearing witness to the unhappy condition of the art, his later works at least describe a reason for despondency. (*Times*, 21 January 1989)

conducting workshop

It is hard to say who learned more: the four young conductors who became Pierre Boulez's apprentices for a couple of days with the Cleveland Orchestra at Carnegie Hall last month, or the audience at this Professional Training Workshop, since the need to explain himself obliged Boulez, one of the most undemonstrative of conductors, to show his hand—or rather, his two hands, capable of maintaining different rhythms quite separately from one another, of thinking apart. That was one problem for his would-be disciples. Boulez's advice was directed solely to matters of technique, and to the musical issues technique can address. Without his technique, the four young men stood little chance of rising to his expectations of them, however straightforwardly and encouragingly those expectations were expressed, and however much support and good will for the brave volunteers was coming from both orchestra and audience. (The only bulls at this corrida were the mutely demanding scores, by Debussy and Messiaen.) No closer approximation to the Boulez ideal could have been expected from conductors early in their careers: few seasoned professionals can chop or mould time with his virtuosity.

But the concentration on the purely musical—on the printed notes, on what can be determined from the printed notes, and on how the fruits of observation can be realized with an orchestra—was at least an education in Boulez's approach. In the introductory session of classroom study, he rapidly passed over the scenario of Debussy's ballet *Jeux*, and said hardly a word about the birdsongs of Messiaen's *Chronochromie*, about that work's concern with the projection of colour through harmony and instrumentation, or about its use of sound to, as the title suggests, give a colour to time. What Boulez asked his trainees to notice was, rather, Debussy's way of transforming motifs, and his own way of transforming Messiaen's metronome marks in order to make the music playable.

In elucidating the Debussy score he was following what he had learned fifty years before when he was a student in Messiaen's class. Messiaen, he said, had pointed out how threads of connection pass through the fugitive melodic ideas of *Jeux*—how an important theme may become secondary or vice versa, how the same theme may recur differently harmonized, how rhythms can be expanded or contracted. 'Maybe you can have an intuition of this, but I doubt it. The relationships are to be'—and here he brought a heavy down-beat emphasis on the participle—'discovered'. There, in a word, was the passion of Boulez's engagement, and also the objectivity, the view of the score as something to be inspected, learned and understood. Once discovered, the motivic relationships are, for him, to be conveyed to the orchestra wordlessly, simply by rehearsing thematically-connected passages side by side. Analysis is for the conductor to do in his workroom; rehearsal is about making things happen, about the activeness on which Boulez was constantly insisting, both in what he said and in his examples of productive gestures.

When, later in the exercise, the question of the baton came up, he looked physically pained at the idea of becoming, as he put it, a sort of Captain Hook of the podium, losing the fluidity and immediacy with which he can work with his hands on the orchestra. Time and again he stressed how the conductor must play the orchestra, must use his hands with a keyboard player's feeling for qualities of attack and volume ('You do yourself what you want to hear'), but always with a sense not of controlling the players but of enabling them, of giving ('You give and you receive. You receive what they play: you listen. And you give them what they need'). To offer a cue, the right hand slices swiftly forward on the horizontal, palm down, and then at the last moment the digits spread, giving the signal to the musicians, not grasping it close to the body, tight-fisted, as Boulez criticized one of his junior colleagues for doing. 'That's not only in order to be precise. That's much more important than to be precise: that's to be'—again an intense final emphasis—'acting.'

Another fault would be—and here, too, an example was provided by one of the students—to do more with the hands than is required, to 'put too much lace around the gesture'. Boulez's gestures, famously economical and exact, are at once controlled and loose: controlled in that the arms move in a shallow vertical space, from waist height to head height, and from a stationary torso; loose in that the hands are held well away from the body, and in that the whole arm, from shoulder to fingertips, works in a single, smooth flow. By comparison with his pupils, whose hands flailed high and elbows chugged, he could often appear to be conducting more slowly, even when his tempos were faster. But though he evidently prizes elegance as a virtue in itself, and said so, there are other reasons for it. A distinct vocabulary of movement clarifies communication with the orchestra. And the extension of the arms is the outer manifestation of an inner attitude: the attitude of giving, of generosity to and care for the players, but also an attitude of distance from the score, of holding the music explicitly at arm's length. Do not come too close. 'You have to be looking at the painting and making the painting at the same time.'

Beyond that, the fluidity of the Boulez style is needed—following his idea of the conductor as super-player of the orchestra—to achieve fluidity in the music, and especially in Debussy's music, and most especially in *Jeux*. He urged his students to find a 'flexibility which does not destroy rhythm', and on another occasion remarked how 'the arabesque in Debussy should be always precise but not rigid', those contrasted adjectives again opening a verbal window into his whole way of thinking. Everything must be thoroughly considered and rigorously executed, and yet the feel must be supple. In his talk about the Debussy piece, and in his answers to questions, another phrase kept recurring: 'But not too much, but not too much'.

Apropos of Messiaen we heard those words much less. The hurdles for the young conductors in *Chronochromie* were, rather, those of acquiring coordination and keeping it all the way through irregular rhythms that would pass at high speed and be suddenly supplanted. Boulez's cavalier reinterpretation of the metronome speeds was a help, relaxing the extreme prestissimos and adjusting neighbouring tempos to simpler proportions—though one was left wanting more justification than the glib assertions that first, Messiaen never objected, and second, composers' metronome marks are always wrong, except in the case of Stravinsky's *Les Noces*.

But even with the path thus smoothed, pitfalls abounded when it came to the practical session on this piece. At an awkward point in the first movement, where an imitation of the Narcissus Flycatcher requires a quick rebound—from high woodwinds and xylophones to low brass, bassoons and percussion, then back again—Boulez asked his student to find the substance of the motif not in imagining the bird but in himself: 'You must live the rhythm in your body.' This incorporation of the music—he shook as he spoke—is probably necessary to the active conducting he demands. Then there was a passage in the Coda where one of the young conductors kept experiencing difficulties with the simultaneous combination of values: thirty-second notes in the woodwinds, triplet thirty-second notes in xylophones, longer durations in bells, gongs and cymbal, and an entry for the brass. 'You forgot your trombones!' The apprentice nodded; it was getting to be too much. Quietly, ruefully, Boulez brought the trial to an end: 'You must try to think of everything . . .'

The trouble is that these things—living in avian rhythms, thinking of everything, and then acting everything for the orchestra—depend on qualities of mind and physique that are particular to Boulez and not easily communicated. *Chronochromie* dates from a period in Messiaen's life, that of the late 1950s and early 1960s, when he was listening not only to birds in the woods and fields but also to Boulez's performances in Paris. Since the sea change in the senior composer's orchestral style occurred between *Réveil des oiseaux* (1953) and *Oiseaux exotiques* (1955–6), across the time of his pupil's debut as a concert conductor, it is tempting to conclude that there was some link, that now he knew it would be possible to compose differently, since he had seen and heard the necessary performing technique in action.

Anyone else who faces an orchestra with *Chronochromie* on the music stand therefore has to become Boulez a little, and it was no surprise that each of the workshop conductors in turn should have found the accommodation tricky when the model was standing behind his left shoulder. If, nevertheless, the four remained good-humoured, that was due not only to Boulez's determination on their behalf but also to the interest, care and honesty of the Cleveland players. The orchestra's musical readiness in the two workshop scores must have been helped by the experience of performing both pieces in Cleveland the previous week under Boulez's direction, in concert and for Deutsche Grammophon. But their responsiveness was just as remarkable: each conductor could see his different exaggerations and faults, and occasionally his different successes, in a perfectly polished mirror.

The permanent mementoes of Boulez's recent time in Cleveland should be interesting. Meanwhile the Debussy recordings he made there two years ago—of the *Prélude à 'L'Après-midi d'un faune'*, *Images* and *Printemps*—have been released, and show the grand sweep and the luxury texture of his current preferences. The contrast with his Debussy of a quarter-century ago, when he recorded the *Images* with the same orchestra, is startling: speeds are much the same, which is to say generally brisk, but the sound is fuller and the continuity more traditional; there is not the quasi-Japanese feeling for fierce tension in a formal gesture, for fire in ice, or the readiness to sound out the weirdness in Debussy. Where Boulez's 1960s view was that of a fellow composer, his new recordings are those of a master conductor, and they provide a more sumptuous sort of pleasure. One also gets a vivid impression, in sound alone, of those separately mobile hands as they trigger an entry or wave in the air an arabesque that is precise but not rigid. (*New Yorker*, 12 April 1993)

at seventy

Boulez's extended, travelling seventieth-birthday party with the London Symphony Orchestra began in London with a magnificent series of eight concerts, a celebration of the music Boulez loves best. That category must surely, and with good reason, include his own works, for he has shown a strong symptom of love in his perpetual anxiety over his music, in his repeated efforts, through revision, to set it on the right path. But his repertory of choice also includes the same works of the same composers he was programming when he began his career as a conductor, in the late 1950s. The first complete concerts he directed in Europe, in January 1959, placed pieces of his own in a context of Schoenberg, Berg, Webern, Debussy and Stravinsky. This 1995 tour adds only Messiaen, Bartók and Ravel.

After the mixed experiences of the 1970s, when Boulez's positions as music director in New York and London led him to take on repertory with which he had little sympathy (Brahms's *German Requiem* represented perhaps the furthest—and furthest possible—alienation of himself from himself), he has returned to the music that for him is home. And his performances with the LSO had the joy of a homecoming. There are places in these scores that open up when he is around: much of Bartók's *Miraculous Mandarin*—especially the last and most lubricious of the clarinet cajolings, and the frenetic chase—or the first movement of Ravel's *Le Tombeau de Couperin*, where he always pushes the oboe soloist to a speed that is just uncomfortable, and thrillingly so. Stravinsky evidently excites Boulez as much now as ever. Berg is another longstanding favourite, not least when Jessye Norman is around to sing, rapturously, the Seven Early Songs and the *Altenberglieder*.

The Seven Early Songs have a wonderful way with nostalgia. Berg wrote the original versions with piano accompaniment when he was in his early twenties, at an age and in a culture (turn-of-the-century Vienna) prone to succulent regret. His orchestration, two decades later, added further layers of distance and enchantment, for while the soprano still sounds out from the comfortable, ripe, Romantic world of 1905–8, the instruments around her are wandering into weirder and wilder regions that are for her a 'not yet', to be discovered soon, as Berg, with Schoenberg and Webern, journeyed into atonality. The singer is accompanied by her composer's own sly, adoring critique of her enthusiasms and her longings. She sings of misty nights, autumn, forest paths and love, and the orchestra tries to comprehend her from somewhere after a catastrophe that is still in her future. The orchestra knows more than she does; Boulez, in the clarity of his performance, shows us how much more. Yet it may seem that the singer knows more than the orchestra, because she glides—and Norman glides superbly—within a world where music comes to meet us with consolation, where it is never strange, where it seems to know us.

This work's special quality depends on its double dating, on the fact that it belongs at once in 1905–8 and in 1928—or, rather, that it belongs wholly in neither. And perhaps Boulez feels a particular affection for it because so many of his own pieces similarly straddle time. His third *Improvisation sur Mallarmé*, which he first presented in the late 1950s as a wonderland of alternative pathways and colliding colours, became a fixed, more uniform monument in the 1980s, and the *Livre pour cordes*, which began as the first movement of a string quartet in 1948–9, was reworked for string orchestra in 1968, and drastically altered again two decades after that. Revision has effectively unhitched these works from history: if we ask when the *Livre pour cordes* was written, there is no easy answer. That makes Boulez's current position very different from what it was thirty-six years ago, however similar his concert programmes. In 1959, by presenting his pieces in the company of the most radical music of his most radical predecessors, he was telling a story of progress: his music was to be heard as uniting and furthering the developments initiated in music between the *Prélude à 'L'Après-midi d'un faune'* and *The Rite of Spring*. But that story has stalled. Since 1959 the great bulk of his music has consisted not of new pieces, continuing the revolution, but of amendments, revisiting it and, by implication, compromising it. So, inevitably, the arrows have fallen out of the earlier music he performs, and out of how he performs it: *The Rite* is now less a herald, more a magnificent achievement in itself. (Yet he shows his continuing attachment to the revolutionary moment in his preference—quite against his practice with regard to his own music—for original versions, including the rarely heard prototypical *Petrushka*, whose added richness he made telling in one of these London concerts.)

The turn in Boulez's concerns from long history (works as points on a line from plainchant to now) to short history (works as fulfilments of their own potentials) may explain the prominence Ravel has come to have for him, for Ravel is all about maximum accomplishment. There was no Ravel in 1959. The awakening seems to have come about in the early 1970s, when Boulez began giving glorious performances of *Daphnis et Chloé*, demonstrating a breadth and an ease that were new and surprising. More recently, he has made an orchestration of Ravel's *Frontispice*, which is his only adaptation of another composer's work other than his replacement for the missing celesta part in Debussy's *Chansons de Bilitis*. Perhaps where once he identified with Debussy, as a liberator of music, he must now align himself, if resignedly, more with Ravel, as one of music's consummate fashioners. There are even direct echoes of Ravel (and, indeed, of Berg) in much of his recent music—for example, the latest versions of *Notations*, *Le Visage nuptial*, and '. . .*explosante-fixe*. . .'—not only in the extraordinarily sophisticated scoring but also in the exquisitely exacerbated harmony, which itself speaks a language more of stasis than of dynamism.

Understandably Boulez wants to see his conducting career as, still, a story of progress, and has pointed out how he not only knows his chosen works better but is readier to listen to what orchestral musicians have to offer. This is clear. Indeed, there would not be much point in playing Bartók's *Hungarian Sketches* other than as a virtuoso conversation-piece, which is what the piece becomes in Boulez's recording with the Chicago Symphony. But a comparison of the 1992 recording of the *Dance Suite*, on the same record, with a 1972 version from Boulez's New York Philharmonic days (reissued by Sony) shows there have been losses along the way. True, the 1992 performance is much more secure. But what was insecure, even reckless, about the 1972 account was part of what made it Boulezian: the lurching tempo changes, the crazy prestissimo in the second movement, the glacial string sound, the separation of colours, the closeness of the music often to a snarl. Professionalism is gained at the expense of personality.

Luckily, though, it does not have to be so. A new Messiaen record—with a *Chronochromie* loud with metal colours and iridescences, and also with subtler shades and sheens, all paraded by rhythm—is outstanding. So too, in its quieter way, is a recent Webern disc, featuring musicians of the Ensemble InterContemporain and, in Christiane Oelze, a singer who can make a two-octave leap not a scream but a delicate flicker of lyrical freshness. This is Webern with the dew still on it. Webern was an ardent naturalist, but where once Boulez emphasized the mineral, crystalline elements of the music—hard form, hard counterpoint, hard pulse—now he shows, in his delicacy with harmony, texture, and phrase, that these pieces are flowers, too.

Also wonderful is his latest Debussy record, in which, as in the Messiaen, he conducts the Cleveland Orchestra. Certainly there is no dilution of individuality here. So many gestures will be immediately familiar as visual impulses to anyone who has seen Boulez conduct: the quick snap of a hand thrust away from the body, the rapid four-four beating that is almost regular pulsation. The recording also follows a Boulezian tradition in varying the sound made by the women's voices in 'Sirènes', from open-mouthed exhilaration to a kind of hardness that makes one think there must be male altos among these sirens. But the sound all through is more glorious, as well as much more secure, than in any of his previous recordings of this repertory. *La Mer* is splendid, *Jeux* is magical, and even the short *Rapsodie* with solo clarinet comes up a masterpiece. (*New Yorker*, 1 May 1995)

Notations VII

As Pierre Boulez explained before Thursday night's Chicago Symphony concert—where he was present not to conduct but to listen, as composer of a commissioned piece—the ending of World War II made it possible for him to hear music that had been banned during the Nazi occupation. Bartók, Stravinsky, Schoenberg and others arrived in a rush, and in a rush he absorbed them and reacted. His whole creative life since then has been one long process of assimilation.

Nothing shows that process better than his *Notations*, a set of twelve piano miniatures he dashed off toward the end of 1945 and has been slowly transforming over the last two decades to create movements lavishly and ravishingly scored for an enormous orchestra. The first four *Notations* emerged in 1980 and were all quite short. *Notations VII*, the piece being played Thursday night, is rather longer, running for about eight minutes. What was abrupt in 1945 is now languorous; what was crude is now done with a lifetime's experience and expertise; what was simple is fantastically embellished, even submerged.

Boulez suggested the metaphor of long-buried grain sprouting, but one might rather think of an oyster making a pearl. As if irritated by the original piano piece, the composer has given it a sumptuous, dense and opalescent coating, not only expanding it but also, in a way, withdrawing its shock. Where the piano piece keeps repeating a loud descending tritone, like a signal that never gets answered, in the orchestral version this motif is always varied, prepared by a rise in tension and followed by a relapse, often a downward ladder of pizzicatos. The violent new influences of 1945 are, in the recomposition, being wiped away. What remains is a closeness to the composer who always seems to have meant most to Boulez: Debussy. In another recent piece, *sur Incises*, there were hints of that composer's *L'Isle joyeuse*. Near the start of *Notations VII* comes a trumpet solo that almost quotes the Scottish folk tune from the orchestral *Images*. The lustre is Debussy-like, too, and Boulezian. In the later stages of the piece, a wind chord shimmers in slow change, like an exotic butterfly's wing flexing. The composition is altogether gorgeous, in a way no budding composer of twenty could possibly have accomplished. It is also, in a way, sad—sad with the loss of innocence and raw vitality.

Two magnificent performances under Daniel Barenboim, the second more positive, were separated by a helpful teaching session, during which Barenboim played the piano ancestor and Boulez talked about the changes, with orchestral examples. This made the second performance of the orchestral version a virtual piano concerto, as one heard the new score against the memory of its keyboard beginnings. (*New York Times*, 16 January 1999)

prescriptions for Schoenberg

Pierre Boulez's first stint in the Composer's Chair at Carnegie Hall last week was brief but busy. Inside four days he spent several hours talking in public, rehearsed a group of young professionals for an all-Schoenberg programme at Weill Hall and presented a concert with the Ensemble InterContemporain in the main auditorium. Those who went to everything, including about eighty young conductors, players and composers chosen to attend the Schoenberg preparations, had a blast of the Boulezian spirit, which, like sharp winter air in sunlight, is exciting and challenging and lets you see clearly. As for Boulez himself, he seemed happy, cordial and relaxed.

It was not always so. But when, in the discussion sessions in Weill Hall that broke up the rehearsals, he was asked about his combative past—a subject relevant in a forum for young musicians—his responses were blithe or humorous. 'Is Schoenberg still dead?' one brave man inquired, referring to the brutally frank obituary, 'Schoenberg is Dead', that Boulez published in 1952. 'No,' the reply flashed back, 'but he needs strong medicine now.'

The strong medicine we saw being applied in the rehearsals. Both the works involved, the Chamber Symphony Op.9 and the Suite for septet Op.29, have been in Boulez's repertory almost throughout the four decades of his conducting career. He does not love them equally: the Chamber Symphony, which he took as a model for his first big composition, evidently stays high in his admiration, while, as he disclosed, he has not changed his view of the Suite as academic. (That was the main charge he held against Schoenberg's later output in 1952.) But nobody could have discerned either warmth or doubt in his treatment of the scores, whether in rehearsal or in performance. He was, rather, scrupulously attentive to the text and to the musicians. Almost never did he speak of the music's character or expressive qualities. Instead his concerns were with balance, rhythmic precision, tempo relationships, all to be tuned to produce the most effective sound and the most natural flow.

The emerging conductors present will have learned a lot. Most scores, Boulez said, require some correction of dynamic markings: Mahler's and Stravinsky's he gave as exceptions. The conductor will need to listen to what the musicians are giving, but must be prepared in advance: 'I cannot conduct a work only by instinct. You have to know how the piece is built, because otherwise you will miss the point.' And the rehearsal will then be a process through which the players learn the form as well as polish the detail. By rehearsing related passages of a movement side by side, Boulez would indicate the relation. 'I take the pretext of the rhythmic or dynamic exactitude to show how the piece is constructed', he said. 'I explain the piece without explaining anything.' Even the point at which the rehearsal ends can be important. Referring to what he had just done with the Chamber Symphony, he disclosed that he had chosen quite deliberately to finish 'at a point they will remember as a turning point in the architecture'.

In the case of the Suite the result was full not only of architecture but also of the character and expression that had so rarely been articulated in rehearsal. It ran fully counter to Boulez's spoken dismissal of it as overly Classical, almost as if he had never heard the humour, suavity and menace in his own performances, or the way those performances—so far from showing Schoenberg pouring new wine into old bottles by using forms like the Baroque overture or theme and variations—reveal the empty bottles dancing, in music that moves with a rhythmic energy very much of the 1920s, when the piece was written.

It was played twice: first in Weill Hall on Friday, with the young players in the middle movements and the Ensemble InterContemporain musicians, who had coached their junior colleagues, in the outer ones, then in Carnegie Hall on Saturday, with the highly experienced French team throughout. Weill Hall was better suited acoustically to the fine textures, the brittleness and the speed of the music, though the young instrumentalists had, understandably, played much better in rehearsal than they did on the performance night. Nervousness seemed to have gone, though, by the time they got to the Chamber Symphony in the second half of their concert, for the performance went like a breeze, with an abundance of highly musical and expressively generous solos, notably from Ariana Ghez on oboe, Timothy Fain on first violin and Jonathan Karoly on cello.

The Ensemble InterContemporain's concert included, besides the Schoenberg Suite, Berio's *Linea* for two pianos, vibraphone and marimba, and Boulez's own *sur Incises* for a similar but larger lineup of three pianos, three percussion players and three harps. Composed between 1994 and 1998, *sur Incises* (*Incises* being the virtuoso toccata for solo piano that provided the seed) is Boulez's most recent long work and as fluent as he is in person, if also as undisclosing. His choice of like but distinct instruments, with the percussionists playing vibraphones and marimba most of the time and the ensemble well spread out, allows him to use his astonishing ear to create effects of harmonic, timbral and spatial echo for which in earlier works he had needed electronic means. The command of musical energy and the sense of drama are also spectacular. At least the first two of the high-speed chases are thrilling, and there are marvellous moments when steel drums come in with their exotic disintonations, or when the harps fall silent for an ominous summons of pianos and bells.

Earlier in the week he had talked about two kinds of artists. 'I admire', he said, 'people who have obstinately gone their way and explored their personalities to the very end.' He cited Beethoven, Wagner and Cézanne, and gave Picasso as a counterexample, 'moving like a rocket', and his hand zigzagged through the air. As a conductor he has indeed travelled toward fulfillment and gone on searching, recently tackling Bruckner for the first time and constantly taking on premieres. But *sur Incises* makes more the sound of that rocket. (*New York Times*, 22 November 1999)

at seventy-five

Pierre Boulez, who will be seventy-five in two weeks' time, is touring the globe for celebrations and hard work. On Friday he arrived at Carnegie Hall with the London Symphony Orchestra for the first of four concerts on consecutive days, playing a new piece in each programme, twentieth-century classics and works by modern masters. The repertory is such as Boulez has been promoting from the podium for nearly half a century: his conviction has not been shaken, not even stirred. But by consistently acting on that conviction, he has helped educate orchestras and listeners, so that the effect of his conviction has slowly changed. There is no battle now. The music has been proved. It just has to be played superbly.

This is what has been happening. The big pieces in the first two concerts, Bartók's *Wooden Prince* and Schoenberg's *Pelleas und Melisande*, are both Boulez favourites, and both succumb readily to his present conducting style, in which his characteristic gifts of clarity of texture and precision in detail and tuning are joined by a grand spaciousness. Both works were given rich and resplendent performances, the Schoenberg beautifully modulated so that it reached its most passionate intensity close to the end. Both also found the LSO—especially the woodwind soloists and the brass—in fine shape.

Even so, the keenest excitement came in the newer pieces, and especially in Ligeti's Violin Concerto, this magician composer's most recent orchestral score. It is music that never comes to ground. Much of it plays in high registers; much of it tricks and delights the ear by giving the impression that the soloist is performing on several violins at once, or that marimbas and other percussion instruments are tucked under the strings. The sounds are like light beams playing through glass, and also like memories of folk music. Abstract and fantastical merges into others earthy and particular. The piece has seemed wonderful before, but this performance, so exquisitely exact in gesture and perfect in intonation, was a revelation. Christian Tetzlaff, the soloist, amazed. His left hand jumped into extreme positions with unerring accuracy, and his playing stayed rhythmically secure and beautifully in tune even at ferocious speeds. The concerto was all spinning brilliance or, in the first slow movement, puzzlement. It was also good to hear that a modern violin, made by Peter Greiner last year, can perform so spectacularly: both in the concerto and in Tetzlaff's encore piece, a movement from the Bartók solo sonata.

There was thus a neat segue from Ligeti's music into Bartók's, in a programme that gained further homogeneity from being all Hungarian. Peter Eötvös's *zeroPoints* had been the whacky opener, beginning from an imitation of an electronic bleep and shooting off in all kinds of directions, from explosive fanfares to a lugubrious passage for low wind, everything finely imagined. The Schoenberg was also partnered by sonic imagination—not so much in Berio's disappointing and raggedly played *Notturno* for strings, but decisively in Sciarrino's piano concerto *Recitativo oscuro*. Maurizio Pollini, the soloist, was typically vivid and alert, but seemed not fully sure of his role in playing chill, bright fragments and explosive chords, while some of the orchestral players wanted to find humour in the music more than unsettling oddity and malaise. Even so, the weird soundscape of scratches, wheezes and whistlings came across. So did the disturbing regular grey tread of a funeral march through much of the piece, and the sense of piano and orchestra as two great animals circling each other in the same cage, ready to fight. (*New York Times*, 13 March 2000)

Le Marteau sans maître

This was *Le Marteau* not *sans maître* but very much *avec*. For a full week young professional players had been receiving coaching at Weill Hall from musicians who have performed the piece many times for the composer: the flautist Sophie Cherrier, violist Garth Knox, percussionist Daniel Ciampolini and guitarist Marie-Thérèse Ghirardi. In between times they were rehearsing—in public, for the benefit of young conductors—with the master himself, Pierre Boulez.

Boulez's experience with *Le Marteau* goes back nearly half a century, to 1952, when he began the score, and he has been performing it regularly through most of its life. Recordings document his progress with it—and its with him. His very first performance, in 1956, gave rise to a recording, which was followed by others in 1964, 1972 and 1985. Next year he plans to record the work again. There is also the recording he made for a BBC television programme, 'Telemarteau', in 1968.

This tape was screened for the gathered instrumentalists and conductors during the week, and it proved a revelation—not only in showing how, thirty-three years ago, an hour of television time could be devoted to presenting and performing a piece of contemporary music. Some of the techniques used to visualize the performance looked dated or misguided: wild zooms, different lighting for the different sets of movements, a wobble effect for vibraphone fermatas. But the short, fast seventh movement stood up well, with its silhouetting of the performers and crisp cutting. What most surprised, though, in the context of these rehearsals, was the speed and the strict-pulsed jagged rhythms.

Boulez, who had never seen the tape before, got up at once after the showing to say that his performance had not changed. When this duly elicited some murmurs of dissent, he admitted that his tempos had slowed, but insisted this was purely for practical reasons. In rehearsal, though, it seemed the practical reasons had a poetic impulse. He encouraged the players—especially the flautist—to take speeds that would allow every grace note to emerge clearly. He also, many times, indicated phrasings by singing—and even recommended the student conductors to adopt this practice with the work. This would help, he said, 'to make things which are very difficult sound as if they are intended'.

But the same passages in 1968 would often sound not so much sung as driven, less intended than compelled, and it was an important question that one of the young musicians asked, about whom should be believed: the man in his twenties who wrote the score, the fully mature musician who recorded it in 1968 or the senior figure who is with us now. Perhaps all of them. *Le Marteau*, with its combination of melody instruments and percussion, is partly about relating different kinds of rhythm, pulsed and free, machine-like and quasi-vocal, digital and analogue. These need not be opposites. Boulez made a central point, not only about *Le Marteau*, when he said that precision was valuable as a way to achieve flexibility.

Many other, more specific insights emerged. In rehearsing the eighth movement—with which he started, because it includes everyone and because it is slow—he remarked how he would only rarely subdivide the bars, so that his gestures in conducting would coincide with the musical content. In this movement, too, he characterized the flute and viola at one point as being 'under surveillance' from the xylorimba and vibraphone—a comment that usefully indicates the kinds of sound drama to be expected in the score. The voice, he pointed out, is progressively 'reduced in its role' from one movement to the next of those in which it appears—though in the performance June Bentley, firm and sure, sounded a strong, oracular note all through.

Meanwhile, the flautist had picked up well the persuasive mellifluousness of Boulez's current style and the percussionists were as alert on the night as they had been from the first. For them, *Le Marteau* is standard repertory, and in that respect passing time has been only beneficial. As Boulez pointed out, in the mid-fifties the test pieces for xylophone players were an extract from *L'Oiseau de feu*, the 'Laideronette' movement from Ravel's *Ma Mère l'oye* and Saint-Saëns's *Danse macabre*. And as 'Telemarteau' revealed, percussionists in 1968 were still using just one stick in each hand, if with extraordinary alacrity. We have all come a long way. (*andante*, May 2001)

the composer's voice

Kagel

An expectant audience has come to the concert hall to hear a new work by a major composer. The stage is set for a large chorus and symphony orchestra to perform. But only about half the performers are in place when the conductor arrives, and he is evidently in distress. He looks as if he is about to say something to the audience, offer some word of explanation. He gapes. No words will come. All he can do is motion to his scattered musicians to draw nearer, and begin.

So starts Mauricio Kagel's *Kidnapping in the Concert Hall*, which was commissioned by a consortium of halls, including Carnegie, the Cologne Philharmonie and the Concertgebouw, to provide a kind of thing such halls often find themselves presenting: an opera in concert performance—except that in this case there would be no theatrical accoutrements to be imagined. The drama would happen on the concert stage.

Kagel was the right composer to ask, for he has been creating dramas in concert halls for nearly half a century. Here was another opportunity, as he said recently at his home in a comfortable suburb of Cologne, to 'try to create absolute music that is at the same time dramatic, that has a relationship with theatre atmosphere: not events, but atmosphere'.

Given the nature of the commission, he wanted to have that atmosphere come breathing out of the very walls of the concert building: hence, with a nod to Mozart's *Abduction from the Seraglio*, his abduction, in which orchestral players, chorus members and soloists are imagined to be prevented from performing because they are being held by a kidnapper. Several times, the kidnapper calls up the conductor, making threats and demands. Noises coming from the corridors outside the hall indicate that emergency services have arrived. Meanwhile, the conductor tries to go on with some kind of musical performance. He knows he is supposed to be conducting an oratorio based on some of the brilliant, strange and fugitive poems of Georg Christoph Lichtenberg (a work Kagel has long been dreaming of). But in the absence of half the performers and under conditions of panic and fear, another kind of music emerges: jittery, subject to sudden changes of mood.

Of course, the audience will know that the kidnapping is an illusion. At a real abduction, musicians would be unlikely to go on performing Kagel's weird but highly sophisticated and disciplined music. 'I make a contract of confidence with the public', he explained. 'I say: "Yes, this is a fiction, but let's think that it's not a fiction." And then each member of the public will be interested in how this fiction is realized, how organic it is.'

Early on the tenor escapes and comes onto the stage. 'In shock, he has forgotten the Lichtenberg text, and the chorus helps him', Kagel continued. 'He keeps trying to start. At one point, he says: "Let's begin at letter B." But after a couple of words he forgets again, because he is so upset.' The soloist's recent 'real life' experiences, as a hostage, have obliterated from his mind the role he is supposed to be playing. One level of the fiction has bleached out another. Musical performance is, as so often in this composer's work, a dicey business, subject to catastrophes and mischances that turn out to be, in a different way, touching and even triumphant.

Also on the programme is another, smaller choral work by Kagel, *Midnight Pieces*. These are four movements 'on texts from a diary Schumann wrote when he was very young, in 1828, as material for operas', Kagel explained. 'The texts are influenced by a German writer who was a friend of his father: Jean Paul. They're the texts that Schoenberg should have used for *Pierrot lunaire*. They have the quality of expressionism without being expressionist. They're very mysterious. Also, they're like the nouveau roman. You get the elements of a scene, the elements of what is in a room, without connection. Absolutely astonishing.'

This is by no means the only work in which Kagel refers to a composer of the past. Bach, Beethoven, Schubert, Brahms and Debussy also appear in his output, though not in expected ways and certainly not in any attempt at easy listening or cheap nostalgia. 'I think my approach to music is a profoundly cultural one', he said. 'I bring to it what I have read, what I'm interested in. I don't think my curiosity about music, about different levels in music, can be satisfied only doing "normal" works. That's a very bad definition. But when I say that I bring my cultural interests to bear, it means I think that in music there are a lot of ways to introduce materials that are not classical, not usual.

'I had no name for my work. Postclassical? Postmodern? I laughed when I heard the term 'postmodern', because I was trying thirty years ago to find what happens to harmony that is not serial harmony. I think the variety and richness of possible musical approaches to musical language are infinite. So why try to make the mainstream?'

It may be that his slantwise imagination owes something to his upbringing in Buenos Aires, surrounded by the diverse languages of his Central European Jewish family and encountering Shakespeare, for instance, by way of a Yiddish theater company from New York. But the autobiographical explanation does not seem to interest him: 'I think my work will be considered like that of a Renaissance artist. I was in Florence a couple of weeks ago, and I bought a catalogue of the machines of Leonardo. He was an inventor, and at the same time he did art in an extraordinary way. The machines are not utopian. This is exactly what I like. I try to be very concrete, using very concrete material, and the result has its own poetic atmosphere.

'But I don't like to speak about culture. You remember the very nice magazine in New York in the forties, *Kulchur*. If I can, however, speak about my sources, it's all this that you can see here'—he gestured around the high shelves on both long sides of his studio, stacked with books, scores and recordings—'without being afraid of producing something that will not be accepted by modern academicism, including the academicism of the avantgarde. My *Sankt-Bach-Passion*, for instance, is not academic. It uses a freeway to the past.'

Often that freeway will come up from underground, and the driver will have a smile on his face: 'I was never afraid of using my irony, my humour. But in the musical world, if you do that, people think the composition is not serious, which is very primitive. What most interests me is the laugh that stops in your throat, because you realize that laughter is the wrong reaction. Or in performances of my *Variations without Fugue*, I've seen orchestral musicians in tears when the actor impersonating Brahms appears on the stage. That's the kind of effect, moving and comic at the same time, you can produce with different levels of fiction, as in *Abduction*.'

Thinking about comedy reminds him of a story from his boyhood. 'I was twelve when I told my mother what I would like to be. She was in the kitchen, and she said: What? And I said: Musician. And the answer was: This afternoon we'll go to Harrod's'—there was a Harrod's in Buenos Aires—'and we'll buy you a black tail suit. She was absolutely serious. This, she recognized, is the musical world. Unfortunately, it was too early, because I grew.

'At that time, I was playing the piano. I also started the cello with a former student of Casals. And afterward, when I was sixteen or seventeen, I became very interested in how music is made. I had the opportunity to study with a very good piano teacher, Vincenzo Scaramuzza, in the same class as Martha Argerich and Bruno-Leonardo Gelber. He said: Look, I have to tell you, you will never become a pianist. I said: Why? You ask too much. Then I realized I was a composer. The wrong use of the tense is right. You are a composer, or you are not. You don't become a composer. You learn to compose.' (*New York Times*, 12 November 2000)

Krenek

Born in Vienna in 1900, Ernst Krenek is our last witness to the cultural turmoil of the century's first quarter: one shakes a hand that shook the hands not only of Schoenberg and Stravinsky, but of Rilke, Berg, Busoni, Adorno, Karl Kraus. . . . And one intercepts a mind, still spry and creative, that has puzzled through the maze of musical developments since World War I.

I ask first why at that time he had elected to study with Franz Schreker rather than Schoenberg. 'Schoenberg did not have such a reputation in bourgeois circles: he was regarded as a madman. Schreker was more reliable. Also, it was difficult, during the war, to get transport out to Mödling. But then after the war I did go to one of the private concerts: one had to ring up one of the "bodyguards" to ask permission to be admitted. And after the concert a little man came up to speak, looking very shy, and I thought: "Who is this person? Can't they find anybody more impressive to make the announcements?" Of course, that was Schoenberg. Then a little later I called on him, and we had a heated discussion for two hours about who was the greater composer, Beethoven or Schubert. Naturally he was for Beethoven. He didn't mind how long he argued, but he had to make his point.'

Krenek has travelled to London from his Palm Springs home to be present at the Almeida Festival concert tomorrow night featuring five of his works. In the early 1920s he moved with Schreker to Berlin: 'It was a more progressive, more aggressive place, and my music took on those characteristics. But then I changed my style rather drastically when I lived in Switzerland in 1923–5 and met Stravinsky: his *Pulcinella* suite made a great impression, though I wasn't so much interested in neoclassicism as in a return to Romanticism.'

Out of that came his 'jazz opera' *Jonny spielt auf*, which had an extraordinary success in the 1920s. I wonder if he has ever regretted that success.

'No! Why should I regret it?' Perhaps, I suggest, because it had so overshadowed his other works. 'Oh yes, I had to make a great effort to cleanse my name, and other things have not become so well known: the Second Symphony, *Orpheus und Eurydike*, the Sixth String Quartet. . . .' While he continues to unroll the catalogue of 237 works in his head, his wife puts in a bid on behalf of the Jason opera *Der goldene Bock*.

But we return to Switzerland, where he met Rilke as well as Stravinsky. 'I visited him in his chateau, and we took long walks, talking. He said he didn't care for people setting his poetry to music, and so I was very surprised a year later to receive from him a beautiful blue envelope, with his seal, and inside were three poems to set. After another year I did it, and I sent him a wire; I got just a pencil note back from the sanatorium, one of his last letters.'

At the end of the 1920s Krenek came, as he says, 'back to Schoenberg'. 'I think I had the impression that I had reached the end of the line with my neoromanticism: it didn't produce any more possibilities. And because of my acquaintance with Berg and Webern, I came to know their music, and studied it.' Were they personally approachable? 'Berg yes: he was a very social person, very easy to talk to. Webern less so. He didn't talk much unless the subject interested him: then he would start a little preachment.'

However, Webern was the greater musical influence, and he has followed Webern's practice of beginning a work with the composition of a twelve-note series rather than a musical theme. 'I also knew Adorno very well, and visited him in Oxford in 1935; he influenced me very much intellectually, and because of that I was separated from Stravinsky—but than I saw Stravinsky often when he turned to twelve-tone music and we were both in California.

'Karl Kraus was also a profound influence on my intellectual development. I read his magazine ever since 1918, and I knew him personally in his last two years. I was very impressed by his moral stature: his integrity, his intransigence. And I was impressed by his poetry. I selected seven poems to set to music, and he came to the first performance; though he didn't understand anything of music, and he certainly didn't like twelve-tone music. Schubert's "Bei dir" was the only thing on the programme that appealed to him: it was the closest to his beloved Offenbach.'

Krenek also admired Kraus as his model in writing German (he has written most of his own librettos and some verse for songs), but then in the mid-1930s he began learning English in the increasing likelihood that he would have to make his home in the US. He had also, I point out, prepared himself for the journey in *Jonny spielt auf*.

'Yes, but at that time I didn't know anything about America except that there were gangsters and there was Prohibition, and I didn't like either. The picture was purely Romantic, in the spirit of Goethe's phrase "Amerika, Du hast es besser". After all, the black man in the opera represents American optimism: if I'd known how negroes are really treated I couldn't have written it.'

It was in 1938 that he made the move to the United States, after which his music began to introduce elements of the newer serialism and electronic material, but without, as he sees it, any further essential change of style.

I ask, finally, whether his unparallelled experience of the range of twentieth-century music has left him with any view of where we go from here.

'I am now an old gentleman living in the middle of the desert. I don't listen to much music. And the little that I do hear, once in a while, I don't care for.' (*Times*, 20 June 1987)

Kurtág

One of Kurtág's songs gives advice to a snail to climb carefully up Mount Fuji: perseverance—never mind how small the present achievement and vast the task ahead—is the great Kurtágian virtue. By the time he had reached the age of forty-five, nearly a quarter of a century ago, he had completed only eight numbered works, most of them very short, and none for a group of more than five players. Latterly, he has been composing more abundantly, and producing works that are longer and bigger; but though this may be partly because growing recognition has brought him growing opportunities, the development must be due largely to his persistence. He began with first faltering steps up the moutain. Now he can look further. Last winter saw the premiere of *Stele*, his first piece for large orchestra in forty years; this summer, his *Rückblick*—an entire concert for four musicans (a trumpeter, a bassist, and two keyboard players)—has been doing the rounds of the European festivals: Holland, Cheltenham, Edinburgh. In Amsterdam, too, there was a hugely successful performance, under Reinbert de Leeuw, of his setting of a late Beckett prose piece, *What is the Word*—a setting which uses relatively large forces (a reciter struggling to utter, a pianist accompanying her, an answering or provoking quintet of singers, and twenty-seven instrumentalists stationed around the hall) and has the unusually long unbroken span of fifteen minutes.

The scale has changed, and yet these larger works are still fragmentary. Kurtág often assembles pieces as chains of short elements: *Rückblick* has more than fifty of them, lasting on average just over a minute. Even when his musical spans are longer, as in *What is the Word*, he eliminates all aspects of formal presentation: there are no preliminaries, no developments and no extensions—nothing that does not exert itself as gesture. And since gesture is a leaping-out from context, Kurtág's art of gesture counters continuity. His music needs, as all music needs, to unfold through time, but its ideal is to exist at the sudden instant, with a fragment's torn edges. Magnificently made as his pieces all are, the best of them have the roughness of immediacy and the rawness of truth. After the performance of *What is the Word*, at a public discussion in a crowded small room of the Concertgebouw, he was asked about his plans for an opera. He paused, then loudly smacked one fist into the palm of his other hand. That, he explained, was his idea of drama.

This Concertgebouw concert had included, before *What is the Word*, the first performance of his *Songs of Despair and Sorrow*, for chorus accompanied by a miscellany of instruments meant to provide, typically, more character than homogeneity: groups of brass and strings, a piano, harps and percussion, two harmoniums and four piano accordions. As the title suggests, these are songs of violence and pathos, and of pessimism that becomes, as so often with this composer, a furious elation. Setting six Russian poets from Lermontov to Tsvetayeva, the music makes the clear, cold light of their vision audible, and creates from their several voices just one, proceeding from a dissatisfaction with life's futilities to a point at which not even the cause or the nature of hopelessness can be expressed. There is singleness of voice, too, in the choral writing. Though the music may be in up to twenty parts, the many mouths seem to make one mouth, voicing itself through them. What one hears is not so much counterpoint as a diversity of surges and sways—urgent, nostalgic, luminous, bleak—within one consciousness. The score is also full of striking images: the stabs of harmonium, normally so felted an instrument; the combination of tollings and sustained tones on the same word, 'night', conveying at once repetition and sameness; the refusal of something like a folksong melody after a few jaunty phrases with a desperate 'No!'; the huge, slow, solemn chords of the finale, when the voices become voiceless. However, the Amsterdam performance, under John Eliot Gardiner, was only partial (omitting the biggest of the songs) and indistinct. This is a major work awaiting its proper birth.

Also this summer in the Netherlands—but at the abbey of Rolduc, in the far south-east of the country, where the Orlando Quartet leads a happy summer academy for amateur chamber ensembles—Kurtág was around to supervise performances of almost all his works for smaller forces. I wanted to be there, because I had heard so much about his strenuous demands—and would hear more, at Rolduc, before I got into the rehearsal room. Erika Tóth, a violinist who studied with Kurtág in Budapest, told me of spending half a year on just the exposition section of Mozart's F major Sonata. Was that, I asked, because he wanted her to try different possibilities? 'No.' Was he, then, working towards an ideal? 'A super-ideal. You could never get there. Nobody could get there. It was wonderful, but then you never want to play the piece again. You could not have a career like that: you would die.' Stefan Metz, the cellist of the Orlando, talked about being coached by Kurtág in a Haydn quartet, Op.64 No.4: 'He would play everything on the piano—and you know how difficult that is, to phrase four different lines at once. It was wonderful.' I asked what happened if the musicians disagreed with the offered interpretation. Metz's reply was quick and short: 'We never disagreed.'

Next morning I was able to watch how Kurtág works. The quality of his attention is evident in his stance: leaning slightly forward from the waist, holding his forearms level in front of him, swaying a little from fullness of tension, his face tightly alert. Nothing matters more at this moment than to get the music right, which means listening acutely to what the performer is producing and might produce. If Kurtág indeed has a 'super-ideal' in mind, the image comes not just out of the score but out of the musician's potentialities. In his rehearsals, as in his compositions, there are no preparations, no explaining. The musician just begins. And, more than likely, soon stops.

On one occasion, the performer being coached by Kurtág was the soprano Susan Narucki, who was starting with the last of his Seven Songs Op.22 for singer and cimbalom—the one about the snail on Mount Fuji. She got through the first two notes before he interrupted. 'More support for the voice.' She started once more, and was stopped once more. 'Not louder! More *weight*.' (This turned out to be one of his commonest requests, for emphasis to be obtained not by a raised dynamic but by another colour: heavy, dark, solid, present.) Again Narucki sang the two notes, which by now were starting to sound momentous—though not yet sufficiently for Kurtág to be satisfied. 'Like Boris Christoff.' Narucki tried again, and was halted again at the same point. 'Like Boris Christoff singing Boris Godunov.' Now, after singing these two notes for the fifth time, she got the go-ahead—'Very fine'—to continue to the third.

In another of the Op.22 songs, where the singer justs repeats three times a glorious long phrase on the words 'Labirintus: Nincs Ariadne, nincs fonál' (Labyrinth: No Ariadne, no thread), Kurtág showed his concern for melody that makes harmonic sense. 'It's a difference to sing correct intervals and to sing within a tonality—and the tonality I miss a little bit.' One note, he suggested, should 'have a spotlight on it'. Narucki sang that part of the phrase again. 'Only don't have an accent!' Here, too, weight was to be conducted onto a note by colouring, not loudening, so that the integrity of the phrase would be preserved.

Throughout these rehearsals, Kurtág stated his requirements entirely in technical terms. He might refer to other music, indicating, for instance, how the plainsong *Dominus ad adjuvandum meum* lies secretly behind one song in *S.K. Remembrance Noise* for singer and violin, or indicating how another song in this set ought to swing: 'Mahalia Jackson is doing this so naturally.' He might also, though more rarely, propose a dramatic situation: the middle song of Op.22 was to begin as if stammered out by someone breathlessly pursued. But the expressive meaning of a song was never a prerequisite: it had to come out of technique, analogy, situation. By the end of the morning, Narucki looked different. She had begun with her weight on her heels, stable, in command of the music. She ended poised, ready, the music in command of her.

That evening her performances were exceptional, and not only in terms of musical force and precision. In one number of *S.K.*, where Kurtág makes a string of operas out of minuscule poems by Dezső Tandori, the soprano sings against—and of—the violin's accompaniment:

> The lawnmower hums (over there)
> My electric razor (over here)

Narucki turned her head slowly and deliberately to look at her musical companion, Arvid Engegård, then turned slowly and deliberately back, then turned slowly and deliberately toward him again. The effect was extraordinary, and I do not fully know why. (Certainly one would not want anyone to imitate her: Kurtág's music asks performers to discover things—whether with his guidance or not—for themselves.) Partly it was that she was showing herself to be thoroughly at one with the songs' voice, resilient.

There was resilience, too, and bite, in Kim Kashkashian's declamation of a sequence of pieces for solo viola, and in the Orlando Quartet's performance of the *Twelve Microludes* which constitute Kurtág's second quartet. As he said afterwards, the Orlando made these brief drafts of music into one whole experience, not a sequence of studies. And again this is a matter of finding the right voice: the voice that must articulate these things, and must do so now.

At these concerts by the Orlando and friends, Kurtág's pieces were being programmed with peaks of the chamber music repertory: Mozart quintets, music by Schumann and Brahms. Not many living composers could exist in this company, and if Kurtág can, that must be because the great tradition is very much his tradition, and has set the exacting standards he demands of himself. Yet his insistence on music that is violently actual, almost physical in its grip, is also a scourge and a challenge to that tradition. In his intolerance of what is good form, he is a thoroughly non-traditional artist. Heard in his company, even Mozart and Brahms seem at times to be doodling. (*Hungarian Quarterly*, XX 1995)

Ligeti

Being inside Ligeti's studio, in a jarring modernist block among the art nouveau residences of a leafy, prosperous part of Hamburg, is a bit like being inside the spectacularly chaotic order of one of his compositions. All is cubic or quadrilateral: the large desk at the window, tables, backless seats, boxes of sketches, and piles and piles of papers, compact discs and scores, which imply a cascading confusion just held in check. When I met him there recently, and carefully perched, we talked about the Sony complete edition of his acknowledged works, among which only the larger pieces remain to be recorded: hence the sequence of concerts to be given by Esa-Pekka Salonen and the Philharmonia this season and next.

'I have no gift for conducting, but I can hear very well all the details, so at the recordings I'm like an audio engineer who is also the composer. And there are things that only I can judge, such as phrasing, articulation, the overall form. What is written in the score is only one layer, and then you have many others, which are tradition. I am specially concerned with the large form, how you have a big arch. For instance, no recording of *Atmosphères* has what Hans Rosbaud and Bruno Maderna gave it in concert performances: the sense of one object—like a painting of Turner or Monet, having one space and blurred details.'

One layer of the Ligeti tradition is the Hungarian culture he brought with him out of Budapest in 1956. 'Of course, the language is a glue. On the other hand, it was a terrible experience when the majority of the population got along with Hitler, so I have no Hungarian nationalist feelings, only very deep connections with the language, poetry, culture. During the three years after the war there was an absolutely wonderful revival of culture in Budapest, but this atmosphere hasn't returned following the dismantling of Soviet control: too much time has elapsed. I have the feeling that everything's become coarse. There's no refinement.'

Earlier this year Ligeti made one of his occasional visits to Budapest to attend a concert which turned out to be more a political occasion. 'Afterwards there was a party, and István Lakatos, a writer and a very good old friend, made a speech. We had founded an opposition circle in 1955, though by the time it became a reality it had already been infiltrated by the secret police. I kept my distance then, so I wasn't a member of the club I founded—not for Groucho Marx's reasons, but because it was immediately under police control. Lakatos was in prison for six years, and he wrote an autobiography. And because I was in the west, he could put all the blame on me, as he was entirely right to do. So he made this speech, again pretending I had a very important role in the revolution, which is not quite true, and afterwards I had the feeling they would put an equestrian statue of me on the hill of Buda.

'If the Soviets hadn't flattened cultural life, if in Hungary there had been normal democracy, I would have had a totally different evolution as a composer. There are pieces from 1946 and 1947, such as the Three Sándor Weöres Songs or the Two Capriccios for piano, that show a searching for a Hungarian idiom in modern music. But then came the censorship, and after that I had so many new influences in the west. So in my music there's no continuity of style. It's always cut, with scissors.'

The cuts have gone on. 'The real detour in the free part of my life, in the west, was the time from my opera *Le Grand Macabre* to my Horn Trio, because this was my postmodern period. It was a reaction against the orthodox avantgarde. All the time I had a very deep love for Boulez—as a person and for his work. Maybe Boulez only. Stockhausen in his early years, later not. Also, it was a reaction against the post-Nono composers, whose work was connected in a very naive way with ideas of socialist utopias. (I used to be on the left, before the Soviet time, when all microbes of socialism in me were killed by the real socialism.) It was a kind of angry attitude against all these people going to Cuba or East Germany, or setting Mao's poetry to music. I hated this: the salon communists. I tried to make a music which was totally different, with a lot of traditional elements. But then my hatred of postmodern architecture, and also of a lot of neotonal postmodern music, pushed me another way—not back, but in another modernistic direction, which maybe the piano études are the clearest product of.

'It comes partly from being open to all cultures. For instance, I have a very strong interest in late fourteenth-century music, because it's a neglected style of the highest complexity. I was always attracted to very complex ornament—like in Maori art, or Viking art, or Arabic decoration in Granada, or the Book of Kells—and therefore my deep interest in African music from south of the Sahara, or gamelan music. I am not interested in non-European music because it's non-European; but the fact that we had no contact with this music means that it's refreshing. The recombination of old, existing traditions can produce something completely new. A very good example is Debussy, who would never have written *La Mer* or some of his piano pieces if he had not heard gamelan music.'

Ligeti is currently at work on the sixteenth of his piano études. 'Then I want to begin the big challenge: *Alice in Wonderland*.' (This is the work that was commissioned for the London Coliseum more than a decade ago.) 'Over the last ten years I've made a lot of sketches, but not really musical sketches. My sketches are rather key words, because to write music down takes too long. When I imagine some music, I label it with a name—like when you work on a computer, you put something on an address. For me, the address might be a Hungarian word, or it might be the name of a composer: Scriabin, for instance—not that you would hear any Scriabin influence, but because a certain harmonic association in the Tenth Sonata would remind me of something in my imagination.'

I ended by asking Ligeti what his *Alice* would be like. 'Very, very light, and full of humour, and moral. Just Lewis Carroll.' And for what kind of singers? 'I could tell you, but I would be gentleman-like if I first told the English National Opera.' (*Times*, 4 December 1996)

Lutoslawski

Lutoslawski is in London for performances of seven of his works by the Philharmonia, mostly under his own direction, during the next ten days. The orchestra's enterprise here needs cheering, especially when the companion works (conducted by Esa-Pekka Salonen) have been chosen as appropriate foils rather than sweeteners, and when the Lutoslawski collection concentrates on relatively recent pieces, leaving out the almost popular Concerto for Orchestra.

Speaking at his club (like any Francophile Pole he appreciates the formalities of British tradition: in his dress and manner he is as courteous and correct as he is in his music), he remarked on this choice. 'The Concerto for Orchestra does not belong to the main stream of my work. I wrote it at a time when I had decided I must begin again from scratch: that was in 1947, when I had finished my First Symphony, and I wanted to study the sound language in detail. I started working with certain scales, which was not terribly successful. Then I began working on harmony, making twelve-note chords, testing them and classifying them. I found some rules. For instance, the simplest is that the smaller the number of different intervals, the more character, the more distinct physiognomy one has in a chord. That was what I wanted: sharp contrasts.

'It's absolutely contrary to Schoenberg's twelve-note method, which did not interest me at all. You see, in the twentieth century there are two traditions. One is Schoenberg and the Second Viennese School; the other is Debussy, early Stravinsky, Bartók, Varèse, Messiaen. I belong to the second.

'Then, when I began to develop this twelve-note-chord technique, I felt it was a little one-sided. It enabled me to work with large masses of sound, as in my Second Symphony, but it was only later, in the 1970s, that I found how to compose thinner textures in the way that I wanted, which made possible various smaller pieces and also the Double Concerto.'

Since the 1970s Lutoslawski has appeared frequently as a conductor of his own music. 'When I conduct, I always feel myself to be a performer who plays pieces by his younger colleague. I don't learn my works by heart: I discover them while performing them and then, knowing better one's own music, one can clearly see what is to be avoided and what is to be developed.'

But if Lutoslawski conveys an image of serene progress from composition to performance to succeeding composition, there are moments of uncertainty, as in the composition of the Third Symphony, which was spread over the years from 1972 to 1983. 'I spent two years on a main movement which I discarded, and then began again from something entirely different.' A difficulty related to the clearer harmonic progression here? 'Yes. Also, I wanted this piece to be completely mature.'

The later works have once again been mostly orchestral, including the *Chain* series and the Piano Concerto. 'The symphony orchestra,' Lutoslawski says, 'is my element. And I like large-scale closed forms. I begin normally with an idea of the overall form and with a number of key ideas, which are abstract groups of notes independent of any context. Those key ideas exert a force pushing outwards, while the formal idea produces an inward force, and the work comes from these two.'

Lutoslawski's manner of working from the germinal detail and the whole at once may help to explain the paucity of vocal works in his output, though he does harbour plans for an opera. 'For a long time I looked for a subject which would fulfil certain conditions. For instance, I can't accept realistic theatre with singing instead of speaking: it would have to be a fairytale, or a dream, or something surreal. Now finally I have found something, but it is a difficult decision to start work: it would take some years, and there are more urgent things. Also, a real problem is the amount of music a sensitive listener is supposed to assimilate. How do I create something which does not tire the audience—and which does not tire myself?' (*Times*, 2 February 1989)

Pärt

Arvo Pärt has the aura of a familiar Russian type: the mystic simpleton. He was born in Estonia in 1935, and at first his career as a composer was well adapted to the Soviet pattern: there were tuneful cantatas for the authorities, and serial pieces for himself. But then in 1968 he wrote *Credo*, whose vigorous choral chanting of belief in Jesus Christ was much less officially acceptable than any amount of serialism. After that came a prolonged study of Renaissance polyphony, followed by an even longer silence, preparing for the breakthrough into utter simplicity, into a music of rhythmic calm and radiant triadic harmonies. Was this something he had been looking for during the earlier period of avantgarde activity?

'I think life is a search. If you offer an infant several fruits, then the child will know by instinct which one is right for itself. But adults are more fractured, and they need time to meditate, to discover their own direction. One day I realized that I possessed a great many things in my music, but I did not possess the most important thing. And so I set about eliminating everything that was extraneous.'

The process of elimination resulted in a style that has drawn comparisons with US minimalism, though Pärt's actionless serenity and his liking for string instruments point to other correspondences, such as with the slow movement of the 'Winter' concerto from Vivaldi's *Four Seasons*.

'I would like to think', says Pärt, 'such a comparison could be made.'

And, like a Baroque composer, he is not averse to creating several versions of a piece: his *Fratres*, for instance, exists as music for Baroque ensemble, for violin and piano, for twelve cellos and for other formations. Does that compromise the aim for simplicity?

'No. There is always the same nucleus, which radiates in different directions. I like to start with a very simple nucleus: I would like to write a piece on just one note, but I have not yet had enough daring, or enough trust in my performers.'

Or enough trust in his audience? 'People should be put in a state of conflict, wondering how long the piece is going to go on, when something is going to happen. Then they may be drawn into themselves.'

Not surprisingly, Pärt sees a great deal of contemporary music as acting on the periphery, not searching for the centre. But what if at the centre there was silence?

'There is. Absolutely. I see my works of the last ten years as a balanced period: five years in the Soviet Union and five years, since 1980, in the west. It was necessary for me to come to terms with the fact of being a musician and having a certain training, but now I would like to stop composing.'

Given the interest his work is arousing in Europe and the US, however, he may find it difficult to be so—to use his own word—decisive. (*Times*, 10 June 1986)

Xenakis

In *Testaments Betrayed* Milan Kundera has told how, soon after the Soviet-led invasion of Czechoslovakia, he found in the music of Xenakis 'a bizarre kind of solace'. On Tuesday there was a rare chance to sample this electric balm at the Cooper Union, at the US premiere of Xenakis's longest concert work, the 75-minute *Kraanerg* for a small but mighty orchestra of twenty or so players and tape. Composed in 1968, the year the tanks rolled into Prague, *Kraanerg* provided plenty of opportunity to savour what most excited Kundera in other pieces: the world revealed as 'rich, vast, complex. . .and without sentiment; a space of consoling objectivity'.

This music has no story to tell, makes no claims on our sympathies and certainly is indifferent to anything that might have passed for beauty of sound or good style. It just is, and spends most of its time just being much the same. There are strident chords with piercing piccolo and oboe at the top, contrabassoon and trombones at the bottom, and nothing much in between. There are grating passages for strings, playing without vibrato and with exaggerated bow pressure. Almost everything has the intensity of a climax, which means that there is no climax at all, but rather a levelness, an absence of growth that must be connected with the absence of subjectivity.

Change, when it comes, is abrupt. Some of the most striking moments in the piece come when the focus is suddenly on one or two instruments: trumpet and trombone in a brief skirmish, oboe tentatively embarking on a solo. More regularly, the orchestra is cut off in favour of the tape (the two are rarely heard together), which seems to feature the same orchestra, but under a hood of reverberation and with the addition of percussion-like electronic noises. In ending with a long tape section, the work ignores even the elementary rule of performance that you cue applause for the people onstage: in this case the conductor, Charles Zachary Bornstein, whose tight, even tense control gave the music strong projection, and his ST-X Ensemble Xenakis USA, who played with heroic attack, sureness and stamina.

The effect was objective, all right, but consoling? One begins to realize that Kundera's experience of the music could only have been from records, and that the shock of a live performance might have pleased him less. With the middle ground of human discourse ripped out, *Kraanerg* is left with things either totally meaningless or at the base level of code, like the loud repeated notes that echo an alarm signal found throughout the world of nature, from thrushes to automobile horns. Like science fiction ('Kraanerg': it could be a rogue planet from *Star Trek*), the piece refashions in technological form the brutest feelings, which are objective only in that we all have them in the same form.

In a revealing preconcert discussion Xenakis spoke of his love for Brahms and his disinclination to interpret *Kraanerg* as expressing the protests and upheavals of the late 1960s. Then a young man got up and said he often played recordings of Xenakis's music to people, 'and a common reaction is that your music is frightening'. There was a pause. How would the composer react to this provocative, possibly hostile remark? He did so by relaxing the ironical wariness he had maintained hitherto. He nodded and chuckled as he said: "That's true!' (*New York Times*, 14 November 1996)

Mozart 1991

With an outpouring of performances, recordings and books to mark the bicentenary of his death, this was Mozart Year.

from Solti

These things are fortuitous, of course, but the bicentenary of Mozart has arrived at an interesting moment of change and possibility in the way his music is performed. Two decades ago the celebrations would have been safely in the hands of standard chamber orchestras—the London Mozart Players, the English Chamber Orchestra, the Academy of St Martin-in-the-Fields—all of them performing a repertory from Bach to Stravinsky without worrying too much about changes in instrumental technique along the way. Now, when the South Bank holds its Mozart Now festival in the late summer, the performing ensembles will be chosen from among those specializing in period style: the Orchestra of the Age of Enlightenment, the London Classical Players, the English Baroque Soloists, the English Concert, the Orchestra of the Eighteenth Century. And the first of these groups has again been engaged by Glyndebourne, this time for two operas.

To see this as a Sarastrian victory for the forces of light against the historically unaware and, of course, totally inauthentic ways of the recent past would be easy, and this conflictory metaphor has certainly been used by some proponents of period style. Allies in aesthetic battles, however, tend to be fighting for quite different ends, and the result is usually something altogether new and unexpected rather than a victory for either side. So it seems to be proving here. The authenticity movement is not one thing but many: the smart, up-tempo Roger Norrington and the yielding René Jacobs, the dancing John Eliot Gardiner and the severe Sigiswald Kuijken. No longer is there any consensus even about fundamental questions, such as orchestral balance or the permissibility of string vibrato. Instead the whole range of musical knowledge and discipline has been broadened, leaving individual musicians to find their own ways. This has made it possible for the 'opposition', represented by established, general-purpose ensembles, to learn and adapt to the new customs, sometimes with the help of 'authentic' conductors (Andrew Parrott, Christopher Hogwood), sometimes without. Of course, there remains the difference that the London Classical Players use copies of early wind instruments, whereas the London Mozart Players do not, but in every other respect the lessons of period style are being assimilated by the more traditional orchestras, just as the back-to-gut-strings school are learning that you do not have to make a scraggy sound in order to prove you have read the eighteenth-century treatises.

One sign of the changing atmosphere came this week in three South Bank concerts given by Sir Georg Solti, whose career as a Mozart conductor goes back to the big-band days of the 1930s, but whose performances with the Chamber Orchestra of Europe showed decisively that he and they have absorbed the developments of the last decade. In his orchestral programme, as in his performance of *Figaro*, he used a relatively small string ensemble, able to take semi-quaver runs at his zestful speeds and still stay perfectly together, and able also to flick quickly between different dynamic levels: this skill, and the breathtaking pianissimo these players could achieve, brought particular musical point and beauty to their performances of the 'Haffner' and 'Jupiter' symphonies. Here too was another 'authentic' trait: the individuality of the wind colours, and the emphasis less on suave blend than on a counterpoint of differences. The flute and oboes of the 'Jupiter' were heard in beautiful interplay; bassoons were nicely prominent; and the horns sounded out with the touch of rustic impropriety they normally have only in period ensembles.

These performances also gave the lie to the notion that ensembles of eighteenth-century size cannot make a full effect in twentieth-century concert halls: when everything is so well played, and presented with such intelligence, keenness and interest, the ear is drawn into the scale of the sound. Nothing could have demonstrated that better than Anne-Sophie Mutter's performance of the Violin Concerto in A. For much of the time, and particularly in the slow movement, she played at levels of extreme delicacy, but her projection was so striking and sure that everything was heard. And Solti and the orchestra partnered her marvellously, covering the gamut from (just to take the finale) the gentle wit of the main theme to the careering wildness of the Turkish-style episode. The days of massed-string symphonic Mozart may be over, but that does not mean there is nothing to be discovered and revealed by outstanding musicians from the mainstream. (*Times*, 25 January 1991)

La Betulia liberata

Painting and music give us an oddly proportioned view of the Bible, one where the Nativity is vastly more prominent than the Sermon on the Mount, and where Noah's brief episode counts for more than Isaiah's sixty-six chapters. The story of Judith and Holofernes is one of these moments favoured by representation, for obvious reasons, and never more so than in the eighteenth century: every big gallery has its lady with the severed head, and Vivaldi was among the many composers to deliver an oratorio on the subject before Mozart, in 1771, set Metastasio's libretto *La Betulia liberata* and created a work that, as Wednesday's Barbican performance magnificently showed, is full of good things.

This was the second stage in the English Chamber Orchestra's Mozart chronology, following last week's *Mitridate*; the boy was now several months older, past his fifteenth birthday, and fiercer in his imagination. Since this is Metastasio, the decapitation of the Assyrian warlord is not enacted but rather described. That, however, is far more useful to a composer of oratorio, and Mozart set Judith's long and sanguineous narration to accompanied recitative that is often juicily illustrative: the little chromatic slithers for the strings at the line 'The severed trunk quivered on the blood-stained ground' are a particularly happy touch. However, in opera seria fashion, the libretto is concerned less with the story than with qualities of human response around it: the determination of Judith, the godliness and guidance of the Jewish leader Ozias, the conversion of the ejected Assyrian soldier Achior from rage to piety, the similar development in Amital from despair to penitent trust. These qualities provide the armature for the arias of which the work is chiefly composed.

Ozias, though certainly the least exciting character, has melting phrases when he leads the Israelites in prayer, warmly and unusually accompanied by slow-moving divided violas against pizzicato violins: commentators like to point to Gluck's influence here. John Aler sang the piece beautifully, and also maintained his fine, lively tone through all the busy decoration of his two arias. Even the long scene at the start of the second part, where Ozias instructs Achior in St Thomas Aquinas's proofs of the existence of God, failed to bore, thanks to Aler's urging of the music upon us. Amital's three arias were also among the treasures of this performance, all of them given unerring radiance by Sylvia McNair: her spectacular leaps sounded completely effortless, indeed inevitable, and she even added one, with glorious confidence, in the cadenza to her first aria. Her second, with twisting modulations in its andante middle section, and her third, with its alternation of two slow tempos, found extrovert virtuosity coinciding with expressive inwardness.

McNair's natural, brilliant ebullience was in effective contrast with the solemnity of Jard van Nes as Judith, whose part gains a severe authority from its relative rejection of florid runs and from its unusual compass, sitting around the bottom of the treble stave and dipping to a low G. The role is further set apart by the fact that there is nothing else by Mozart in this deep contralto register, which even Van Nes found less than comfortable. Achior's two arias were done with nice storming vigour and chastened calm by Stafford Dean. There was also a very beautiful performance, true and poignant, of Chabris's slowish G minor aria by Rosa Mannion, and Gillian Webster waited patiently to give an elegant account of Charmis's F minor aria. The orchestral players, and their conductor Jeffrey Tate, seemed more spirited than in *Mitridate*, perhaps simply because this is a more interesting score. There can be no complaints about Wolfgangolatry when the result is occasions like this. (*Times*, 1 February 1991)

two historic concerts

Our cheese-paring ways of concert giving, with no more than one soloist engaged and the whole thing over inside two hours, can normally give no flavour of the ample, multifarious programmes of two centuries ago, but the South Bank's Mozart Now festival offered an ear into the past in this respect as in so much else. Two concerts last week, roughly reconstructing the programmes Mozart gave in Leipzig in 1789 and Frankfurt the next year, each duly presented a banquet of symphonies, piano concerto and arias lasting for nearer three hours than two, and the Leipzig night even brought, from Robert Levin, a revival of Mozartian skills of improvisation. For once one could share the assurance, which Mozart's audiences would never have had reason to doubt, that one was hearing new music (from which pont of view a Berio concert with the London Sinfonietta is a closer representation of eighteenth-century practice than any amount of gut-string fiddling).

Levin's announcement that his cadenzas for K.503 would be completely impromptu came over as a touch cocky, and a dubious departure from authentic practice, since Mozart seems always to have played from written-out cadenzas. No doubt, too, if Levin had prearranged things he could have avoided long runs of conventional pattern, however adroitly dispatched. But his spontaneous solo fantasy on four themes was great fun, right from his good-humoured choosing from a basket of vaguely Mozartian ideas scribbled by members of the audience (although the best was the invention of the orchestra's principal viola player) to the brilliant, inventive and amusing thing itself. Levin's keyboard style—erect, sprightly and extrovert—was in complete contrast with Melvyn Tan's poeticism only a few days before, and again with Malcolm Bilson's unassuming gentleness a couple of days later. There is certainly no danger that the period-instrument movement is aiming towards a cramping orthodoxy—a welcome message vigorously endorsed by the shuffle of so many quite different orchestras across the stage of the Queen Elizabeth Hall. The Orchestra of the Eighteenth Century, arriving to join their conductor Frans Brüggen for these two concerts, showed off a beautifully, even sensuously blended woodwind ensemble, especially delectable in the slow movement of Levin's piano concerto. But perhaps their most remarkable distinction is in the clarity and variety of their strings' articulation, enabling Brüggen to draw phrases as if in light pencil strokes. Their close familiarity with him was shown too in a spectacular tutti crescendo in the comic-opera Symphony No.32, as well as in infectiously fast finales.

Other great pleasures of these concerts came from the singers, and particularly from Cyndia Sieden, who went straight from a wondrous performance of the high, haunting aria 'Vorrei spiegarvi' into an equally amazing account of the other, much more fiery coloratura show-stopper Mozart devised for insertion in the same opera, 'No, che non sei capace'. Pure and composed, but also with a native human freshness, Sieden's voice presents a very plausible image of what captivated Mozart in the singing of Aloysia Lange, who was still only in her early twenties when he wrote these arias for her. Sieden sounds young; she also contrives to project the virtuoso high notes, warblings and leaps of Mozart's Aloysia style without strain, and at the same time to convey the expressive character he admired in his favourite singer. 'Vorrei spiegarvi' was a nobly plaintive withdrawal, 'No, che non sei capace' a fierce, scorched repudiation. In this same concert Luba Orgonasova offered a contrastingly majestic sound, but agile in movement, for the Andromeda scena 'Ah, lo previdi', and then joined Sieden in an astounding performance of the duet from Act 2 of *Mitridate*, ending with rippling flourishes of vocal brilliance and confidence from both singers. Different again and gorgeous in every note, intelligent in every phrase, Diana Montague distinguished the earlier evening with perfection in the two grandest soprano concert arias of Mozart's Vienna years, 'Ch'io mi scordi di te?' and 'Bella mia fiamma'. (*Times*, 9 September 1991)

Mitridate

Listening down from his perch in eternity, where infinite things can be done at once, Mozart will have been able to drop in on all the thousands of commemorations happening as the night of December 5 rippled around the world. No doubt, so many requiems had their due response: perhaps mostly one of frustration that none of us down here can hear the completion. One can imagine him looking more kindly, if surely with astonishment, on the Royal Opera's production of an opera he wrote when he was fourteen and never troubled himself with after the first couple of performances in Milan at Christmas 1770. This was a bold choice for Covent Garden, and yet also an apt one. For one thing, *Mitridate* was itself dead for two hundred years before its first revival, at the 1971 Salzburg Festival. Even now it is very far from being a repertory piece: this is its first production by a British company, providing an altogether fitting celebration.

It is also a quite spectacular success, thanks in equal measure to a superlative assembly of voices and a splendid staging by Graham Vick and his designer Paul Brown. The set is fiercely coloured and simple, a versatile arrangement of large planar objects in crimson, with hints of red lacquer or sanguine marble, seen against stark black or searing blue. A few beautiful images stand out from these backgrounds: an obelisk, an outcrop of slatey rocks, a moon, a magnified antique globe, a tree. But the oddest things here are the people. Brown's costumes reinstate the vastly wide farthingales to be seen in theatrical engravings of the period: the hero Sifare, with his hank of hair swept back from a high brow, his swathing of royal blue and his extrapolated skirts, looks like a cross between a lifeguard and a clothes brush. Vick and Brown seem to accept that there is something ludicrous about the effect, but the lasting impressions are the right ones of strangeness and extravagance, and they are reinforced by the beauty and surprise of other marriages in the wardrobe. Sweeping coats, figured fabrics and turban-like wigs entwine the Turkish and the eighteenth century; there are strong samurai elements too, and African masks, and a visitor from Mughal India. The synthesis is strong, however, and yet of course these are not normal people. The costumes have a practical advantage in obliging their wearers to move with circumspection, and so to strike formal attitudes without their seeming empty. Dressed so, too, these are not so much characters as singing structures, the beings that opera seria is about.

This is also the singing that opera seria is about. The challenging tenor title role is sung by Bruce Ford, who makes up in confidence and resolution what he lacks in sheer vocal power, and whose decoration in his first aria is stunning. Jochen Kowalski as his turncoat elder son gains in force throughout the long evening, and gives it a moving close. Lillian Watson is bright and touching as Ismene, Patrick Power majestically sure in his flamboyant single aria as Marzio, and Jacquelyn Fugelle brilliantly pure as Arbate, a creature appearing in severe black triplicate as if to intimate the three ladies of an opera twenty years in the future. Further presages come in the music for Aspasia, which Yvonne Kenny, particularly in an enraptured account of her third-act scena, makes us hear as anticipating Ilia and even Pamina: the view is distant, to be sure, but it is clear. And Ann Murray as Sifare offers more than support. She has another of the opera's great numbers, 'Lungi da te' with horn obbligato (the latter a bit rough, like most of the orchestral contributions under Hartmut Haenchen), and she makes it a superb display of controlled phrasing and shading, the centrepiece of a superbly accomplished performance. Hard now, just afterwards, not to hear Mozart smiling. (*Times*, 7 December 1991)

so many Mozarts

Nobody could wish the bicentenary bookshelf any longer, not when Mozartian volumes published in English alone this year stretch on for a good couple of feet, and yet it is impossible not to be struck by a singular absence, that of any new comprehensive biography. The last was Erich Schenk's, published for the birth bicentenary in 1956; a whole lifetime has passed without a life. Meanwhile there have, of course, been biographical studies, but the most important of them have been presentations of the sources or else existential speculations: on the one hand H.C. Robbins Landon taking his readers gently on tours through libraries and archives in search of the facts concerning Mozart's Requiem or his masonic affiliations; on the other Wolfgang Hildesheimer offering a severe portrait of the loneliness of genius. Lacking the long broad narrative, we have to look to other stories, other contexts, other embeddings for the works, and there are several proposals here. Or it may be that these other frames are put forward in the suspicion that biography cannot tell us very much.

The irrelevance of Mozart's life is silently suggested by Cliff Eisen's *New Mozart Documents*, a supplement to the collection published by Otto Erich Deutsch in 1961, and quiet not only because these are scrapings from a very thoroughly scoured barrel. Most of Eisen's snippets are certainly of pretty meagre importance: concert announcements from the infant prodigy years, or listings of Mozart works in publishers' advertisements. But even where more of the composer is implicated, the glance is tangential. Take this, from the diary of Wilhelm Backhaus—not the great pianist, of course, but the man who was Antonio in the first Mannheim *Figaro* in 1790:

> I embarrassed myself with Motzard. I took him for a journeyman tailor. I was standing at the door during the rehearsal. He came and asked me if one could listen to the rehearsal. I sent him away. 'But surely you would let Kapellmeister Mozart listen?' he said.

This appears to be one of the rather few Mozart anecdotes recorded soon after it happened, and the artlessness of the reporting (leaving aside the role the man was singing) vouches for it, even if there must be some question as to why Mozart should have asked permission from a member of the cast to be present at his own rehearsal. But perhaps what counts most in its favour is its very ambiguity. It can be quoted as evidence of Mozart the dandy, or of Mozart the little man of unimpressive appearance. It can prove Mozart's humility or his pride. It can suggest either the isolated dreamer or the convivial wit.

These and all the other representations of Mozart's character that have been offered over the past two centuries are the subject of William Stafford's *Mozart's Death*. In one respect the title is misleading, since the events of 5 December 1791 are Stafford's concern for less than a third of his book, where he follows the generally respected diagnosis of rheumatic fever exacerbated by the bleedings and emetics administered by the composer's doctors, a view put forward by Carl Bär nearly twenty years ago. But after the death Stafford turns to the life, and puts to more original use his principle of marshalling all the evidence in favour of some hypothesis and then knocking it soundly on the head. One by one they go: Mozart the German nationalist, Mozart the social reformer, Mozart the angel in the body of a brat, Mozart the unknowable, inscrutable even to his own interiorizing, Mozart the man of destiny who shaped the musical world to his dictates, Mozart the victim of circumstance. Not too surprisingly, given that his whole method has been based on argument and counter-argument, Stafford's conclusion, too, is in a pair of opposites. Either we can take the view that, beneath all the wishful thinking, all the attempts to enlist Mozart in some cause, all the Procrustean efforts to fit the evidence to some pattern, there exists a body of discernible objective facts, or else we must accept that any endeavour to understand Mozart's life will fail as inevitably as all those which the book has paraded before us.

Such a conclusion will come as no surprise to historians, while to musicians it may well recall the argument about performance practice, whether it could be possible, through a thorough examination of the sources, treatises and other contemporary evidence, to establish ground rules of 'authentic' style, or whether all performances are bound to be partial representations, cramped not only by imperfection of knowledge but also by the assumptions, tastes, histories and period of those performing. Equally one can see biography and performance practice not as mirroring one another in their essential dilemma but as rival founts of endorsement and energy in efforts to understand the music—as rival stories into which the works can be fitted.

The message from Stafford as from Eisen is that we seem to have passed beyond a time when anything from Mozart's life could be useful in interpreting his music. Imagine this. Robbins Landon, or some other scholar-detective, discovers in a remote Swiss monastery the lost manuscript of the D minor Kyrie, on the back of which is written, verifiably in Mozart's hand, a piece of prose headed 'What I Meant to Achieve in My *Don Giovanni*'. Once the dust had cleared, one might wonder how brightly even the composer's own interpretative views would shine against the light of E.T.A. Hoffmann, of Kierkegaard, of all those who have contemplated, sung, conducted or produced the work through two centuries. So much less do we need to know about Mozart's sex life.

If we now look for validation and assistance much less to the life than to the instrumental and vocal practices of the time, *Perpsectives on Mozart Performance*, edited by R. Larry Todd and Peter Williams, might seem likely to be more use than any biography. Unfortunately, though, the authentic sound emerging most noisily from this volume is the unmistakable one of scholars grinding axes. Of course, this has an entertainment value all its own, particularly in the case of Frederick Neumann's 'A New Look at Mozart's Prosodic Appoggiatura', whose wonderfully undangerous title shelters a blast of fury, indignation and rebuttal directed at Will Crutchfield for daring to propose a viewpoint different from that espoused in our author's magisterial survey of Mozartian ornamentation. But other contributions are not so heartwarming. There is a stimulating and nicely written examination of Mozart's tempo indications from Jean-Pierre Marty, and the views of distinguished performers, such as Paul Badura-Skoda, Eduard Melkus and Jaap Schröder, will command their colleagues' attention, and no doubt refutation. However, the pieces by the editors are, rather strangely, focussed on side issues: Todd writes on Mendelssohn's relationship with Mozart (this is the cutting-edge of authenticity, to recreate Mendelssohn's performance of Mozart's arrangement of Handel's *Alexander's Feast*), and Peter Williams lets loose some thoughts on the chromatic fourth motif in what is pure musicology, if modishly argued in terms of rhetorical *figura*, rather than advice to performers. It is bad luck, too, that the last contributor—Christoph Wolff, writing on cadenzas and improvisation in the piano concertos—should have to end on the saddest of footnotes: 'An important article by Robert D. Levin . . . published after the present essay was written, explores a broader range of pertinent issues.'

If the study of performance practice is a frail and forked crutch, then perhaps we should go to the works themselves to find their story, a narrative they could unfold independently of the life or of the hazards of the prosodic appoggiatura. And yet we cannot altogether avoid the life when it was Mozart himself who made the first exhaustive catalogue of his works, who gave the story an outline plot. Given the problems in dating pieces that are not in his catalogue and whose autograph manuscripts have disappeared (that D minor Kyrie is an example, dated to the period of *Idomeneo* by some authorities, to that of *Don Giovanni* by others), one can easily imagine the debates there might have been had we not had this *Verzeichnüss aller meiner Werke*, in which the composer carefully listed and dated almost everything he wrote between February 1784 and just twenty days before his death. This central document has now been published in a fine facsimile by its holders, the British Library, reproducing not only the pages Mozart covered with details of titles, instrumentations, occasions and incipits, but also the thirty that remain blank.

Blank. One hesitates over the adverb.

One of Stafford's alternative false Mozarts is the composer who had completed his journey, who had attained a late style, and whom we, without alarm, can see lying on his deathbed as the calendar closes on the bicentenary—false because this 'late style' is, of course, late only in retrospect, because the alternative to his death is too staggering to dismiss, and because of the blank waiting pages and the cover label in Mozart's hand, indicating that his catalogue runs 'vom Monath febraio 1784 bis Monath 1 . The lack of a 7 in the terminal date is suggestive. Alan Tyson, in an introduction to the facsimile, points out that the blank pages are too few to have carried the catalogue on into the nineteenth century: at Mozart's rate of production it would have been filled around the end of 1795. But of course, if Mozart scribbled the label when he began the catalogue, he need not have known just how prolific he was going to be. In any event, there is no evidence he was ready to fill in 'December 791'.

But to go on from there, to mentally venture even the incipits, is unimaginable. What we find in the works of 1791 are foretastes of Schubert (the *Ave verum corpus*), of Weber (*The Magic Flute*), of Berlioz (*La clemenza di Tito*), but not of what Mozart might have become. It is a moot point too how these composers—and still more so Beethoven—would have been affected by a Mozart alive and composing into the 1820s.

If those blank pages must remain forever blank to all enquiry, the catalogue can tell us of Mozart's professional care and pride. As Albi Rosenthal notes, in the facsimile's other introduction, the document appears to have no parallel. It descends, in a nice process of internalizing, from publishers' lists of wares, through inventories drawn up by Leopold Mozart to publicize his son's achievements to this aide-mémoire that Mozart must have made for his own eyes only, and that he kept up meticulously through nearly eight years of creative and performing activity, of family hurly-burly, of house moves and journeys. That alone must counter the image of him as feckless, especially when one considers how very few compositions he omitted to register.

What is remarkable, too, and testifies to the attentiveness of Mozart's successors as well as to his own tidy housekeeping, is how very few of the compositions he catalogued have been lost. Here are tantalizing blanks of another kind: a German aria, a slow movement for a violin concerto, a final chorus for an opera buffa by Sarti, which Mozart entered only a few months before his death. Any or all of these might yet turn up: only two years ago a missing sheet from a horn rondo was discovered. But that beguiling-frustrating repertory of compositions known to be lost is very small—much smaller than in the case of Haydn.

Mozart's cherishing of the record of his work—a record which, unlike musical manuscripts, can have had no financial value to him—is one of the rare and indisputably heartening signals we have from his life, one where he speaks to us directly, not to a correspondent he wants to impress, reassure or tease, and says: yes, rest assured, I knew my worth. It is greatly satisfying to have this beautiful facsimile in one's hands, and a special pleasure, also, to be able to see the original, together with a great many autographs, scribal copies and early printings, in the exhibition 'Mozart: Prodigy of Nature' at the British Library.

Many of the manuscripts belong, like the *Verzeichnüss*, to the library, whose Mozart collection was started in June 1765 when Leopold presented it with the short and rather rough unaccompanied chorus *God is Our Refuge* (though the exhibition booklet is not quite right that this 'was to remain his only setting of English words': Nardo in *La finta giardiniera* has something to sing on that matter). However, an assembly of Mozart manuscripts on this scale is surely unprecedented since the publisher Johann André's holdings, bought from Mozart's widow Constanze, were dispersed after his death, in

1843. And blame for the crass title can be placed on the hardened shoulders of Leopold, who, during their long London visit, advertised his eight-year-old son as 'a real Prodigy of Nature'.

The exhibition is a reminder, sobering but also cheering, of Mozart's productivity, and of the extent to which his music, bodily before us here in hundreds of pages, not merely charts but indeed was his life. With 626 Köchel numbers to get through in under three decades, he wrote a musical movement every fortnight on average. Sometimes he would have got through the quota in a single day, as we know he did in the case of the odd little gigue he wrote into a Leipzig organist's album, leaving plenty of time for playing billiards, carousing with Schikaneder, bedding Frau Hofdemel and doing all the other things ascribed to that filmy Mozart between fact and fantasy. But he must have spent a lot of his time at work.

If that collapses the biographical perspective, there remain other stories that can be woven to give the works a unity, other contexts, other frames, even if changing the frame changes the object under scrutiny. Seen as a set of problems in performance practice, the output is dominated by the sonatas and concertos for piano and violin. Viewed as a journey in human understanding, as in Ivan Nagel's tight-packed fist of ideas and insights *Autonomy and Mercy*, it has the operas as its main stages. Or if we are concerned with the dissemination and influence of Mozart's music during the decade after his death, within that critical period of somersaulting revaluation when the journeyman tailor became the great composer, then domestic music looms largely into view.

This is the stuff of reception history, exemplified by Gernot Gruber's *Mozart and Posterity*, which presents raw materials, untempered by anything more than an approximate chronological organization: here is the great meandering river of Mozart reception, going sometimes into regions that now seem remote—in the 1830s, for example, we find the resoundingly named Anton Wilhelm Florentin von Zuccalmaglio adapting the operas to contemporary taste, so that *Idomeneo* becomes *Der Hof in Melun*, a Hundred Years War drama concerning Charles VII of France and Agnes Sorel (surely something else due for authentic revival)—then swerving back close, as in Grillparzer's reference to 'an alien figure of greatness', which seems to convey a modern sense of distance, loss and immeasurability in the face of Mozart.

Gruber's book was originally published in German, but that is not the only reason German sources preponderate. German artists from Goethe to Stockhausen have taken Mozart as one of their own, whereas the neglect in Italy even of the Italian operas appears to have begun during Mozart's lifetime, after his boyhood success in Milan with his first essays in opera seria. Perhaps a non-German author would have leaned less heavily on German and Austrian stage history in the twentieth century, but Gruber is more than fair on Mozart as a figure in English verse. He gives the last word to Auden, and includes this couplet from Keats, even if he exaggerates a little in suggesting it shows how the poet 'found wonderful things to say' about the composer:

> But many days have passed since last my heart
> Was warm'd luxuriously by divine Mozart.

If 'reception history' can thus be hardly more than a grand name for anthologizing, its current vogue is itself a cultural marker, showing a concern for the attitudes of other times and places that can be seen either negatively as a symptom of disintegration and self-doubt or positively as a sign of openness and curiosity. Response to Mozart's last two operas, both through history and now, is germane here. Gruber's material shows how *The Magic Flute* has always had a high place in popular and cultural regard, and this is further documented by Peter Branscombe in his Cambridge Opera Handbook on the work, a volume valuable especially for its full and sensible treatment of the opera's sources, first performances and narrative problems. If Mozart had lived only three more years, Branscombe reveals, he could have seen Pamina onstage in just about every major city from Budapest to Amsterdam, from Danzig to Freiburg. Maybe his financial circumstances would not have been much different, but certainly later generations would have been unable to conclude he died neglected.

And yet, as Gruber hints, his immediately posthumous fame may have needed to be posthumous. It was his death, occurring at a moment when European musical culture was closing around a canon (publication of Burney's history was completed in 1789), that made him a classic: the acknowledgement was there in the newspapers within days. The works would become a complete collection of specimens (Köchel, one may recall, had been a classifier of plants and minerals before compositions), to be placed among the musical scriptures that helped give post-Revolution Europe a sense of homogeneity. Aristocratic culture had valued living composers, who could be told what was needed; bourgeois culture venerated dead ones, who could be learned. Mozart happened to be the first dead composer on whom the wreath of greatness could be bestowed, precisely because of the complexity that had hindered his music's progress under the old order.

In Deutsch's collection of documents, and now also in Eisen's supplement, this problematical difficulty comes up again and again, as for instance in a letter from Dittersdorf (in Eisen) referring to Mozart's quartets, 'which, indeed, I and still greater theorists consider to deserve the highest praise, but which because of their overwhelming and unrelenting artfulness are not to everyone's taste'. In an age when music was to be played once and set aside (Stafford reminds us that *Idomeneo* had only four performances while Mozart was alive), Mozart was with some justice less successful at the Viennese Burgtheater than Paisiello, Sarti and Martín y Soler. In an age of classics, developing to the point where one could hear that same *Idomeneo* in four different recordings any day, the judgement is necessarily different.

Idomeneo was not, though, one of the classics right away—nor did *Der Hof in Melun* make it one, for that well-wishing farrago may never have been staged. Its rise began half a century or so ago (though Gruber makes surprisingly little of this), with Strauss's 1930 Vienna version and the Glyndebourne production of 1951. A view of the classics not as an immutable body but as subject to additions and substitutions, quite apart from changes in interpretation, may be the principal lesson of reception history, in its relevance at a time when the notion of a fixed canon is under examination.

In that debate *La clemenza di Tito*, with *The Magic Flute* the other opera of Mozart's last year, provides an even more challenging exhibit than *Idomeneo*. The modern revival of the latter did justice by a piece that had been overlooked, and so simply extended the canon. But *Tito* was once among Mozart's most successful operas—the first to be staged in London, in 1802—and the current change in its fortunes, a phenomenon entirely of the last quarter-century, is a reinstatement, not a widening of regard, suggesting more worryingly a fickleness in canonical evaluations.

There is a further difference, even more crucial. The retrieval of *Idomeneo* was stimulated by, and in turn fostered, a feeling not only that it was something special in Mozart's output, being a combative confrontation of Gluck's heroism of the solitary and his choral spectacle inherited from French opera, but also that it was something the same, that Ilia and Idamante and Idomeneo were embarked on journeys of self-discovery not unlike those taken by the central characters of *Die Entführung*, *Figaro*, *Così fan tutte* and *The Magic Flute*, and flamboyantly, vehemently, shockingly rejected by the protagonist of *Don Giovanni*. But nowadays no one—not even John A. Rice or any of the witnesses he calls in another Cambridge handbook published aptly in tandem with Branscombe's on the *Flute*—is seeking to claim that a similar self-realization is attained by, or by the music granted to, the figures of *La clemenza di Tito*.

Nagel persuasively argues the centrality of *Idomeneo* to the humane project of Mozart's operas as dramas of free characters, and the exclusion of *Tito* from that project. His title provides the key. *Autonomy and Mercy* is a beautiful sequence of reflections, ranging in size from fully advanced essays to apophthegms, and in topic as far from Mozart as to Kleist, Kafka, Stravinsky and the sinister Nazi jurist Carl Schmitt, though all circling round and touching pointedly on the theme, which is that the glimpsing of truth gives a character power over her fate, and thereby gives her power also to bring liberation into her world. And this does seem to be a female prerogative: Nagel tracks the moment in the singing of Ilia, of Konstanze in *Die Entführung*, of Beethoven's Leonore and most especially of Pamina, whose proud line in the first act finale of *The Magic Flute*—'The truth, the truth, and though it be forbidden'—resounds through these pages. Perhaps this has to be a woman's part, for reasons of the exposure, force and word-dissolving power of the soprano voice. Through one clamant vocal act, of a kind far beyond speech, the female hero wrests for herself autonomy, and for herself and others mercy.

Many marvellous things spring out of and around this pinpointing of where enlightenment musically happens. Nagel has a good piece on 'Atmospheres', appropriately dedicated to Ligeti. 'No one until Debussy', he begins, 'was able to compose the music of the air like Mozart', and he goes on to indicate how this aeriform music, still 'striking and strange' in *Idomeneo*, becomes recognized by the characters as their common atmosphere: 'They cannot lose one another, since they are embraced by one animated world'. He is excellent too on the particular musical junctures at which autonomy and mercy are unloosed, as at the end of *Figaro*, where 'mercy itself seems to glide down to earth in the unison of the violins', or in the first act finale of *The Magic Flute*, where Pamina's resolve to tell the truth is immediately succeeded by her doing so to Sarastro:

> But not until Sarastro's bass is imitated by the solo bassoon (deep under flutes and strings, affirming their gesture of renunciation) do two half-measures encompass what cannot be said—what Tito's entire part with its private sighs and public sermons tried in vain to express. Leading out of a shadowy minor into brightness, the instruments tell of the enigma of mature melancholy: how it is at once the painful offering and the comforting reward of human kindness. Again, anticipation appears as the transient signal of autonomy: Sarastro frees himself before he frees Pamina, with the decision

> that the orchestra speaks for him while the voice pauses and gathers strength to repeat it.

The candour and the eloquence here are characteristic; so too is the quiet listening, and the richness of intimation. One could write a whole essay out of Nagel's exposition of instrumental verbalizing in this score, and indeed Thomas Bauman has done just that, independently of Nagel, in a sensitive contribution to his edition of *Mozart's Operas* by Daniel Heartz.

But the swipe at *Tito* is typical of Nagel, too, and calls for investigation. Nagel does not take either of the old views: that the opera was lamed by its composer's illness and haste, or that Mozart could not rouse himself to any interest in the moribund genre of opera seria. Rather he seems to feel that *Tito* is the genre's own expression of its moribundness, that the theme of the clement autocrat—one of the great plot lines of Metastasian opera seria, and predictably brought out once again for performance on the day of Leopold II's coronation as King of Bohemia—could no longer be sustained, not in 1791, not when the emperor-king's sister was about to keep an appointment with the guillotine. This is tempting. But then we have to ask whether Tito is really very different in his enfeeblement from his counterpart in Mozart's previous treatment of the theme, *Lucio Silla*, written nearly twenty years before, far from the brink of revolution. After all, Silla has only two arias in his opera, and though one of them is active enough, if in the conventional vengeance mode, the other is a threat that trails off into recitative for a central quandary of vacillations. Also, Silla, exactly like Tito, deigns to take part in ensembles, a concession Nagel would see as abdicative.

The suspicion arises that everything Nagel holds against *Tito* he ought to hold against *Lucio Silla* too, that his dissatisfaction is with the genre. To say of Tito's role that 'the strained tenor has the effect of being not a man and sovereign, but the true castrato' is to ask whether Silla and Mitridate, and a thousand other tenor kings, generals and emperors singing in the opera seria of the period, are so much more robust. And the straining here is as much Nagel's as Tito's. If singers in this part do indeed often sound forced, that could be because they have to sing it in theatres much too large, or because they come to it, through their training and experience, from a world radically unlike their eighteenth-century colleagues'. The invocation of the castrato, too, is sleight of hand. The music castratos had to sing, not least that written for them by Mozart, is not at all castrate in effect: it could be outrageously, splendidly erotic; it could alternatively be bold and noble, as in the role of Sesto in this very opera. Also, if indeed a particular impotence is written into Tito, that could be because Mozart was writing the part for the man who had been the first Don Ottavio, not one of the heroes judged most sympathetically in Mozart reception.

If *Tito* fails to match up to Nagel's model of the Mozart opera, as it surely does, then perhaps the fault lies not in it but in the paradigm, for all Nagel's daring and thoughtfulness, luminous clarity and hard grace, in which case readers will have to move on to Rice and Heartz. But just a moment. If the characters of *Tito* are truly 'bloodless', to use Nagel's word, perhaps they are so only because they have not been blooded in dramatic and written interpretations through two centuries. The people of *Idomeneo*, with stage careers of several decades behind them and an even longer history of critical appreciation, have now been restored to life. Perhaps we must just wait for those of *Tito* to rouse themselves.

Meanwhile, Rice's immediate and engaging espousal of the opera appears to concede its statuesqueness, and so too do the essays by Heartz and Bauman. The G major chorus in the second act is honoured by Bauman in a fine phrase as 'the greatest compliment ever paid to the aspirations of Metastasian opera to idealize the worth and dignity of those who hold temporal power' (though some will still prefer the earlier F major chorus, the greatest compliment ever paid to *Così fan tutte*, in particular to its garden serenade). Rice, too, scans through the opera to Metastasio, quoting lengthily and approvingly from Vernon Lee on the Caesarean poet as Romantic. However, if we want to hear what Metastasio wrote, we have to go to Caldara's original setting of 1734, not Mozart's, for which the libretto was chopped and changed—'ridotta a vera opera', as Mozart put it in his catalogue—by Caterino Mazzolà. And the scenes that remain from Metastasio are by no means the best.

One such scene, much admired in the eighteenth century, is the interview between Tito and Sesto, a dialogue prolonged because Sesto is held back from speaking by love and nobility while Tito is held back from acting by friendship and uncertainty; it is a model Metastasian situation. We entirely miss the point, Rice insists, if we bring with us from opera buffa the view of simple recitative as just a way to move the plot along to the next concerted number, for opera seria has its narrative life in recitative, where for once the librettist is the dramatist. Nor can we avoid the issue on the grounds that Mozart did not have time to set the recitatives, and so they, as Heartz puts it, 'lamentably, had to be entrusted to another hand' (probably Süssmayr's, which has been roundly slapped over the years for its supposed inadequacy). As Rice proves, conventions in recitative setting were well defined, so that there is a close similarity between what Gluck wrote for this text in 1752 and what reached the ears of Leopold II in 1791. (Perhaps the dormant ears. It appears that the empress's description of the opera as 'una porcheria tedesca' belongs among the Mozart fables, but happily Rice has salvaged her opinion from a letter to her daughter-in-law that is also in Eisen: 'the gala opera was not much and the music very bad so that almost all of us fell asleep. The coronation went marvellously'.)

But leaving aside Metastasio and Süssmayr and Maria Luisa, what are we to make of Mozart's part in the piece? Rice envisages nothing like Nagel's attentive sympathy but rather a passive capacity for admiration, wonder and the receipt of pleasure. If, he proposes, we could hear 'Deh per questo istante solo' sung by a soprano who could 'bring Sesto's words and feelings vividly to life' and could 'ornament the vocal line spontaneously and beautifully' (but following Neumann or Crutchfield?), the great rondò 'could represent musical drama at its most intense and memorable'. However, the conditionals here are advised, for Sesto is a castrato role, and we can only imagine the effect in the theatre of a person of this rare and special type, created for such moments of performance alone.

A more fundamental objection to Rice's invitation would be to its generality, to its defence of *Tito* merely as an example of its genre, however outstanding an example. That is also the drift of his quotations, such as those from an unnamed Italian poet, rhapsodizing over a castrato rondò in a Sarti opera, or from Lord Mount Edgcumbe, lamenting the demise of opera seria around 1820, or from Stanley Sadie, praising the tide-turning 1969 Cologne production because 'Ponnelle tackled the opera on its own ground, that of eighteenth-century emotion and eighteenth-century classicism'. Just as those who deplore the opera, like Nagel and Hildesheimer, are dismissing a whole species, so those who speak for it are admiring one. Heartz, too, is in this camp, noting that opera seria was nowhere near extinction in 1791, for Paisiello and Cimarosa went on pursuing the form until the end of the century, but seeing Mozart in *Tito* as 'trying . . . to challenge Paisiello and the Italians on their own terms'.

Like everything else in this author's essays, the point is learned, eminently plausible, smoothly expressed and also practically useful, in this case because it should alert opera companies to an under-regarded repertory. But what if we want to see *Tito* in Mozart's terms, give it a context not from Paisiello's *Fedra* and Sarti's *Giulio Sabino* but from *Idomeneo* and *Figaro* and *Così*, make it a chapter in the Mozart story? There is instantly a problem, and not one of genre or farmed-out recitatives. One of Heartz's masterly essays on *Idomeneo*, which he edited for the Neue Mozart Ausgabe, shows how the work's genesis can be illuminated with reference to the French source and to Mozart's correspondence. Similar evidence is not available for the six subsequent operas, he remarks, but: 'What can be learned here applies to all that follows.'

It simply cannot apply, though, to *Tito*, where, for the first time since his previous Metastasio setting, *Il re pastore* of 1775, Mozart was working with a given libretto. Even if he had Mazzolà to change it for him, a lot of the aria texts remained from the original, as did the plot. Space was thus severely limited for the kind of freedom Heartz and Bauman want to see Mozart exercising, and passionately encourage the reader to see Mozart exercising, over his other librettos: the freedom to modify and enrich the ending of *Die Entführung*, to choose *Figaro* as the locus for an answer to Paisiello's adaptation of its predecessor in Beaumarchais's trilogy, to develop *Così fan tutte* as a threading of references back to the earlier operas, and especially to *Figaro*. All this is scrupulously researched and appetizingly displayed. And though Heartz is by no means indifferent to the artistry of librettists (he has a piece on Metastasio, Goldoni and da Ponte in their roles as stage producers as well as providers of words), the Mozart he and his colleague present is the Mozart we want to see, the man who had the guiding hand not only in pacing and characterizing his dramas but in shaping them.

Perhaps what is most essentially disconcerting about *Tito* is that it cannot have come about in that way. The tracks were laid down. The people in this opera are singing Mozart, and in doing so, because character in opera is made by the voice, they come to us as Mozart creatures. But they are placed in a drama alien to them. That is their tragedy.

One way in which the mismatch between characters and drama expresses itself is through the strong connections between these opera seria figures and their fellows in the quite different world of *The Magic Flute*. Heartz points to the likenesses between Sesto and Tamino, Tito and Sarastro; he also notes how, on the broadest harmonic scale, *Tito* is the *Flute* turned inside out. One could add that *Tito* is full of tunes which, like the much castigated quick theme of Sesto's rondò, call across to the simplicity of the fairytale.

However, another link may give a warning. Erik Smith, contributing an essay on the music to Branscombe's *Magic Flute* handbook, remarks how a certain violin figure, a twiddle followed by a skipping staccato arpeggio, turns up in the score on two quite dissimilar occasions: at the start of the Act 1 quintet, where Papageno has had a lock put on his mouth, and in the finale to the same act, when Tamino tries the three doors. Since this same figure recurs often in the High Priest's narrative of doom and destruction in the third act of *Idomeneo*, it is hard, Smith says, to be sure what it can mean. And it becomes even harder when one adds the example of Vitellia's recitative before her rondò in *Tito*. Maybe one could get away with saying that both the *Flute* occurrences are in connection with locked entrances, but that does not cover the case in *Idomeneo* or *Tito*. And indeed the figure sounds less like a symbol than like a rhetorical gesture, a call to attention. A very clear motivic correspondence may, then, be empty of significance: we may be looking at a punctuation mark. That must make us wary of treating Mozart's operas as instalments in a super-*Ring*.

Heartz is not shy of subscribing to that view: 'all seven master operas of Mozart's last decade', he concludes these essays, 'belong to the same family. They constitute an interrelated cycle within the larger corpus of his works'. And by that point he has certainly shown how profitable such a perspective can be. If one wants to maintain, though, that the 'interrelated cycle' may be a rather complicated contraption, and in particular that *Tito* stands fundamentally apart, Nagel can be of help again. His contemptuous aside that Tito's benevolence is nothing like Sarastro's demands the rejoinder that it cannot be so, because the crucial moments of truth-telling and mind-changing come in recitative. There is, nevertheless, a descent of grace such as Nagel would have to admire, and it comes from Servilia in her only aria, a minuet of sustained soft radiance. The words would seem to be calling for something harsher, more affirmative: Servilia is pointing out to the self-serving emotional weathercock Vitellia that tears are not much use to Sesto at this point, arraigned as he is for conspiracy against the emperor. But Servilia, the Servilia created by the music, is not listening to the words. She has to take this opportunity, the only opportunity that can be squeezed into the drama, to open the way to self-understanding. That way stays, though, as blocked as Sarastro's temple doors and Papageno's mouth. What comes next is Vitellia's recitative and rondò: not self-understanding but self-pity.

La clemenza di Tito is a place where different stories gash one another. There is the Metastasian drama of the forgiving emperor and his fallible subjects. There is the postscript to *The Magic Flute*, in which we should perhaps see Tito not as a quasi-Sarastro but as Tamino, overparted now that Sarastro has yielded power to him and disappeared. There is the story of the ruler, his son and his son's beloved, the story travelling on from *Idomeneo*. No single story will do, not for the works, not for this composer. (*Times Literary Supplement*, 29 November 1991)

a decade of Don Giovannis

The dark centrepiece of the three operas Mozart wrote with words by Lorenzo da Ponte, first produced in 1787, had messages of sex and death for two centuries later.

English National Opera 1985

Jonathan Miller's production may not be the first *Don Giovanni* to be clothed uniformly in black and white, but it perhaps breaks some records in placing this night piece so much out of doors. The stage is dominated by three corners of anonymous buildings, or giant book-ends, revolving to provide a variety of half-evoked interiors and street scenes. They are lit, by Robert Bryan, harshly, the cold white light coming straight from overhead as if from a spectacularly fierce full moon (if one that switches on and of rather brutally). But behind and all around there is darkness. This is the night of eros let loose, and the only people who thrive in it are Don Giovanni and, a shade more surprisingly but very aptly, Zerlina.

The others come from the daytime of moral respectability and decent social behaviour, and the figures they cut in this blackness teeter on the edge of caricature. Don Ottavio is a stuffy bore with the air of a Georgian clergyman; he leaves Zerlina and Masetto, then stops and returns to lecture them with his aria 'Il mio tesoro', and Maldwyn Davies's willingness to lose sweetness for plain speaking here is typical of the whole cast's readiness to follow Miller's cues to character even when these act against vocal beauty. Fecility Lott's Donna Elvira is another case in point. Miller responds acutely to the tone of fussy properness that is announced right there in the orchestral introduction to her first entry: she is conveyed in a chair. And when she steps out, we see a lady well past her prime, with rouged cheeks and a slightly ridiculous mantilla; she might be a duenna. Of course, the spinsterish aspect makes her pursuit of Don Giovanni across Spain more plausible, but it is perhaps in living up to it that

Lott makes her singing a little dry of tone and shortwinded of phrase, even if the basic sound is still the sheer pleasure we know. Josephine Barstow both looks and sounds more comfortable in her personification of Donna Anna. This is a woman again beyond her first youth, but one who has learned nothing from experience. Her most characteristic vocal gesture is to move into a pianissimo as if she were about to fall into a swoon, and when she has to be more positive, one hears through the attack the plangent hopelessness. Nor does this Laporello have much fun. Richard Van Allan's grave tone must be an invitation to make the man dour, but Miller has him thoroughly embittered as well, except for one moment of voyeur-like glee. He thus lacks any kind of moral kernel that could be the ground for his pleas to his master to change his ways—but this absence provides the occasion for a performance of dark wit from Van Allan.

Don Giovanni in these surroundings ought to shine like a lyrical god, and William Shimell certainly looks the part: he might have stepped from the cover of a romantic novel, and his fantasy handsomeness could well be irresistible to this Anna and this Elvira (this Zerlina would see through it, but still take pleasure in what she found: this is a gorgeously sung, vital, sexy performance from Lesley Garrett). Shimell's singing lives up to his appearance when he is alone, but last night his voice tended to be covered in ensembles, robbing him of authority. He scored a coup, though, in imitating Van Allan so successfully for Mark Richardson's stalwart Masetto.

The single set makes possible an uninterrupted performance of each act, and the flow is further assisted by the musical decision to use piano and cello continuo: their harmonic support is exceedingly discreet, and Miller encouraged his cast to bend the recitative towards speech. Moreover, the absence of clattering harpsichord cadences removes the frames around numbers. As for the orchestral accompaniment, that is not discreet at all, as is perhaps inevitable in a house of this size. One jibs a bit seeing so many chances for elegance pass by, but perhaps Mark Elder makes the wisest choice in playing the score for its dramatic, symphonic potential. More than once one feels Beethoven leaning over Mozart's shoulder, and snorting no doubt at Miller's vision of hell. (*Times*, 5 December 1985)

Scottish Opera 1989

There is a lot of death in this production. Virtually the only piece of furniture, recurring to a point where it becomes more wearily amusing than sinister, is a great ebony casket; Donna Anna and Don

Ottavio re-enter for the quartet at the tail of a funeral procession; and the costuming (by Eleonore Kleiber), though non-committal as to period, is pretty definite about its dominant tones of black and a little white. The major exception is the Don himself, who comes in blood red and a curious ensemble of leather trousers and beret with a wide-necked top of fur and velvet. This looks like an outfit designed to bring out the womanizer's often-supposed secret proclivities, and it says much for the strength, bleakness and persistence of Jonathan Summers's performance that such an impression is rapidly banished. If the detail and polish of the music sometimes have to be sacrificed, he provides the image of a man physically superb but internally ravaged. There is no real enticement offered to Zerlina, only a snap command, nor is there anything alluring in his serenade, sung without hope or sentiment, or any expectation of those things, to an empty window. The Champagne Aria, taken at a gallop, is one more staging post on this dead soul's race to hell, which is where he knows he is aiming from the start. What attracts the women is not Giovanni's appearance, nor his sensuality, nor his charm, all of which are seriously undermined; his zest is abandonment, and his glamour the enthusiastic embrace of extinction.

Being death-bound, the production has to underplay the life of the opera: the life of the city, and of different classes. David Walsh, the new head of production for the company, places everything within a high-windowed palatial saloon, which has the effect of making all the action look formal. The peasants' wedding-best is quite as smart and proper as the clothing of the aristocrats. By this stage, of course, one is not surprised that they look dressed more for a burial than a marriage. What is slightly bewildering, though, is that the Commendatore (majestically sung by Oddbjørn Tennfjord) should appear not as a statue but as a man ruefully sitting on the tedious coffin: this is one of those cases where the contradiction of the text just looks like some weird oversight, making the performance, and not the action, the subject of one's anxieties.

However, the ending is good. The back wall ruptures, and smoke and fire are seen, but the Don is cheated of the destination he has been careering willingly towards. Instead it is the coffin that awaits: his fate is not punishment but memorial. And when the chorus has gone, the remaining principals are strikingly revealed in silhouette at the rear, ready for the coda. They are a good team. Jane Eaglen sings with marvellously polished tone and cultivated phrasing, presenting Donna Anna very much as the grande dame; only the cruel ornaments of 'Non mi dir' find any unpreparedness in her performance. Kathryn Bouleyn finds it hard occasionally to sustain tone at the top, but hers is also a composed and musical performance as Elvira. Judith Howarth's Zerlina is rather more than that, her voice honeyed and caressing yet precise, bringing a rare access of wit and voluptuousness into this otherwise severe evening. Jan Opalach, making his European debut, took a while to get the measure of the theatre, but his acting of a Leporello out of *Waiting for Godot* was effective from the beginning. Glenn Winslade nicely retrieves the fineness of Don Ottavio by his lyrical singing (one wishes he could have been given his second aria, 'Dalla sua pace'), and David Marsh is a firm, dark Masetto. John Mauceri conducts a generally quick performance, with the orchestra singing and silky to the limits of its capacities. (*Times*, 10 February 1989)

Opera Factory 1990

Opera Factory's attempt to present a Vienna version of *Don Giovanni* interestingly introduces a sequence in which Leporello is subjected to death by a thousand cuts at the hands of Zerlina, but of course this is by no means the only new scene of the evening; for though David Freeman's production is not a transposition in the manner of his beachwear *Così*, the masquerade and the sex in the piece become rumbustiously and roughly explicit. David Roger's travelling-theatre set provides an arcade of curtained bodegas with stairways and ladders, and even a trampoline-cum-bed: an arena for the athletes all Freeman's singers have to be. The crux concerning whether or not Giovanni has enjoyed Donna Anna at the start is solved by a mime show during the overture, though the Don's orgasm looks painfully sudden, in accord with a bleak view of the sexual huntsman. Within a staging that has so much activity, his dead still, dead cold delivery of his serenade is particularly striking: Elvira's maid is bathing naked within view, but he stares out at the audience, seeing, one supposes, only an emptiness within himself. Omar Ebrahim, normally such a vigorous singer, seems obliged to rein in his lustiness, though it may be that Mozart suits him less well than Cavalli or Birtwistle.

The enjoyable sex is mostly for Zerlina and Masetto, which makes the former's cries for help in the Act 1 finale appear rather unfair, though it may be that she has switched nature here along with almost everyone else: the three toffs change into homespun, and the peasants are grotesquely got up as parody aristocrats. This is one scene in which Freeman vividly brings out the threat in the Don's amoral amorousness, and it makes the Act 2 finale look tame and affected, with its writhing naked bodies. But the epilogue is smartly done, the challenge to the audience intensified by the lack of any clear boundary at the footlights.

The cast is dominated by the women: a brilliant, bell-clear Marie Angel as Donna Anna, sounding at once lascivious and vulnerable; a radiant Christine Bunning making Donna Elvira passionate and believable; and Janis Kelly as a bright and caressing, as well as sexually active, Zerlina. Clive Bayley makes a nicely grave-voiced, downbeat Leporello who has seen it all before, and Meurig Davies has the makings of a serious Masetto. Paul Daniel converts the London Sinfonietta into a fine Mozart orchestra. (*Times*, 13 February 1990)

Maggio Musicale 1990

Anyone arriving at Jonathan Miller's new production for the Teatro alla Pergola, in Florence, after seeing his ENO *Don Giovanni* is likely to be drawn beguilingly, disconcertingly into a Sevilian maze of real and false memories. There is a new designer, Bob Israel, but still the uniform colour is the dark grey of slantingly moonlit facades for this opera of city streets and night. The look is new, but the same. This goes, too, for much of the production detail. As before, we first catch sight of rather more than usual of Don Giovanni as he comes rushing away from Donna Anna's bedchamber, though one may well still feel that a wobbling willy has limited erotic appeal. Perhaps the suggestion here is that Miller is concerned more with the anatomy than with the physiology of the opera, with groupings and movements and gestures rather abstracted from any implication. The characters are put on display against the blank walls and blind classical porticos of the set, and there is very little touching in this production, which seems to have its centre not in the Don but in the fastidious asexual partnership of Ottavio and Anna. But the coldness is a reasonable response to all these creatures, and the flashes of emotional communication are the more telling for their rarity, showing up like the occasional pink against the general creams, slates and blacks of the costuming. At the end of the first act, for instance, Giovanni contemptuously tosses his sword to Ottavio, who of course does not know what to do with it: a nice point in itself, and a marvellous solution to the problem of how to wrap the act up. Then in the sextet, Masetto seems attracted towards Elvira, and Zerlina, on grounds of social decorum as much as sexual jealousy it seems, gently draws him back. Less plausible is the ending, which again repeats the novelty of Miller's ENO version, with Don Giovanni being dragged off by a few dishevelled representatives of his catalogue entries: hell is other women. Once more, as with the pendulant member, the value of the point is emblematic rather than dramatic: one can interpret the moment as meaning that Giovanni's evaded past is crowding in on him, but as a stage spectacle his fate looks forced, and a little silly.

Samuel Ramey's Giovanni fits in with Miller's cool view almost too well. His singing is grave and solid, with very little of the carnal about it: a matter of his staid rhythm and constancy of volume as much as his tone. This is a man of force and breeding, but perhaps more a Count Almaviva than a Don Giovanni. Claudio Desderi's Leporello, by contrast, is full of sweaty life and colour, using every word, and every nuance. Carol Vaness repeats her superb, grandly aristocratic and polished Donna Anna, unfussed by such minor problems as a weak Ottavio. Daniela Dessì makes a striking Donna Elvira, her tone held to a dreadful coldness throughout singing of great artistry: it is as if her emotional fires have burned out through so much abuse but she still goes on through the same motions of passion and outrage. Adelina Scarabelli and Natale De Carolis are a likeable couple as Zerlina and Masetto, and Peter Rose, with a voice of booming power but fine control, is a magnificent Commendatore. Zubin Mehta conducts. (*Times*, 20 June 1990)

Opera North 1991

No, taking pleasure is not the same thing as having fun. It is a dark-hearted, troubled and troubling vision of Mozart's dramma giocoso that Tim Albery and his designer Ashley Martin-Davis offer in this Opera North production, and it is swept into being by orchestral playing under Paul Daniel of extraordinary speed and fizzing vivid allure. The music begins with the summons to hell, and by abolishing the curtain Albery can justify placing the action there from the start. At the rear of the stage a screen carries an unrolling abstracted image of the passing from night to day to night. But this is a kind of mnemonic, separate from the set, where there is nothing of the exterior world: no natural light, no buildings. Instead, the main structural feature is a red-black wall reaching to the back, looking like the side of a boat, though it also suggests a wave of fire caught at the point of breaking. Much of the action hangs on this precipice, but often the characters are slumped on the level in upholstered armchairs and sofas which, like most of the costumes, are jet black and look as if they have been rescued from a conflagration. This is an opera of charred beings. But there are exceptions. When the Commendatore is killed, a child angel in a pure white costume comes slowly on to lead him away. There are more such angels, now in copper uniform, in the graveyard scene, and the white one returns to take Don Giovanni's hand at the end. In every case the effect is touching, but also a mite absurd. That may be the point. By kicking the ground from under his own feet, by walking a tightrope in full view (like his cast on the crest of the fire wave), by inviting ridicule, Albery provides an image of life being lived dangerously. This intensity of challenge comes out, too, in the production's treatment of charm, which is brisk. Zerlina and her chums, for instance, deliver their chorus in a line staring straight into the theatre: there is absolutely nothing light about it. And the same provocative manner is used for Don Giovanni's serenade and for the final sextet, where triumph is replaced by anger: after all, the sinner has not just been driven to hell (the vapour and the demon here are pantomime stuff) but escaped from it.

So risky a production will obviously vary from night to night. One daring gambit that came off brilliantly on Thursday was Giovanni's assumption of a magenta evening gown and gloves while singing the Champagne Aria: another number flung straight at the audience as an affront. It happens that this Don's most erotic relationship is with Leporello, but the transvestism has less to do with his sexual psychology than with exemplifying a world of overturned values: a bleak carnival world that we then see in the first-act finale. This is a daring, urgent production: its weapon is the knife, not the gentlemanly sword. That it so often cuts to the bone is largely because of a cast utterly bound up in what is going on. Robert Hayward looks and sounds superb in the title role, his singing big and violent with cruelty, defiance and despair. John Hall partners him wonderfully as Leporello: his are the hardest tasks in dealing with the tempo and in making all the humour black. In both the quality of his success is almost shocking. Helen Field as Donna Anna may be charred with the rest, but she is also on fire with passion: her big number in Act 2 is a tour de force, courting its own dangers of insubstantial tone, but magnificent in a manner that has nothing to do with good Mozart style. Jane Leslie MacKenzie as Donna Elvira gradually rose to an impressive brilliance and agility; she may be hampered by the fact that the production is uncertain about her seriousness. The seriousness of Don Ottavio, though, is not in question. In this world of extremes, of sopranos and basses, he alone holds the middle ground, and he alone in this production is consistently reasonable and affecting. It may seem a backhander to say that Paul Nilon is best in the recitatives, but his singing there is so beautiful that his problems in the arias are all the more poignant. Lynne Davies and Peter Snipp are a likeable peasant couple; Sean Rea a splendidly sonorous Commendatore. (*Times*, 6 July 1991)

Covent Garden 1992

Given the way that *Figaro* and *Così* have passed across this stage under his hands, nobody can have expected the *Don Giovanni* that completes Johannes Schaaf's Mozart–da Ponte threesome to stake out the work's claims as opera buffa. No, the feeling is big, black, oppressive and cold, cold, cold. The only laughter of the evening comes from Don Giovanni—a sudden, powerful reinvention of the part for himself from Thomas Allen—and it is a harsh, cruel mockery directed at all the Leporellos of this world who expect to be snug.

The aura of the production owes a lot to Peter Pabst's sets, which have a tilt of beautifully projected sky on a great panel up above, but which are dominated by high, black and featureless walls. Black is the main colour of the costumes, too, with all the gentry looking like anxious courtiers of the Spanish Hapsburgs, so that the tumble of creams, azures and browns with the arrival of the peasants is a very welcome breeze of life. Many different configurations of the walls are possible, none more effective than the narrow channelling of entrances and exits straight down the middle of the stage in the garden scene towards the end of the first act. The arrival of Giovanni and his bevvy of long-haired minders (the same ones who are to make good his escape in the next scene) is a particularly powerful moment in a production lean in dramatic braggadocio.

Most of the 'ideas' similarly depend on extras. A female servant hangs around the spot where the Commendatore was killed (a rude stabbing by this scorner of human hopes and pretensions, not a duel), bringing flowers and kneeling in prayer, and it is to her that Elvira goes for consolation at the end of Leporello's catalogue aria. Rather similarly, Donna Anna has a confidante to whom, more than to Ottavio, she addresses 'Non mi dir'. But the touch of female fellowship is weak without support in the music. There is also something ill-fitting about the collection of human statues in the cemetery (one is just amazed that they can all stand so still, which is not really the point of the scene), and about the nude young lady gracing Giovanni's supper table: the piece is about seduction and conquest, not having it put in front of you on a plate.

Much is said about the completeness of Allen's portrayal by the fact that his Giovanni is here for once unsettled and confused, or seems unsettled and confused, bothered by an irrelevance. It is remarkable to hear this singer creating a character so bleak and unengaging, finding the voice for such a chill and chilling soul. The man is a kind of insatiable zealot. He knows hell before he gets there.

When there are so many Glyndebourne regulars onstage—and of course in the pit, where Bernard Haitink conducts a performance full of demonic drive, incisive points of detail, and many moments of an opening beauty—one misses the possibilities of intimacy. Carol Vaness never slips a trick as Donna Anna: she is a magnificent blend of the imperious and the impassioned. Claudio Desderi offers a characteristically rich and appealing Leporello, and gets away with pretending this is Glyndebourne in his conversational manner (and in an unforgettable close to his catalogue aria, the one sexy moment in the whole evening). Hans Peter Blochwitz makes a fine case for Ottavio as a young man whose ardour is constrained by a fierce sense of honour and propriety (again very much a Spanish figure); his singing is captivating and precise. Marta Marquez is a lively, bright Zerlina, Bryn Terfel an admirable, very sympathetic Masetto, and Robert Lloyd a luxury Commendatore. Patricia Schuman, entering this giant cast in place of an indisposed Karita Mattila, will no doubt settle; her vulnerable flame of an Elvira could be touching. (*Times*, 7 February 1992)

Glyndebourne—Salzburg—Munich 1994

All operas invite us to hear through the character to the singer and through the singer to the character; the form is founded on the art of half-impersonation. But *Don Giovanni* asks us particularly to wonder about the way a character is imposed—and imposed not so much by the composer as by the interpreter. Because four of its roles—Giovanni, Leporello, the Commendatore and Masetto—are set in the same vocal range, and because this common range is that of the bass voice, which in Mozart's style exacts relatively little variety (unlike the soprano), we differentiate these characters largely by virtue of the singers' particularities. And we do so especially when, this being a night piece, the eyes are secondary. Episodes in the action—Leporello's comic uncertainty as to whether his master or the Commendatore has survived their duel; the exchange of clothes, and superficially of roles, between master and servant—depend on the closeness of these uniformly bass characters. We should consider, too, how much Mozart might have expected his audience to recognize that the singer of the Commendatore returns as the singer of Masetto. Nowadays these roles are almost never doubled, as they were at the two productions, in Prague and Vienna, with which the composer was associated. Should we glimpse, in Masetto's resistance, a warning from the shrouded Commendatore? Should we then understand, when the Commendatore starts to sing again, that a certain layer of subterfuge has been discarded, for the reason that now more serious measures are needed?

The superficial confusions and interchangeabilities of the four bass roles may indicate that we are dealing not with four characters but with a single being who appears in several aspects. One of those aspects, known as Don Giovanni, kills another, known as the Commendatore; but this self-mutilation cannot be an actual death, and that is why the Commendatore-Masetto remains to stalk the would-be assassin. Don Giovanni's crime is not homicide; it is not even multiple rape and breach of promise. His crime—gross enough to make a statue sing—is that of laughing at Leporello, of despising this mask of himself. Here da Ponte made a crucial alteration to his immediate sources: Molière has Giovanni's fatal offence as hypocrisy, and in the libretto Giovanni Bertati wrote for the opera by Giuseppe Gazzaniga, the Don seals his fate by mocking heaven, not scoffing at a character. Da Ponte's indictment seems more just, more true, because Don Giovanni has seemed all through the opera a man who fails to see other people as real. To him, all men (Don Ottavio, the un-man, excepted) are himself: a person he scorns. And all women are, as he tells us, mere assuagers of bodily need, like food or air.

If the opera colludes with him in his view of men as replicas of himself, perhaps it does so in order to show us that this is his hell: not the hole that opens at the end, but the hole of solipsism that has gaped all through. The demon chorus that awaits him is a herd of basses, of facsimiles. His damnation will be to go through his career again and again: killing himself, deriding himself, in a world otherwise unpopulated. (*New Yorker*, 20 November 1995)

Henze

Never mind the physical strains of being sixty-seven years old, Hans Werner Henze was in buoyant mood. Despite a wrist injury, he had finished his new symphony. Now here he was in Symphony Hall, doing his utmost to disregard a damaged knee, marching down the aisle without his stick to acknowledge the applause for that symphony's first performance, by Seiji Ozawa and the Boston Symphony. The spectacle was that of a man still robustly upright in his bearing: in the dark three-piece suit and bow tie he chose for this premiere, he looked like a count, or the director of a Gymnasium. And the formal attire set off the pushing energy of his head, a head which seems to have been not only baldened but dynamized by time, so that it is now a vigorous egg of flesh, fronted by a muscle of a face.

As is the physical appearance, so is the music: thoroughly groomed, making a proud show of the most conventional dress, and bursting with being. The bulging catalogue tells the same story of capability. One could build a whole orchestral season out of Henze's works—symphonies (the Boston commission is No.8), concertos and other pieces—or a whole opera season out of what he has produced for the stage. He is, in everything, the complete professional, fulfilling those nineteenth-century demands of form and genre which continue to rule our concert and operatic life. Or, to view the case another way, his music is comfortable with the world in which it has to live. Even his exercises in music theatre and his other efforts at confrontation, written when he had a rush of revolutionary blood in his forties, belong to the same pattern, reflecting a momentary imposture of liberalism in the dominant culture at the time. And the longstanding unease of his relationship with his native Germany—a complex affair of repudiation and love on both sides—has not kept his music off the schedules of German concert halls and opera houses.

His success has, inevitably, been accompanied by charges of opportunism, and by unflattering comparisons with Richard Strauss, both composers being presumed to have gone some way with musical progress (Strauss as far as *Elektra*, Henze perhaps as far as his Second String Quartet, written in 1952) and then jumped off in favour of pleasing the audience: hence *Der Rosenkavalier*, or in Henze's case *König Hirsch* ('King Stag'), the lush fantastical opera he wrote following his permanent move from Germany to Italy. But this is too simple a picture of Strauss's course, and much too simple a one of Henze's. His participation in the postwar avantgarde was never more than a brief encounter; he was, from the first, set on the career he has kept to, and there are heady things in the works he wrote before his flight to the Mediterranean—things such as his Third Symphony of 1949–50. Nor could one easily maintain that composers who kept faith with the European avantgarde through the 1950s and 60s—Pierre Boulez, for instance—were therefore spurned by the cultural institutions to which Henze is presumed to have prostituted himself.

Undeniably, Henze's music is infused with a wish to please, and very often a wish to please in ways that have pleased before: his almost erotic way of teasing and treating the ear is an abiding characteristic one may find either enchanting or supine. But his artistic motivations are more easily understood as matters of personal choice and disposition than as tactics to gain influence and reward. In particular, his difference with the avantgarde was a dispute not about the audience but about the nature of music. At a time when composers were discovering that the substance of their art is notes, sounds, lines, planes, Henze stayed resolute that music was constituted of melodies and feelings. He was a Romantic—the last of the Romanstics, one might have said, until the overflow of the past two decades. But he had learned enough from Stravinsky to know that the Romanticism he wanted—the nineteenth-century romanticism of Schubert, Weber and Schumann, of Bellini, Donizetti and Verdi—was over. Besides, Romanticism was for him, as it was for so many Romantics of the nineteenth century, a frustrated longing for a presumed Classical perfection, so that he was doubly distanced from the objects of his desire. In such circumstances, what could he do but dream?

Hence the atmosphere of prevarication and play, the apprized unreality, in so much of Henze's music, which differs from that of younger would-be Romantics not only in sheer expertise but also in this awareness that there is something hopeless and helpless in the yearning to compose as before. There are moments when Henze seems to be protesting against his predicament, though only to find that even protest is permitted within the rules of the dream game. Many such moments came in his politically engaged scores of the late 1960s and early 70s; another arrived in the symphony preceding this

Boston one—the Seventh, written in 1983–4 for the Berlin Philharmonic. But much more frequent are the sweeter dreams, in which he reconvenes the forces of music past, and contrives pleasures that are also, because these are only dreams, sadnesses.

His fluency in doing so is matched by his selfconsciousness: he suffers no illusions about musical history, or his own place in it. 'Old forms appear to me as Classical ideals of beauty,' he has written, 'no longer attainable but still visible from a great distance, arousing memories like dreams.' Or again—though this was in a spirit of self-criticism at the time when he was writing a symphony for Cuba—there is his description of his earlier music's qualities of 'nostalgia and scepticism'. Nostalgia is the mode of a man dreaming up the past; scepticism is the reaction he must have when he knows himself to be dreaming, when he places his dreams before us not in any Berliozian way as actuality, but in the dream light of his harmonic and orchestral sophistication. Henze's only mistake was ever to assume he could break out from this circle, since nostalgia and scepticism were still the over-riding characteristics of his revolutionary music, as in *El Cimarrón*, a concert-length piece he wrote in 1969–70 for baritone and three instrumental players. Here the memoirs of a runaway slave engender not so much a mirror of present abrasions and contempts as a hallowed image, communicating the message—profoundly welcome in a middle-class culture—that the only good or necessary or achievable revolutions are all in the past. 'Back then. . .', the work begins. With his opera *We Come to the River*, produced in 1976, he brought this period of idealized political combat to a climax and a close, and his later music has been a return, though with increased range and richness, to earlier ways of dreaming.

His new symphony is not only a dream but the dream of a dream: the dream of, specifically, *A Midsummer Night's Dream*. Undaunted by Mendelssohn or Britten—or indeed by his own *Royal Winter Music* for guitar, a set of portraits from Shakespeare that included sketches of Oberon and of Bottom in his own dream—he presents us with three movements that are musical interpretations of images and episodes in the play. Perhaps disregard of obvious predecessors is a symptom of the dreamer, who exists in an imaginary world that includes only him and the object of his dreams. Another such symptom would be Henze's frequent recourse to literary models—librettos, poems, plays, histories—that give him something to dream about.

The first movement refers to Puck's line 'I'll put a girdle round about the earth in forty minutes', spoken as he leaves to fetch Oberon the magic flower. 'Well,' Henze wrote in a letter to his conductor, 'I composed this girdle'—though it takes not forty minutes but only the few of Puck's absence in the play. As so often in Henze's music, and particularly his later scores, a highly enriched tonal harmony allows him to proceed at two speeds simultaneously, so that in this case the fleetness of Puck's orbit is conveyed in a soft presto of flickering scales over slow song strains in other parts of the orchestra. Equally characteristic is the way one texture, one passage of movement, begins before the last is quite over, rendering a journey that goes in overlapping stages, and that suavely maintains momentum through opalescent plays of colour. Apart from suggesting fast and weightless travel, the music also implies a Puck remembering what he has just heard from Oberon. The instrumental vocalise, going on under the waves of speed, is perhaps that of the 'mermaid on a dolphin's back / Uttering such dulcet and harmonious breath / That the rude sea grew civil at her song', and the movement's climax, according to the composer, is the noise of 'Cupid's fiery shaft / Quench'd in the chaste beams of the wat'ry moon', with the words' sexual imagery made explicit as rising trumpet calls are enveloped in reiterated fortissimos. Finally comes Puck's offering of the flower, which Henze conjures as a gift to his orchestra and his audience: a slowly unfolding chord for muted strings.

After this we jump to the scene between the flower-drugged Titania and the ass-headed Bottom, their discourse presented as a dialogue of two very different kinds of music. Bottom begins the show with a galumphingly grotesque Latin American dance, heftily syncopated and making much use of the orchestral heavyweights. Titania wakes, and sings an aria on violins that begins gently but soon becomes passionate, to which Bottom responds with a canzonetta on trombone. From this point the conversation of folly goes on, mostly in Bottom's rumba or tango, though with interventions of Titanian song and dance for an orchestra predominantly of strings, and with each kind of music seeming to reflect the pertinent character's image of the beloved. It is all great fun; the movement could even make it into the pops concert repertory. But if one forgets for a moment the Shakespearian programme, the sound of ugliness at once glorying in itself and enraged is disquieting. Bottom becomes ever more enthusiastic, and the movement ends, as it must, with a bang.

The finale is an adagio that, in the composer's words, 'has something to do with the peaceful and gentle and lovely epilogue of the play', and peaceful and gentle and lovely it duly is. The exquisite extension of the main material is broken off several times, as if the music wanted to visit other possibilities—other pools, featuring small groups of woodwinds with harp—but then it goes on, reaching towards the high equipoise of the final chord, which is again luminously scored for muted strings. 'And this weak and idle theme, / No more yielding but a dream.'

Henze's only other symphony for an American orchestra—his Fifth, written for Bernstein and the New York Philharmonic in 1962—had more of an American sound and feel than this new one has. (However, his statements about No.5 have been contradictory, sometimes invoking 'Manhattan, mon amour', sometimes 'the sensuous happiness of twentieth-century Rome'.) No.8 is, at least in the movements around the central comedy, altogether more serene and softer—music of silks, requiring care in balance and refined solo playing. Ozawa and his orchestra presented it expertly.

In its three-movement form and its under-half-hour duration, this Eighth Symphony makes a return to the design Henze had preferred in earlier symphonies, as if slimmed dimensions would enable him to slip out from under the yoke of German symphonic history. Being essentially a lyric composer, Henze would rather sing than argue; being an artist of nostalgia, he could not be expected to sympathize with a musician whom history has made into a symbol of challenge and self-determination. In that respect his Seventh Symphony was an anomaly, being on the Beethovenian scale of four movements playing for close to forty minutes, and by happy chance a magnificent first recording of this anomaly, by Simon Rattle and the City of Birmingham Symphony Orchestra, comes along just as the new symphony is having its first performances.

'My Seventh Symphony', Henze declares in his note, 'is a German symphony, and it deals with matters German.' (His ironic portentousness is characteristic, an indication of the man who cherishes no fantasies about himself.) He goes on to remark how the first movement is a German dance, an allemande, and how the last is 'an orchestral setting' of a Hölderlin poem: again the dream object from literature. Again, too, there is the dreamer's solitariness, for in what is perhaps an unconscious chain of thought he sees the slow movement as 'a kind of funeral ode, a song of lamentation, a monologue'. What he does not say is that each of the four movements ends with the shattering arrival of aggressive, repetitive march music, of ruthless force that grows blacker from movement to movement. That was the nightmare; after it comes the dream. (*New Yorker*, 18 October 1993)

operatic passions

Arianna, or Rewriting Monteverdi

Monteverdi's second opera, *Arianna*, somehow got abandoned when musical history sailed away. It was written in 1608 for a Gonzaga wedding, and revised by the composer for later productions, but until recently nothing was known of it except for Ottavio Rinuccini's libretto and a fragment of the music—though a substantial fragment, the heroine's lament, comprising fully a tenth of the score and surely representing the opera's apex. How that apex was approached and left could only be imagined. Now, however, the whole opera has been imagined for us, in what the title page of the vocal score aptly describes as a 'lost opera by Claudio Monteverdi . . . composed again by Alexander Goehr'.

For Goehr, whose father was a leader of the Monteverdi revival in Britain, the recomposition of *Arianna* is the culmination of a slow progressive encounter that began in the 1950s with incidental evocations of style, moved in the 1960s to emulation of genre (in the music-theatre piece *Naboth's Vineyard*) and wholesale translation (a clarinet 'paraphrase' on *Tancredi e Clorinda*), and just a few years ago reached a thorough-going modern Monteverdianism in the cantata *The Death of Moses*. Influence and imitation presume separation, but *The Death of Moses* begins to suggest the earlier composer working from just under Goehr's skin: if Monteverdi had been alive in the 1990s, and commissioned by the Proms, this is the work he would have produced. *Arianna* merely takes the identification a step further, so that the Monteverdi inside Goehr returns to reproduce a work from a career not finished but suspended in 1643.

That step is, though, a momentous one, and it could not have been made by a composer lacking Goehr's qualities of selflessness (allowing the internal Monteverdi to exert himself), technical adroitness, taste and intelligence (all lending that Monteverdi the necessary tools); nor could this *Arianna* have been such a delight without his charm and lightness of touch. The task was not to embed the surviving lament in pastiche: that would have been to create a fake opera, not a lost one, and for Goehr it was a preliminary stage. Having set the slightly cut Rinuccini libretto in Monteverdian style, as a sequence of melodious dialogues, madrigalian choruses and sinfonias, he went on to vary, to elaborate and to play with what he had fashioned—and indeed with what Monteverdi had fashioned in 1608, since the authentic lament is also transformed, and also honoured, by Goehr's attentions: the melody ranges more widely (magically so after the familiar opening phrases), the harmony is enriched, and the accompaniment is laid out, as it is throughout the opera, for an ensemble of seventeenth-century scale but twentieth-century colour, featuring flutes and saxophones, high string trio, percussion, harp and electric guitar.

Sometimes, whether in the lament or in what surrounds it, the musical language of 1608 sounds through freshly; more often it is patinated, or observed through layers of pearl. Harmony and texture haze the image, and there are passing references to what has been happening in the interim between Monteverdi's Baroque dormition and his modern awakening. Goehr invites us to hear a little of Debussy's Mélisande in Arianna, and there are teasing touches of Puccini occasionally at the ends of phrases. Harder to know is whether the echoes of Strauss's Ariadne opera come from the composer or from us, watching similar events—especially the arrival of Bacchus—unfold in music. After all, the question of the author's authority is being posed gently and gracefully throughout this entertainment, by an author—Monteverdi—whose death could hardly be more certain (for we can visit his grave in I Frari) or now more unsettlingly insecure. However this music arrived, it is riddled with Monteverdianisms: in the vocal decoration, in the dancing character and brightness of the sinfonias, in the keen expressiveness and tonal lucidity of the melody, in the repeated notes to finish clauses, in the brushing of the accompaniment into and under the vocal line. At the same time, harmony and instrumentation are almost constantly telling us that this is not Monteverdi, and so reinforcing our knowledge of the case (if we can hold on to that amid all the pleasure and opalescence). The Monteverdi we hear is an absent Monteverdi. This is still a lost opera.

Francesca Zambello's production of it is very fine. Alison Chitty's designs are brilliant, and in tune with the music's treble-register brightness, elegant simplicity, colourfulness and joy: gods fly on and off within box frames; children dart about dressed as cupids in acid pink or as miniatures of the small male chorus, in antiqued armour or stage-fishermen's clothes of turquoise, eggshell and ultramarine. Robed in white, and relatively inactive, Ariadne is set up as the fantasy's heart, as much as her lament is maintained as the heart of the score, and Susan Graham magnificently fulfills the role. Voiced by her, the music sounds rich and natural; it also sounds passionate, in a way that accords with her persona, which is one of dignity raised to a point where it becomes challenging. Goehr sets his heroine's final words ('Rejoice in my rejoicing') so that she accepts Bacchus as she accepts the inevitable: with dismay, foreboding and a new self-awareness. This is the moment towards which Graham drives: her powerfully sung lament is not a wallowing in grief but a deliberate, difficult rescue of the self.

Zambello accommodates the range from this serious central progress to the frolicking of the children and the superfluousness of the gods. She also registers the oddity and festiveness of the occasion: the little orchestra is set in the middle of the stage (from where they are not ideally well heard: the instruments will sound better when the opera is played in smaller houses), and towards the end players on Renaissance instruments drift down towards the front. The masque of divinities and seafarers begins to peel off; the fantasy starts to dissolve. This would be another reason for Ariadne to redefine herself in the closing moments, another reason for Graham's resolve to outface shame.

There are some in the cast who cannot match Graham's appreciation of the opera's marriage of old formality with new sensibility; there are some who substitute an all-purpose modern-opera bawling for the composer's scrupulous lines. Principal among the others are Axel Köhler as Bacchus, and Gidon Saks and Christopher Ventris as messengers—particularly Saks, who is strong, urgent and vigorous in relating Ariadne's hopeless venture into the ocean after Theseus. Nothing in this marvellous passage was written by Monteverdi, and yet what drives through it is everything we have always thought Monteverdi to be about. *Arianna* is a triumph of musical resuscitation (perhaps someone could now give us Mozart's *Semiramis*), and because it presents us with Monteverdi composed now—with a Monteverdi who can write for electronic sampler, and who knows about Schoenberg as well as Debussy and Puccini—we rejoin the audience of 1608, confronting something which did not exist hitherto, and which is therefore uncategorized and unpredictable. This is not the *Arianna* that was performed at the Gonzaga court, but it might be how it felt. (*Times Literary Supplement*, 29 September 1995)

Handel, or The Chevaliers of Eros

Don Quixote, who loved to read about the exploits of Amadis of Gaul, might have been perplexed and disappointed by the showing his hero makes in the Handel opera on the subject, *Amadigi di Gaula*. One can imagine him tapping Sancho Panza on the shoulder, or more likely kicking his squire awake, and traipsing sadly out to resume his own enterprises. Not that there are many windmills these days in Brooklyn, where *Amadigi* is being presented at the Academy of Music's Majestic Theater.

Amadigi is in love with Oriana, who is also loved by his comrade, Dardano. This triangle fulfills the basic requirement of a Handel libretto, that it should offer plenty of opportunities for elation and despondency. Then the whole thing is complicated by the interventions of the enchantress Melissa, who is herself in love with Amadigi, so she claims, and whose supernatural powers provide her with the means to make the others elated or despondent whenever she fancies. A strange image of the world is offered. There are only four people in it. And those four exist only in and for the emotions of lovesickness, with the addition, in Melissa's case, of the delights of pulling nasty tricks on the others. The arrival of a fifth character near the end is the principal dramatic shock of the piece, after two hours when we have been in the company of just the fighting, jealous, adoring, despairing, triumphing quartet.

The main reason for them to behave so, and for us to endure them, is that they are thereby caused to sing. *Amadigi* may not be Handel's most persuasive narrative, but it does have some beautiful numbers. In a slow aria, Amadigi, Narcissus-like, looks into a magic fountain and sings dreamily to an accompaniment that includes, for the only time in the score, two recorders. Dardano has a marvellous, ardent piece with solos for oboe and bassoon before his death, after which he reappears as a ghost to deliver a short and chilling song with staccato strings. Melissa's music covers a huge range, from frustration to exultation, and it is for her that a trumpet enters the orchestra in the third act. Oriana, more gentle, is no less passionate.

These errant creatures are excitingly sung by the cast of a production brought from Ireland by the Opera Theatre Company. In the title role, the countertenor Jonathan Peter Kenny gives the impression of a well-tuned sigh; his singing is unforced, consistently fresh-toned and pliable. Dardano, as sung by the splendid Buddug Verona James, makes a nice contrast. James is a decisive performer, and her quick, wide vibrato gives a metallic gleam to her rounded tone: she sounds like a Brancusi. Majella Cullagh is fiercely impressive as

Melissa, being unsparingly agile and always on target, yet with feeling in her brilliance. On this female side, too, there is a useful divergence of vocal styles, for Anne O'Byrne as Oriana puts the emphasis on feeling and naturalness, but without distortion to a well-made musical line. Nicholas Frisch, a boy soprano with his feet on the ground, is the deus ex machina. Further excellence comes from the small period-style orchestra, conducted by Seamus Crimmins. (*New York Times*, 13 March 1997)

◆

The New York City Opera's production of Handel's *Partenope* is a treat. Six young singers give the firm impression that Handel wrote this music for them, so fluent are they in the vocal athletics and expressive delirium of their roles, and so youthfully fresh, enough to make the music sound fresh, too. By their voices they create a magic world, and a magic world is what the director, Francisco Negrin, and designers have created for them onstage. John Conklin's set provides an elegant palace chamber, which can turn into a boiler room under intense orange light (Robert Wierzel's lighting is a joy all through, and fire, including real fire, is a motif of the show), or which can calmly accept other wonders happening: walls opening to reveal trees, mysterious symbolic objects, a garden or, in a striking image of mental disturbance, a billowing sheet of indigo cloth. Paul Steinberg's costumes are of our own time but neatly echo the music's stylization by their colour coding, which is also handy in helping us identify the characters and learn something about them.

Partenope—a queen and, for most of the time, ostensibly the only female character—is in a dress of body-hugging pink wool. Of her two principal suitors, the unreliable Arsace has a sporty outfit of peacock blue jacket and white pants, while the ardent Armindo is more loosely dressed in tones of red. Rosmira, pursuing Arsace in male disguise, wears greens. Ormonte—the queen's confidant, aptly made here into a priestly figure—is robed in yellow and white, and has a white Hare Krishna seal on his forehead. Emilio, a warrior prince, invader and potential seducer who rather oddly turns into a grinning onlooker at the happiness of others, trades his leather-boy kit for soft grey.

Lisa Saffer plays and sings Partenope as a butterfly brain, being agile, clear and brilliant in this high-lying part. Jennifer Dudley, as Rosmira, offers an alternative view of the female heart in singing that is warm, luscious, noble and constant. Eduardo Chama executes

Ormonte's solemnity with a light touch, being nicely unfazed by the others' amorous cavortings. John McVeigh makes a striking entrance as Emilio near the end of the first act, with a vocal show of male bravado that is at once thrilling and dexterous, and he is excellent too in the sweeter, calmer music his character so strangely arrives at.

All these are splendid portrayals, but the action of the opera is essentially in and between Arsace and Armindo, two castrato roles sung here by the countertenors David Walker and Bejun Mehta. They are appropriately, magnificently different. Walker is a poised and cultivated artist; Mehta is a sheer singing animal. He sings his arias, and his final duet with Saffer, with full-throated passion and voluptuous tone; everything he does seems natural and expressively direct. Walker's delights are more ordered. His Arsace is, rightly, for most of the time pettish and juvenile, until he emerges, after being crushed by events, into a sore but secure self-knowledge.

Negrin's work, in bringing out these performances and creating a habitat for them, is characteristically sophisticated, touching and attuned both to eighteenth-century formality and a modern immediacy of feeling and gesture. The orchestral performance, under George Manahan, is less classy, but has exuberant contributions from the wind players. (*New York Times*, 14 September 1998)

◆

Opera is many other things besides, but it can also be a parade of gorgeous voices, one after another, in thrilling and touching songs. Handel's *Giulio Cesare* returned to the Met on Friday with most of the same outstanding principals it had last season.

In the title role Jennifer Larmore stands on the ground as if she owns it and sings with the same command. Her tone is bright and eager, and her phrases leap into action. She is especially good in Caesar's martial numbers: she seems to enjoy the scent of musical battle and the chance to engage vividly and vigorously with the orchestra. She also has fun with the cross-dressing. Though she looks good as a man, her voice is richly and gloriously female, and in playing the world conqueror she is humorously aware of the deception she is imposing. One hears the smile behind the mask.

Handel's two contrasted heroines, the noble and the naughty, are presented by Stephanie Blythe and Hei-Kyung Hong. Blythe, as Cornelia, is magnificent. In everything she does, she combines poignancy with stateliness, true in that to the aesthetics of the

Baroque. Also very much in style is her use of vibrato as an expressive device. She thereby brings forward a remarkable range of vocal colours, from the stony to the feather light or creamy, all apt to the meaning of the moment and smoothly worked into the phrase. Hers is a resourceful and even daring performance, too, in how she allows her voice to fall to the level of the instruments at times, or to bloom slowly out from instrumental tone.

Hong is a brilliant performer, and in this she is the image of her character, Cleopatra. Her voice shines, and her projection is unerring, as is her agility. Though she sings marvellously in one of the great Baroque laments, 'Piangerò', from a quiet centre and with beautiful ornaments falling into the repeat section like slow tears, one is never quite sure of her emotional truthfulness. And this is right: after all, Cleopatra spends most of the opera using the guiles of love to further her familial-political intrigue, and at the end, just as one begins to think she might really be in love with Caesar, cheerfully exchanges his heart for his hand in helping her onto the throne. Hong excellently conveys the character's sense of singing as power, and in her fast arias her decorations are as exact, dazzling and effective as the rhinestones on her several tiaras.

There is a nice and useful difference, too, between the countertenors, David Daniels and Brian Asawa. Daniels, as Sextus, is characteristically and exquisitely sweet and yet also completely fresh, as if singing this way were the most natural thing in the world. Generally he comes to the same position for each of his arias, centre stage left, and just sings. This is all he has to do. In a similar way, he maintains the same vocal character—honeyed, sensual—within which he can run the gamut from mourning to protest. It is quite an achievement to present a character for whom sex is not an issue, to do so frankly and believably, and yet all the time to be singing so seductively. Asawa accomplishes a difficult task, too, in singing and acting the weakling schemer, Ptolemy. He uses the coolness and artificiality of falsetto to convey the character's decadence and nastiness, but at the same time his singing is immediate, forceful and alert. He also moves well and uses a series of extravagant costumes to his advantage at every turn.

Among all these high fliers, Julien Robbins has the bass role of Achillas, in which he is appropriately soft and strong. With his height and by his singing, he suggests a big, simple soul misled by love. John Nelson conducts an able, straightforward orchestral performance, with luscious plucked strings in much of the slow music, capable obbligato soloists and some electric uptempo movements. (*New York Times*, 3 May 2000)

The Queen of Spades, or The H(a)unted Man

Many of the pleasures and pains of the Met's new *Queen of Spades* are well on display before a note is sung. Valery Gergiev, conducting, is characteristically in command from the very first bars—even though here the tone of that command is to educate the players in a certain suspension, a gathering up of music forever awaiting the downbeat. In later episodes, too, there will be these musical clouds, edged with moonlight by prominent and sweet-toned solo strings, but always chilly from the precision of articulation, pulse and phrasing. The other sort of weather in this opera—sudden thunderstorm—is no less vivid and beautiful, and no less icily delivered. Passion, in Gergiev's musical vocabulary, is violent, overwhelming and fierce, and though he can produce suavity, such an effect is the wonderful pretence of someone with a savage gleam in his eye. The grand dances that occupy so much of the score (not just in the ballroom scene but, for example, in the opening chorus of the gaming-room finale) go with pride and splendour, and also with a vehement and even cruel push behind them. Occasionally the zip is achieved at the expense of faltering ensemble; however, what matters so much more is that the orchestral performance has the excellent and very Tchaikovskian virtues of bravery and accomplishment—virtues that, when so firmly installed, eliminate the possibility of sentimentality.

Here, then, is one big plus. Another is the design, which again proves itself in the opening minutes. Mark Thompson sets the opera within a great gilt frame, and the first picture we see inside it is of a solitary, stooped figure in a near-black box, with febrile illumination (designed by Paul Pyant) that ripples the perspectives. Just in this momentary vision a great deal has been conveyed about Herman: his apartness, the weight upon him, his instability, and the instability too of the opera, which recklessly keeps making the leap from objectivity to identification, from giving an account of the hero to becoming his own account of himself and of the world—an account that seems to be the sound of his delirium.

At this point, unfortunately, the figure begins to move, and we move with him from the powerful image of a lone man swept by hurricanes of sound and shadow to the banality of a poor guy getting a deck of cards out from his pocket. This immediately weakens the atmosphere in many ways: by suggesting the audience has to be given a visual clue to the man's identity, by anticipating what the opera will tell us in its own good time, by asking of Ben Heppner, who takes the role of Herman, a gesture that he cannot (as nobody could) execute with conviction.

What Heppner can do is sing. He does so with straightforward, simple force, quite enough to sustain a note at firm volume without a flicker of vibrato or extend a phrase without seeming effort. His performance is impressive, but not as *ex*pressive as it might be if he could find some colours other than the dark grey of consistent gravity and the occasional gold (albeit beautifully done) of head voice, or if he could make the words work for him, instead of having them appear a kind of bland treacle through which he must swim. (This last comment applies to several others in the cast.) With tousled hair and beard, and with his heavy frame made monumental by the greatcoat he wears throughout the opera, he looks like the Repin portrait of Musorgsky defying death, but in his singing he does not seem a man ravaged and possessed, and in his acting he is not much helped by Elijah Moshinsky's production, which is effective in the grouping and movement of the chorus but not at all in the detail of personal relationships.

The big spectacular scenes get a lot of assistance, as the opening did, from Thompson's designs and Pyant's lighting. There is also a neat use of toy-town models—of St Petersburg buildings, and of boats for the canal-side scene—which not only look good but also operate dramatically by implying a world where human beings, their thoughts and their feelings are the biggest things around. Since the set and the costumes are mainly monochrome, moments of colour can be jolts of significance, either of a generalized kind, as in a patch of blue sky and a sailing red balloon exhilaratingly revealed at the back of the first scene, or made particular by the production, as in the appearance of the Countess's ghost in the red dress of the painting we saw of her in her Parisian youth. (Leonie Rysanek is a jolt of significance all by herself as an old woman who is ruminatively self-obsessed and is capable, in the odd brilliantly clear note, of making the memory of youth become its retrieval.)

Twice the production's feasting of the eyes tastes wrong. It is a pity to spoil the tease planned by the Tchaikovsky brothers (Pyotr and his librettist Modest), that of Catherine the Great's not arriving: an ermined supernumerary propped on walking sticks cuts against the mounting anticipation and the music. Possibly more serious, because more connected with the main substance of the piece, is the realization onstage of a funeral procession to accompany the quasi-liturgical music that enters Herman's solo scene at the beginning of the last act. The procession is, like so much of the production's visual apparatus, elegant and emblematic, but it should not be there. This is one of those crucial moments when we ought to feel unsure whether what we are experiencing is Herman's hallucination or an event in the exterior world—in this case, the Countess's requiem. By acting out the music, the production tilts interpretation in the latter, less interesting direction.

What tilts it back is Gergiev's fervent exhibition of how so much of the score develops out of ideas that are associated not only with Herman but are signalled as the sound of his mind. We are left in no doubt but that Herman was Tchaikovsky's reason for composing this opera, which otherwise he peopled with characters who are almost repetitions of prototypes in *Eugene Onegin*: Lisa a second Tatyana, Yeletsky another Gremin. (To perform duplicates is not easy. Karita Mattila, as Lisa, was further troubled by uneven registers; Dmitri Hvorostovsky, making his house debut as Yeletsky, had to endure the exquisite discomfort of a heartthrob playing the dull and decent loser. He sang ably, but his stage presence is not at all what the glamorous photographs might indicate.)

If we can accept *The Queen of Spades* as not just centred on Herman but moving into the disconcerting realm where he, a character, appears to be the work's author—and we still can, since the opera outpowers any attempt to tame it, and since the music, which is what matters, is impeccably untamed in Gergiev's handling of it—then we have found the work's most Mozartian quality. Tchaikovsky's pastiche, even when he is using Mozart themes, is porcelain stuff, limited by his age's view of the composer and totally without the eroticism we would now expect to find in any Mozart, late or early, real or unreal. But the sense here of a world taken over by one of its inhabitants—of a night world, where that could be believed possible—brings this opera into the neighborhood of *Don Giovanni*. The difference is that what Don Giovanni achieves by will, Herman is driven into by his blinding obsession with gambling.

That, at least, is the story the libretto wants to tell us. However, we do not see Herman at the card table until the very last scene, by which time his music may have suggested that what harries him is of a different nature, for here the music has the ardour—certainly as Gergiev delivers it—missing from the rococo intermezzo. Herman—like Manfred in the symphony Tchaikovsky based on Byron's play, or like the nameless protagonists of the Fourth and Fifth symphonies—is set apart (and indeed set upon) by fate, and whatever one may make of Tchaikovsky's biography, one cannot easily avoid feeling the drag of fate in these works as the drag of sexual desire against some psychological resistance. Herman, of course, knows nothing of this, and it would be crass of any singer or producer to tell him. Heppner and Moshinsky, by leaving the hero in a state of shambling ignorance in the face of the compelled music he seems to stimulate and expire, speak loudly of his frustrations.

This was the first new production at the Met to benefit, if that is the word, from the electronic libretto crib available in front of every seat. These 'Met Titles' are markedly superior to the systems at most theatres: you can switch them off, and they do not become part of the performance's public discourse. They are private, and a gifted comedian can make a joke of their closet presence, as Bryn Terfel did as Leporello earlier this season. But they have their own problems. The screens are dim. There is the bother of refocussing one's eyes all the time. And in such a complex polyphonic art, does one need a new rude, irregular bass line? As simple a thing as Yeletsky singing 'Ya vash lyublyu' has so much going on: a character in a story addressing another in speech; a character onstage addressing another in song; a singer performing a role; a composer conveying, as a sober ideal, a love he cannot share; a scale ascending; four fingers moving on a keyboard. To add, in illuminated letters, 'I love you' is to add nothing. (*New Yorker*, 20 November 1995)

Wozzeck, or the Power of the Powerless

One of the Metropolitan Opera's great recent productions, Berg's *Wozzeck*, is back, demanding to be seen and heard and felt and thought about. The cast is superb, from Franz Grundheber and Hildegard Behrens in the main roles to the players of bit parts. Not only is every scrap of vocal music put across with startling force, but the acting in Mark Lamos's production is consistently vivid.

Wozzeck is an opera that dares to work like a play, and here it does, not that the orchestra is in any way subservient or incidental. It could not possibly be, with James Levine and his musicians making the score sound beautiful always and sometimes, in perfectly tuned wind chords or a viola solo, breathtakingly so. Performances of *Wozzeck* usually suggest that Berg's early language of rampant atonality with an enfeebled but still beating tonal heart gave him the means to illustrate savagery with savagery, eeriness with eeriness, desolation with desolation, in a succession of violent discords, hollow timbres and melodies pushed to an extreme pitch of intensity. All these things are there in the Met Orchestra's performance, of course, but their unpleasantness has gone. And surely Berg never meant *Wozzeck* to sound ugly but rather to be, as it is here, shocking and ravishing at the same time. The beauty does not cover the shame but uncovers it.

The people of *Wozzeck* are pawns of bestial hierarchy and instinct, distinguished from animal life in little more than their cruelty and degradation. God has gone, and moral authority with Him, as the

Captain makes clear in the opening scene. But the soldier Wozzeck and his mistress, Marie, are still human, still suffer and hope and try to do better, and the thoroughgoing beauty of Berg's music, as the Met performs it, insists that the characters' humanity is not an add-on but a continuing, deeply integral part of what they are. The drama has them careering from incident to incident, but the music is whole and fully developed. Levine brings out the descriptiveness of the score, how it responds to emotions, to gestures and to the natural phenomena the characters talk about, but at the same time the music swings forward with its own energy, passion, lustre and determination.

Grundheber makes Wozzeck, the put-upon victim, a study in grey, and yet suggests within that greyness the emotions that are waiting, and that will erupt in Marie's murder. Every word tells. The interior light is alive, for all the numbed demeanour. Behrens, as Marie, sheds decades and sings with exhilaration in her voice, the exhilaration of someone whose love of existence is heightened by the knowledge of imminent death. Her singing is strong, rich with compassion and vital. Kenneth Riegel provides a peppery Captain, afraid of his own shadow and so all the shriller in exercising his power of command. Franz Hawlata sings the Doctor's part with a marvellous, sharp blackness and portrays the character as a maniac in love with his madness. The two of them work excellently together. Everyone else onstage contributes magnificently: the chorus, Mark Baker as the bull-man Drum Major, Wendy White in showing Margret as a Marie who has gone past caring, David Kuebler as the gentle Andres, James Courtney in a striking moment as the First Apprentice, Jonathan Press as the boy who ends the opera parentless and alone. So are they all, parentless and alone, and, in this production, emphatically present. (*New York Times*, 19 April 1999)

Die Eroberung von Mexiko, or The Shriek

Perhaps it is a kind of arrogance to suppose that the main thing we have to do with the conquest of Mexico, or by extension with the whole whitening of America that haunts the Columbus quincentenary, is make a moral judgement. Wolfgang Rihm, whose opera on the subject has just opened, is not in the business of giving easy answers. What he brings into the theatre instead is a massive exploding question, not a taking of sides but a mounting of the collision between Aztec and Spaniard.

The meeting of Cortez and Montezuma is an encounter of irreconcilables: of dynamic and static, human-centred and earth-centred, rational and spiritual. Accordingly the opera itself can hardly hope to maintain a stable partnership between its own irreconcilables of words and music, except at the slippery pinnacle where they meet in crying and screaming. This shriek—of rage, fear, lamentation, ecstasy—comes out of people in extremis. In myriad forms it dominates Rihm's opera, though achieved characteristically with extraordinary fastidiousness, almost gentleness, and with care for the grain and substance of instruments and voices.

The distinction between these two resources is another dividing line which becomes in the opera a line of force: the teasing of them together produces effects of miraculous beauty and electric tension at once. There is also a fierce exposure, a glaring light through the orchestra, that makes instruments as potently expressive as the work's heroic vocalists. An incandescent high soprano in the pit (Carmen Fuggiss) is equalled by two sky-skimming violins up in a gallery, while the animal passion and vehemence of an unnamed character, 'Der schreiende Mann' (Peter Kollek), is matched by the pit orchestra of wind, percussion and low strings. The use of the whole house, with not only the stereo violins but also some percussion and wind placed high in the auditorium, is one more aspect of Rihm's exploration of boundaries, having the music break into 'our' space.

Yet another is his decision to cast Montezuma as a dramatic soprano, and so to make the central impact of the piece the impact also of male on female, female on male. Cortez and Montezuma, the latter powerfully a woman by voice and costume, circle around each other; the music is that of bristling fur and friction. Finally they come together in a kind of Liebestod, but the two wide-spanning voices are now unaccompanied, and the feeling is exceedingly tentative and taut. The idea of a pair of male and female demigods comes from Antonin Artaud, as does the whole groundplan of the opera.

This collaboration of composer and writer-seer is the work's one aspect of consummate fusion. Like Artaud, Rihm pushes right to the edge; like Artaud he is at once contemporary and primitive, with little in between (a couple of bursts of something like sixteenth-century Spanish music sound blurred, as if through Mexican ears). But his Artaudesque passion is achieved by sophisticated means, by a musical sculpture of scintillating, glass-sharp splinters, a piece of shattered granite evoked with painstaking but self-obliterating skill.

The projection of this rock or sculpture through time, under Ingo Metzmacher, is powerful and magnificent, and the performances of the fiercely demanding central roles, by Richard Salter and Renate Behle, are astonishing feats of strength and stamina. Peter Mussbach's production responds to the challenge of the piece by pushing the action out halfway over the stalls on a great walkway, and some of the stage pictures, achieved with lighting and planar geometry, are spectacular. It might be possible to retain more of Artaud's frenzy, perhaps, but there is that in the music, which remains quietly startling the memory. (*Times*, 14 February 1992)

Thérèse Raquin, or Hearing Zola

In *The Visual Novel: Emile Zola and the Art of his Times*, William J. Berg is concerned among other things with matters of viewpoint in the Rougon-Macquart books: how the writer can set his readers' minds aflicker by changing between, or confusing, what the narrator sees (and understands) and what a character sees (and, inevitably to a lesser extent in a naturalistic story, understands). Sometimes this can happen inside a single sentence. Taking an example from *La Conquête de Plassans*—'He appeared quite annoyed in seeing the visitor, whom he pretended at first not to recognize'—Berg notes how we begin the sentence looking through the narrator's eyes ('he appeared') before our view slips into that of the character ('seeing the visitor'). One might add that the swivel seems to take place within the word 'annoyed', which takes us from outside to inside the character. As for the latter half of the sentence, it is a nice point who is noticing the affectation. Are we back with the narrator, as Berg suggests? Or are we still with the character, as annoyance slides into pretence, in which case the sentence's second 'he' is partly an 'I'?

Berg would like to understand such switches and ambiguities of narrative viewpoint in terms of Zola's lively interest in contemporary painters: this same section of *The Visual Novel* includes an analysis of *On the Balcony, Meudon*, a watercolour by Berthe Morisot (whom Zola repeatedly praised) in which a woman watches a child looking out over Paris, so that we see the cityscape all at once from the position of the 'narrator' (the imaginary person whose view the artist has framed for us), the child and the woman. However, this trick of spliced viewpoints is not wholly an invention of late nineteenth-century realism. Consider another sentence: 'And God saw the light, that it was good: and God divided the light from the darkness.' Here too we start by sharing the narrator's viewpoint, seeing the character see (and yet who could this narrator be in a universe that so far has only the single character in it?). The judgement 'that it was good', more subtly than in the Zola, swings us partly into the character's viewpoint, and then we withdraw again to rejoin the narrator in observing the character decisively from the outside.

Opera extends the possibilities for such complexities of viewpoint—or perhaps one should say 'hearpoint'—since it adds to the space occupied by characters and implicit narrator a new dimension, that of the music, which has its own ways of instructing us how to hear. Once again, this is not something confined to Zola's world, though it might be profitable to pursue Berg's lines of thinking into the several operas on which Zola collaborated with Alfred Bruneau. As *The Visual Novel* exhaustively demonstrates—and the great mass of evidence suggests there may after all be something in the argument for the specialness of sight in Zola—not only are the Rougon-Macquart novels quivered with different viewpoints, but they are crammed with visual imagery and with people looking, and they include, in *L'Oeuvre*, the story of a painter. One wonders if Zola's librettos could similarly be shown to be full of hearing and of characters who listen.

This is the way of Michael Finnissy's libretto for his chamber opera *Thérèse Raquin*, which was put on last month by the Royal Opera House's Garden Venture in consort with the Eastern Touring Agency, and which arrived in London as part of the French Institute's celebrations of the centenary of Zola's first trip across the Channel. Finnissy based his text on Zola's early novel of the same name, and on Zola's own adaptation of the book into a play; the language is correspondingly imbued more with sight and touch than with hearing, as it follows the tale of Thérèse and her lover Laurent through the murder of her husband Camille to the resulting long annulment of their passion, and so to their deaths under the horrified-satisfied gaze of Camille's mute mother. However, it is hearing that turns out to matter.

On the face of it, the story is an odd one to find appealing for music. Much of its power comes from visual evocation, in which respect it supports all Professor Berg's assertions about the later books: this is a dank nocturne, of characters riddling through the streets of Paris, and its big set-piece is a description of Laurent at the morgue, searching for Camille's drowned body (here, with a vengeance, we are watching a character watch). It is, too, a novel in which the narrator's voice sounds out more loudly than those of the characters, and in which that voice can undercut its own power by excess of brutality. We are told in some detail how guilt so fastens on Thérèse and Laurent that they cannot make love after murdering Camille; then suddenly Thérèse is pregnant, but only so that she can provoke Laurent into kicking her in the belly and so bringing on a miscarriage.

One miracle of Finnissy's opera is that it is not at all the kind of latterday expressionism one might have expected from the subject and from Zola's treatment. There are no violent acts onstage—unless one counts as violent the act of giving voice at this level of intimacy and intensity, or that of inflicting the verbal and non-verbal savageries in which people who live together are expert. The entire scene of Camille's drowning is sung offstage by Laurent and Camille, while what we see, according to the stage direction, is 'Thérèse alone onstage—outside specific time or location—crouching in intense concentration, listening.' And though the final scene of murder-suicide would seem to run against the opera's disturbing quietness, by this point the killing-off of the central couple (Thérèse stabs Laurent, then herself) is inevitable, and more kind than shocking.

Musically, too, the work is delicate—though its delicacy can be pained and painful. There are just four soloists (the essential quartet of woman, lover, husband and mother-in-law) and a piano: this is a sinister sort of drawing-room entertainment, and it will surely have a continuing life in venues small enough that the characters can indeed seem to be singing at home. (Even the little Théâtre Artaud at the French Institute was a bit big, forcing the excellent cast to project more than was comfortable for them or the music.) The score leaves some fear of a piano-accompanied rehearsal or cut-down version, but in the performance any such impression lifted after about five seconds, once it was abundantly clear that this was real piano music.

Like many Finnissy's concert works, especially those for piano, *Thérèse Raquin* is an elaborate musical parody. It draws, he has said, 'on the predominant melodic characteristics of French opera of the period 1850–65 [roughly the period from the action of the novel to its writing], also on its stock-in-trade dramatic "gestures" (tremolandi, diminished seventh chords)'. His note further specifies references to Meyerbeer's *L'Africaine* (not an idle choice, for Zola introduces Thérèse to us as having been born in Oran, to 'a native woman of great beauty'), to folksongs from Haut-Normandie in the countertenor part of Camille (again the model is pertinent, since we are told the Raquins moved to Paris from Vernon), to a Fauré song, to *Tristan*, and less expectedly to a Bach chorale prelude.

One could not have guessed all this without the composer's help: the climbing gestures, the diminished seventh harmony and the trammelled ecstasy in much of the piano writing might suggest a later nineteenth-century world, closer to Scriabin than Meyerbeer. But the essential point was sure, that this was domestic music, saying rather more than domestic music should. And the connection between Camille's part and folksong was unmistakeable. That connection, and the unearthly ring of the countertenor register (especially of Andrew Watts's countertenor register), made Camille sound precious and alien: a fairy being, and a man maintained as a fairy being by his colluding family. In the book the man is a milksop. Here he became something more interesting and more tragic: a neutered toy, providing his mother with a patient and a pet, Laurent with an object to despise, and Thérèse with a reason for dissatisfaction. This was the hideous status quo of Finnissy's second scene; by murdering Camille, in the central third scene, Laurent and Thérèse changed the rules, only to find they had no clue how to play the new game.

But the references and models are not the music's only source of a power to insinuate malice and undercurrents, for Finnissy's piano can, on its own account, enter, shadow or colour the action in various ways. Sometimes its music is richly textured, following the manner of the prelude and interludes, sometimes the keyboard voice becomes straw-thin, a melody in the upper treble. There are also places where the piano falls almost silent, as in the scene of Camille's murder, or where it adds only a punctuating chime (the scene between Laurent and Thérèse at night), or where it answers a voice in dialogue (this is the remarkable next vignette, a solo for Thérèse), without one being quite sure whether the character knows she is being accompanied—accompanied by the piano and by the audience.

Another special aspect of this opera's gentleness is the range of opportunities opened for listening: the audience's listening and the characters'. There is the central scene of Thérèse listening, as if reliving the moment; there is the sense that what we hear from Camille is not his own voice but rather the persona his tiny entourage has foisted on him: he sings what they want to hear, in the way they want to hear it. These are not isolated instances. The opera begins with two people onstage, Thérèse and Laurent, but with only one of them—Thérèse—singing. We come to feel that we are hearing Laurent listening to her more than we are hearing her sing. When this opening scene moves into dialogue, the interaction is stilted, and the conversation presents itself as taking place between the Thérèse that Laurent wants to hear (the unsatisfied wife) and the Laurent of Thérèse's dreams (the bullish suitor). Thérèse's solo scene much later is perhaps sung by the Thérèse of the audience's or the composer's desires, and the finale of double death surely expresses the deep wishes of Mme Raquin, whose presence as a silent witness, following her stroke, gives us a character who can do nothing but listen.

Finnissy's concentration on a minimal cast is essential if this drama of listening, of hearing hopes and delusions, is to make its points. We and he were lucky to have so persuasive a pianist in Christopher Willis and so committed, if not equally steady, a quartet of singers. Besides Andrew Watts's silvery Camille, there was Richard

Jackson dark and urgent as Laurent, Heather Lorimer courageous and often exquisite—an exposed nerve—as Thérèse, and Linda Hirst forbidding as Mme Raquin. Wilfred Judd directed and David Blight designed, but this was an opera principally for the ears. (*Times Literary Supplement*, November 1993)

Snow White, or The Liars' Fairytale

Heinz Holliger is probably still better known as an exceptional oboist than as a composer. But the ECM recording of his opera *Schneewittchen* (Snow White)—his biggest work of recent years, completed in 1998—should help shift that imbalance.

Forget Disney. This Snow White is based on a deeply unsettling play by Robert Walser, a writer with whom Holliger has had a special relationship, across the sixty years that separate them. What they share is not just Swiss nationality but, much more important, a quality of searching, a pushing at boundaries, a distrust of what everybody knows, and a sense of humour.

In Walser's version of the fairytale, the whole action has already happened before the beginning. The four main characters—Snow White, the Queen, the Prince and the Huntsman—speak of the glass coffin, the attempted murders, the awakening kiss and (briefly) the seven dwarfs as all in the past. They cannot escape that past; they go on trying to explain it and even relive it. But they are also wearied by it. The plot of their drama has become for them a shrivelled husk. So they make things up. They fly off on wild tangents of invention. They say things for effect: to shock, puzzle and wound. Their words are full of snares, falsehoods and alarming, possibly unconscious disclosures. They gave up caring a long time ago. But they did not give up loving and hating.

Full of passionate expression and cast in unrhymed ballad metre, Walser's play makes a wonderful libretto, and Holliger honours it with a setting in which its words are clear. This is opera as song, in an intense lyrical style recalling its composer's admiration for Webern. The lyricism and the intensity extend also into the orchestra, where lines, colours and textures flick past almost before they can be recognized, producing a constantly renewed stream of expression and character. It is this perpetual renewal, this vivid pulse of life and thought, that counteracts and contradicts the bleak vision of pathological fantasts, even while it creates that vision. There is something childlike in the eagerness of Holliger's music, as there is in Walser's text, an adolescent delight and disquiet.

The turbulent, torrential flow of the score does have stabilities. Holliger's music—like that of many Swiss musicians, including Honegger and Frank Martin—sometimes echoes with Bach, and occasionally the highly active, modest-size *Schneewittchen* orchestra will settle into a chorale or a contrapuntal invention, thoroughly reimagined for the late twentieth-century context.

Snow White herself, a high soprano, generally has a glacial accompaniment of glass harmonica, flutes, celesta, string harmonics and an extravagantly but tightly virtuosic solo violin. This high, white music is another constancy and another Swiss aspect of the opera, along with the intermittent oom-pah-pah wheeze of an accordion recalling leather-shorted folk musicians and the sweet but blood-stained craziness of the text; Walser was one of several Swiss writers in the early twentieth century to wind up in a mental institution.

A few examples may convey something of the remarkable musical richness and dramatic force of Holliger's score. In the last big scene, when the Huntsman asks Snow White whether she still believes he meant to kill her, she swings back and forth between 'yes' and 'no' before ending on 'yes', and this final 'ja' is wonderfully extended as an orchestral concord. The gesture is luminous and sure, and comes like sudden sunlight through haze, but it is also, in this score, a fabrication, a white lie—or more, a golden, glorious lie—and it speaks of the groundlessness in Snow White's mind, where any affirmation can only be a momentary tactic.

In another scene, Snow White is discoursing with the Queen on love and hate. Love is boundless, she sings to a descending line, against which the orchestra comes forward with a rising gesture, as if—it seems for a moment—to join her and underline her statement with an emphatic cadence in the manner of nineteenth-century opera. But the harmony drifts and hangs in the air, and turns into a long exhalation, with Snow White joining in. This is just one place where Holliger's music profits from his practical and imaginative experience of what were once marginal effects. Love's boundlessness is exhaustion, and Snow White is exhausted.

A larger instance of musical imagery comes in an earlier scene, where the Prince is rapturously telling Snow White what he can see in the garden: the lovemaking of the Queen and the Huntsman. Moaning wordless voices in the orchestra help express a queasy sensuality, a disturbing uncleanness, in a depiction of voyeurism that can stand for its power with Debussy's in *Pelléas et Mélisande*.

This recording was made with the cast and orchestra responsible for the Zurich Opera premiere. Juliane Banse is formidable in the title role, winging effortlessly and musically into the high register, ice-cold but burning with pent-up emotions and questions. The contralto Cornelia Kallisch majestically embodies the Queen's tired abandonment of morality in favour of sex and lies (black ones in her case). These two characters dominate, but there are also excellent performances from the tenor Steve Davislim as the jejune Prince, the baritone Oliver Widmer as the lusty Huntsman and the bass Werner Gröschel as the King, who arrives in the epilogue to lead everyone to a slow, uneasy peace, a congelation rather than a conclusion. The composer conducts. (*New York Times*, 17 June 2001)

The Dangerous Liaisons

LETTER 70,156: *The Marquise de Merteuil to the Vicomte de Valmont*

One alters the tedium with letters—with letters and with outings. I was at the Opera the other evening. (Some day, perhaps, I will tell you with whom.) Despite the fact that the performance—I mean the performance onstage—was excellent, what chiefly attracted my interest was the intrigue, since this purported to present a story with which you and I, my dear Vicomte, are somewhat familiar. I need hardly say more than that the piece was entitled *The Dangerous Liaisons*, and that the libretto was an adaptation, by a certain Monsieur Philip Littell, of that book of our correspondence which was published to such gratifyingly scandalous effect by the Capitaine-Commandant Choderlos de Laclos. I did not note the composer.[1]

To see ourselves singing upon the public stage might have been a cause for some merriment. However, that was not to be. I cannot tell you how little the Merteuil of the opera resembled myself—leaving aside all question of her clothes. Of course, one cannot avoid the comparison with the cinematic version, in which I was personified with such bewitching subtlety that I almost felt myself to be living there in flickering light on the screen and not in my seat. Never was there any question of that in the case of the opera, for reasons that have to do, I believe, principally with the language offered in the libretto. We live through our words. We are our words. I have always thought it one great virtue of the epistolary form that the reader is apprised of one solely by means of one's own words, and I feel sure that here is a principal reason for the success of Monsieur de Laclos's book, in which we come into being through what we utter on paper, and in which the

1. The name which eludes the Marquise is that of Conrad Susa.

participation of the compiler is restricted to the occasional, merely efficient footnote.[2] As I say, we are our words. But am I to concede that I am this: 'He usually doesn't drop in here so often'? How could I say such a thing? How could I sing such a thing? It is not the anachronism to which I object, nor yet the misplaced adverb, but rather the inelegance to which both contribute—and not so much the inelegance for its own sake as for what it bespeaks of an absence of style. Without style there can be no irony; without irony there can be no Merteuil. There are, it is true, instances in the libretto where the words are more knowingly fashioned: I refer to the sudden outbreaks of rhyme. But these have no rhythm or finesse. I—if it is indeed I who speak in this libretto—hurtle from the drab to the witless:

> Her intended will not find a maid
> His insult to me will be repaid.

This is poor substitute for the intricacy of the letters through which our history originally came to the public—and no substitute at all for the intimacy our readers must feel as they finger what was private, and read us in words we intended for other and quite particular recipients. Film can offer that illicit intimacy in another way. We can linger on faces and features as otherwise only lovers can. The image soaks up our gaze without embarrassment and asks for more. And we give it. But at the Opera the other night, with the singers far away and their words as I have said, it seemed to me that all the lustre of these episodes was lost: here were shadows singing to us of matters that had nothing to do with them.

In the foyer, as I was going out, I chanced upon the pretty little Danceny. (Delicious the rumours about quite how, and quite where, he was stilettoed in Malta.) Since he seemed in a hurry, I asked that he would write me his opinion of the music. I enclose his letter for your perusal.

I finish without the usual appendages of date and place. Death has among its solaces the redundancy of the calendar, and as for my address, you know where to find me.

LETTER 70,157: *The Chevalier de Danceny to the Marquise de Merteuil*

Madame, I hasten to accede to your request, but must first apologize for my abrupt behaviour last evening. The truth is that I was overcome with shame, yet again, at the rehearsal of these long past events, and

2. The Marquise surely underestimates the author of these footnotes.

still more so with anger that the music had displayed such want of feeling. Since it is the music that must be, by your express wish, the subject of this communication, I fear I will make a doleful correspondent. Pray forgive an offence which you, sweet Marquise, solicitted!

I do not complain so much about the presentation of myself. I was a minor character in the business, and to show me as I was, it was enough to let a lyric tenor have a few unfinished phrases followed by—in your presence—some pleasant ardour. All young men sound the same. But you, Madame! In you was the occasion for a role of huge and various powers: your teasing prevarications, your seductiveness and your knowledge of it, your majestic self-defence, your feigned sympathy with Cécile, whom you had obliged Valmont to deflower, your stern command to him to discontinue his connection with Madame de Tourvel,[3] your final magnificence in ruination—these were opportunities for music to coax, caress and—yes!—alarm us with its knowledge of the heart. Instead we heard a vocal part that, perhaps attempting the ambiguous, achieved only the neutral. So many phrases that simply declined with the words! And such strange thinness and nonchalance in the orchestra! Often there was nothing more than a sequence of blank, elementary chords, or a meandering line that seemed ignorant of what was occurring onstage—if anything was. For fully the first twenty minutes one waited in a perplexed stagnation for something to happen, and in all the whole opera the only moment of musical passion arrived when Valmont failed to use quite to the full the whore Emilie.

The didjeridu. . .[4]

LETTER 70,158: *The Vicomte de Valmont to the Marquise de Merteuil*

You are quite wrong, of course, about that opera. As chance would have it, I caught the PBS telecast,[5] and though I can confirm all that you say about the words, they are not the cause of your dissatisfaction, nor are they of mine. In opera, all problems are musical problems. But Danceny's shafts, too, though well aimed, hit only the outer rim of the target. He laments that this was not an opera by Tchaikovsky; I would rather say I wish it had been one by Mozart.

3. Curiously, nothing from Madame de Tourvel has been found among these posthumous letters. It may be that persons in her present situation have not the leisure of correspondence.
4. There is much more from the Chevalier in the same vein.
5. This would enable us to date the Vicomte's letter to soon after the 17th of October, 1994, could we be sure that dates in his realm have any relevance.

And so perhaps would the composer, who has been quoted as remarking that 'Mozart stole a lot of my best melodies'. At least that would explain why they were not present in his music.

So why do I find Mozart when I look for what this opera was not? Surely not just because Mozart was our contemporary. No, but because Mozart's music lived, as our letters lived, on that precarious edge where what has been controlled, even counterfeited, comes to be what is felt, and where what was felt is lost among the byways of masquerade. And also because such uncertainties breed the erotic, where nature is on the point of escape from, or subjection to, taming.

Let me add at once that Mozart is not the sole custodian of the erotic in opera: the art is erotic through and through, and it astonishes me that you can have been so right about the intimacy of the stolen letter or the film close-up but failed to observe that opera, too, gives us access to the forbidden: to the voice raised in the extremity and nakedness of excitement. The voice, my dear, is our other genital organ, and one that partakes of both female and male: its dwelling is an orifice, and yet it projects.

However, for the probing of boundaries between the civil and the erotic, between order and desire, Mozart above all other composers is your man. What was needed in this opera was not Danceny's 'feeling' but your 'style'—though in the music, not in the words. We should have felt ourselves to be always unsure, as in Mozart, whether what we were hearing was convention or meaning. This need not have entailed Mozartian pastiche: conventions can be convened for the occasion, as witness the example of *Der Rosenkavalier*, to which our composer quite evidently refers in his writing for a trio of women's voices—not to mention his intimation of you, my love, as a kind of sister to the Marschallin. He also goes a little way toward subterfuge in his use of a minuet and a sarabande, and of the sound of a harpsichord in the pit—though, fatally, these are items of sonic decor; they do not buckle the music into duplicity.

How typical of you that, in your own condemnation of the opera, you should fasten on the figure you cut in it! And how typical of Danceny that he should move to your excuse! Poor me: I had rather thought myself to be the principal character. If you ought to have been a Marschallin, with your passion turned to pride and your mercy to vindictiveness, then I should have been a Don Giovanni, propelled not by desire, nor even by the notion of desire, but by the drive to win. Perhaps another Mozart opera, *Così fan tutte*, would offer at once a closer parallel and an antithesis. In that piece, a game becomes real: toying with emotions, the characters come to feel them. Whereas for us the game was already the only reality: emotions were to us a superfluity—all emotions, that is, except those we felt in the play for power. You found the pleasures of the escritoire to be more consuming and even—was this not so?—more satisfying than those of the bedchamber. And here was another problem for the opera. People so in command of themselves do not sing. We two, you and I, we should have been speaking players in a drama of singers: manipulating those poor fools, but all the time their lessers. I might have begun to sing with Madame de Tourvel, at the end. I do not know. I am beyond being aware of what I did not feel.

So too, I fancy, the gallant gentleman playing me in the opera. Thomas Hampson—genial, warm, candid—seemed to be benignly watching over the action rather than fulfilling it. There was the release of tension one feels when Leporello has to take on the role of Don Giovanni: if the buffoon is now impersonating the villain, nothing serious can transpire. The fault is, of course, in how the part is composed—or in that it is composed at all. Frederica von Stade had the other struggle of singing you, and her effort to make something of that struggle was an opera all its own: the determination, so aptly betraying a note of harshness in her tone; her valiant attempts to make words work where the music would not. Bravo. I liked the young Australian, David Hobson, for his ingenuousness as Danceny. I liked Mary Mills for her quickness as Cécile, and I liked Renée Fleming for her passionate gravity as Madame de Tourvel. I liked the efforts of Colin Graham, the director, and Gerard Howland, the designer, to make a small budget go a long way: one knows, even here, of the financial woes of the San Francisco Opera, who commissioned the work. I liked the tireless spirit of Donald Runnicles, conducting. It was all so likeable and all so . . . null.

Were we ever null, my dear? Were we ever null? Ah yes. Always. But our nullness mattered.

Hell, some wit once said, is other people. But no: hell is ourselves, when ourselves are being portrayed without the constant accomplishment we know those roles to exact.

I could continue, but I would fear to make this letter into a review—a genre which I know you to detest. As to the identity of the person with whom you attended the Opera, my love, did you really not penetrate my disguise? (*New Yorker*, 26 September 1994)

Vivier

I first met the Canadian composer Claude Vivier ten years after his death. Someone had sent me a tape—the piece was *Lonely Child* for soprano and orchestra—and what I heard was as simple as a nursery rhyme, as tragic as a Mahler adagio, as formal as a noh play. It went on its way with harmonies glistening high above the slow vocal melody. It was like nothing I had ever heard, and it was beautiful. To be drawn into this music was indeed to meet another person and, through that other person, another world.

Such experiences, arriving out of the blue, are rare: I had to hear more, know more. I got hold of all the Vivier recordings that were available, all of them Canadian releases, and from the liner notes I gathered a few items of information about the composer, though not much more than the fact that—after just a decade of accomplished work, and little more than three years of total mastery—he had been killed in Paris in 1983, at the age of thirty-four. The fuller story—the story of a life lived, right to the point of death, for music—only began to come together after I had spent a while in Montréal, studying the scores at the Centre de Musique Canadienne, reading the composer's articles and interviews, and talking to people who had known him.

Vivier was born on 14 April 1948, in Montréal, and put into an orphanage. He never knew his natural mother: that was the first big fact in his life. The second—the fact of his homosexuality—emerged several years later. He had been adopted, when he was two and a half, by a working-class couple who already had two children of their own, both by then in their early twenties; the family lived in the industrial suburb of Laval. He did not speak comprehensibly until he was six years old, but his sister Gisèle remembers him affectionately after that as a little boy who would bombard her with questions, and who discovered a love for music. 'He was always in the church playing the organ: that was why my parents bought him a piano.'

Gisèle Vivier seems to have been the first of the many surrogate mothers he found for himself. Thérèse Desjardins—whose comfort- able and civilized household was open to him during his last years, and who clearly still thinks of him warmly as a son—told me the story he had told her, of how, as a boy of eight or nine, he had been seduced by an uncle.

'He had to tell the priest, in confession, and the priest said he had to tell his mother. So eventually he did. It was a storm. They sent the uncle away from Montréal, and they put Claude in a church school—which saved him. Suddenly he was in a place where people were nice, he had his own piano with a key, he had friends who would listen to his music, all boys, good meals, no worries about money, and he could study: it was perfect. He needed nothing else.'

No doubt Vivier felt that too. In a contribution to a gay symposium, published in Montréal in 1978, he recalled his awakening to his vocation during his schooldays. 'From that time dates my encounter with music, at a midnight mass. That would change my whole life. Unconsciously I had found the ideal instrument to express my search for purity, and also the entire reason for my future existence.'

He seems to have had no anxieties about coming out, for the simple reason he was never in. The 'search for purity' (the word recurs in his writings) was to take place not through a denial of his sexuality but through a rejoicing in it, through a living of life to the utmost, to come as close as possible to what lay on the other side. There—at the point of death, of eternity, of recovered innocence—he would find music.

His way toward that goal took him from the seminary—from which he was expelled at the age of eighteen, allegedly for being sexually too hot to handle—to the Montréal Conservatory, where he studied composition with Gilles Tremblay, himself a pupil of Messiaen and one of Canada's most prominent composers. Walter Boudreau, who was in the same class, remembers his first impressions of the young Vivier: 'Horrible. Noisy. Obnoxious. Very self-centred. A bit condescending on everything that was not part of his world. He smelled really bad. And that's about it.'

Not much was to change—certainly not the obliviousness to personal hygiene or decorum. Flamboyant, theatrical, extravagant, ostentatious in his sexuality, exaggerated in his behavior: these are the terms in which he is recalled by all who knew him. As Georges Nicholson, a musician who now works for the Canadian radio, put it to me: 'The switch was always *on*.' Vivier was evidently an embarrassing friend to have—one who would think nothing of charging across the street, or across a crowded concert hall, to come shrieking your name and embrace you. Yet he was also generous with whatever money he had, with his time, and with his consideration, outside of any sexual encounter. Rober Racine, an artist and writer some years younger, remembers these aspects of his personality with obvious fondness: 'He lived well. He was a fine person. I had a lot of pleasure with him, a lot, a lot.'

In 1971 Vivier graduated from the conservatory and went to Cologne, in the hope of studying with Karlheinz Stockhausen. But Stockhausen sent him to spend a year in Utrecht first with Gottfried Michael Koenig, one of the earliest generation of Stockhausen associates. He then went back to Cologne, and, as Professor Tremblay tells it, Stockhausen asked him why. 'Vivier said: Because you are the greatest composer in the world. That was enough: the only entrance test!'

Vivier arrived at an opportune time. Stockhausen was working on a new version of his *Momente*, an exuberant festival of love and music for a cheerful soprano soloist with choirs, brass, percussion and electric organs. For the young Canadian, following the rehearsals 'revealed the very essence of musical composition, and brought about a sort of baring of my soul'. In December 1972 he began a new work of his own, which he would think of as his opus one: *Chants* for seven women singing.

Chants started with a visionary night, as Vivier's works seem often to have done. 'My whole life unfolded before me, allowing me to glimpse in filigree the face of a sad child who would have liked to express something grandiose, and who had not yet been able to do so. These memories tumbled together into a bizarre dream: in a great cathedral there were three tombs; one of them broke open; I ran to alert the priest. This good old man spoke to the dead person who came out of the tomb, and who strangely changed into a white eagle, which seized me in its immense talons to carry me over the earth.'

Typically untroubled by all this news from Eros and Thanatos, he set about making the dream a reality, feeling he must create 'a veritable ritual of death' for 'three women in the presence of death and their three shades', the seventh voice being his own, that of the sad child. This was not entirely a new departure. *Musik für das Ende*, a choral piece dating from the year before, is also a requiem, apparently prompted in part by the suicide in 1970 of a close friend, the young Canadian actor Yves Sauvageau. *Chants* is different, though, in being about birth as much as death. It is amniotic music—music that floats in the gentle, warm support of static harmonies, that babbles with the syllables of the 'invented language' Vivier used in all his subsequent vocal works (which means the great majority of his works altogether), and that hears almost nothing outside women's voices and odd percussive knocks. It is also music that looks back toward the origins of the art: one can imagine it in an Anonymous 4 concert. Finally, it is music in which Vivier effects his own birth as a composer.

The piece he had written immediately before, the balefully titled *Désintégration* for two pianos, had been 'entirely predetermined: no note at any moment was left to chance.' Now he sought just the reverse: music that would flow, like water, from one situation to another, supported by no conscious system, channelled by words and images that came in dreams. To use terms he would develop later, *Désintégration* had been the triumph of Idea: a work entirely objective, saying nothing about its creator other than that he had taken the decision to initiate it. *Chants*, on the other hand, is the projection of the 'Moi,' the first-person singular. It is the piece in which Vivier began to teach his music about what mattered to him: the hope for purity, the fear and lure of death. It pointed the way he would go.

'Purification' was his first idea for a title: the piece was to be, in German, 'Reinigung'—until he discovered it would then sound like a laundry. 'That period in my life as a composer', he recalled, 'had, on the one hand, to purify me from all influences, allow me to rediscover the condition of a child; and, on the other hand, it had to express me, express the me that I am.' Yet, for all the cleansing of language going on in *Chants*, the piece still owes something to Stockhausen, whether by way of influence or confirmation. Like Stockhausen, Vivier was offering his works as sacred ceremonials, elaborating them from melody (though here Messiaen was also an important example), and seeing them as communicating with the self and—beyond the self—the divine.

The last piece he wrote in Cologne, *Lettura di Dante* (1973–4), brings a glimpse of his mature style—a style which lay only five years in the future, though in his case that was half a creative lifetime away. Slow, and ample yet light, the music unwinds as long melody for a soprano with instrumental septet, though with the need for a *coup de théâtre* to compensate for what the music cannot yet express: the soprano, who hitherto has sung from behind a curtain, is disclosed deaf-signing and then speaking the words 'I have seen God'.

Vivier returned to Montréal, and in his note for the first performance of *Lettura di Dante*, which was given there in September 1974, he said he was no longer thinking of the future, nor of the past, but of 'a sort of vanished present, a sort of impalpable joy mixed with the sadness of a child who has lost his mother'. This image was to recur in his music, not least in *Lonely Child*. The personal relevance is obvious. From the age of six, Vivier recalled, his knowledge of his adoption allowed him to 'make up my origins as I wished, pretend to speak in strange languages'. Here surely is one of the origins of his 'invented language'—of such phrases as 'ku-ruk-shé-tra' and 'pu-ru-sha-ti-ca-se' that calmly interpose themselves among the words of the

Divine Comedy in *Lettura di Dante*. The fact that he was late in speaking, too, might help explain his predilection for prattle, as well as his use of deaf-signing. And the notion of the 'vanished present' comes out strongly in his recollection that as a child he had felt 'reality was not the one I was, in fact, living but one I was taken from in a very strange fashion'.

The idea of an alternative, better present—which would have to be an absent present—was also to become important in his musical theorizing. A late note, written half a year before his death, asks: 'What does music provide, if not a disposition into "historical" time of an opening into another temporality? Music rends historical time and, for brief moments, shows us the beyond-time, ambiguous flow of musical space.' Expressing the same thought on an earlier occasion, he had said how music allowed human beings to 'transgress the great order of celestial mechanics. . . .That's why people construct their time machines known as music'.

However, for Vivier to make his own vessels time-tight would take a little while. He had no other aim. He taught for a short time at the University of Ottawa, in 1976, but otherwise he was determined to live as a composer, supported by grants, commissions and performing rights. And he was no slouch. During the two years after his return from Cologne he wrote two big scores—*Liebesgedichte* for four singers and eight wind players (1975) and the orchestral *Siddhartha* (1975–6)—as well as a bunch of solos and duos. *Liebesgedichte* is, like *Lettura di Dante*, a sprawling piece that keeps flashing forward to the later Vivier. It has some wonderful moments, as when the bass whistles and sings at the same time, or when oboe and clarinet jostle against one another in a faintly Iranian melodic interplay. It also suggests another virtue of the 'invented language', to camouflage the names of lovers. In *Bouchara*, a subsequent love song, the soprano keeps singing the name of one of Vivier's Montréal boyfriends, to whom the work is dedicated. In *Liebesgedichte*, the tenor comes back again and again to 'Dieter'.

Siddhartha is a more expert composition, but also a less individual one, close to the recent Stockhausen (especially *Inori*) and at times to Varèse or Scriabin. Vivier never heard it. He had written it for the National Youth Orchestra of Canada, who turned it down on grounds of difficulty, and the disappointment would seem to have been one of the spurs that sent him on a long journey through Asia in 1976–7. First he visited Japan; then he spent several weeks on Bali.

'Here I've been given a Balinese name, Nyoman Kenyung (the laughing third-born)', he wrote back to a Canadian music magazine.

He studied Balinese music; he took part in performances; and he discovered how hard it was to maintain a regular rhythm. (By all accounts he had no great skill as a practical musician; creation alone was what was important to him.) Finally he had to leave. 'A lesson in love, in tenderness, in poetry and in respect for life: that was my journey on Bali. These words may seem strange when I am talking about music', (again he was writing for the monthly *Musicanada*) 'but how can one not speak of love when a friend dances for me as a way of saying farewell, when this old woman offers me a fruit for my journey to Java, because that for her is as far from Bali as one can go!. . .One thing on Bali: music has its ultimate place in the depths of the heart; one understands music because it speaks to the heart.'

While still there he had said: 'I absolutely don't want to write Balinese music!' Once back, though, he found it hard to resist exactly that. *Pulau Dewata* (The Island of the Gods)—written for the McGill Percussion Ensemble, and recorded by them on an array of xylophones and metallophones strongly suggestive of the Indonesian gamelan—is Bali come to Montréal, and in two other works composed soon after his return, *Love Songs* and *Nanti Malam* (Later this Evening), he tried for a Balinese integration of music and dance in ritual.

The music became more interesting as the memories dimmed, and sank to a deeper musical level. One of the features of Balinese music that had most impressed Vivier was what he called 'interlocking'. One pattern (note-rest-note-rest-note-rest) is played simultaneously with its displacement (rest-note-rest-note-rest-note), and so the result is a regular rhythm (note-note-note-note-note-note). This duly happens in *Pulau Dewata*, but the principle is used more subtly in the virtuoso piano piece *Shiraz*, which was completed later in 1977, and which also introduced another kind of mobile interlocking, between melody and harmony. With *Pulau Dewata* Vivier had divested his music of counterpoint, to leave just a melody line and accompanying chords—chords which at this stage were blissfully elementary. *Shiraz* has more complex harmonies, often Messiaenesque, and by its speed and fracturedness it suggests a facetted jewel: the eponymous town, which Vivier had visited on his way back from Bali, he described as 'a pearl of a city, a roughly cut diamond', and he included in the dedication of the piece 'two blind singers I followed for many hours in the market place of Shiraz'.

He had always identified himself with the rejects and misfits of society. In one of his earliest interviews he had talked about an encounter on a train in Holland, during the time he was studying in Utrecht: 'I met an old Corsican, completely drunk, of whom everybody was afraid. I, for my part, decided to make conversation with him, and I got the idea to record him discreetly with the little machine I had with me. I wanted to eternalize him, transcend him, take him out of the context of the train, transform this meeting into an ecstatic vision.' The result was his 1972 electronic piece *Musique pour un vieux corse triste*.

Later, when he was in Montréal, he used to frequent not only the favourite artists' bar of the time (The Pit, on the Avenue du Parc), and not only gay bars, but also another establishment that Rober Racine told me about: 'He took me once to a place on the Rue St Laurent where all the prostitutes and tramps and transvestites hung out. It was like the whole of human misery was there. And he told me he'd spent Christmas there once, and he introduced me to some people who'd been in the same orphanage. He was thoroughly at home there: that was his family. And he said that these people were the inspiration for his music.' Indeed, *Greeting Music*, a piece for five instrumentalists written in 1978, was intended as a greeting to the growing numbers of people living on the streets.

In *Greeting Music*, and in another chamber piece from the same year, *Paramirabo* for four players, he continued his explorations into the strange world of high-treble harmony, letting his ear scan overtones on strings, sounds sung into the flute, and, again, whistling. In this world, as he was evidently aware, the abrasion of frequencies on each other can produce ghostly lower pitches and natural harmonics can interfere with tones played in the equal temperament that western music has made normal; sound becomes misted, iridescent. But still these works of 1978 are only foreshadowings, and the same is true of Vivier's second work for orchestra, *Orion*, which goes a bit too eagerly after effectiveness and likability, with its brave trumpet calls and its chugging minimalism. Only near the end does it open into new space, when forward drive gives way to more listening upwards, and a percussion player twice sings 'Hé-o' into a tam-tam, the second time to be met with silence—silence which is the seventh, unsaid part of the score.

Orion was composed in 1979 for Charles Dutoit and the Montréal Symphony, whose first performance of it, in 1980, was not a success. That same year, though, Vivier made a breakthrough with his first opera, *Kopernikus*, which became a signature piece for the concert series he had founded with some friends, Les Evénements du Neuf (*neuf* for the newness of what went on, and also for the fact that the 'événements' always took place at 9 p.m. on the ninth of the month). *Kopernikus* is not, though, his best piece: it is another ritual of death, bubbling with the infantilism that was also an embarrassing feature of his choral autobiography *Journal* of 1977. Both are among the works in which his attempt to recuperate childhood experience resulted in kitsch. 'You always feel like a little child anyway,' he said in an interview. 'You don't see yourself grow old. I think that's what makes the unity of a human being.' So it may be, but he had to find a way to speak as a child, not show himself as an adult playing children's games, and he discovered his infant voice much more by pursuing the untoward harmonies of *Paramirabo* than through the miminy-piminy fairy talk of *Kopernikus*.

Then suddenly that infant voice arrived. In March 1980, just five months after finishing *Orion*, Vivier completed *Lonely Child*. Thérèse Desjardins, whose closeness to him dates from this period, told me something of how he was then.

'When he finished a piece, during the two or three days following the *point final*, he was out of his mind with nerves, because for him the only point in life was to compose. I don't think he could have lived with anybody, because he had to compose, and for that he had to be alone. He had a very structured life. He would wake up at seven, go to the same restaurant every morning for his breakfast, come back to his place, and compose. At eleven he would call me and other people, put the telephone on his piano and play what he had just composed.' (Everyone I spoke to told me of this habit.) 'I heard *Lonely Child* like that, day by day. I remember once I said: I don't like it. And he said: Who are you? I don't *mind* if you don't like it!'

Lonely Child, which plays for about twenty minutes, concentrates even more than the preceding works on slow melody, but with harmonic auras that are suddenly more complex. The change is striking: we are in a new world. And the fantastic orchestration—which is what makes this world new—has not been prepared by anything in Vivier's earlier music, or anyone else's. It is possible he had learned something from French composers of his generation, such as Gérard Grisey and Tristan Murail, who were working with natural harmonics; however, his music does not sound like theirs. It is also possible he had been listening intently to bells and gongs, for the huge chords that march along with—around—the voice in *Lonely Child* commonly have deep fundamentals with a fizz of interfering higher tones, rather as metallic resonances do. Vivier's own explanation, though, was in terms of his spiritual quest: 'This urge for purity, it's created a style of its own.'

Purity, he seems to have felt, entailed polishing the music with his preoccupations until it would shine. *Lonely Child* moves that way on the level of its text, which is intimately personal in being partly the lullaby of an idealized mother, partly a prayer to the Virgin Mary, partly a love song addressed to the boy in *Death in Venice*. But where these urgings might imply a deep holy-carnal sentimentality, the work is redeemed by its candid gaze. It sounds innocent—a voice we have not heard before, and could not have expected. It evades camp, which can only arise where there is shared experience and prevarication. Everything in this music is open to view: the slow melody, and the wide chords that chime with each note, while often suggesting a different fundamental. Vivier's harmony works as it had, for instance, in the short piece *Pour violon et clarinette* of 1975: there are essentially two lines, which come together (often in a major third) and meander away from each other. But perhaps what makes *Lonely Child* importantly different came from its sexuality.

In an interview he gave in 1981 to a French gay magazine, Vivier suggested a link between the traditional view of manhood ('strong, big, dominating') and the traditional view of music as moving toward a goal, which he rejected. Other statements of the same period, without making that link explicitly, say how, in his music, something quite different was happening—how, for instance, 'I just have statements, musical statements, which lead nowhere.' Vivier was not claiming that this was entirely new. 'I could compare myself', he went on to say, 'with some Japanese musics or Balinese musics. Among the western composers I could compare myself with Mozart and Chopin.' (Louise Duchesneau, who came across Vivier when she was a student in Ottawa, told me that he was always playing the same two pieces on the piano, Mozart's 'Rondo alla turca' and Chopin's 'Revolutionary' Etude, and that he never got to the end of either of them before breaking off into improvisation.) Nevertheless, what certainly was new in *Lonely Child* was the particular form taken by the directionlessness, by the dropping into our time world of moments of eternity.

During the year and a half after *Lonely Child*, Vivier wrote *Cinq Chansons* for mostly Asian percussion instruments, *Wo bist du Licht!* for mezzo-soprano and orchestra, and a group of works centred on the figure of Marco Polo: *Prologue pour un Marco Polo* (more suite than overture, consisting of eight linked scenes devised for radio performance), *Zipangu* for string orchestra (named for the Japan that was, for Polo, unreachable), the wordless love song *Bouchara* and *Samarkand*, a big slow movement for wind quintet and piano. Discussing Marco Polo on tape, Vivier used words that echo what he said of his self-projection in *Chants*: 'I have the impression that Marco Polo is above all, also the image of this one who has tried to say something and has not succeeded. I find that, as an image, I find that quite desperate.' It is moving to find Vivier still feeling this, just as he was musically coming into his own.

Hitherto he had written his own texts, sometimes incorporating or embroidering on classic poetry or the words of the Catholic liturgy, but on *Prologue pour un Marco Polo* he worked with the poet Paul Chamberland, who gained perhaps the greatest insights into Vivier as an artist.

'He was inhabited', Chamberland told me, 'by his figures: Mozart, Lewis Carroll, Copernicus, Marco Polo. The figure of Marco Polo he already had in his head, and so for me it was—well, "easy" would not be the word, because I had to work, but it was a question of being on that level. And that excited me. From the beginning I listened attentively to what Claude said, and to the rhythm of how he spoke, which was very rapidly, staccato. What was very important, quite apart from the musical aspect, was his way of describing the character of Marco Polo. He was always very precise—above all, what he said always had this seriousness. When I got home I wrote down things, sometimes phrases, and let that work, one might say. Then I would go to his place—which was in indescribable disorder, scores everywhere. He played what he had written at the piano, and I came with my words, and a kind of circuit was formed.

'He was a seer, a *listener*. There was one writer we had in common, as a reference: Aurobindo. What fascinated me was that he already was in that visionary world, as if mental structures had become physical structures. But it was completely natural: that's what struck me. He was not an adept of any particular theory or doctrine: of course, nobody is entirely self-sufficient, but he had an autonomy in his thinking. He had a passion to make something *be*. He felt himself—the term is over-used, but he felt himself inspired, at the service of something. Yet at the same time he wasn't egocentric. There was a complete absence of vanity in him, and never the slightest trace of wanting to convince. Either you play with me or you don't: it's all the same.

'He was a complex person, but relatively transparent. There coexisted in him an abandoned child and a kind of being like an angel, who had completely a sense of his gravity.'

Prologue pour un Marco Polo and the other works of 1980–81 find Vivier, Polo-like, exploring the continent that had loomed into view in *Lonely Child*. *Bouchara* is the most perfect of them. *Wo bist du Licht!* is an elegy for our age, and owes its power much more to the long lament sung by a low mezzo (perhaps a portrait of the composer's grandmother, 'who I knew only very slightly, but who was for me a little island of affection and security') than to the incorporated news recordings, which include Martin Luther King's 'I have a dream' speech and noise of Robert Kennedy's assassination. Perhaps that is the point. Vivier was, as he said, removing his work from history—both from the course of human events and from the course through time that western compositions had sought to make their own. *Wo bist du Licht!* goes in search of non-history, or trans-history, with the figure of a blind singer (memories of Shiraz) from a poem by Hölderlin. 'In a divine sound landscape', the composer's note on the score concludes, 'there still rings out the voice of the wounded man, who incessantly repeats to God his despair, without which he would not even be sure that God exists.'

Soon after finishing *Wo bist du Licht!* Vivier celebrated his thirty-third birthday, with Thérèse Desjardins and her family. As she told me: 'He played "Happy Birthday" with my mother at the piano, and he had this cake I'd made, with thirty-three candles, and he didn't want to blow them out. Normally after dinner, when my daughters were there, they would help Claude with his make-up, because he was going out to the park, or I don't know where. But that night he didn't go out. And he started to cry, because this was the first time in his life that he'd had a birthday party.'

Apart from the works in highly refined, teased-out harmonies ('great sheafs of colours', as he called them), Vivier also in 1981 worked on and starred in a short videotape, *L'Homme de Pékin*: movies were important to him, and he spoke of doing more in this line. Then, toward the end of that year, he returned to bald octaves and a joke. *Et je reverrai cette ville étrange*, the octave piece, locks together six instrumentalists in melody almost without colour, and *A Little Joke* for chorus is the odd, tiny fruit of a one-night stand with a woman. After that he was silent for some months. He felt he had to leave Montréal once more for the sake of his musical development, and in June 1982 he went, to Paris. Most of his Canadian friends never saw him again.

The letters he wrote back to Thérèse Desjardins, however, give us windows into his life during the nine months that remained. In July comes the first idea for 'a dramatic work without subject, where the drama would be the music itself'—a notion he was later to develop into the project of an 'opéra fleuve' that would move through *Prologue pour un Marco Polo* and the pieces he had placed along the Silk Road: *Shiraz*, *Samarkand*, *Bouchara*, *Zipangu*. By August he was composing *Trois Airs pour un opéra imaginaire*, which he felt represented a stage he had to get through before he could write the new opera: 'a rediscovery,' as he said, 'of counterpoint and of a more dramatized musical time'. In September he heard Mahler's Seventh Symphony at a concert, and reported that: 'Mahler is perhaps the musician to whom I feel closest—an exacerbated sensibility, schmaltz, and at the same time profound desire for purity, but for a purity that's almost libidinal.' Relevant here is his intuition that he might be Jewish himself, and his horror at the racism he found in Paris directed against Jews and North Africans.

The next month he announced definite operatic plans: the work would have the form of a Requiem mass, out of which would come scenes from the martyrdom of Saint Sebastian and from another martyrdom, Tchaikovsky's, with singers doubling roles (the tenor would be Sebastian and Tchaikovsky, the bass Emperor/Alchemist and Tsar, the coloratura soprano Sorceress and Mme von Meck), and with Joan of Arc and Gilles de Retz also among the dramatis personae. That Vivier should be attracted to homoerotic hagiography was inevitable; the appeal of Tchaikovsky would have been heightened by the story, then gaining currency, that the Russian composer had been forced to commit suicide in order to avoid involving his old school in the shame and scandal of a homosexual liaison. 'I place the opera,' Vivier stated with his unaffected boldness, 'in the line of Dante, Mozart, and Bataille.'

By November 1982 he had a commission from the Groupe Vocal de France, and was planning a *Dies irae*, which presumably was to be related to, or part of, the Tchaikovsky-Sebastian opera. Meanwhile, he was living ever more dangerously, as Philippe Polini—a video artist who had worked with him on *L'Homme de Pékin*, and who was now in Paris—told me.

'It was very frenetic, but with an energy that doesn't go towards life: it goes towards death, somehow provoking death. That wasn't completely new: he had always walked a thin line between life and death. Because he was adopted, he was alone. He had no connections: no family, no stable lovers, no real parents. He was suspended, and in a state of constant vibration. In Paris it just got more. It was a very clean energy that he was putting into his music, but as soon as he left the composition—outside of that border—everything was disorganized.'

More testimony to the danger and chaos of his life at this time comes almost certainly in the pages of Christopher Coe's novel *Such Times* (1993), for there is compelling evidence to identify Vivier with the composer Claude of that book. Coe's Claude is said to look like the Memling 'Portrait of a Man' in the Frick Collection in New York; Vivier's photographs show a longer face and a more down-turned nose, but the mouth, chin, prominent cheekbones and thinning hair are similar. Timothy, the narrator of the novel, hears a six-minute piece by Claude for oboe and piano, and thinks it sounds like Xenakis; Vivier wrote a piece of that sort of length for flute and piano, and the similarity with Xenakis is plausible for a character who does not know much music. Claude lives in squalor; so did Vivier. But what really clinches it is the laugh. Everyone I spoke to mentioned Vivier's laugh, which he unleashed—whether the occasion was appropriate or not—to show what he thought of people or of music. His laughter was, Louise Duchesneau told me, 'very loud, very Mephistophelean.' The musicologist Jean-Jacques Nattiez imitated it for me: a harsh cackle. Gilles Tremblay told me of a time he had been at a concert in Paris, and had not known Vivier was in the auditorium—until he heard the laugh. And this is the first sound that greets us from Claude in *Such Times*: 'He let out the highest, most out-of-control laugh I had ever heard. . . .It was the laugh of someone who probably didn't care much, or at all, about what people in a place like this thought of him. Or it was the laugh of someone who doesn't know how to laugh.'

Not knowing how to laugh, Vivier had discovered how to sing. In early January he made a last attempt to escape his fate, writing to Thérèse Desjardins of his wretchedness at having 'nobody to telephone when I compose, nobody to confide in, nobody with whom I can talk about my anguish of spirit'. Parisians were cold; most of his fellow composers were useless; he would come back to Montréal in April or May. Only four days later, however, he could write reassuringly that 'the crisis has quite passed', and that he had completed six minutes of his new piece, which was now not a *Dies irae* but had the title *Glaubst Du an die Unsterblichkeit der Seele?* (Do you believe in the immortality of the soul?).

Also in January 1983 he wrote of a love affair with 'an American', Christopher (who must be Coe), and of being violently raped. 'I don't think my music can be the same after what I've just lived through. . . . I'm afraid, Thérèse, and I think it's myself I'm afraid of. I'm afraid of this infinite void that I'm not afraid of. Death is totally demystified.

'You know that this year in Paris has been vital for me', he went on. 'I'm maturing at an absolutely phenomenal speed, and the music I'll write—in particular my opera—will have a human meaning that no music has been able to achieve until now. . . .I must compose on the hoof, give human beings a music that will prevent them once and for all from making war. A phrase comes to my mind: "It's my own death I will celebrate." I don't know why, it seems to me I want to conquer death on its own ground, make it the liberator of beings open to eternity, give humans such a music that their consciousness spills directly into eternity without passing through death, without paying tribute to the old Ferryman of Acheron!'

Such hopes. They were the hopes they had always been: to counter the aggressiveness written into the conventional role of the male, to feel the silent pulse of heaven. They were hopes that could only be entertained by one who was risking a martyrdom of his own—one who was, as Philippe Polini records, spending his nights drinking heavily, having lots of partners, not asking questions, and behaving that way in preparation for the next day's work on *Glaubst Du*.

'Listen to me, listen to me!' says a tenor near the start of the piece. 'You know I always wanted to die for love but. . .how strange it is, this music that doesn't move.' 'Speak', says a contralto, and the tenor goes on: 'I never knew—.' 'Knew what?' 'Knew how to love.' The contralto then asks him to sing a love song, and one follows—in the 'invented language', as usual. But it fades away, and the voices turn to what sounds even more alarmingly like autobiography. One of the synthesizer players, speaking into a vocoder, recounts an episode that Vivier told as a dream in a letter to Thérèse Desjardins. The narrator is attracted to a young man on a Métro train, who sits down next to him, introduces himself, pulls out from his black jacket a dagger, 'and thrusts it right into my heart'. There the score ends.

On 12 March 1983, Vivier was found in his apartment, where he had lain dead for five days. There were forty-five knife wounds in his body.

His death appalls by its inevitability. 'You know I always wanted to die for love.' His whole life, quite apart from his erotic life, seems to have been headed in one direction. Nobody I spoke to could imagine a Vivier grown middle-aged; everyone saw him as blazing towards extinction. And he probably had the same certainty himself. In one of several depositions he made against the conservatism and provincialism of cultural life in Québec, he listed some of the artists who had killed themselves or died young. 'It seems to me that in Québec people die easily, and it's in a completely Québecois (adolescent) sensibility that we must look for the solution. Extreme sensibility which, alas, because of a pseudo-male environment, very often cannot but suffer.' What Vivier seems to be describing here is a retardation that must be countered by retardation, by a celebration of adolescence, such as his later music achieved in its freshness, its libido, and its tenderness—a celebration that machismo and conformity would have to want to terminate.

The judicial case concerning his death was soon resolved, and a boy of nineteen was convicted of the murder. Justice for the music has been longer in coming—partly because of the musical remoteness of Montréal, partly because of tussles between the composer's friends and his adoptive family, partly because of an excess of protectiveness on the part of those who have taken responsibility for the scores. But with the new recording of *Lonely Child* and other works conducted by Reinbert de Leeuw—the composer's first international release—Vivier may at last be crossing the threshold from death into life. (1996)

at the movies

with Tarkovsky

Most film directors come to have an effect on composers during the course of their work; not many continue doing so from beyond the grave, as Andrei Tarkovsky has. In 1987, the year after his death, two distinguished composers, Nono and Takemitsu, independently wrote musical memorials to him. Four years after that Abbado put on a concert in Vienna to include the Nono piece, commissioning for the occasion further tributes from Kurtág, Rihm and Beat Furrer. Now a recording of that concert has been released as 'Hommage à Andrei Tarkovsky', whose appearance, coupled with the recent screening of Tarkovsky's films at Anthology Film Archives, prompts some thoughts about why this director has become such a talisman for musical creators.

Part of the answer, surely, has to do with his persona as an unreconstructed Romantic, with his insistence on the high calling of the true artist, his impatience with mere entertainment, his assertion of art as an ethical force, his total unwillingness to compromise. In his book *Sculpting with Time* he speaks in terms that could have been endorsed by Schoenberg, even Schumann. He belongs philosophically to another age, yet there he was, in our own time (or something not so distant from it), making films unlike any that had been seen before.

That would be one reason for composers to honour him, but there are others that have to do more specifically with how he used music in his films and how he handled film as a musical medium. Music for him had precise meaning. It could be a symbol of hope, however much he decried symbolism. The finale of Beethoven's Ninth Symphony, barely audible above mechanical noise, is used that way in both *Stalker* and *Nostalghia*.

He could also get good things out of the composers with whom he worked. The flatcar sequence in *Stalker*, where the three central male characters are travelling along a railroad, includes one of the most persuasive uses of music in all of cinema. At first there is the regular rhythm of the rail joints, but then this rhythm bends out of the world of realistic sound effect to become the stuff of Eduard Artemyev's electronic music. Instead of hearing the sound from outside, we seem now to be hearing it from within the three heads we see on the screen—hearing it as the characters hear it, dimming and floating in consciousness as their thoughts move elsewhere. Instead of separating us from the action, as most movie music does (for what is a modern symphony orchestra doing in seventeenth-century Salem?), the music here takes us right inside.

But perhaps the most remarkable music in Tarkovsky is neither in the classical extracts nor in the virtuoso modern cuts but in the general sonic texture with which each film is imbued—especially those textures of drips and splashes that suggest vast resonant space, beyond the reach of modern 'dynamic digital sound'. Someone blind and unconversant with Russian might anyway enjoy a Tarkovsky film as music.

There is a sense of music for the eye, too, in what Tarkovsky shows on screen: a music of different colours, tempos, rhythms, spaces. In most movies these things are subordinate to the story: we move to a fast car or a rural landscape because that is where the characters are. In Tarkovsky, though, the logic is not of events but of shots, and in that respect he worked like a composer, creating unreal worlds we recognize inwardly as real.

Of the unreal-real music created in homage to him, Luigi Nono's *No hay caminos, hay que caminar* (There are no paths to travel, only the travelling on) and György Kurtág's *Samuel Beckett: What is the Word* are alike in many respects. Both have groups of musicians distributed around the hall: instrumental ensembles in the Nono, singers as well as instrumentalists in the Kurtág. Both move forward tentatively, subject to fearsome setbacks.

Nono's piece, one of the last he wrote, has been analysed as an analogue of Tarkovsky's final film, *The Sacrifice*, but this is surely to misread the tribute. Nono admired Tarkovsky's moral stance and his imagination, not the mechanics of any particular production. His music is not looking across at the director but forward with him, in company; the instrumental groups offer tenuous, suspended sounds—usually G in one octave or another—and keep going despite the hammering they receive from percussion.

The figure of resilience in Kurtág's extraordinary work is a singing actress, Ildiko Monyok, who struggles to enunciate a late Beckett text. Her disjointed phrases —

folly seeing all this here
for to
what is the word
see
glimpse
seem to glimpse

— are prompted and supported by a pianist beside her and echoed over a wider plane by the musicians at a distance. The piece is cruel and tender; it is also, in this premiere performance, fiercely dramatic. In subsequent performances and recordings (one was made at the Salzburg Festival two years later) Monyok has dealt less histrionically with her predicament, and perhaps more powerfully, though what she does here is chilling. Born six years before Tarkovsky, Kurtág did not need to learn from him. Instead he moved in parallel to reach the same position: that of not being afraid of life, to observe closely and create. (*New York Times*, 9 March 1997)

with Prokofiev and Glass

Nobody is surprised when quite a conclave of violinists turns up in a motel bathroom to help murder the leading lady. Nobody turns a hair at the presence of a symphony orchestra while the army of Novgorod is battling it out with Teutonic knights on a frozen lake in the thirteenth century. Nobody minds that an orchestra is there when Robin Hood and his companions ride through the forest, or when Cleopatra has herself unfurled from a carpet before Antony, or when any number of nameless monsters emerge from any number of gleaming steel pods. Movie music is not just a convention; it is a habit. Just as nature abhors a vacuum, so the cinema abhors silence, and when there are not people talking, we seem to need music to maintain a human voice, a human rhythm. This may even be the main purpose of the film score: not to tell us what to feel but to reassure us that someone is there, that this vision we have been forced to take over does not have to be our responsibility—someone else is looking after it for us. After all, this is how Muzak works, giving real life its backing score, in the hope that we will feel consoled by the implication that somebody out there is in control.

Just as music was introduced into the movies to alleviate the embarrassment of there being nothing to hear, so we now seem to be witnessing the backwash of movies into the concert hall to lift what anxiety we may feel, in an age dominated by visual imagery, at having nothing to look at. Recently the New York Philharmonic gave some performances of Prokofiev's score for Eisenstein's *Ivan the Terrible*, with scenes from the film to accompany the music; at the Brooklyn Academy of Music last winter Philip Glass provided an entirely new score for singers and ensemble to accompany a screening of the Cocteau movie *La Belle et la Bête*.

Ivan the Terrible was the second Prokofiev-Eisenstein project to be mounted by a team including John Goberman as producer, William David Brohn as musical arranger and Yuri Temirkanov as conductor. A few years ago they presented *Alexander Nevsky*, whose complete score is now available on compact disc and, with the film, in video formats. According to Goberman, the principal object with *Nevsky* was to bring the music out from behind the heavy veil of the 1938 soundtrack, and to do so not by reproducing the original film score, which is laid out for a studio orchestra, but by presenting a new orchestration for symphonic forces. Brohn based his work on the concert version Prokofiev made soon after the movie was released; additional sections he painstakingly transcribed from the soundtrack. So now we can hear, in brilliant modern sound, musical sequences that, because they did not make it into the concert piece, had not been played since 1938—sequences such as the one for percussion alone where the ice breaks under the battle.

An interesting issue is raised here. If we can replace a score we deem inadequately recorded, we could also replace a scene we think did not come off, or, with the right technology, an individual performance we consider could be improved upon. You did not like Jean Simmons in *Spartacus*? O.K., shoot Michelle Pfeiffer in the role and edit her in. Film, which has seemed a cryogenic kind of drama, is on the edge of a new age of flexibility, and we can look forward to having our favourite movies available in multitudes of different versions, starring performers of diverse generations.

More immediately, these Prokofiev-Eisenstein revitalizations make film into a real-time performance art, since it is now possible for the score to be performed by live musicians in synchrony with the picture show, as at the Philharmonic's *Ivan the Terrible* concerts. The movie itself becomes the subject of the performance. With an orchestra playing along beneath the screen, we seem to be at a re-enactment of the soundstage recording of the score, and the drama of the forging of the Russian state takes second place to the drama of the forging of the film. In the case of *Ivan*, that internal drama has some power. Eisenstein's movement, by jump cuts from one image to another, has a completely different rhythm from that of Prokofiev's symphonic sweep; the long sequence portraying the siege of Kazan becomes a dialogue between two kinds of time: brutal instants and grand progress. This rhythmic discord may, paradoxically, be crucial to the success of Prokofiev's collaborations with Eisenstein (though that success is diminished in *Ivan* by comparison with *Nevsky*, possibly because Prokofiev could not raise the same enthusiasm twice, as witness his blithe re-use for the Kazan scene of a big tune from his current opera *War and Peace*). Film, like music, is polyphonic, moving simultaneously at different speeds: the speeds of the camera, the action, the dialogue, background events. Eisenstein's willingness sometimes to freeze movement—even more than his willingness also to include song and dance episodes—allows music to come forward and steer us through time in its own manifold ways.

More momentary sorts of drama are possible. Close to the start of the Philharmonic performance, in the coronation scene, there was a magical transition when the old soundtrack was quietly joined by the live sound of women's voices in chorus. However, Prokofiev's score barely justifies the attentions of a crack orchestra for ninety minutes. Temirkanov and the Philharmonic may have had similar doubts, for there was sometimes, and especially at the end, a sense of people shouting to make themselves heard against some distraction. Also, the exercise seemed a bit like a CD-ROM session brought awkwardly to life. The performance had a general shape, thanks to the retention of most of the film narrative (the flashbacks in the second part were the main casualties) and to the use of the scene in colour as a finale, but it was—as much as Eisenstein's cinematography—full of stops and starts: sections of music without film, sections of film without music, of which the latter included, for no obvious reason, the long scene between Ivan and Metropolitan Philip. Deconstruction without reconstruction is more the nature of life at the computer than of time spent in the concert hall. From the musical point of view *Ivan the Terrible* is not a big cultural item; its value is rather as a collection of materials that can tell us something about the combining of sight and sound. It is something to play with, not to sit in earnest witness of.

Glass's movie opera offers a more integrated and cogent experience. Because he accepts Cocteau's vision as given, he may appear to be adopting a subservient attitude, and yet his music runs sublimely on its own course. Contrary to what happens in the Kazan scene of *Ivan the Terrible*, in *La Belle et la Bête* the score is static while the pictures flow on. The music resituates the movie in a dream time of eternal repetition; it also shows a splendid disregard of events. When, just occasionally, a diminished chord seems to chime with some ominous turn in the story, so that one has the brief feeling the music really is noticing what is going on, it is as if a robot were to smile. But what the score cannot ignore is the text. Glass's music is designed to synchronize with the film, which means that the words, all sung, sometimes have to be enunciated at quicksilver speed, well beyond what is natural for singing characters. So one gets to feel that in fact these are not singing characters at all: they are ministers of words, for strangely silent creatures on the screen—assistants to those creatures, rather like the people in a noh play who support an actor's costume or reclothe him. The film looks cherished, fragile and, because the instrumental music stays in a very different rhythmic world, out of reach. Glass has pressed his music into the mould of the movie, and produced something quite different—so different that it works extraordinarily well on record, separated from the movie. This is the best sort of film music: music that could not have existed without the movie but does not need it now. (*New Yorker*, 3 July 1995)

brief encounter

[commissioned for the summer 1996 film and television special issue of the Chester house magazine *The Full Score*]

(Torchlight on carpet in a Hollywood movie theatre in the early forties. Cut to rear view of STRAVINSKY being shown to his seat by an usherette. STRAVINSKY sits down and, with a start, recognizes the man next to him, who is eating from a large bag of popcorn.)

STRAVINSKY: Herr Schoenberg! I don't believe we've met. . . (He offers his right hand.)

SCHOENBERG: (keeping his eyes on the screen)
And you are?

STRAVINSKY: Stravinsky!

(SCHOENBERG, himself startled, turns his head rapidly towards his new companion, brushes his right hand against the front of his jacket, and takes STRAVINSKY's hand in his.)

SCHOENBERG: Delighted! I am Schoenberg. But of course, you recognized me.

STRAVINSKY: Only I hadn't expected to see you here.

SCHOENBERG: I come for the newsreels. The only way to get accurate information about what is happening in Europe.

STRAVINSKY: Indeed.

(There is a long pause.)

SCHOENBERG: Would you like some popcorn?

STRAVINSKY: What flavour is it?
SCHOENBERG: Butterscotch.
STRAVINSKY: Then I will, thank you.
(Schoenberg offers the bag, and Stravinsky takes a large handful.)
STRAVINSKY: Do you know what the main feature is?
SCHOENBERG: *The Great Dictator*.
STRAVINSKY: Ah yes, Chaplin. He once asked me to work with him, you know. Didn't work out. Never does—except when you'd rather it hadn't.
(Pause. Both composers go on eating popcorn.)
STRAVINSKY: Did you see *Fantasia*?
SCHOENBERG: I *heard* it. Had to close my eyes. Not too bad a performance of *Der Zauberlehrling* of Dukas. Or the Beethoven. The rest of the music, of course, was stupid.
STRAVINSKY: Indeed.
(Pause. SCHOENBERG goes on eating popcorn. STRAVINSKY glances at the bag. SCHOENBERG finishes, and screws the bag into a ball.)
SCHOENBERG: Stokowski is not an artist. Disney is not an artist. Film is not an art form—not here in America. The audience watches its own lack of culture.
STRAVINSKY: Then Pabst?
SCHOENBERG: Perhaps. Perhaps with Pabst it would have been possible. You know my *Begleitmusik zu einer Lichtspielszene*, of course. Pabst without pictures. Something like that. (Pause.) It was the *development* in certain films that interested me, the foreshortening of time. Events that in real life would have taken many hours—a journey, a sleepless night—could be presented within a minute, or still less. The idea would be there, and all its implications cascading after it. That was what was important: film as an image of fuller, faster time. (Pause.) But then, it may be that this is only a musician's view. What do *you* think?
STRAVINSKY: My opinions, my dear Schoenberg, are of little concern to those with *no* concern for my works. Not that the two should be confused.
(Pause. SCHOENBERG goes back to watching the film.)
STRAVINSKY: Since you have the goodness to ask, however, I would say rather that what interests me is the *structure* of film. Surely no composer in our age has been able to ignore what the cinema can do with time—not make

it fuller or faster, as you say, but on the contrary hold it stationary. A film take is a moment that can be run again and again—exactly the same in this theatre here as it will be in fifty years time. Frozen. This is something quite new, this opportunity to fossilize time. And not only that, but the fact that portions of time can be spliced together—close-up, long-shot, close-up again: this must change how we make musical forms.

SCHOENBERG: But the editing is only a trick. What matters is the progression *through* from one take to another, the progression of the idea.

STRAVINSKY: Or is *that* only a trick?

SCHOENBERG (stiffly):
No. It's name is thought. The rest is presentation.

STRAVINSKY: And to that we give no thought?

SCHOENBERG: Only secondarily. Only to secure the idea. This is why American film cannot rise above kitsch, because presentation—

STRAVINSKY: Lana Turner?

SCHOENBERG: I make an exception for Lana Turner. Because presentation—

STRAVINSKY: Rita Hayworth?

SCHOENBERG: I make an exception for Rita Hayworth. (Pause.) Where was I?

STRAVINSKY: I think we were agreeing that what the cinema *should* be doing is offering opportunities to composers, and I mean *serious* opportunities, not just to supply background music like some paid lackey—

SCHOENBERG: Exactly.

STRAVINSKY: —but to contribute to the creation of a new art form, requiring music in action with words, movement, design. . . . I believe that with such means you might have been able to complete your *Jakobsleiter*.

SCHOENBERG (smiling):
Or you your *Dialogue de la Joye et de la Raison*.

STRAVINSKY: Precisely. This is what people of our stature *should* be doing for the cinema.

SCHOENBERG: This is what the cinema should be *expecting* of us.

STRAVINSKY: Shall I go and get some more popcorn?

SCHOENBERG: Why not?

(STRAVINSKY rises from his seat, but is stayed by the arrival of the MANAGER at the front of the auditorium to make an announcement.)

MANAGER: Ladies and gentlemen: I have to tell you that this afternoon's feature has been supplied to us with no music score. Is there a composer in the house?

(STRAVINSKY races down the aisle with his hand up, closely followed by SCHOENBERG.)

Schoenberg on the stage

Arnold Schoenberg's biggest work was an opera to his own libretto, *Moses und Aron*, of which he wrote the first two acts in 1926–32 and left the third, despite repeated promises and hopes, unset. Moses and Aron (i.e. Aaron) are the Biblical patriarchs, Moses being the visionary who cannot readily communicate his vision, Aron the spokesman inclined to sugar the message. Since its posthumous premiere, at Hamburg in 1954, the work has been one of opera's great challenges. So has the composer's short opera *Erwartung* ('Awaiting'), whose sole character is a woman seeking her dead or departed lover.

Salzburg 1987

Salzburg has at last produced Schoenberg's *Moses und Aron*, and a mightily dramatic event it proved. In that heaven where perfect operatic performances exist this work is being played by the Vienna Philharmonic under Mahler, but if that maestro is beyond even Salzburg's means, the Vienna players are there, and show what abundant strengths and beauties this score contains, whether in the potency of its long melodies, in the freshness of the scoring for flutes and mandolin, or in the extraordinary mixture of snarl and seduction in the Golden Calf scene. And the force of James Levine's conducting is enough to overcome any misgivings about his concentration always on a single prominent line, even in a work which is so full of cross-currents, which exists so much under the sign of 'but yet'.

Not at all less remarkable, in this first Salzburg staging of what is arguably Schoenberg's central achievement, is the production by Jean-Pierre Ponnelle. Though one might question his view that a respect for the historical setting would inevitably result in a sort of 1950s Hollywood biblical epic, his situation of the action in the twentieth century is as apt as it is visually striking: Schoenberg was indeed writing at a time when the Nazi advance seemed inescapable, and *Moses* is, musically, inescapably a work of the 1930s. It is more doubtful whether this has to mean an opening scene, before the music has begun, of synagogue-desecration and Jew-hunting carried out by abstracted storm-troopers with flashing lights and whistles. The atmosphere of a despised Jewry could be left simply to the stage picture, which must be one of the most effective to have been placed within the stone arcades of the Felsenreitschule. Tombstones, many splashed with yellow paint, indicate a disfigured Jewish cemetery; there is also a massive overturned menorah in the same grey of stone or ash, together with a pair of swinging, smashed sanctuary lamps. This is, very simply but powerfully, the land of oppression, and Ponnelle's use of recent history does not appear presumptive when the history is one that the work shares—not even when the chorus appear as 1930s orthodox Jews, all in dark grey, with a liberal sprinkling of Homburgs, side-curls, skull-caps, prayer-shawls and Stars of David.

Aron, as he must, fits very easily into this environment: dressed in a morning coat, he is the successful bank employee Schoenberg might have become if he had thrown over his artistic pretensions. Philip Langridge, in a greatly distinguished performance, plays him as the soul of plausibility and smugness: a natty operator who has always foreseen every eventuality and always knows best. A favourite gesture has him holding an arm forward in order to demonstrate that things indeed turned out exactly as he predicted. And how he predicts them! This is, even for Langridge, an astonishing performance, seeming to gain rather than falter in strength, delivering the words with force and precision, sounding always lyrical, never finding the line wilfully awkward. This is essential: Aron, unlike Moses, must appear to be in his element, a fish in water. Langridge conveys this quality so well that the part suddently seems to have been misplaced when given to richer, fruitier tenors.

Theo Adam's Moses is perhaps more in the conventional line of rugged, intemperate prophecy, but it is a great achievement to have let some warmth into the singing without any loss of gravity and fierce purpose. However, one major flaw in the production is that this Moses is still a Michelangelesque figure while all around him belong in the European ghettoes. Of course the Jews do not understand him: he belongs to a quite different script. And so, by providing a ready explanation for Moses's isolation, the staging stems a vital source of conflict: one sees an opera that is more about Jewish steadfastness in the face of adversity than it is about the comprehension of God.

However, the work's more essential meaning is urgently communicated in the dialogues for Moses and Aron, which come across with unusual clarity, thanks partly to the width of the theatre but also to the diction and sensitivity of the principals. Smaller parts, too, are excellently taken in what impresses as a deeply committed, intended performance. The work of the Vienna State Opera Chorus is quite magnificent, at once workmanlike, resilient and luminous. And praise must also go to the 'movement group', who disappointingly—and surely uncomfortably, since they have to daub one another with yellow paint—become themselves the image of the Calf. However, by concentrating the eroticism in the writhing concourse of gilded bodies, Ponnelle leaves the stage free to show the separate episodes of this scene with great lucidity; eqally clear is his handling of the miracles in the first act, despite the excesses of live snakes and multiplied hands. The success of any *Moses und Aron* must depend on the extent to which philosophical argument and drama are mutually beneficial: in Salzburg there is no doubting either the message or the spectacle. (*Times*, 21 August 1987)

Toronto 1993

Arguments about proper opera production, fierce now, were no less so sixty-three years ago, when Schoenberg wrote to the director of the Berlin company due to stage his one-acter *Erwartung*, cautioning him with characteristic severity: 'I believe that you are *not* one of the producers who look at a work only in order to see how to make it into *something quite different*.' 'Such a wrong', he went on, 'could never be greater than if done to me, since while I was composing I had all the scenic effects in mind, seeing them with the utmost precision.' He might have added that they did not stay in that interior theatre: his stage directions stipulate every setting and every move for the solitary character, the unnamed Woman looking for her lover at night in a forest, and his sketches for costume and decor further suggest that what he saw as he wrote was something dark and unsettling in the line of Edvard Munch.

Is a modern director at liberty to go for 'something quite different'? Well, no, of course not—not if that is the intention: Schoenberg's formula begs the question. But 'something quite different' may arise after a director has considered all the evidence contained in the libretto, the music, the stage directions and the drawings, just as different conclusions will always be reached by different singers and conductors who come to interpret the score. No doubt Schoenberg not only saw but heard the piece, during those seventeen days of manic creativity, in the summer of 1909, when he is alleged to have written it down. But what did he hear: Jessye Norman's performance or Anja Silja's? James Levine's or Pierre

Boulez's? The score, even a score as finely detailed as that of *Erwartung*, cannot tell the whole story, and no more can the instructions and guidances presented to the director. If we seem to trust the musical prescriptions more than the dramatic ones, the reason lies more in the relative developments of notation and of perception than in any principle. There are a million ways of performing any phrase in Schoenberg's score, and a million ways of bringing the moon onto the stage. The life of any art depends on there being always the possibility of 'something quite different'.

That is certainly what we get from Robert Lepage in his new production of *Erwartung* for the Canadian Opera Company. The work is being given as an antithesis or sequel to Bartók's *Bluebeard's Castle*, and Lepage takes advantage of the three supernumaries needed for the Bartók opera in order to increase the dramatis personae of Schoenberg's 'monodrama'. When the performance starts, in silence, the Woman is cowering at the side of a bare wall, while a man in a white coat sits ready to take notes. One's heart sinks at the prospect of an 'explanation' of the work as psychoanalytic session: that was where *Erwartung* began, in the experiences of its librettist Marie Pappenheim as a medical student in turn-of-the-century Vienna, not where it ended, or should end. However, the realism is only there to be turned into the chilled, poised surrealism of Lepage's production, which demands, and gets, feats of gymnastic control from his extras. The next time we see the psychiatrist—the set repeatedly darkens to focus on the Woman and allow nimble scene-shifting—he is still sitting, but bizarrely turned through ninety degrees, as if the wall were his floor, while another man, later identified as the Woman's lover, dangles alarmingly through a hole in the wall, supported by only one heel.

But wait a moment. Schoenberg's stage directions unambiguously indicate that the action takes place in a forest. And his letter to the Berlin director insists that it has to be 'a real forest', because the Woman is afraid of the forest, and how could anyone be afraid of something that is not real? How? All too easily, one might want to answer—and add that real things might easily inspire awe, or fright, or alienation, but that fear is much more likely to be engendered by what is not real. This is dangerous ground, but there is some justification for regarding Schoenberg's requirement in this instance as naive, and for concluding that what is most important, to him and to the work, is not the forest but the fear. If we can take that step, then Lepage's resituation of the opera in a coldly lit dream space, where one perturbing image glides into darkness to be replaced by another, can be hailed as a realization of, if not Schoenberg's intentions, then the intentions behind his intentions. What helps settle the issue is not only the precision of the execution but the tightness of Michael Levine's designs and Robert Thomson's lighting.

What further helps is the proof—in the large number of Schoenberg's and Pappenheim's ideas taken on board—that Lepage's ambition is to render the piece as accurately as possible, and not simply to create 'something quite different'. The moon—that potent symbol of Viennese musical expressionism, of light after the sunset of tonality—is present in the form of a wildly floating illuminated globe, which strikingly helps create the double space at the beginning, of open night sky and clinic. Later, in the episode in which the Woman thinks she has stumbled upon her lover's body but then decides that what she saw or felt was only a log, Lepage presents both objects in turn, and so in this case exceeds Schoenberg's literalism, since the stage directions remain silent on how, if at all, the Woman's confusion is to be realized. (This silence is perhaps more evidence of the composer's uncertainty about how to stage fear.) In the fourth scene, which occupies the whole second half of the piece, the house Schoenberg wanted visible at the back of the stage is duly present, in a powerful image: it is a small-scale cutout, with a woman's arm reaching out through one of the windows to lure the lover in.

For the earlier scenes, the production's imagery had been generally static around the Woman, as if we as spectators were watching a Magritte slide-show with a single living, breathing human being caught up in each of the frames. Now, in the final, fullest and climactic scene, the stage begins to draw itself into movement, as an appropriate response to how the libretto and the music begin to root the Woman's fears in her lover's presumed or actual affair with a rival—the woman 'with white arms', as she is repeatedly described, perhaps in a reference to the Tristram story. Once again, Lepage's staging, though visually as far from Schoenberg's milieu as 1930s Paris or Brussels, takes care with the images that are important in the text.

The scene slips to inside the house; the lover is pulled in through the window by the other woman, and they tumble together up the stage and onto a bed. None of this is in the score, of course, but it is plausibly the reason for what is in the score, the reason for the music's gathering pressure towards its bursting point. And there, in a gesture that none but a master of the stage could have achieved without bathos, the Woman kills her lover, using the only possible weapon that could allow both a violent slicing action and an aim at the genitals: a scythe. After this, in the adagio whose length is extraordinary by the quick-flicker tempo standards of the piece, the lover's naked body rolls slowly down the stage, with the Woman stumbling after watchfully as she sings. The whole sequence, from bed through murder to threnody, has an acute force, for which it depends squarely on how well it fits the trajectory of the music.

Contact between the stage and the score is further enforced by Rebecca Blankenship's imposing performance as the Woman: she nurtures her phrases, never makes do with hysteria, and sustains the dislocation from surrounding events that the production seems to require from her—the sense that she is wandering through actions remembered. Richard Bradshaw's conducting effectively feels for the delicacy—the lunar-light delicacy—of the score, though some of the orchestral detail was lost in the wide space of the O'Keefe Centre in Toronto. (*New Yorker*, 15 February 1993)

Amsterdam and Brussels 1995

The two grandest European festivals, Salzburg and Edinburgh, will be featuring Schoenberg this year, in stage productions that were recently tried out in the Low Countries. *Moses und Aron*, due for Salzburg, opened in Amsterdam with a gathering of big names: Pierre Boulez conducting, Peter Stein directing, Chris Merritt as Aron, Karl-Ernst Herrmann designing. The Edinburgh evening, which started out in Brussels, is a portmanteau occasion that moves without a break from *Erwartung* through the *Accompaniment to a Movie Scene* (with movie) to a danced *Verklärte Nacht*, and it too boasts important talents: Anja Silja as the protagonist of *Erwartung*, Klaus Michael Gruber directing it, Antonio Pappano conducting the whole programme. Both ventures hearteningly suggest that Schoenberg's theatre works are beginning to be relished for the very reason they were so long neglected: they challenge the habits of opera houses, and place on performers the onus to exceed.

Moses und Aron may be Wagnerian in its leitmotifs and in its prevalent types of situation—moral debate between two characters and choral spectacle—but Moses' mistrust of imagery is taken into the work as the opera's mistrust of its form and even of itself. Schoenberg probably recognized that his first solution, to compose the piece as an oratorio, was too neat: better to accept the theatrical nature of his material and question it. In the role of Aron (the spelling Schoenberg preferred, in order to avoid having an unlucky thirteen letters in his title) he required a big tenor—the kind of voice that is used to expressing an opera's central passions and purposes, Otello's or Siegmund's, but whose mellifluousness is here opposed by the nature of the vocal line, as well as by the drama, in which ingratiating charm is the character's only quality, and a damning one. We seem to be invited to put more faith in Moses, who speaks principally of God, in absolutes ('Single, eternal, omnipresent, invisible', as the opera begins), and whose utterances, in pitched speech, act to castigate the genre in which they appear. So the brothers are enabled and hampered in equal measure. Aron is a natural operatic being, but in the wrong opera; Moses is not an operatic being at all, but needs opera as the vehicle of his dissent. The work ends with Aron's success, as the people of Israel march off guided by images: the pillars of fire and cloud. But what matters so much more to us, in the great final scene, is Moses' failure.

Schoenberg dismissed the idea that *Moses und Aron* was the dramatization of his own dilemmas: those of an artist who, like Moses, has ideas and, like Aron, must make them public, or of one whose big new idea—the twelve-tone principle—had to be promulgated with the means of the old musical language and to audiences familiar with that language. Indeed, it might be truer to see, in reverse, his creative life as strengthened and disciplined by the example of the Moses-Aron story, whose importance to him is attested not only by the opera but also by a play he wrote shortly before, *Der biblische Weg* (1926–7). In the play, which concerns a modern exodus of Jews from Europe and the United States to a new state, the leader, Max Aruns, is killed by protesters among his own people. However, his Zionist project will survive, under a Joshua-like figure who arrives to take command, and to Schoenberg this was what counted. Through human tragedies—the disappointment of a Moses, the self-hollowing of an Aron, the pride of a Max Aruns—the good idea would unfold as of itself, needing those tragedies, and able to survive them.

For this triumph in *Moses und Aron* to be seen, heard and felt, though, there must be some arching unity through the production, and this the new version so far lacks. Boulez's sense of the score is brave and beautiful, but not so special in sonority as when he recorded it, in 1974, and less inclined to rapid-fire regular rhythm. His distaste for twelve-tone Schoenberg used to express itself in an insistent fury; now he has learned acceptance, which sounds less interesting. Acceptance does leave more room than fury for the choir to project themselves, and the choral contribution in Amsterdam was outstandingly clamorous and luminous, thoroughly prepared, and splendidly sustained. The two main roles were also well taken. Merritt showed immense strength in throwing his voice through the switchbacks of Aron's line, and so using power to the ends of weakness and lack of support. David Pittman-Jennings's Moses was, unusually but aptly, an ordinary man forced to do the extraordinary: not a commanding figure, but a stubborn one. Among the bit parts, those of the Young Man in the first act and the Naked Youth in the second were given the right wild adolescent intransigence by John Graham-Hall.

That Graham-Hall and his companions should all be really naked in the orgy was one of the production's profitless literalisms: naked people onstage (unless the music is very different from Schoenberg's) look vulnerable, like children, not erotic. Nor did we need four straining horses for the arrival of the Ephraimite, or a poor bullock to be threatened by knives in the Dance of the Butchers. (The choreography for the second act, by Ron Thornhill, had altogether too much shivering.) Stein and Herrmann also funked the magic: their pillars of fire and cloud were galvanized chimneys flying aloft. And this was symptomatic of the production's prosaic response: in the scene where Moses and Aron, approaching the Israelites, should appear to overtake one another, the use of the revolves looked like a faithful rendering of the stage directions, not like something happening. Even the one strong visual effect—a burning bush with real flames—was spoiled by being labelled with the tetragrammaton, as if the image were not enough. Possibly this is a production in progress. The massing of the chorus onstage, like the massing of their voices, was often effective, and a start had been made in showing Moses and Aron locked in fraternal struggle: they might make more use of the jagged nook of stage that juts out over the pit—part of a floor whose stark geometry was unnecessarily outlined with yellow and white strip lights.

Erwartung is another magnificent problem. It takes up an archetypal operatic phenomenon, the soprano aria, and exacts the high standards only a leading company could attain, but it counters all routines of the opera house, having no plot, no supporting cast, no room for extravagance other than extravagance of expression, and no obvious companion piece. At the Théâtre de la Monnaie, in Brussels, the answers to these various challenges were enterprising, even thrilling. Antonio Pappano, the theatre's US chief conductor, unfolded a consistently sweeping, surging, searching account of the score. As the unnamed protagonist, Silja proved the continuing force of that harsh, white, steady flare she can bring to her voice: the sound of an emotional wound. The confession of fear, doubt, love and jealousy spilled out of her without her accord, hammered or drawn out of her by the orchestra, and that impression of involuntariness is intensified by the bold, bald stare with which she confronted the audience.

Gruber's production had her as an old woman, shuffling forward on slow traverses of the stage with the help of a stick. Perhaps this singing victim was blind. The only decor consisted of one slumped tree-trunk and a transparent screen of abstracted autumnal woodland, with the singer at first behind this, then in front, and finally, after the curtain had descended, alone on the proscenium. Perhaps we were being introduced to her blindness by this disappearance of the visual world. On the other hand, the growing concentration on the narrating woman gave her—bowed yet still singing—the poignant, exhilarating force of a Beckett heroine.

From *Erwartung* the programme moved to another forest nightscape of despair, love and hope, written a decade earlier: *Verklärte Nacht*. (Less happily the move came by way of the later movie music, done with an utterly inappropriate sequence from *A Night at the Opera*.) Pappano and his orchestra were again outstanding. Right from the start, where the trudging weight invested in simple repetitions of a low D was astonishing, the musical performance had authority, drive and passion. The elegant choreography by Anne Teresa De Keersmaeker, for six couples and two extra girls as children, was capable of sudden gusts of emotion—in, for example, the simultaneous turns of the six men, who had been standing with their backs to us since the piece began, or the inrush of a child to join and separate her parents. The six couples were really only one, whose movements and feelings rippled out through more than two bodies: when, at the climax, there are just two bodies onstage, the result was a luminous and moving love duet, with the hint of rehearsing the loss and separation to come in *Erwartung*. (*New Yorker*, 15 January 1996)

Met 1999

It happens in front of your ears and eyes: a great work comes rolling off the stage. The Metropolitan Opera's production of Schoenberg's *Moses und Aron* was glorious when it was first presented, in February. It is now overwhelming.

Here is one moment, among many. Moses is off up the mountain, receiving the Ten Commandments. The Jews who have followed him are anxious and angry, furious and frustrated: the combination of feelings, very true to life, has been powerfully projected by the music. They look to Aron for some explanation of what has become of Moses, and Aron dreams. Perhaps this, perhaps that. The orchestra plays delicate changes on the lustrous chords of God, making beautiful sounds, and the whole tragedy of the piece is revealed. Moses' idea, of the almighty, invisible God, could be stated in just two chords. The idea becomes theatre only because of Aron's fascination with it—a fascination that leads him to imagine, play, distort.

At this point the last of his distortions, the last of his 'perhaps' speculations, is to suggest that perhaps Moses has been killed by his God. The people, surprised and appalled, repeat the idea: 'Killed by his God?' And as his words come back to him, Aron (Philip Langridge) widens his eyes. It is not that he wishes his brother dead; what delights him, even more than his power over the crowd, is the notion of drama. Here again, on an intimately human scale, is the entire tragedy. Aron's weakness for drama at the expense of truth, as represented by Moses, will lead to an orgy of bestiality in the 'Dance around the Golden Calf' and then to a permanent impasse as the opera ends, decisively and necessarily unfinished.

The moment is a key one, but the strength of this production rests on no single scene and no one performance. It is everywhere. As Moses, John Tomlinson has the same look he had before, of an ordinary man, deficient but unshakably determined. His voice, though, has grown. He sings less, using the freedom of Schoenberg's speech-song to find fiercely expressive regions of growl and lament. There is nothing bombastic. He is a heroic figure, but flawed and gnarled and touching. Langridge fits perfectly with him as a mirror opposite. All the fluency and lyricism this Moses lacks, this Aron has. 'Unrepresentable'—one of Moses' string of adjectives about God, which sounds utterly resolute as Tomlinson delivers it in the German form, 'Unvorstellbare'—becomes in Langridge's supple voice a whole aria. He is persuasive, capricious, unrepentant, clever in everything except knowledge of himself: with his voice and his eyes and his nimble movements, he provides all the role requires, and he makes each word count.

Smaller parts are finely done. Matthew Polenzani projects an ardent tenor as the Youth. Sergei Koptchak makes a robust, no-nonsense Priest. Jennifer Welch, Heidi Skok, Andrea Trebnik and Malin Fritz tune their music beautifully together as the Four Naked Virgins. Graham Vick's production is running more smoothly than before, and Ron Howell's choreography in the orgy fits the music, being at once brutal and clean, with moments of eeriness and shock. The members of the chorus are as physically present in the action as the dancers, and their singing is magnificent, at the thrilling close to the first act and everywhere else. As for the orchestra, it is impossible to imagine the score sounding better, fuller, more expressive or more dramatic. James Levine, conducting, encourages his players to render it all: the hot, intense sound of one instrument at a time, like a desert horizon against Moses' voice in the opening scene, the luscious Viennese waltzes, the weird tones in the orgy of mandolin, tuned percussion and high woodwinds (a wild leap from E flat clarinet), the tightly contained passion in solos for violin and cello. You just have to forget to expect major chords, and listen to what wonderful and meaningful sounds music can make without them. The final orchestral passage—the yelling unison string melody that accompanies Moses' hard self-recognition—makes the taut, sinuous, inevitable line of a whiplash. (*New York Times*, 30 September 1999)

five British composers

Dominic Muldowney

It could never have been predicted that Mrs Thatcher would preside like an Astraea over a renaissance of British music, but the past seven years have proved astonishingly productive, and the summer festival at the South Bank is reflecting some of the dazzle. Just twenty-four hours after the premiere of Birtwistle's new opera, the London Sinfonietta were back with a programme of new and very new music by younger composers. Apart from two contrasted dawnscapes, Simon Holt's ominous . . . *era madrugada* and George Benjamin's celebratory *At First Light*, all the works came from the past year or so.

Dominic Muldowney's new Sinfonietta is an exceedingly smart piece. It takes on the challenge that Schoenberg took on in his First Chamber Symphony, that of creating a continuity that functions both as a sonata allegro and as a complete four-movement composition: in other words, one gets to the end of the first movement and finds one has reached the end of the whole. *Rheingold* might be another example, though there, of course, when one comes to the end one is just in time for the real beginning. Muldowney anticipates Wagner by starting with something that is both beginning and end: a tick-tock downward phrase makes an opening gambit, while the brass rush up in a staccato jazzy closure, a gesture that will often be repeated in varied forms.

Then the machine is off. It slows for the 'second subject', marked by solos for oboe and viola, and speeds up for the scherzo cum development, then eases itself towards a moment of repose for strings with piano and marimba, the only passage where the juggling with tonality almost relaxes into concord. But most of the recapitulation-finale is as tricksy, rhythmically surprising and harmonically needling as this work requires. The difference from Schoenberg, whose parallel work seems to hover in the wings, is that Muldowney is not sure the game is a serious one. But this is not at all a frivolous work: he is very serious indeed about the business of playing the game, and his own appeal to Stravinsky rather than Schoenberg as mentor is entirely apt. This is as fascinating a recomposition of the past as his concertos and quartet of recent years. It is also a very virtuoso piece, and the Sinfonietta, under Diego Masson, performed it exhilaratingly.

Also on the programme was Steve Martland's mind-numbing *Orc*, with Frank Lloyd as solo hornist, and Mark-Anthony Turnage's marvellously curious *On all fours*, which is a Baroque suite and much else. It is typical of him—or could be of Muldowney—to have an Allemande recalling a flute-clarinet duet from *The Rite of Spring*. (*Times*, 9 August 1986)

Brian Ferneyhough

Like a nude ice-skater, Brian Ferneyhough places a great deal of faith in his technique. He also exposes himself to an inspection avoided by so many composers who cover themselves with earlier forms and manners. There is nothing 'quasi' here, nothing 'neo', no quotation marks. Even the notorious complexity of his music seems more an avoidance of backward reference than the obfuscation often inferred—though such charges are beginning to wear rather thin now that he is emerging from his forests of heavily qualified demisemiquavers to execute elegant figures in an open-air of his own discovery.

His recent *Etudes transcendentales* for soprano and instrumental quartet is a thoroughly remarkable essay in daring, being not only the lynchpin in his concert-length *Carceri d'invenzione* cycle but also, by aspiration, a companion piece to *Le Marteau sans maître* and *Pierrot lunaire*. These are tough acts to follow, and if there were any doubts about the success of the work, Ferneyhough would be feeling chilly in some pretty uncomfortable places. But there are none. Simply that. We are dealing here with something very special and rare, something which eases back, against so great a resistance, the boundary of the beautiful. The journey, from Schoenberg to Boulez to Ferneyhough, is one of a lyric impulse ever more embattled, and the world of the new piece is, as the heading of the penultimate movement has it, 'cold but under great pressure'. The composer refers to a line of Trakl, 'The pain face in the stone', to suggest this emotion that is petrified (in both senses), and his nine poems, by Ernst Meister and Alrun Moll, pick at ancient, distant, icy, but still furiously alive, images—as furiously alive as his own wheeling oboe solo with vocal support, his brilliantly numb, dark song with harpsichord and pizzicato cello, his duet for voice and a flute, at first aerated by scale passages, his adagissimo of muted congealing around a vocal part of soft, detached sounds and his quite extraordinary finale. This opens with a strident, high, unison F sharp, a signal of music squeezed to the limits, and ends with a resigned cessation of the war to weld music and words together. Jane Manning was, by this stage, clearly in trouble from a throat infection, but she had sung like a manic angel to press home the importance of this work, very eloquently aided by Lontano under Odaline de la Martinez. (*Times*, 12 November 1986)

Robert Simpson

Symphonies, even ninth symphonies, are no longer the rareties they were twenty years ago, but Robert Simpson still stands powerfully alone in his symphonic single-mindedness, in the insistence with which his music presents itself, in his total lack of pretence or conscious irony. The first performance of his Ninth Symphony last night by the Bournemouth Symphony Orchestra under Vernon Handley was predictably an emphatic occasion.

Also predictable by now are Simpson's symphonic premises. His own note refers to Bruckner and Bach, both of them clear points of reference; his description of the first part of his immense four-movements-in-one structure as a vast chorale prelude is apt, but it could apply to much else in a work so directed by a purposeful bass line and so solidly ordered in its counterpoint; and equally the spacious opening and the massive harmonic architecture can be related to Bruckner, though it was hard to detect the specific homage the composer challenges his audience to identify. Other ancestors, however, are very evidently lending support, not least Sibelius in the ostinatos of gathering tension and Nielsen in the energized angularity and the inextinguishable force of the major climaxes: both are, of course, composers on whom Simpson has written with the insight of a comrade at arms. More surprising is the echo of Tippett, in the first part particularly, thought perhaps this is merely an adventitious result of working so much with fourths.

However, the shadow of Shostakovich, which darkens over a string elegy at the midway point and again over the final slow, ethereal coda, is more pervasive, and perhaps more indicative of the compulsion that lies behind this music. Though Simpson seems to work naturally with assumptions that were imposed on Shostakovich—those of music as essentially tonal, progressive and even heroic in its aspirations—one senses something of the suppression that has been necessary for him to achieve that 'naturalness'. One senses it not only in the symphony's bleaker moments but right through in the striking absence of large thematic ideas. Given that the work lasts for more than three quarters of an hour, it is extraordinarily lacking in tangible tunes: Simpson's effort is all towards the harmonic growth of his music, with the result that melodies tend to be journeys through pitches made inevitable by the harmony.

The work was conducted by Handley with all the required energy and largeness of thought, though it will surely receive performances that are better played. (*Times*, 9 April 1987)

Michael Nyman

Michael Nyman is not so much a composer, more a malfunctioning compact disc player, which stores and jumbles snippets of music and then keeps repeating them until you think you're going mad, going mad, going mad. Of course, this is standard minimalist practice, but in Nyman it has a particular charm, thanks partly to the occasional wit of his musical allusions (so often a ground bass of Baroque solidity will suddenly start sounding like the backing for an early Beach Boys number, and sometimes one smiles) and thanks also to the crudity of his sound world. In the company of Steve Reich, Philip Glass and John Adams, Nyman is the poor relation: his raw amplified mix of buzzy saxophones, strings and metallized piano is at the furthest possible remove from their slick, glamorous ensembles, and the bright dancing of scratchy violins on the surface of his textures provides a cheerful homespun note. US sophistication has become English eccentricity.

Perhaps this is what has endeared him to an audience composed entirely of people with shaven heads wearing charcoal grey suits two sizes too big for them. Last night at Sadler's Wells they turned out to hear him and his ensemble perform an hour-long concert version of his score for the new Peter Greenaway film, where what drowns musically by numbers is a four-bar extract from the slow movement of Mozart's *Sinfonia Concertante* for violin and viola. This parentage was clearest in the opening section featuring the string ensemble of three violins and cello, where gestures from the Mozart were isolated and given three times each with terrible and frustrating inevitability. But there were echoes too in the other movements, including what was perhaps the 'Wedding Tango' (the programme notes were carelessly unhelpful), which sounded like the eighth funeral procession of a steamy day in Costa Rica. The score also has instances of Nyman's neat knack of launching out on harmonic progressions that appear predictable but then turn corners into labyrinths: one might wish for more of these and rather fewer of the hammered eight-bar periods, but that would be to rob Nyman of his street-kid punch. Besides *Drowning by Numbers*, there were mementoes of earlier Greenaway-occasioned assaults in selections from *The Draughtsman's Contract* and *A Zed and Two Noughts*. (*Times*, 12 September 1988)

Nicholas Maw

And an hour and a half later they were still playing. . . . Clocking in at a hundred and two minutes, Nicholas Maw's *Odyssey* must be one of the longest continuous stretches of music ever conceived for the concert hall, and its transgression of the normal bounds takes one into a quite new musical world where, in a Wagnerian or a Proustian way, internal relationships are far more important than any connections with the universe outside. This was already apparent when the piece enjoyed or suffered a three-quarters performance at the 1987 Proms. Now, after a quite heroically sustained full account in the Festival Hall by the BBC Symphony Orchestra under Richard Bernas, the work's individuality is even more obvious.

So although there are plentiful memories of other music—of Tippett in dancing violins over distant horns, of Strauss, Bruckner or Mahler in the immense climaxes, of Bartók in string fugatos, of Sibelius in the alternately dour and abrupt gestures at the start of the big slow movement, of Berg in the poignantly adult arrangement of nursery tunes, of Copland in the rising fifths of his declamatory manner, of Wagner unavoidably in the final settling into *Rheingold* E flat—the terms are so changed by the time scale that there would be no question of pastiche even without Maw's ability to reimagine things one easily thinks outworn.

Of course, the two things go together. A work which aims to exceed the excessive, to challenge late Romantic symphonism on its own ground, can only do so on the basis of ideas which measure up to the standards and then go further. For instance, the most gigantic climax of the lot is a hair-raising moment, with the principal horn whooping stark mad (David Lee thoroughly deserved his solo ovation) while piccolo trumpets burn white-hot at the top of their range. But commentary of this sort is abashed not only by the length of the piece but also by the length of its writing: a work which took its composer fifteen years to complete, and which is both the route and the report of his creative development from his late thirties to his early fifties, is hardly to be discussed in a few paragraphs after a couple of hearings.

Nevertheless, it seems clear that *Odyssey* is not only an unusual but also a complex and majestic achievement, magnificent as well as magniloquent, and that far from being an attempt to re-establish the old values (despite Maw's being a son of Grantham), it is a response to symphonic rhetoric as something almost vanished and to be found now only through extreme effort. Maw is as distant as may be from cheapjack neoromanticism; this is, rather, continuing Romanticism, but needing in the present age exceptional resources of time and imagination if it is to retain its validity.

One of the works included in the related afternoon concert was Maw's choral setting of *The Ruin*, that fragmentary eighth-century vision of Roman walls in dilapidation. His project in *Odyssey* is nothing less than the construction of a new Aquae Sulis from within the Dark Ages, and future performances will, though inevitably rare, equally inevitably testify as this one did to the work's extraordinariness and scope. (*Times*, 12 April 1989)

Lachenmann

Widely esteemed in mainland Europe from the late 1960s onwards, Helmut Lachenmann was slow to gain performances and appreciation in Britain and the USA, where the view stemming from the writings of Theodor Wiesengrund Adorno—that music, inescapably reflecting the disintegration in western societies, must advance into the previously unheard, marginal and rejected, avoiding the easy options of regression to older norms or compromise with popular music—had less hold. By the end of the century, though, his importance was inescapable.

Mouvement (vor der Erstarrung) and Salut für Caudwell

The ICA's concert series, returning for another summer season of Sunday nights, can be relied on to be stimulating. This first evening was devoted to the music of the fifty-year-old German composer Helmut Lachenmann, who has been played and talked about with increasing partisanship on the Continent, but who had not been much performed before in this country.

Lachenmann's starting-point would seem to be the familiar one that the house of music has long lain uninhabited, that all a composer today can do is to kick over the dust, shake a few bones and listen to the rodents behind the walls. These things he does with some assiduousness. The most characteristic sound of his music, to judge from the two pieces played on Sunday night, is a soft dry rattle, the noise very often of instructments being played in unconventional ways: air blown tonelessly through wind instruments, palms brushed over guitars, violins bowed on the neck. Lachenmann's problem is that people will go on listening for something pleasant, and it is awfully hard to avoid providing it.

His (*Mouvement vor der Erstarrung*) for eighteen-piece ensemble is quite successful in the avoidance: it was laid out by Circle under Ingo Metzmacher as a landscape of rustlings, scrapes, electric bells and pointless percussion toccatas. But in *Salut für Caudwell*, for two guitars, it was difficult to remain entirely impervious to beauty. As played by Wilhelm Bruck and Theodor Ross, Lachenmann's marginal effects produced magical sounds: the sounds of two small chambers echoing with noise and chiming. And the very end, with the desert journey finally reaching some quiet brushed flamenco rhythms, had a poignancy quite beyond the composer's intentions, at least if one is to take seriously his appeal here to the aesthetics of Christopher Caudwell. In introducing the piece he spoke of composing not sounds but 'ways of hearing'. Sounds, though, may be easier to control. (*Times*, 8 July 1986)

Harmonica

With a coloratura soprano and a tuba as the two soloists, this BBC Symphony Orchestra evening at the Festival Hall was a concert from the outer edges: yesterday's music and today's (extremes indeed, since nothing now seems more alien than what was written 15 years ago), Italian exuberance and German weight, finesse and crudity.

The older pieces were Maderna's *Aura* and Zimmermann's *Photoptosis*, both done by this orchestra during the Boulez years, though here given gleaming and, in the cse of the Zimmermann, riotous new life under Peter Eötvös. This performance was enough to persuade one that *Photoptosis* is some kind of masterpiece, beginning with veils of quarter-tones, mostly from between the notes of the piano keyboard, to suggest a tenuous grasp on new territory, then falling through the dismissive fanfare of Beethoven's Ninth Symphony into a pool of more or less submerged quotations from Scriabin, plainsong, Wagner, Tchaikovsky and Bach, and finally mowing home in savage noisiness.

Also mightily impressive were the two newer pieces, Donatoni's *Arias* and Lachenmann's *Harmonica*, the former a sequence of exultant, frenzied love songs in which the skimming and scrambling vocal line is accompanied by heavy, charging orchestral gestures. Sarah Leonard voiced the excitement with a cool freshness.

Donatoni's superb technique would perhaps be scorned by Lachenmann, who comes from the punk end of contemporary music and in *Harmonica* creates a non-concerto in which both the tuba player and the orchestra use a lot of banal and improper sounds: there is, in particular, a great deal of breathing in this score, justifying Lachenmann's description of his solo instrument as a giant lung.

But there is another important fact to the tuba's personality. Because the instrument conceals much of the player, including most importantly his face, it seems almost to be playing itself, like a ventriloquist's dummy. In *Harmonica* this produces the extraordinary effect of an orchestra being led by a silver monster, which shuffles and grunts and squeaks and belches, and finally delivers an oracular prouncement in words from Ernst Toller: 'Mensch, erkenn Dich doch, das bist Du'. What we are, the work suggests, is a farrago of meaningless trifles; though unregenerated humanists will have taken some comfort from the stamina and virtuosity of James Gourlay behind the presumptuous coil of piping. (*Times*, 5 November 1987)

Gran torso and Serynade

Occasionally there comes along a concert that takes you by surprise and starts you listening all over again. It happened on Thursday night at Miller Theater when, as part of Helmut Lachenmann's weeklong residency, the programme included his classic *Gran torso* for string quartet, performed by members of the Ensemble Sospeso, his much more recent piano work *Serynade* and his teacher Luigi Nono's late composition *La lontananza nostalgica utopica futura* ('The Utopian Future in the Nostalgic Distance') for violinist and recordings.

Gran torso is music of noises: scrapes, taps and rustlings achieved by means of painstaking notation that prescribes the necessary actions. The viola player draws the bow slowly over the instrument with almost zero pressure, to make a sound that stays close to or below the threshold of audibility—a sound, therefore, as much seen as heard. Violinists generate patterings with the wood of the bow bouncing on the strings. The cellist digs in to create a guttural rasp.

There is something provocative here: a wilful misuse of the most prestigious medium in western music. But that was only a very small part of the story as told by the Sospeso players: Mark Menzies and Calvin Wiersma on violins, Lois Martin on viola and Christopher Finckel on cello. Their execution of the sounds was breathtaking, even lovely, and they also conveyed unerringly and rivetingly the special time sense of Lachenmann's music, how it moves steadily and quietly on with hardly any propulsive force. This is music that, refreshingly, is not trying to persuade us of anything. It is just there, an invitation to sharpen our perceptions. The audience was rapt.

If *Gran torso* is very old music in its references, backed by the two or three centuries of tradition, here it seemed also, and more so, utterly new. Where so much music of the last thirty years is borne down by the burden of history, in this work one feels the composer's own weight as, with precision, agility and care, he manoeuvres himself on the cliff-face of the past. It is free music, and liberating.

So is *Serynade*, which lives in the same hovering time and also displays remarkable sonic invention, even if the virtuosity of both composer and performer is more regular. Its chief features are ghost resonances produced when the pianist nimbly moves from a loud chord to silently hold down other keys, these resonances enhanced by amplification. There are also flowing ribbons of fast figuration that seem to blow in from another possible world and disappear again, as well as single notes, intensely insisted upon, and some effects toward the end made by fingers on the strings—a touch from the composer's earlier self.

Lachenmann wrote the work for his wife, Yukiko Sugawara-Lachenmann, whose first initial is responsible for the little distortion in the title. She played it here, with magnificent dexterity, strength and ease.

The Nono piece was superbly done by Menzies. Much of the part consists of very high notes, to be maintained at an even low level for a long time: it is at once strenuous and unassuming, and Menzies found its true character. He also made it sing, projecting consistent beauty of tone. And he was effectively unpretentious in executing the drama of the work, pacing from one music stand to another in a journey of search. The end, when he walked off still playing, was a touching farewell. (*New York Times*, 9 April 2001)

Mouvement again

Who is the most influential European composer of the moment? A few names come to mind, but none more immediately than that of Helmut Lachenmann. Many of the most energetic composers under forty have studied with him, and his music has been a subject of intense debate and excitement for the last quarter-century and more. His importance as a provocative teacher and guide alone should have brought his work more attention than it has so far had in the US. Perhaps the neglect can be blamed on so banal a thing as the way he looks in photographs, often having the austere expression of a man racked by anxiety and oblivious to charm. The image fits all too well with the vulgar idea of contemporary European modernism as crabbed and embattled. Listen to the music, though, and you hear a different story.

Take *Mouvement (vor der Erstarrung)*, where the instruments of a mixed ensemble are more often used in unconventional ways: there are a lot of whirrings, scrapings, knocks and breathings. But not only are these noises beautifully made in themselves, they also add up to a bracing musical design. They are the noises of instruments discovering new possibilities within themselves, and using those possibilities to connect. Indeed, so strong is this impulse that what is superficially destructive and negative—the sound of instruments being brushed, tapped and blown in ways unlikely to produce normal musical tone—becomes constructive, even thrillingly so.

Lachenmann simply draws the obvious lesson from the rise of the percussion section in the music of the last hundred years. Instead of seeking to maintain a nineteenth-century hierarchy of tone producers (strings and winds) over noisemakers (percussion), he finds ways to deal with all the instruments equally. That means removing, generally, the advantage the strings and winds had in making presentable notes and chords; it is, to that extent, a levelling down. But it is also, and much more so, a levelling up. New sounds and new combinations stand revealed. Even more important, the instruments can join together on an equal footing. The gaps between percussion and others—and the gaps within the others, between strings and winds—are closed. Sounds of similar kinds, whether a soft, continuous rustling or a sudden abrasion, can come from anywhere.

This omnipresence of sheer sound contributes to the poetry of *Mouvement*, which seems like Caliban's isle 'full of noises', and the availability of similar sonorities in almost any instrument or section contributes to the formal strategy, allowing the work to become the music of instruments listening to one another. Sounds and gestures ripple through the ensemble: soft but insistent ringing trills like those of electric bells, a high note emerging and staying, wooden knocks and—drawing all the instruments most closely together—a moto perpetuo full of vim and ostinatos. This arrives about a third of the way through the twenty-two-minute piece, soon vanishes and is then tensely awaited before its rampant return toward the end.

Lachenmann's own understanding of this process seems to accord with the grim face he presents to the world. The title can be translated 'Movement (Before Paralysis)', and the composer's note begins by describing the piece as 'a music of dead movements, almost of final quivers', and soon invokes the unappealing Kafkaesque image of 'a beetle floundering helplessly on its back'.

Certainly the music can be heard that way. But it can also seem restorative, outgoing and optimistic: optimistic because it does not deny or flee but rather embraces and transcends the state of cultural disintegration in which we find ourselves, and because it uses materials that are not hard and leathery with age but soft, supple and fresh.

What he is after, Lachenmann has said, is music that 'does not require a privileged intellectual training but can rely uniquely upon its compositional clarity and logic'. The best of his work achieves just that. It comes as if from nowhere, takes you firmly by the hand and will not let go until it has shown you things you could not have suspected. (*New York Times*, 4 November 2001)

mapping Mtsensk

Shostakovich's opera *The Lady Macbeth of Mtsensk* was first performed in Leningrad in 1934, and for two years was highly prized as a major work by the Soviet Union's outstanding young composer. Then Stalin saw it. The piece was denounced and withdrawn, and though Shostakovich was able to put out a modified version in 1963, the original version was not seen again until after his death.

English National Opera 1987

The official banning of Shostakovich's second opera has often been seen as evidence that Stalin had no ear for music; but perhaps the father of his people saw and heard right enough what was going on, and detected in *Lady Macbeth* a four-act shriek of outrage, an explosion of total cynicism. Such is the shocking effect of the new English National Opera production, which brings the original version of the work to the British stage for the first time.

This delayed arrival, though it has had different causes, is just one of many parallels between Shostakovich's opera and the exactly contemporary *Lulu* of Alban Berg. Both works take their heroines from empty marriage to amoral ecstasy to degradation and death; both have a host of subsidiary characters presented in caricature; both suggest that the only dependable relationship between people is one of unmediated lust, and that the only proof of lust is the willingness to murder. Then again, Stalin ended the career of *Lady Macbeth* the month after death ended that of Berg, and so prevented the completion of *Lulu*.

There is, however, a crucial difference between the operas. Where Berg is prepared still to countenance love—of his heroine and of death, and finally of both—Shostakovich is not. Sergey is throughout a bull male, kin to the Drum Major in Berg's other opera, and his connection with Katerina is nothing when it is not being physically expressed and noisily accompanied in the orchestra: the rhythm of copulation, which is also the rhythm of marching, drives a great deal of this opera. And that is another central departure from *Lulu*. Berg places himself onstage in the character of Alwa, but we hear Shostakovich in the pit, as the hugely magnified ghost of a cinema pianist thumping out motor rhythms to pretend he is in control.

This cinematic nature of *Lady Macbeth* finds an excellent response in certain aspects of David Pountney's production: in the fixed, dispassionate expressions of Jospehine Barstow as Katerina, for example, or in the sudden mad tableaux of workers and policemen. But at other points the attempt to mirror the music's power and rhythm leads to bathos. The crashing climax to the great funeral march-passacaglia, for instance, is not much helped by a dozen women throwing bunches of flowers to the ground in unison. What is also unfortunate is the overdose of angst in Stefanos Lazaridis's set. We are not in a bourgeois household but a meat warehouse, a dark grey and steel-laddered box hung with carcasses. Accordingly, the Ismailovs' servants are converted into butchers, and the savagery of the music is given a false turn: Shostakovich is delivering a Gogolian, vituperative, appalling, clear-sighted challenge to the whole human race, not a defence of vegetarianism.

The cast is led by Barstow, in a role where her highly strung ardour can flare all the way from depression to manic exultancy: hers is not, of course, at all a Russian voice, but she makes the part entirely her own, not least by the dead-cold intensity of her acting. Willard White is a bleak-hearted but roundly sung villain. Jacques Trussel rampages as Sergey, and Stuart Kale is effectively ineffectual as Zinovy. There are also striking cameo appearances from Maria Moll, Malcolm Rivers, Wills Morgan and Dennis Wicks, to mention only a few in this torrent of nihilism. (*Times*, 23 May 1987)

Met 1994

The stage is full of machines. This is the first presentation of Shostakovich's *Lady Macbeth of Mtsensk* at the Met since 1935, and a huge crane rears up at the back of the set. There are scenes featuring gantries, an earthmover, an automobile for the hapless husband to drive off in, a crushed replica of it to store his body. And all the while we see, cavorting and killing, those other machines: human beings.

Lady Macbeth is a savage piece, a hysterical piece. It has been remembered in the history books as the opera which—soon after Stalin had seen it (or most of it), in 1936, by which time it had been playing in Russia and abroad for two years—was fiercely condemned in a *Pravda* editorial, removed from the stage (two productions were then running in Moscow), and taken as the occasion for a crackdown on the composer. Now, at the Met, we can all hear the alarm bells that must have rung in the Great Leader's ears, and we can hear, too, how the anonymous *Pravda* writer was not such a bad music critic in remarking how 'snatches of melody, embryos of a musical phrase drown, struggle free, and disappear again in the din, the grinding, the squealing'. That is pretty much how the score sounds—if we interpret 'melody' to mean any kind of lyrical cantabile, as opposed to the perky little tunes on which Shostakovich based what James Conlon, conducting, reveals indeed as mostly din, grind and squeal.

Soulfulness is all but extinguished because, in this gallery of bullies, villains and hypocrites, souls are all but extinguished: the rare visions of a less driven, riven world arise around musical reminiscences of *Boris Godunov*, and they are generally slammed shut fairly fast—perhaps nervously fast, as if they were temptations that had to be rejected. For Shostakovich the notion of human aspiration singing itself out in G minor had been revealed as an illusion by both the great revolutions of his time: Stravinsky's and Lenin's. *The Rite of Spring* had asserted that music's business was not with the expression of an individual psyche but with the structure and action of society, and to that extent, its composer had shown himself a faithful follower of Marx: at least, that was the import his message had in the way it was understood and transmitted by Shostakovich.

Lady Macbeth is a post mortem on Romanticism. What had been the great sustaining metaphor of Romantic music—love—is in this opera displaced by brute sex. The only character who makes any attempt to reveal an inner life is the antiheroine of the title, Katerina Ismailova, and what she shows of herself is a wasteland of Chekhovian boredom, musically voiced in a kind of Soviet blues. Maria Ewing's performance in this role is a key element in the Met triumph. She starts out slumped in a flabby armchair, singing with a passionate disdain—the passion in the attack or the gleam she periodically injects into the notes that otherwise come out of her mouth and pass her by, almost as if they belonged to someone else. And that is how she goes on. She does not get excited by her serial murders: of her father-in-law, her husband, her sexual rival. The only moment when her voice is thoroughly, violently present and engaged comes in the yelping of the first bedroom scene with Sergey, the labourer with and for whom she goes on her track of homicides. Life for this Katerina is either orgasm or nothing. Mostly, of course, it is nothing—though this nothing, as Ewing expresses it, never for an instant ceases to fix attention on her singing and her person.

The emptiness inside Katerina is one element in Shostakovich's autopsy; another is the ripe vitality of movement in his score. Rhythm here is, most frequently, mechanical repetition, and the musical forms that the nineteenth century had made to seem agencies of pleasurable relaxation and social intercourse—the dance forms of waltz, polka, galop—are pressed to a point where they suggest rather the tyranny of a military regime or the control of a circus whip. They do not swing hearts; they drill bodies. And bodies are what Graham Vick, the director, brings onto the stage, in a production that combines amazement with parodic self-deflation. Vick's sense of the outrageous is finely tuned. When Katerina's lascivious longings are answered by the advent of a set of hunks who could have stepped off jeans posters, together with a row of other men in shower cubicles, or when the double bed of adultery arrives—with sheets of shocking pink—in the embrace of a fork-lift truck, or when the funeral party goes off with candle-carrying mourners solemnly gliding up and down through the air, or when serried policemen show off lurid T-shirts under their uniforms, the production is laughing at itself, so we are encouraged to laugh with it, and with the piece. And that laughter keeps us in there, keeps us mindful of the cynicism and the viscerality.

Vick and his production team—designer Paul Brown, lighting designer Nick Chelton, choreographer Ron Howell—are all making their house debuts, and they bring more life to this stage than it has seen in years. They use its space, by means of their machinery, their vibrant colour, their aerial ballet and their sense of spectacle as comedy. They also get around the chief problem of space: lack of immediacy. Partly because of the lighting, partly because of the way the set is tilted, and partly because of the effrontery of so much that goes on, this is a show that, emphatically, comes across. Apart from one early scene of happy peasants and workers casting down red roses, there is no totalitarian camp. By placing the action in the 1950s, as it seems from Ewing's flaming dress of red-dashed yellow and from items of interior decor, Vick and his colleagues are able to give a quick image of the bourgeois dream from anywhere. And the jumbling of the code objects is right for a piece so stylized: the eternal summer sky is painted across the walls and the many doors; the neatly rolled lawn is a carpet. The irruption into this environment of heavy industrial equipment is, again, a nice equivalent to the way the music goes, at the point where the opening private scene, largely Katerina's, is invaded by the chorus (singing with excellent fullness and spirit) and by blasting ostinato.

The opera is mainly about this opposition between the vacant, unrooted, washed-out, frustrated individual and the vigorous commonality, and since Katerina is onstage almost throughout—and always then dominant—there is not much glory in most of the supporting roles. There are moments for a Shabby Peasant (Dennis Petersen, shambling well) and an Old Convict, the messenger of resolution, if not of comfort, in the final act (his solo beautifully sung by Alexander Anisimov), but only the lover and the father-in-law have any more consistent importance. Vladimir Galusin, the Sergey, has a very Russian tenor, which he uses to convey not emotional fragility but a springing natural urgency and a zeal for sex. The dark grey bass of Sergei Koptchak, in the part of the father-in-law, is all gloom and disapproval. Having these Slavic singers on board provides some justification for performing the opera in the original language, though here surely was a case for the Met to make an exception and translate. *Lady Macbeth* is not about getting the right phonemes.

Its concern is rather, as Stalin surely understood, with continuing the revolution by other means. 1917 had unthroned authorities; *Lady Macbeth* mocks everything except desolation. There is no reason to suppose Shostakovich was not committed to the revolution at this time. Several of his works of the 1920s are overtly political, and if there are signs in them of bad faith, the reasons are over-eagerness and lack of precedents more than compulsion. *Lady Macbeth* perpetuates the overturning of the old world and their search for the new: it is in this search, as the convicts shuffle off, that the opera comes finally to a note of grim hope—of hope that might, at the 1934 premiere, have included the hope of more Shostakovich operas to come. Two years later that possibility ended, because Stalin was not interested in revolution and had a fair contempt for hope.

Hence the inevitable domino-fall of ironies. A revolutionary composer, among the first raised in a revolutionary society, was castigated by the leaders of that society. Forced, then, to write about the only society left to him—that of himself—he became the outstanding example of everything he had earlier spurned and derided, the outstanding creator of music as individual expression. *Lady Macbeth* may leave us with little solace, but it does leave us with the irreverent, exuberant, fearless image of Shostakovich before that last long martyrdom. (*New Yorker*, 28 November 1994)

Stockhausen

In the early 1970s Karlheinz Stockhausen was the most highly regarded member of the brilliant generation that had emerged soon after World War II. His renown depended on works that were already old, such as his electronic piece *Gesang der Jünglinge* (1955–6) and *Gruppen* for three orchestras (1955–7), but it held, and large concert halls would fill for his works. He was an inevitable presence at the great European festivals of new music, which still existed, if with less authority than they had enjoyed in the 1950s and 1960s. (See the report below from La Rochelle and Royan in 1973.) But the excitement had been partly that of a composer constantly beginning again. After he had settled into a mature style based on slow melody in long, loose forms, and particularly after he had embarked on the enormous project of dramatizing this style in a sequence of science-fantasy operas, both his audience and his critical reputation steeply declined.

London 1971

The English Bach Festival and the Institute of Contemporary Arts gave us five consecutive evenings with Stockhausen, a rare opportunity to catch up with his recent thought and works. Since his intuitive music depends so much on close contact over a long period between composer and performers, the four concerts given by his chosen singers and players were specially valuable. Apart from a short piano piece, all of the music played dates from the last four years, and three of the programmes were devoted to works not previously heard in Britain: *Stimmung*, *Hymnen* (version with instrumentalists) and *Mantra*.

In the 1950s Stockhausen's music arose naturally from theoretical considerations of musical time and from experiments into the nature of sound; his theory today presents a more confused picture. His lecture at the ICA on 'Four Criteria of Electronic Music' was substantially the same as a radio talk he wrote ten years ago, and was likewise illustrated by reference to *Kontakte*. It had little relevance to the more recent *Hymnen*. Also, where at the lecture he said that 'these are the sort of discussions I like to have, not talk about Zen Buddhism and aleatory music', in his programme notes for *Stimmung* and *Mantra* we find him writing about communicating with higher planes of consciousness, the Vedas and the Upanishads. Then again, when he introduced *Mantra* before the performance we had none of this but instead a twenty-minute technical analysis of the work. The conflict seems to be between Stockhausen the artist and Stockhausen the guru, the intellectual and the spiritual, the west and the east.

Unfortunately the contradictions are carried over into the music, which—particularly in the case of *Stimmung* and *Mantra*, most closely linked with Stockhausen's mysticism—seems to be falling between all possible stools. Perhaps Stockhausen's Wagnerian egocentricity will not let him relinquish conscious control over his work, which would be necessary for it truly to be a 'speedy aircraft making for the Cosmos and the Divine'.

Stimmung is for six vocalists who intone into microphones. Each singer uses only one note (from the overtones of B natural) throughout the work's seventy-five minutes, although he or she may slide above or below to some extent for brief periods. The number of singers singing at a time is continually shifting. The vocal material consists of 'magic words' repeated over and over again, so that the sound has a pulsating quality, and is usually sung with a nasal inflection, recalling oriental chant. The work proceeds as a transmission of magic words, which individuals introduce and others take up, in combination with what they were singing previously. There is also spoken material: selections from the erotic writings of Karlheinz Stockhausen and days of the week in English and German. The hypnotic effect was broken every few minutes by risible sequences; the Collegium Vocale Köln have given more than a hundred performances, but they still found the jokes funny.

Mantra is Stockhausen's most recently completed work, fully notated for two pianos with electronic modulation operated by the pianists, who are also required to play tiny cymbals and woodblocks. The work received a dedicated performance from the brothers Kontarsky, who gave the premiere in Donaueschingen last October. Electronic transformation was used to produce gamelan-like sonorities (close to those of a prepared piano), glissandos and some rather unpleasant sounds which resembled what might be obtained from very poor loudspeakers. The work is founded on a thirteen-note series (Stockhausen calls it the 'mantra'), which is played three hundred and twelve times in various transpositions and combined with a series of thirteen qualities (in which are included modes of attack, trills and introductory figures). But this is not a return to the serial methods of the 1950s. Then these procedures were used to elaborate forms in which melodic and rhythmic figures never returned, whereas repetition is of the essence of *Mantra*.

The other two concerts were given by Stockhausen's regular instrumental group: Aloys Kontarsky (piano), Christoph Caskel (percussion), Harald Bojé (electronium) and Peter Eötvös (electrochord—a multistringed board which may be bowed, plucked or struck, sometimes betraying the nationality of its inventor-player by sounding like a cimbalom). All four were involved in *Prozession* and *Hymnen*, which lasts for two hours and is the work in which Stockhausen demonstrates that the world is his tamtam. Tchaikovsky managed to work only two national anthems into a piece but Stockhausen uses many more, although rarely as recognizable tunes. The contribution of the instrumentalists was disappointing, picking out and completing fragments of anthems when these appeared and adding little in the long static sections, such as the ten minutes of heavy breathing in which the work dissolves. At times *Hymnen* sounded like a crazy Olympic Games where no one could agree on the winner. The remaining concert included—besides *Prozession*, where the most interesting passages occurred when one player was clearly in control—*Spiral* (Bojé), *Pole* (Bojé with Eötvös) and *Klavierstück IX*. (*Musical Times*, July 1971)

La Rochelle and Royan 1973

Although its nucleus had been transplanted to La Rochelle, the Royan Festival continued as before. There was the same packed timetable of up to five concerts a day (with films in between for the most voracious) and the same concentration of world premieres—indeed the organizers felt that an apology was necessary if a work had been played before in France. In the first days of the La Rochelle Festival the schedule was more humane, and the repertory generally restricted to established and dependable composers. If the organization at La Rochelle was not entirely smooth, it was a paragon of efficiency by Royan standards. Harry Halbreich, the new artistic director there, had to announce alterations and cancellations at almost every event, and his continuing cheerfulness was not always shared by the audience.

The main feature of the early days at La Rochelle was a Stockhausen cycle. There were old favourites (*Zyklus*, *Refrain*,

Kontakte), played by Christoph Caskel, Aloys Kontarsky and the composer but marred by the noise and the glass walls of the yachting centre. Another programme coupled Intermodulation's reading of the text *Kommunikation* with the *Indian Songs*, a recent work for soprano and tenor. The two sing simple phrases to each other, or else together, and the piece is fully written out, even to the extent of the singers' actions and gestures.

It was heard again as one element in *Alphabet pour Liège*, which was performed in a long attic gallery, with each of the twelve 'situations' in a recess at one side or the other. These situations are explorations of the physical, psychological and metaphysical properties of sound—for example, breaking plates of glass by setting them in vibration, or making love with sounds, or blessing food with song. Interactions are rare. However, at regular intervals all activities are brought to a sudden halt by a signal from the musical director, producing powerful moments of stillness and silence. Apart from its qualities as an exhibition and an experience, *Alphabet* suggests a mode of life in which all activities are accompanied or even instigated by sound, an essential role for music such as it has progressively lost in western societies.

Another composer prominent at La Rochelle was Xenakis. An evening of his music included *Persephassa* for a battery of six percussionists surrounding the audience and *Persepolis*, a long tape piece consisting of massive, slowly evolving slabs of sound. In a later concert *Eridanos*, for brass and strings, was performed for the first time: a fiery torrent.

At Royan the composer most in the limelight was Cristobal Halffter, whose orchestral *Requiem por la libertad imaginada* received the most appreciative applause, perhaps as much for its title as for its 'tragic' rumblings and 'painful' slow crescendos. Fellow Spaniard Luis de Pablo provided an audiovisual piece, *Historia natural*, which was mounted in the early Gothic abbey church of Sablonceaux. A television set flickered on the altar; rubber balloon dolls rose to the last trump and fell back disappointed, all by means of piped air; several sources of electronic music continued; and the composer struggled with TV men making their own strong contribution with blazing lights and whirring cameras.

Other specially featured composers were Ligeti, Zimmermann, Donatoni and Schnebel. Typical of Schnebel's work was *Ki-No*, a sequence of films and slides to spur a performance from the audience, many of whom responded vigorously (a performance in Britain would probably be a disaster). Siegfried Palm worked wonders with a sonata and four studies by Zimmermann, and with Penderecki's Cello

Concerto. He was also the soloist in the first performance of Feldman's *Cello and Orchestra*, turning it into a Romantic concerto (if turning it needed). Roger Woodward, given an intolerable piano and inadequate rehearsal facilities, still showed something more of Barraqué's sonata in a performance prefaced by a few diffident remarks from the composer. His *Lysanias* was to have closed the festival but is still not ready.

A festival should be more than a series of concerts, and the coherent plan of La Rochelle was more successful than Royan's bits and pieces. Also, there has to be some reason for taking music to small towns which lack ideal concert halls. La Rochelle attracted a considerable local audience (with middle-aged ladies arguing vociferously about Xenakis during the interval), while at Royan there were precious few who were not making notes in their programmes. (*Financial Times*, 10 May 1973)

Donnerstag

There was a strange little item in the programme book for the original La Scala production of *Donnerstag aus Licht*, where Stockhausen gave snap answers to thirty-seven questions. What, he was asked, was his besetting sin? That of taking everthing seriously. But this should not be a problem for anyone else attending his opera: one can hardly respond seriously to a work which itself shows such a deep lack of seriousness in its treatment of its basic theme, which is nothing less than the salvation of the world. The real reasons for going to see *Donnerstag* at Covent Garden—and they should be enough to persuade anyone—are that it contains much quite extraordinary music and that Michael Bogdanov has produced an evening that is breathtakingly spectacular yet honest in taking account of the opera's discrepancies of vision and its weird mixture of cosmic imagination with juvenile smut and artistic shoddiness.

There was never any question of the thing working at face value, as a ritual of the redeemer Michael's education, earthly journey and return heavenwards. Even Stockhausen himself, at one level, is not convinced by it: hence what must surely be a deliberate marring of the grand strategy in his introduction of an old woman to interrupt the triumphs of the last act and be futilely attacked by a toy tank. Idiocies like that, and there are others, do not withdraw disbelief from the rest, as Stockhausen would seem to intend, acting like a satyr play to point up the seriousness of the main business. They cannot serve that purpose because one sees through Stockhausen's attempts at comedy, poignancy, celestial splendour or any of the other cards he plays. But if the opera never for a moment works as the mystic revelation it pretends to be, it remains utterly fascinating as a document of a great creative mind talking to itself.

Obviously the three main characters are projections from within the composer's psyche: they are even intended as such. Michael in the first act is made to relive aspects of Stockhausen's own remembered and idealized past; Eve is the sunny mother figure who first appeared as his female alter ego twenty years earlier in *Momente*: and Lucifer is the intellectual planner in him, counting out steps before he takes them. Beyond that, the whole of *Donnerstag*, and perhaps the whole of the *Licht* project to which it belongs, is a Luciferian construction into which has been shoved some Michael-style vision and a touch of Eve-style humanity. It is as if some elaborate machine were held together with bits of muscle and internal organ. It cannot conceivably function, but it is very wondrous to comtemplate—wondrous, that is, when it is not just silly.

Bogdanov succeeds so well with the piece because he takes it as it comes. If there is realism, as there is when Michael's mother is taken off to a lunatic asylum, then it is done with brutal simplicity. If there is adolescent sexual fantasy, then there it stands: the breasted bird-woman is just brought on, and only Suzanne Stephens, who has to play the role, seems embarrassed. Bogdanov also accepts the nightclub aura of the second act, and with no cue from the libretto dramatizes it by means of neon lights and nifty sterotypes of the characters Michael meets in his journey around the world: mechanics in Cologne, sumo-wrestlers in Tokyo, a dancer in Bali, a drum majorette in New York. This is not to ridicule the music but to justify its being as it is, and in the third act too, the production achieves the astonishing along with the vulgar and banal.

Both these later acts depend on outstanding work from the designer Maria Bjørnson and lighting man Chris Ellis. The earth for Michael's journey is a rotating sphere of scaffolding with a central stairway, seen against the constellations. It is a magnificent vehicle for a trumpeter to stride about in, and a beautiful object for illumination. Ellis comes into his own, though, in the 'light compositions' with which Eve greets Michael in the third act: a shower of spangles through rainbow clouds, a great rising disc of multi-coloured flashes, and a spectral display brought on by 'moon children' bearing giant prisms.

On the technical side, there must also be praise for the sound team, working under Stockhausen's direction as aural projectionists. The singers, and the solo instrumentalists whose roles are quite as important, are all amplified and so are the orchestral players, but that does not disguise either the richness and power of the score as conducted by Peter Eötvös or the feats of memory, virtuosity, conviction and tact achieved by the soloists. Annette Meriweather's laughing presence is a delight as Eve in her soprano persona. Markus Stockhausen as the trumpeter Michael looks and sounds the golden hero, while Julian Pike, with something of the aspect of the young composer, progresses with firm authority from baby talk to visionary pronouncements. Lucifer's starkness and severity are well-represented by the bass Nicholas Isherwood and the trombonist Michael Svoboda; his dangerous, feline plausibility comes from the dancer Alain Louafi. David Smeyers and Beate Zelinsky are splendidly funny clarinettist-clowns, and Bow Street police station does Stockhausen proud in providing accommodation for the trumpeters who fanfare the audience away after this astonishing evening. (*Times*, 18 September 1985)

Montag

At this stage, with three of the seven operas completed, Stockhausen's week of festivities is beginning to make sense, up to a point. The appearance first of *Donnerstag*, the 'day of learning', may have misled, since learning is progressive and implies a work with some narrative continuity. In the unavoidable comparison, *Samstag* then seemed bewilderingly heterogeneous, being a sequence of four utterly dismissimilar episodes, each of them essentially static and repetitive. But now *Montag* is even more a succession of bits and pieces: the three acts simply assemble twenty items which belong together only in the way that the prayers and readings of a liturgy belong together. The absence of drive, of drama, is inevitable; the whole nature of the project is ceremonial.

Since *Montag* is the day of Eva, the Venus-Mother of Stockhausen's pantheon, it is pre-eminently the day of birth, though the emphasis is on the prenatal, the potential, the unformed. The music seems to exist in the state of gestation, enveloped in the same harmony for long periods, embedded in the continuous sounds of synthesizers (a trio of these with a bellhop percussionist have the function of orchestra throughout). The theatre becomes a womb, bathing the audience in the amniotic fluid of diffuse electronic tones, and allowing the outer world to penetrate only as sound: farmyard noises, motors, national anthems and even a snatch of Hitler, promptly flushed down the loo, all make this Stockhausen's biggest essay in musique concrète since *Hymnen*.

In other respects the connections are with his celebrations of sexuality and the eternal feminine in *Stimmung* and *Momente*, works of similar ecstatic prolongation (the total duration of the three acts of *Montag* is almost three and a half hours, and some of the scenes seem to drift on endlessly). As in those earlier works, too, the closeness of mother and lover in Stockhausen's erotics is marked: sex is joined to birth not by causality but because the male in sexual activity becomes infantile. Hence the prominence of children (the exceptionally secure and confident Radio Budapest Children's Choir) in all three acts, and hence too the regression to nursery rhymes, to a powerful focussing on the breast, and to a giggling babble of punning, compound words and nonsense in most of the text.

The cover of the programme book reproduces the 'Montags-Lied' dedicated to Suzanne Stephens, who is in many ways the adored instigator of *Montag*. Stephens, as the basset-hornist persona of Eva (though called 'Coeur de Basset'), dominates the last two acts of the work, but in the first, 'Eva's First Birth', the goddess is present as a trio of sopranos, singing from the shoulder of an eight-metre-high female idol that is the spectacular main feature of Chris Dyer's set. Supporting herself in semi-recumbent readiness, the idol gives birth to seven animals and seven dwarves: implicitly to the days of the week and to fairy stories. The ensuing celebrations include a wonderfully silly close-harmony trio for tenors arriving as sailors, and an inordinately long ballet for baby buggies, after which Lucifer bursts in for a big anger aria in nonsense syllables progressing through the alphabet: Nicholas Isherwood was splendid here.

In the second act, 'Eva's Second Birth', the focus shifts to instrumental soloists, reminding us that the use of instrumentalists as mime artists must be Stockhausen's most fruitful operatic innovation. Pierre-Laurent Aimard comes to impregnate the idol with Piano Piece XIV, played on a comically extended grand thrust between her legs. Then the days are born again, explicitly this time, as naked children to be taught their songs by Coeur de Basset, who afterwards calls for replicas of herself from the breasts and vagina of the idol. The act thus moves from the clear innocence of singing girls in candle-lit procession (albeit dressed with rampant symbolism as arum lilies) to the dark, damp sensuality Stockhausen finds in the bassethorn.

The third act, 'Eva's Magic', makes a reverse transition, beginning with Coeur de Basset playing to an adult chorus of admirers, and ending with a flautist (Kathinka Pasveer) and the Hungarian children enacting the Pied Piper story.

With so much input from the composer and his long-standing collaborators, Michael Bogdanov's contribution as producer is facilitatory rather than creative, and similarly Mark Thompson in his costume designs has been influenced by Stockausen's tastes for breast ornament, eau-de-Nil Lurex and split skirts (the sailors, though, dressed as clowns in fruit-print Bermuda shorts, are an independent triumph). Essentially this is Stockhausen's show, with hardly anybody from the Scala allowed anywhere near it. It is, of course, an act of gigantic egomania, but it is also intermittently delightful and, not least, pretty alarming in being a ramshackle enterprise that we all merrily accept, perhaps have to accept, as a masterpiece. (*Times*, 10 May 1988)

Freitag

Imagine that beings from another planet have picked up a television broadcast of a play from Earth. The signal is badly corrupted: not many of the characters can be made out, almost none of the text, and whole scenes have been lost. Still, the beings decide to put on their own performance of what they can piece together. Their drama, like the original, lasts for three hours, but the only characters are a man in black, a woman in white with flowers, and a king, all moving through elongated versions of the scenes that could be partly deciphered: Ghostly Apparition, First Self-Communing and so on. This is approximately the impression made by Stockhausen's *Freitag*, the fifth opera to be completed of his *Licht* cycle, which had its first performance last week.

Each of the *Licht* operas so far has had less plot than the last, and *Freitag*'s main action is pared to a few moments. Friday is the day of temptation, and the day also of Eve and Lucifer. Eve is persuaded by Ludon, an emanation of Lucifer, to bear a child by his son Kaino. Meanwhile, the theme of miscegenation is played out on another plane by twelve couples (human, animal and inanimate) represented by dancers, and there are troops of children who, though doubtfully fixed to the storyline, contribute liveliness and charm. The sense of witnessing something from outer space is intensified by the continuous electronic music on tape, and in particular by that component of it which was presented in the Amsterdam planetarium last year as *Weltraum*: a two-and-a-half-hour meditation on a few notes, most prominently a high E flat. Recorded passages of musical love-talk, featuring the voices of the composer and Kathinka Pasveer, are added to this when the couples appear, and the electronic music is also the warm, fluid medium which supports the soloists onstage: three singers in the named roles, plus flautist (Pasveer again) and basset-hornist (Suzanne Stephens) as shadows of Eve.

This almost amniotic bathing of electronic music, the slow motion and the presence of children, all link the new opera with *Montag*, the segment of *Licht* that was principally Eve's and concerned with birth. But *Freitag* is distinguished by its pairings, and by how those pairings are musically reflected in twinned melodies that often move in contrary motion. The melodies avoid, often by slowness, any conventional expressive effect: such things as the love scene or Eve's aria of repentance are big musical moments but psychologically null. This is Stockhausen's way. Each of his operas is an instruction, not in how to feel, but to listen: hence the importance of instrumentalists as stage performers and the motif—emphasized here by the children—of education.

In Leipzig the joy of the children was infectious, and a great lesson in how the very young can relish the challenge of new music. Less happy, though, was the division of the cast into white (a blonde-wigged Eve, with pale children in pastel blue) and black (Ludon, Kaino and more children all made up as stage Africans), with a strongly implied connection to the cycle's central metaphor of light and darkness. It is not enough here to be naive. The vocal soloists all commanded the necessary statuesque manner and effortless delivery. Angela Tunstall was the angelically bright Eve, and Nicholas Isherwood the stentorian Ludon. There was also excellent work from Uwe Wand (director), Johannes Conen (designer) and Johannes Bonig (choreographer). (*Times*, 18 September 1996)

New York 2001

Thirty years ago Karlheinz Stockhausen was the most prominent composer in the world, sustained in place by spectacular performances he was giving internationally and by Deutsche Grammophon's prompt and opulent release of each new major work. That great river of success has thinned to a trickle, but Thursday's exciting concert at Miller Theater both caught the earlier force and suggested what went wrong.

Presented by Ensemble 21, the programme started and finished with works from around 1960, Piano Piece IX and *Kontakte*, representing a period when Stockhausen was burning up a whole new compositional approach in each score. In the piano piece he combined the most brutal minimalism—an ugly dissonance hammered in insistent regular rhythm—with airy, unpredictable figuration. In *Kontakte* he placed a pianist and a percussionist within a swirl of electronic music.

Marilyn Nonken gave a luminous account of the piano piece, showing how the extremes of regularity and irregularity dovetail. The chord repetitions were tense and lifted as much as they thudded; the surreptitious detail of changes in balance and resonance came through, partly thanks to the use of moderate amplification, as Stockhausen prefers. Nonken also captured the marvel of the moment when monotony gives way to the first melody, and maintained a sense of purpose through all the beautiful, wavering music that results, right up to an extraordinarily quiet but intense close that clinched the whole piece.

Kontakte grew here from the paradox that the artificial sounds, laid down by the composer on tape, seemed to come straight from nature: sounds of rushing winds, thunder, the cries and bellowings of animals, a distant human choir, falling water. The pair of performers—Nonken again and Tom Kolor—were like Eve and Adam in a harsh Garden of Eden, flooded with information about the world and racing with supreme energy and agility to keep up with the flow. Their music-making created a further flood of beautiful, bewildering information and was thrillingly dramatic. A classic was refreshed.

Between the piano piece and the live-electronic storm, the later *Tierkreis* could offer little. Stockhausen's arrangement of his twelve zodiac melodies is oddly insensitive to textural niceties in its scoring for flute, clarinet, trumpet and piano; the tunes sound much better in their original form, chiming from music boxes. David Fedele, Jean Kopperud, Carl Albach and, once more, Nonken did what they could, but the music is at an astral distance from *Kontakte*. (*New York Times*, 28 February 2001)

behind the rusting Curtain

Tbilisi 1989

One of the destinations has been whited out on the placard of excursions that the wide, empty Intourist office will organize from your Tbilisi hotel. You can still go to Metskhita, the ancient capital of Georgia, where within a stone-walled stockade you will see the thirteenth-century cathedral, a great block of green and ochre stone sculpted with vines, beasts, saints, zodiac signs and, reaching to measure the top of a high arch, the proud arm of the architect and his signature. You can still go to Borjomi, 'world-famous mineral spa'. You can still see Georgian bread being baked, Georgian wine being made, Georgian folkdance being folkdanced. But what you cannot see, though the words can still be made out under the fresh snow of anonymity, is the birthplace of Joe Stalin.

Having held on to some renown here, if only as a local boy made good, Stalin no longer quite fits the mood since April 9, when the Red Army moved in on a peaceful demonstration with spades and ice axes to kill twenty people, most of them young women. Stalin, I was told, was not a real Georgian: he belonged to some mountain herd. The distinctions now are important. The massacre of April 9—'our tragedy', as everyone calls it—has inevitably stirred up something more than the natural devotion of a small nation to its literature, its music, its long history of fidelity as the easternmost stronghold of Orthodox Christianity, its even longer history of vassaldom to foreign empires. The recent events and the distant past echo one another, and it is hard to see where and how the reverberations will end.

Maybe, as has happened before, even the script of the impenetrable Georgian language is on the move. When Constantinople held sway, Georgian lettering had the square detached style and the elisions of Byzantine Greek. Later inscriptions, from the time when Tbilisi was an Arab emirate, fly off in festoons, spitting diacriticals.

Shop signs and street names put up in the present century squash and formalize the alphabet so that it looks like a variety of Cyrillic—but the poems, prayers and testimonies posted up at the Siony church in memory of the victims of April 9 suggest a particularly Georgian style, the characters curling like wisps of smoke.

The place to start looking for the distinctive Georgia, however, is in the Museum of Fine Arts, on the ground floor, in the twelfth century. This is where, under David IV, Demetrius II and the Amazon introduced to me as 'King-Queen' Tamara, Georgia suddenly parted from Byzantium. The figures in the superb metalwork gain a new elasticity: the Jesus on a crucifix has the caved-in stomach, the lapsed muscles, the sagged features of a dead man; the two women in an image of the Visitation clasp and fall into each other's bodies; angels supporting the ascending Christ flick their heels into the air.

A little further along, the curator, the elegant daughter of a family of painters, points out the difference between Byzantine and Georgian panels and medallions of cloisonné enamel. The Georgian work is, she admits, less fine, but look at the colours! 'That is the colour of Georgian wine. It is special to Georgia. It is found only in the work of Georgian masters.'

It is the colour of the roses and carnations that people come to heap under the photographs of the twenty martyrs that are displayed in the courtyard of the Siony church, and will remain displayed for forty days of mourning. Such a public memorial to dissident victims seems extraordinary in a major Soviet city, but though it was not permitted on the site of the killings, it goes on here without hindrance. At any hour a crowd is in solemn attendance, bringing flowers, reading the messages on the wall, signing a book, lighting candles, or just silently standing. There is not a soldier to be seen.

In the evening there are more flowers strewn, and a dead tree stands tied with twenty black ribbons on the stage of the new Tbilisi Musical Cultural Centre, which was due to have opened with an international festival, but which instead is being dedicated in a national act of remembrance. The black programme leaflet is inscribed: 'To the holy memory of the innocent souls who perished April 9', and the week-long festival is withered to three evenings: two of excerpts from the works of the first Georgian opera composer, Zakhary Paliashvili, interspersed with old Georgian liturgical chants, the other devoted to performances of the Verdi Requiem.

The numbers from *Abesalom da Eteri* and *Daisi* sound like Rimsky-Korsakov or Borodin with coriander, but they are flung out with fierce passion by Georgian State Opera forces, under Jansug Kahidze. In the Verdi, Kahidze's command brings steel into a variable orchestra and a solo quartet who are on slippery ground in the ensembles, but there are no problems with the massive, enfolding sound of the Armenian State Choir, turning pianissimos to velvet and fortes to thunder: collaboration between Armenians and Georgians, traditionally at odds, is another sign of something new since April 9. And it is again this hot sound of souls on fire that draws me one afternoon up the hill to the Armenian church and so on up to the citadel, a bare dust-blown ruin.

Once through the gatehouse I find two men working lackadaisically at rebuilding a wall that has crumbled to a height of no more than three feet, while perhaps twenty other men are gathered in a hut. Seeing a lone visitor, one of them rushes out and hails me. I have no idea what he says, or even whether he is speaking in Russian or Georgian, but I know the answer to give: 'Angliya.'

'Angliya!' He beams, strides forward to grab my arm, then wonders quite what to do. Another burst of what I tentatively identify as Georgian. I smile. He smiles. We go on smiling. The two workers go on patiently smoothing mortar. By now all the rest have gathered round, and I notice a boy who might just be old enough to be learning English at school. I point to him and ask: 'He speak angliyskiy?' But they all shake their heads, mutter and turn aside, clearly thinking it a foolish idea to expect a child to serve as interpreter.

Defiantly I persevere. 'What is your name?' And back the reply comes with the immemorial, universal lesson learnt that answers must always be given in complete sentences: 'My name is Lasha.' Encouraged, I go on, but the men have drifted away. 'How old are you?' 'I am threaten.' 'Thirteen?' I ask. He nods. There is another, smaller boy hanging by. 'Is he your brother?' We are obviously reaching the limits of Lasha's angliyskiy now, but he hesitantly nods. 'What is his name?' 'His name is Tata.' 'Tata', I repeat, and the little one almost rolls on the floor in merriment. I tell myself he is charmed to hear his name spoken by a stranger from the fabled west.

But now the men return with a new idea. 'Jimmy Greaves!' cries one. 'Jimmy Greaves!' I reply. 'Gary Linacre!' This one foxes me. And then, four or five of them together: 'Margaret Thatcher!' It is a limited form of communication, but at least it has brought up the matter of politics. The first man says 'England, Georgia', seizes one hand in the other, and repeats his broad smile. Then the expression changes. 'Georgia russkiy kolonia.' I nod sympathetically. 'Russkiy kolonia', he repeats more quietly and turns his face away, then quickly looks back as another new idea occurs: 'Germanskiy?' 'Deutsch, ja', I say, and hurriedly he packs someone off to find a German-speaker. Meanwhile he points out the black flag fluttering from the castle defences. 'Tragediya', he explains. And he indicates the wall where the two workers are still lovingly preparing their patch of mortar. 'Kloster.'

Then all at once there is movement down below, and we go to meet the German speaker. 'Sie sprechen Deutsch?' 'Ein sehr klein bisschen.' 'Ich auch', Shota politely lies, and explains what is going on up here. 'These are professional people poets, writers, the chief of police' (for the first time in my life I shake the hand of a shyly smiling Soviet police commander: the police are popular here now, having helped save people from the army) 'who work without pay to rebuild a great church that was founded in the fifth century.' At last, I notice, a thin tile is being carefully laid in place. Then I hear from Shota the story of April 9.

'The soldier-pigs—excuse me, but there is no other word—came with spades to kill women, and the bodies they just piled into lorries: their parents have not been able to bury them. The next day the army returned with fire engines to wash the blood from the streets, and the people came to sing and dance in front of the fire engines and tanks. The soldiers could not understand that. And you heard about the gas? Many people were poisoned: I too was poisoned, and was very ill for several days. Some were worse and are still in hospital. Would you like to go and see?'

I would. Shota's brother drives us down the hill and across the city to a bus stop, and we wait. Meanwhile Shota fills me in on the background. 'People say that the demonstration here was just because Georgia wants to have control of Abkhazia, but it's not true. It was a demonstration against the Russians. We hate the Russians. I see them on the streets and I hate them. You know, the Russian soldiers think that when a Georgian girl is thirteen she is a woman. They are disgusting.'

We arrive at the hospital, and go up to a tranquil corridor, with doors opening on to double rooms with their own lavatories and showers. It is considerably more welcoming than my hotel. We enter a room and speak to two women. Another is occupied by a law student who was on the demonstration. 'The army smashed the windows of houses and squirted the gas inside. My mother and my sister were affected.' Nurses and a doctor gather in the room. 'The doctor is Russian', Shota explains when he is out for a moment, 'so I speak to him only in Georgian and force him to speak Georgian.'

'Would the student go on such a demonstration again?' I have Shota ask. 'Yes!' the reply comes yelled back immediately in English. Incautiously, perhaps, I mention the name of Gorbachev. 'Gorbachev dictator!' yells the student again.

We leave the hospital and walk back towards the bus stop. 'You don't believe in perestroika?' I ask. Shota, normally quiet and intense, for once erupts in laughter. 'No! We have had four years of perestroika and still I cannot buy soap in the shops. You know who perestroika is for? Perestroika is for Gorbachov and Raisa.' I remark, nevertheless, on how excellent the hospital is. 'Oh, but this is a hospital for those who are working with the regime', Shota says. 'I could not show you the other hospitals. . .'

I look back. 'Is that why', I ask, 'there are red flags hanging from all the windows?'

'Noooo! Those are not Soviet flags! This red: it is the colour of Georgian wine. It is special to Georgia. Those are the flags of Georgian independence.' (*Times*, 3 June 1989)

Budapest 1989

For three decades, after the 1956 uprising, music and religion were just about the only spheres of dissent permissible in Hungary. Now, of course, dissent is so widespread as hardly to count as dissent, and though the churches are still full, Hungarian composers have obviously lost something of their prerogative. The new ungrateful circumstances were very evident at this year's contemporary music festival in Budapest. In the world outside, the party congress was unpinning itself from Marxism-Leninism and the bookshops were full of people buying what has so suddenly become accessible: Orwell, biographies of Stalin, Varlam Salamov's account of the Gulag, even Virginia Woolf (and Budapest is one city where everyone in a bookshop has to be a local). But in the concert hall audiences were sparse and underwhelmed.

The single reference to topical events came in László Vidovszky's A-Z for piano duet, one movement of which bore the title 'For Changes in Hungary'. But Vidovszky is the last composer to offer a political message, or indeed any other kind of definite statement. A concert devoted entirely to his music revealed a continuing ability to puzzle, not least by the variety of the puzzles. Here were computer-generated pieces of lengthy, bubbling but aimless note-spinning, a scrap of material salvaged from a computer brainstorm and gently laid out for six players (*Soft Errors*, based partly on a Joplin rag that trickled to the surface near the end) and two sets of solidly crafted and yet not-quite-right studies, works that sound at once perfectly normal and disturbingly odd, maybe because one cannot take their normality at face value: the piano duet pieces and Twelve Duos for violin and viola.

The four-hand pieces, played by Zoltán Kocsis and Adrienne Hauser, range from a slow 'Intrada' entirely in abrupt startling chords to quick canons. There is a good deal of canon in the string duos, too, though the instruments are almost always in stately rhythmic unison: one might be reminded of medieval organum one moment and Bach the next, though the references are always tangential because the music's substance is so sound. Perhaps this perverse seriousness (unless it is serious perversity) is the one common feature among Vidovszky's works: Gavin Bryars would be Britain's nearest equivalent.

Nowhere, though, is there a composer at all like György Kurtág, who once again provided the festival with its most striking new work, his *Officium breve in memoriam Andreae Szervanszky* for string quartet. This is a continuous sequence of fifteen fragments, paying homage to Endre Szervánszky by gradually moving through hints towards an open quotation of a C major melody from his Serenade for string orchestra, while at the same time there is an arch-shaped progression towards and away from a quartet arrangement of the final chorale-canon from Webern's Second Cantata. The fragment and the homage are familiar forms with Kurtág; what is remarkable here is the net of cross-references that keeps so many disjunct pieces together. Some recur with variation (there is a fine re-drawing of the Webern canon, as well as a pair of episodes in which the Szervánszky tune is dismembered, Webernized); elsewhere the relationships are more indefinite. The only worries in this performance by the Keller Quartet were that the Webern quotation, retaining the threefold repetition of the original, threatened the formal balance, and that the ending, with the Szervánszky tune hesitating then left in mid-air, might easily sound sentimental.

Otherwise the best things in Budapest were British and Italian. Two concerts by the London Sinfonietta under Diego Masson offered twentieth-century classics little known in Hungary (Varèse, Ives, Henze) and new British works; there was also a long late-evening recital respectfully dedicated to the small instrumental productions of Howard Skempton (curious to encounter a hundred people, many of them highly distinguished composers and musicians, sitting down to hear a full programme of music which in London enjoys a fringe, semi-private circulation). Italian music was represented by a brilliant evening with the duo pianists Bruno Canino and Antonio Ballista, and by a programme of pieces published by Ricordi. Among the latter was an excellent set of miniatures by Bussotti, *Le bagatelle da camera*, touching on Webern, Proust and folksongs, and also a soft, slowly turning, opalescent piano quintet by Sciarrino, *Le raggioni delle conchiglie*. (*Times*, 17 October 1989)

Budapest 1990

The fate of Jenő Bors—dismissed after twenty-five years with the state record company Hungaroton, simply because he served under the old regime—illustrates some of the frustrations of freedom in Hungary. The outcome has been inevitable. Most of the leading Hungarian musicians, and most of Hungaroton's own staff, promptly left the firm to set up a new company around Bors, with US financial backing. In such ways the national economy, already suffering after the collapse of Comecon, divests itself of potentially profitable enterprises. More problems are also added to those of high inflation, lack of fuel, apathetic polls at elections and chauvinism. Then there are the peasants, freed by the new capitalism to choke the streets with tacky embroidery and other wares on display. In this context, the annual festival of contemporary music in Budapest is curiously a calm reminder of the old Hungary. The only change is that the audience has diminished, perhaps because new music has lost its rarity as a permitted avenue of free thought. And perhaps also because of that loss, there is a sense of less excitement among composers.

György Kurtág, however, remains as intense as ever. His festival offering, being played for the first time, was a trio for clarinet, viola and piano with the title *Hommage à R. Sch.* But it approaches Schumannesque fantasy and codedness very much in his own vivid terms, in music whose gestures—from the most aerial, charming and elliptical to the most savage—seem indelibly inscribed. Partly this must be a matter of economy. Each of the first five movements of the new trio is a tiny miniature: an exchange of flights between the clarinet and the viola, doubled by the piano; a three-bar canon on 'Der begrenzte Kreis', one of the composer's *Kafka Fragments*; a brief altercation ending in emphatic chords; another miniature canon; a rippling of overlapping scales. But then comes a five-minute slow movement which, in this mayfly time scale, seems an immense adagio, grounded on low chords and tolling semitone falls in the piano, but full of wild and strange things from the other players, as if releasing monsters from the encapsulated ideas of the earlier movements.

Otherwise, the most impressive Hungarian music came from Zoltán Jeney, one ofthe minimalist-oriented New Music Studio group. His *El silencio*, *Cantos para todos* and *Spaziosa calma*, all for combinations of voice (the ferociously ethereal Luisa Castellani) and ensemble, revealed a crystalline purity of system. The last work also showed a becoming frailty and a challenging push to extremes, so that there is a feeling of necessity but also of emptiness and extent—of, indeed, 'spacious calm'. A record of the last two of these works, coupled with the extraordinary Twelve Songs for soprano, violin and piano, is worth seeking out before Hungaroton disappears. (*Times*, 12 October 1990)

Verdi at the Met

Stiffelio

Suddenly coming upon a new one—*Stiffelio*—makes you notice what odd things Verdi operas are. Maybe this is a special case—an opera that is odd only because it is new to us, and new to us only because it was judged odd in the past—but that is not the whole story. Certainly *Stiffelio* is strangely formed in ways that are particular to it: the central character engages directly with the audience hardly at all, being heard mostly in duets and ensembles; his wife's lover, who would be the clearcut villain of a more conventional tale, lives in the shadows; the orchestra is full of bizarre notions. But one could point to features just as outlandish in *La Traviata*. Verdi made an art out of dealing roughly with his material and with his chosen genre: trying the untried, not disguising the carpentry. This strikes us in *Stiffelio* because we are not prepared by familiarity.

Indeed, nobody at the opening of the Met's new production can have been entirely prepared for what we were hearing and seeing, since this was effectively the world premiere of the score Verdi wrote in the summer and fall of 1850. When that score was first produced, at Trieste, the libretto was stymied by censorship (unsurprisingly, given that it is set in Austria and puts clerics, albeit Protestant clerics, on the singing stage), and in revivals the minister Stiffelio became a German prime minister, necessitating the new title of *Guglielmo Wellingrode*. Dismayed by this ridiculous and unwanted turn of events, the composer adapted the piece several years later to make *Aroldo*, performed in 1857, but his cobbling has been regarded by many Verdi experts—perhaps most—as a desperate attempt to retrieve a messy situation, and the resulting score remains the least loved of the post-*Rigoletto* operas. According to those same experts, *Stiffelio*, written immediately before *Rigoletto*, is the real thing. For them, then, the Met production will have been an occasion of some moment. Here at last the piece was, realer than ever, with the music not used in *Aroldo*—music long thought ditched or lost, and recoverable only from copies—played in a new edition benefitting from the rediscovery last year of the autograph material.

Whether *Stiffelio* will now join the regular Verdi canon remains to be seen. Probably it will not. After all, it is not so entirely new: various versions of the score have been circulating for a quarter of a century, and there was a Boston production in 1978. All one can say is that at present *Stiffelio* provides a cold encounter with otherness, and that this is only partly the fault of history, since it seems to have been part of Verdi's plan in this opera to plunge his audience into a state of ignorance.

The unusual period (contemporary) and the unusual location (Salzburg, unlikely as that might seem for a Protestant community) may have been chosen to that end: these were Verdi's decisions, in that he picked the subject, a French play, from among several suggested by his librettist, Piave. However, the location seems quite incidental, and it is hard to be sure whether the placelessness is an accidental fault or a strategem to help create puzzlement in the audience. Other cases of absent definition are much more plausibly deliberate. For example, in the opening scene we are confronted almost at once by seven characters, of whom only two—the elderly minister Jorg, who begins the opera with dark threats of impending disaster, and his younger fellow in orders Stiffelio—have had much opportunity to make themselves acquainted to us before they are all joining in the first of the work's majestic ensembles. We know that the anecdote Stiffelio has recounted just before this, about an amorous escapade he heard about, has caused consternation in his wife Lina and in a nobleman present, Raffaele, and we can guess why, but neither of these characters has yet sung alone.

In the Met production, directed by Giancarlo del Monaco and designed by Michael Scott, our immediate disorientation is nicely accentuated, since the curtain opens not on Jorg in solitary contemplation but on him and five others, with only Stiffelio to arrive later. Who are all these people? What kind of nasty business out of Edgar Allan Poe are we to expect in this enormous dark-panelled, gothic-arched library? The few clues—Raffaele's bottle-green velvet jacket, sinisterly flash when everyone else is in severely dark clothing—only quicken wondering. It is a striking stage picture, and one wishes there were more of them. (The reason there are not is that this is an old-fashioned Met production, with grand naturalism triumphant in the decor and nothing in the action to trouble the thought that you stage an opera by staging the libretto.)

The opening confusion that Verdi engenders, or at least permits, is dramatically functional, since it thrusts us into sympathy with Stiffelio, who also, plainly, does not know what is going on. (It is perhaps in order not to damage our feeling of being at one with Stiffelio that Verdi keeps him from addressing us directly, and thereby calling attention to our difference from him.) When everyone else has left he challenges his wife and begins to suspect the truth: this number counts as his only aria in the opera, though it is virtually a duet, and significantly so. He is prevented from unburdening himself by the rules of the opera and by the rules of his calling; also, he discovers himself through the discoveries he makes about other people. We then see and hear, as he does not, Lina in anxious-contrite entreaty to heaven, but it is only along with him that we gather clues, through the second act and into the third, as to the nature of her relationship with Raffaele.

Raffaele's motivation stays obscure to the end. In the first act he features as an individual in just one scene: a scene so tiny as to be almost comical, in which he slips back into the room to hide a letter to Lina inside a locked book. (Messages we cannot see—letters that are never read out—occur three times in this act, and do nothing to dispel its secretive atmosphere.) In the second act his main function is to shove Lina from cantabile into cabaletta. And in the third he gets killed—by Lina's father Stankar, to save her honour—almost without opening his mouth. One has the impression of a character who is refusing to take part for fear of self-incrimination. His silence, and his burying of himself in the work's ensembles (other characters are buried there too: Dorotea and Federico), help to perpetuate the pall of guilty uncertainty that has been giving the opera, right from the start, its quite particular colour.

Lina—as the living embodiment of guilt, and in sharp contrast with Raffaele—is heard a great deal alone. From her prayer in the first act she goes deeper, into a grand scena and aria at the start of the second act, where she is wandering in the churchyard by moonlight and arrives at her mother's tomb. The part is one that profits in this production from Sharon Sweet's stately demeanour, from her rich tone, and also, though not always, from the scale of her singing. What it needs besides is some sense of the gentle and, most crucially, some ability to hit notes other than by way of a creamy slide: her cadenza at the end of the largo of her second-act aria showed lamentably what can happen when she tries for a more staccato kind of delivery. However, if the pathos of Lina's music appeared calculated—something to be regarded, not felt—that may have been because Verdi's design is to hold Stiffelio as the figure with whom we identify. (Odd, this, from such a convinced anti-clericalist: maybe the reformed clergy were exempt.) We are with

Stiffelio not only in his gradual awakening to the truth, but also—since we never learn much about Raffaele—in his moral resolve to deal with the present rather than rake over the past.

This central role is another of the work's unusual attributes. Stiffelio is propelled not by jealousy but by the stern demands of truth. (Verdi must have relished giving a spin to a tired operatic theme.) This is a man who needs to know, so that he can deal honestly and adequately with the case. In terms of the plot, his austere and heavy virtue means that he has to surmount not one but two catastrophes: learning of his wife's unfaithfulness is no greater hardship than having his conciliation pre-empted by his father-in-law's murder of her lover (an event this production diminishes by enacting). In terms of the composition, it means that lyricism is the way he behaves only when under delusion, as in that beautiful barcarole near the start, where, with an orchestra mellowed by horn tone, he tells of a boatman who has unknowingly seen Lina and Raffaele. Thereafter his big numbers are all duets and ensembles, and his vocalism becomes urgent, declamatory, baritonal. The part could have been made for Plácido Domingo at this point in his career: what might otherwise be faults—the hefty projection, the top beginning to sound fragile—become the means by which he conveys the man's solidity holding against extremes of pressure. There is no refuge here in piety: his great cry of 'Sacerdote sono!' (perhaps not the likeliest words for Piave to have put into the mouth of a Protestant pastor) sounds out with the force not of self-restraint but of self-realization.

What we may well feel to be Verdi's robust sympathies for and with his central character are compromised only by the presence among the dramatis personae of another, more frequent conduit of his musical emotions: a man who is a father, and the father of a daughter. Apart from Lina's solo scenes in the first and second acts, the only substantial passages in which Stiffelio is absent from the stage are devoted to Stankar: a duet with Lina in the first act, in which he prevents her from writing in explanation to her husband (this is another of the concealed missives) and, to open the last act, a magnificent aria, which is, like Lina's in the second act, a triple-decker of recitative, slow song and cabaletta. We were lucky to have Vladimir Chernov in this role. Though asking our indulgence on account of a throat infection, he gave a splendid performance: his grey, grave tone was vigorously focussed, his phrasing pliant and moving, his pacing of his aria unerring. Doing the right thing by his character and doing the right thing by his music were fused into a single purpose, achieved.

No one else in this opera has much opportunity, Raffaele (Peter Riberi) being such a vaporous presence and Jorg (Paul Plishka) only a meddler—no one else, that is, except the conductor. James Levine let us enjoy both the extravagances and the banalities of the score: the introduction to the moonlit churchyard, with chromatic curlings from divided strings and a jamming together of unlike themes, and the bouncy measure to which Stiffelio makes his first entrance; the dissonance as he pauses before starting his final sermon of forgiveness (at which point we realize there are two audiences held in doubt: one in the church onstage and one in the theatre) and the more ordinary uses of discord to create worry and alarm. This was a fine performance, right from the overture, which is a brittle melange in the inexplicable brightness of D major (wind pipings cruelly hard to play, a broad trumpet tune, a shameless dance), and in its inconsequentiality maybe not so unfitting a start to this eccentric piece.

But then one has to face the question as to what oddities are peculiar to this opera and what belong to Verdi more generally, on account not only of his creative wilfulness but also of our distance in time. The revival of *Stiffelio*, nearly a century and a half after its first, hampered hearing, may be justice coming too late. What the Met offers is, in a certain sense, authentic: here is what Verdi wrote. However, this is authenticity of a uniquely modern sort—an authenticity that places stringent requirements on what is under scrutiny (every quaver, every syllable must be in accord with the composer's original), yet asks for no guarantees from us that we will approach the piece in the same period spirit. History has taught us how to react to *Rigoletto*. It may even have taught us how to react to *La forza del destino*. (The first duty of performances, of course, is to show us how history has mistaught us, or only partly informed us.) But *Stiffelio*, coming out of the blue, shows up as acutely alien all the things we casually take as normal: these singsong ensembles driven along by the orchestra, these melodramatic settings (graveyard, church), these arias bound to move from legato to athletics, these cautioning fathers and wayward daughters, these splendid costumes and elaborate sets, these machineries of the form—including, and not least, this all too audible prompter. The efforts of musicologists, not to be decried, have assembled for us a work; the performers, most of them admirable, have set it in motion. But nobody can tell us what it is for. (*New Yorker*, 8 November 1993)

I lombardi

Coming only six weeks after *Stiffelio*, the Met's second new homegrown production of the season was again devoted to an early Verdi piece the company had never staged before. But that was where resemblances ended. *Stiffelio* held its fascinations and posed its queries as an unfamiliar arrangement of familiar items of vocal and dramatic furniture; *I lombardi alla prima crociata* demands rather less of us—perhaps little more than that we be prepared to be continually astonished by a slapdash spectacle of fraternal rivalry, changed allegiances, betrayal and baptism, hermit and heroine, battles and blessings, all set among the Milanese and their combatants at the time of the First Crusade. After these mad fireworks, the drama of the Salzburg pastor in *Stiffelio* begins to appear in retrospect like some triumph of sober maturity and depth.

It is not surprising, then, that *I lombardi* should have been the victim of time and of the critics during the century and a half of its existence. When it was first heard in New York, in 1847, it may have represented Verdi's US debut. (There is some doubt about whether it was this opera or *Ernani*, which a Havana company brought to the city the same year, that had the privilege.) But it was rapidly overtaken by later works, and Verdi himself perhaps hoped to hasten its burial by recasting it as *Jérusalem* for Paris, also in 1847. Italians went on ostentatiously preferring the original version, possibly because this is one of Verdi's remarkably few operas in which most of the people who sing are themselves Italians, but in the long view of Julian Budden, writing in his definitive study of the composer's output, *I lombardi* is 'an agglomeration of heterogeneous ideas, some remarkable, some unbelievably banal'.

This judgement the Met production cannot but uphold. Beautifully modulated responses to Bellinian cantabile (Verdi, like Stravinsky, learned by theft) flow in rich and subtle rhythms; then suddenly you find you are into one of those bang-bang choruses that have all the musical interest of a child at a tin drum, and equivalently zero charm. There are similar let-downs in the orchestral writing. Fine moments—upward spirallings of woodwinds and violins together, passages of delicate chamber music—exist alongside raucous march tunes, the supererogatorily elegant jammed up against the downright rude. There is the feeling of a sensibility at war with itself, which may be the composer's response to the bellicose subject matter, but which may also be the flailing of a young artist beginning to gain possession of his talents but not yet certain how to use them.

One result of the internal confusion is conspicuous wastefulness. The opera is almost baroque in its scenic demands, requiring at least ten different sets and several costume changes for the chorus. Happily these are areas in which the Met excels. John Conklin, the set designer, provides a useful unity and grandness of image by keeping a row of great gold-panelled doors along each side of the stage, and his conjurings of the different locales are quick, emblematic and strong: a Romanesque arcade and rose window for the basilica of Sant' Ambrogio in the first scene; Moorish arches for the tyrant of Antioch's palace when we jump to the Near East at the start of the next act; a painted landscape for the River Jordan; a cyclorama of mustard light for the desert. Dunya Ramicova's costumes are also simple and colourful—especially the patterned robes of the Antiochans and the copper armor of the crusaders. Nowhere is there much effort at historical accuracy: these are broad, swift, modern reactions to Romantic reactions to crusaders, and their aim, rightly, is more to be smart and effective than to be integrated.

Quite apart from its spilling over so many settings, *I lombardi* is also wasteful in its treatment of minor characters. Viclinda, cause of the dispute between the brothers Arvino (her husband) and Pagano, sings briefly in the first scene; by the next act her daughter is praying to her spirit, without anyone having bothered to tell us she has died. The tyrant of Antioch has his hot moment at the start of the second act, goes off almost at once to fight the invaders, and returns as a corpse. Sofia, his wife, appears in just one scene, where her sole function is to serve as an admiring audience for her son, Oronte.

Since this is Luciano Pavarotti's role, she acts as the embodiment of the entire house—or certainly did so on the opening night, when Pavarotti was at his most mellifluous and persuasive in this mama's boy aria. His tone was unfailingly sweet, his comportment of the voice between registers assured, and his decoration nimbly executed without disturbance to the line. He was all the time driving along securely, holding plenty in reserve, keeping to the style. If he seemed also a little careful, that was perhaps a touching disclosure of artistic bashfulness and loneliness. Nobody in the world is more fearsomely exposed, more alone, than Pavarotti in embarking on a new role; here he produced, out of that condition, simply the finest he could offer: singing of silvery appeal, and a marriage of his natural gifts with the artistry he has assiduously developed and sustained.

Sadly, he slackened his concern and awareness in his later scenes—or, more likely, found them slackening inside himself against his better intentions, as well might have happened under the unhelpful circumstances. In the love duet of the third act, he had to hold to his line—and he did—against Aprile Millo's disturbing mistunings as Giselda (and she was as determined in holding to her quarter-tone at the cadence). His character's death, during the course of another ensemble with Millo, may have come to him as hoped-for relief. Then, when he was obliged to reappear from the dead, it was perhaps the dreadness of that eventuality, together with the absurdity of the drama and his backward placement on the stage, that was responsible for encouraging out of him a more uniform, and uniformly loud, treatment. Spirits—even spirits who come on to bring good news to distressed Europeans of a handy water supply—ought to coax rather than trumpet.

Samuel Ramey, as Pagano, was more consistent in his singing, and in his vivid presence: he alone onstage conveyed the impression he thought he was in something that mattered. And he did so despite the fact that the piece required him to present not one character but two, with no opportunity for developing one out of the other. In the first act, Pagano is naked villain: Ramey aptly and ably used that bark, particularly on long 'a' sounds, which he can produce without damage to his melody. (Part of what makes his singing special is his strange ability to enunciate and colour the words with the strength of speech while letting forth a sway of pure music: you seem to hear the words and the musical line separately, but at the same time.) In the three acts following, where the move to the Holy Land finds the wicked brother become a somber eremite, Ramey softened in tone, but not in power. Even when prayerful and subdued, he was in command.

The honours belonged to him, to Pavarotti in his first aria, and to James Levine and the orchestra, whose leader, Raymond Gniewek, played decorously in the violin concerto which suddenly pops up as an interlude and stays around to underlie the whole last scene of the third act. Bruno Beccaria was stark as the good brother Arvino: the part could take more ring, more music. (Maybe this could still be an opera in which Pavarotti and Domingo might share the stage: they would not have to sing together, for Verdi and his young librettist, Temistocle Solera, had enough experience to keep their fighting-cock tenors apart, never mind what the result might be in making a switchback of the drama.) Anthony Laciura, in a brief appearance, offered a startling moment of high-tenor intensity well suited to his role as the Milanese grandee who comes rushing into the opening scene to announce the crusade: Mark Lamos's production, otherwise pretty straight, had him look like a Russian holy fool, which was striking.

This might be the moment to consider the plot, even at the evident risks of muddle and disbelief, but in this opera it is secondary. What matters is the subtending geometry—the geometry that makes it possible for an aria to happen here, a duet there, a concerted finale some place else—and, particularly in the case of this work, the atmosphere. Responsiveness to place and time matters less. There is not much difference between the Milanese of the first act and the

Antiochans of the second; the strands of church music probably are not to be inspected too closely for signs of Ambrosian chant; and one listens in vain for any musical realization of the parching sun or its effect on the crusaders. When they are supposed to be on the brink of dying from thirst, they fling out a grand hymn Verdi evidently modelled on 'Va pensiero', the hit of his immediately preceding opera, *Nabucco*. History, geography and dramatic plausibility were all pretty much closed books to Verdi at this time. But where the music certainly does find itself in accord with the character of the libretto—however hard it would be to maintain Verdi was directly stimulated by Solera's text or the subject—is in the above-mentioned belligerence.

The roughness in the piece may be the roughness of a raw, as yet unformed and undisciplined creativity, but it fits all too well, almost sinisterly well, with the dramatic proceedings as realized by Lamos. Several of the Holy Land scenes are dominated by ranks of coarse-cut crosses, covered with the scarlet gloss of new blood—and we remember that the priests of the Sant' Ambrogio scene were also vested in brilliant scarlet. What we have here is a portrayal of the church militant as the church barbaric. The tableau of crosses, an image repeating until the very end of the opera, comes on each time seeming more threatening, in an appalling crescendo that is thoroughly in keeping with the music. Nastiness on this scale may not be what Verdi intended, but it is the way he sounds, and in making the nastiness functional—in fixing it on the crusaders—Lamos puts a little power into the dramatic shambles of the score. He also provides—faint praise though this must be—the most thought-provoking new production at this theatre in a couple of seasons. (*New Yorker*, 27 December 1993 / 3 January 1994)

Otello

There are softer ways of suffering than to be up there singing Otello, but this is the public purgatory Plácido Domingo has chosen, and you have to admire him for it. You also have to admire the achievement, as well as the simple fact, of his performance in the new Met production of Verdi's opera—an achievement all the more fascinating, moving and meaningful for its edge of frustration and distaste. His characteristic ring of brightness is proudly there, in his first appearance and in much that follows, but it seems not to be coming easily to him; it has to be striven for. It even seems an artifice he would rather be without, and which perhaps the character would rather be without. After all, the Othello story is rooted in the myth of the noble

African, and the voice of that myth is cavernous and bass: Olivier, when he played the role, seemed to be speaking from the very bottom of his lungs. Verdi's setting of the part for a tenor was perhaps culturally forced, since only a Russian composer could have imagined a bass Othello and a tenor Iago. But at the same time, the contradiction of the archetype has rich repercussions. Otello is assigned a voice not ideally adequate to his purposes; he would rather not be singing to us in this way. Domingo makes that voice the voice of the inner man: Otello as subtext to Othello's text. When the character exhibits power, at his arrival or in breaking up the sword fight, Domingo shows not only the charisma but the fragility, the nervousness, the insecurity that has to be there for Iago's scheme to work. When he exhibits affection to Desdemona, the warmth and the gentleness are cut with worry, perhaps even with self-doubt. At other points the sense of strain can produce either intensity or an exquisite discomfort, but always it is true to the expressive moment. The command holds, superbly. And if we begin to notice the cost, we notice it not at all as vocal deficiency but as the cost exacted by the score on the wretched victim it makes its chief character.

Just once, in the terrifying monologue in the middle of the third act, Domingo takes the opportunity of low-lying and quiet music (*voce soffocata* is Verdi's marking) to leave aside the demands of heroic brilliance and appear vocally naked. There are no fronts or delusions now, no gap between what the character wants to sing and what he sings. Text and subtext are one, and the voice of both is, as Domingo performs it, bleak, grim and heavily baritonal, revealing the raw grain of the wood, without the polish.

The purpose of the evening was to honour Domingo on the silver anniversary of his first appearance with the company, and honour him it did, as much as he honoured it. Originally a new production by John Schlesinger had been intended, but that plan was dropped at almost the eleventh hour, on the grounds that William Dudley's set would have been too complicated for the necessary shuffle of a repertory house. At that juncture, with less than a year to go before opening night, the Met had to find something proven: hence the invitation to the director Elijah Moshinsky and the set designer Michael Yeargan, who had staged the work for Covent Garden. The result, while not quite a remake of the London production, has many of the same features, including especially the feel of Venetian painting—not so much in the huge art works actually on display, which oddly suggest Siena (a crucifix in the first act) or Rome (a faintly Michelangelesque exertion of some sort in the second), and which wreathe the production in a faint sniff of religiosity, but decisively in the look of the stage: the immense neoclassical columns that reflect Carpaccio's spacious vistas, or the Bellini-like luminosity of the second act, with its blue sky and huge white awning, or the Titianesque sumptuousness of colour and texture in Peter J. Hall's costumes (Titian hair, too, for Desdemona). Here the production follows the librettist's vision, for Boito wrote to Verdi hoping that Carpaccio and Bellini might inform the costumes. More to the point, Yeargan and Hall provide a feast of visual splendour. When the Venetian ambassadors arrive in the third act, they do so as a strong forward wave of crimson brocade and fur, shamelessly spectacular.

Shamelessness and spectacle are also what Moshinsky is about. His handling of the crowd scenes is extravagantly busy and brilliantly managed: the slicing apart of the curtains at the beginning reveals a proscenium at once filled with activity in an exhilarating chiaroscuro—activity going on right up to a top level of soldiers and cannons. Exactly what kind of structure is being represented here is unclear, just as the architectural purpose of the grand columns is never fully explicit. But the function of the sets is not to portray a city (in any event there is not much aura of Carpaccio in Famagusta) but rather to provide sufficient space and splendour for action, or contrariwise for the effective stillness, emptiness and isolation of the more intimate scenes. In these, Otello and Desdemona are often pinned against the base of a pillar; Duane Schuler's lighting examines them mercilessly. Only Iago has the freedom to wander and lean.

Iago is our master of ceremonies; *Otello* is his theatre. In a much-admired production that Peter Stein made for Welsh National Opera, it literally was so, in that Iago could stand outside a great box containing all the other characters. Moshinsky's realization is much more in the line of Met-style lavish naturalism, but it exacerbates that style to a point where naturalism becomes neat artifice. Not only do the set's columns have no architectural reality, but the movement of the chorus is sharply choreographed (not least in the fight, directed by B.H. Barry, which for a few seconds looks like fifty pin-ball machines in action at once), and the expanse and lighting together focus on the principal characters as performers. Only Iago moves with ease and casualness in this painted, harsh-lit world; he seems to claim the follow spot, not have it dog him; he is the one for whom the others perform.

The production is fortunate in having in Sergei Leiferkus a Iago who can express the ruler not only by demeanour but also by being effortlessly in control of his vocal equipment. His gentlemanly correctness—the way he sounds as if he had just swallowed a pebble but were far too well-bred to let such a vulgar mishap discommode him—begins by seeming perhaps even too finely modulated: evil, one may feel, ought to spit more, be more scarred. But this Iago is not evil, except in being the supreme manager. What delights him is regulation, efficiency, the ability to manipulate scenes and emotions. The 'Credo', in which Leiferkus does bare his tone and show us some vocal fangs, seems an act, a momentary slippage into performance rather than observation, necessitated by the score but not by the drama we are in.

Carol Vaness's Desdemona is a less effective piece of casting. She is a mettlesome stage personality, not used or suited to presenting what Verdi insisted was 'the type of goodness, of resignation, of sacrifice!' She gives the appearance of a precarious restraint: left to herself she would surely be clouting Otello back, and scorning his jealousy in a huge D minor aria. Nor is it just a matter of how she looks and acts, for there is an evident carefulness too in her singing. She can produce beautiful sequences of rounded, gleaming melody in the middle-high register, soft and yet carrying; but the notes have to be held in place and warily balanced. It is a near miracle that they almost always are so, but one cannot quite believe in the purity, and without purity Desdemona does not have very much personality or, indeed, point.

The other parts are paltry in this cruel opera, cruel by no means only to its titular hero. They are adequately done. The conducting is far more than adequate. Valery Gergiev, normally associated with Russian repertory, proves he can be just as passionate in and about Verdi, and there are moments, notably the close of the third act, when the passion he encourages in the orchestra threatens to drown out even a stage full of voices. Detail is zealously brought forward; sometimes rather ordinary music is obliged to come up with some significance. The chorus interests him rather less, and his tempos in the first act can leave voices hurrying behind. But the orchestra, in its display, equals the savage magnificence we are witnessing onstage. (*New Yorker*, 11 April 1994)

La forza del destino

St Petersburg was as far from home as Verdi travelled, and the opera he wrote for that city, *La forza del destino*, has a lot to say about exile. Part of its message comes, as James Levine and his musicians wonderfully display throughout the new Met production, in the quality of the orchestral music, which moves away from anything noisy or ordinary, as if trekking off towards polish. Some of its stories are fortuitous—like those that depend on the responses it elicited, by virtue of where it was done, from Russian composers. For instance, the shift between the first two acts, from high seriousness to conviviality, looks a tempting precedent for how Musorgsky was to move in *Boris* (another of his steals might be the offstage monastic choir), and the use of a fate motif could have impressed Tchaikovsky before he found the same thing in *Carmen*. Verdi's opera thus gained a certain Russian colour, but that is not at the heart of its strangeness.

Verdi presumably had plenty of opportunity to hear the orchestra of the Imperial Theatre before he completed his score, in 1862, and presumably this prior experience accounts for much of what is special about *Forza*: the refinement, the lack of weight and splash, the engraving of expression, the superb long instrumental melodies. Levine and his players make it all song and fine gesture, represented by the clarinet solo at the start of the third act—grandly and nobly phrased, with an almost flute-like purity of tone—and by the impellent drumming in the finale. But the drama begins in the overture, and since this was added for the 1869 revision, Verdi must have been responding here not to his personnel but to his work. The 'force of destiny' is a musical idea. It is the abrasion of urgency on repose, and it is figured for us first of all in the overture, in the assault of repetitive music—which not only symbolizes but realizes the call of progress in being beat-driven and in marking time through its iterations—on cantabile melody. The insistent circlings can belong only to the orchestra; the tunes are evidently meant to be sung. And so the orchestra sets up a demand that it will reinforce in not overly subtle fashion at the first turning-point in the drama (the reappearance of Leonora's father to confront her nocturnal visitor, Alvaro) and again at the start of the last scene, and which it will imply all through: the demand for control.

That is why the libretto has to be such a mess. If one looks for justification of the title in the text, one is bound for disappointment. Nowhere is it explained why Leonora and Alvaro, on the point of leaving together at the end of Act 1, should become separated, or why Alvaro should soon afterwards believe Leonora dead. Far from being forced by fate, these people are condemned to an unmotivated wandering, and Leonora's brother Carlos—though having the motive of revenge for an affront to family honour—necessarily wanders with them. The whole opera is a protracted, dislocated prelude to the moment when its three central characters finally meet, and the further irony of the title is that Verdi had second thoughts about what should happen then. Should all three die, in a rapid fall of bodies (which early audiences seem to have found more gross than ridiculous) to be followed by a choral prayer, or should Alvaro survive, and the opera end more intimately?

Levine's choice—the 1869 version but with the 1862 order for the third act—allows him to end that act with the focus on Alvaro, which is where anyone would want it when Plácido Domingo is singing the part. His interpretation is keen. The sound is dark and taut; its gleam is the gleam on old wood, and Domingo's vocal joinery is as expert as ever, the phrases integral and the ornaments fitted in justly. There must be a word in Spanish for the robust yet aristocratic distaste he conveys—not only in this role but especially and rightly here. His Alvaro is a man who is trying to conduct himself with dignity through a world without scruples—a world that will buffet him from palace to battlefield and on to monastery without any satisfactory logic, and in which the people to whom he is closest will either be removed from him without cause or be present in disguise. It is a world in which time and place, as measured by words, have lost their grip, and the characters, in as much as they are made by words, have lost themselves, preserving only, but crucially, what is defined for them by music, which is their emotional core. Domingo's Alvaro is this: not Alvaro at all, but a nameless one who has to behave as if he were Alvaro, in situations in which he has been suddenly and inexplicably inserted, at the behest of the music. Music, in this most experimental of Verdi's operas, takes off on its own. We can see no reason for what happens, but we can hear every reason.

One can imagine ways in which a production might connect with the work's rootlessness, its disesteem of consequence in drama or location, by providing settings and actions to suggest the dangerous insubstantiality of nightmare. There could be nothing onstage but mist or a labyrinth. Duets could be duets of search rather than of arrival together. Religious retreat, to which both Alvaro and Leonora resort, could be shown as an almost autistic reaction to a prevailing unanswerability in the universe.

It was not, of course, in order to explore such possibilities of stagecraft that Giancarlo del Monaco became the Met's director of choice in the Italian repertory, and yet his production does—thanks to its monumentally stagy decor, by Michael Scott, and to its calm failure to be surprised by anything the scenario can throw at it—amount to one huge alienation effect. To begin with, del Monaco and Scott seem to be playing a more sophisticated game, for the initial couple of sets are presented boxed and tidy. But then the production team—including the lighting designer, Gil Wechsler—defiantly throws caution to the winds. We get a wide wall of fake tombs, a candle-lit Franciscan church interior that comes sliding forward, a battlefield of tree stumps and feeble fireworks, and a spread hand of towering ruins as container for the second ebullient scene with

Preziosilla and her various entourage. This is all nonsense, of course, but in being nonsense it makes no claim to be embodying the real action of the piece, and thereby serves the opera admirably. There is a moment, too, in the first church scene when the set is used to create a striking acoustic effect, that of the chorus lying face down and singing into the floor.

Altogether *Forza* comes boldly across as a drama in which some of the characters—those going under the names of Leonora, Alvaro, and Carlos—are never where they hope to be, while others, including most notably Preziosilla, would never think of being anywhere but where they are. That could define the difference between tragedy and comedy, and Verdi's alternation of the two (which is another experimental feature of the work, perhaps contingent on the first) is excellently manoeuvred, as it must be, by Levine and the orchestra, who make fifes and jingles as demanding of our interest as suavity and catastrophe. It also helps to have a decorous Preziosilla in Gloria Scalchi, who suggests the untamed by means of strong white tone—particularly in the second act, where her interlacing with Sharon Sweet's Leonora is startling for clarity and contrast—rather than posturing.

Sweet, after some initial problems, was beautifully consistent and consistently beautiful. As Carlo, completing the triangle, Vladimir Chernov was a singing muscle: fit, bang on the note, nothing wasted, and as vigorous and trim in his movement as in his singing. Another fine performance came from Roberto Scandiuzzi who sang the Padre Guardiano with the inevitable gravity but also with grace, the brief notes feathered into the line. Bruno Pola was the nicely greasy Melitone; Michel Sénéchal gave a veteran's show of health as Trabuco. (*New Yorker*, 18 March 1996)

a quintet of singers

Song recitals are theatre, in which singers become other people, usually several at once. Cathy Berberian, in 1972, became a salon diva of the Edwardian era, and the review was an attempt to travel part-way with her.

José van Dam

By this point in his career José van Dam has seen a lot and been a lot—everything from St Francis to the devil. His performance of Schubert's *Winterreise* at Alice Tully Hall on Thursday conveyed, in every breath, that length and breadth of experience, that variety of self-projections, all of which have also been self-examination.

The expressive stance was one of utter candour. Van Dam does not sound like a young man anymore. Come to think of it, he never did. That was never the point. And now, in *Winterreise*, was no time to start. These were emphatically not the songs of a swain disappointed in love, but those of a man disappointed by life—or not so much disappointed as confirmed in his low expectations. And out of his suffering, out of the bleakness, he comes up with the means to tell his whole story. You listened as if to someone buffeted but robust, looking at you flat-lipped and staring.

Lyricism was no more the issue than youth or love. Christopher H. Gibbs's excellent programme note told us that when Schubert first sang these songs to his friends, they were perplexed and liked only the fifth number, 'Der Lindenbaum'. Had they heard Van Dam's performance, they surely would not have liked even that, for by this stage, having reached his stride in the song before, he was making everything sound like the most extraordinary, direct and compelling recitative, as if the notes and the rhythms were always and only the best means of giving utterance to the words—or rather to the feeling, present or remembered.

The words and the notes were the means, to be transcended by being lived, to the ultimate. In one of the most moving songs, 'Wasserflut', Van Dam showed how different syllables at the same acute point in the recurring melody could each have a different weight, intensity and sway, a different way of rearing out of the line, like a thorn, yet integral to it. Each had a different way, too, of pulling the heartstrings when you thought you knew what was coming.

And what was the piano thinking at this point? Maciej Pikulski's playing was superlative throughout: highly refined, light and poetic in sound and sensation, a delicate yet thoroughly decisive and dependable support for the singer. What it was for the singing persona—the voice that Van Dam was bringing so immediately into the hall—was another matter. There were times when the accompaniment just enfolded and concurred, as in 'Wasserflut', where Pikulski's playing of the shifting, settling cadence after the first two lines was breath-stopping. But elsewhere the piano appeared to have thoughts of its own, and not very comfortable or comforting ones. In the next song, 'Auf dem Flusse', it kept breaking the journeyer's thought. In 'Einsamkeit', it seemed blithely negligent of his distress—an image, rather, of the calm world he was railing against. In 'Irrlicht', giving him his lines, it was teaching him how to sing. Then finally in 'Der Leiermann', of course, it was the little tune—sweet, consolatory and deeply uncanny as Pikulski made it—of Death the organ-grinder, greeted by Van Dam with complete, naked simplicity, all rage and anguish gone. (*New York Times*, 26 October 2002)

Dmitri Hvorostovsky

Maybe it was not planned this way, but Sunday night's recital at Carnegie Hall by the bass-baritone Dmitri Hvorostovsky, with Mikhail Arkadiev at the piano, provided a kind of sunset postscript to the festival of Russian music that had been brought to the hall in four preceding concerts by the Kirov Orchestra. Tchaikovsky and Rachmaninoff were on the programme (as they had been for the orchestra): nine songs by each. The sound was superb, the mood glowing.

Tchaikovsky's songs—superior domestic music—may have been a bit too frail for these circumstances, but it was good to hear Hvorostovsky sounding so ardent in 'Why?' so melodious in 'I bless you, forests'. He also did well in his manner and stance to give the songs some dignity even while showing a sense of humour. Touching a hand to his silver locks, smiling easily, he made his good looks a joke he shared with his appreciative audience.

After intermission, the Rachmaninoff group was more serious and more varied. It also gave Arkadiev a chance to sing. He is indeed an exceptionally tender and sensitive pianist, with a fine feeling for songful phrasing and resonant tone. Meanwhile, Hvorostovsky just seemed to get better and better, increasing his range of dynamics and colour, driving deeper into the music.

His last encore, though, was something else. Brought back again and again, he had already sung a piece from Rachmaninoff's opera *Aleko* and two outrageously sentimental songs. Then he returned without Arkadiev to sing, as he said, his favourite Russian folksong. The house went silent, and he threw himself back into the primeval present. Grace notes were beautifully articulated and integrated into the ululation. Extraordinary pianissimos happened. Head tones were fully integrated into the chest voice.

What was being said? Who knows? This was a voice communicating beyond language. (*New York Times*, 22 December 2001)

Ewa Podles

Inside any singer lies an expressive persona that generally comes to the surface just fitfully: in a phrase, a cadence, maybe a single note—things of utter rightness. With Ewa Podles, who gave a recital with Garrick Ohlsson (in superb form) on Sunday afternoon, this interior being is there all the time, out to the level of the skin, taking over the entire body. When performing she stands with her head slightly tilted back, and one can almost see her voice as a flame hovering over her mouth. Her whole body seems tuned to create that voice. Her demeanour is that of a person consumed by singing.

She is nominally a contralto, but she belongs to no category. She does indeed stalk the lower depths of the female voice, but without the thickness, the cream, that is often found there. This is not particularly a voice of comfort. Her basic tone, though perfectly formed and extraordinarily adaptable to different colours, has something bare about it, even something a little harsh: harsh with the harshness of grief (the subject of so many of the Rachmaninoff songs she chose here) being exposed. This is a voice that has been expertly trained, but not tamed.

If in the Rachmaninoff sets she was a sybil, standing monumentally proud in her scarlet robe to pronounce the truth of sorrow, suffering and bitterness, in Musorgsky's *Nursery* cycle she became nanny and child. She did so physically. She can do things with her body that from most other singers would be cute and selfconscious. She can raise one arm in a dismissive gesture. She can seal her lips and widen her eyes. She can respond to a harmony in the piano with a downcast look. She can do all this because her behaviour is being ruled by her voice. Her voice has taken over.

Where her singing was concerned, her identification with the characters was so complete it could be slight. She might bleach and diminish her tone for a brief while to suggest the child, but then she would range over her whole repertory of ways to fill out or skim a note without losing the effect of the child's voice. The pitfalls of potential embarrassment in this music are everywhere. She went right up to each one of them, looked in deep and never stumbled. (*New York Times*, 21 November 2001)

Hermann Prey

'It is so still, so secret here: the sun has gone down, the day disappeared. How quickly now the evening greys!'

These were the first words sung on Wednesday night at the 92d Street Y, and they set the tone for a concert that was all about lateness. In the first place, the event was a postscript to the Y's Schubertiade, which had begun in 1987 with the magnificent aim of presenting all Schubert's music within a decade. Also, the programme consisted entirely of songs from the last year of Schubert's life. And the singer was Hermann Prey, the moving force behind the Schubertiade and a man who has been singing these songs for half a century. As he reminded the audience in one of his genial introductions—some members of the audience gasped as if they had not thought of this before—Schubert died at the age of thirty-one. His music is a young man's music. The poems he set in his songs, even at the end, are a young man's poems. Love is in the air. Nature is experienced with freshness. Everything springs from the hero's heart. But it is part of a young man's sensibility, too, that all these things should be felt as evanescent. Love goes. Nature is heedless. Everything slips through the hero's hands. When the voice in the poem is speaking of joys, the voice in the song is usually placing them in the past tense. From this Prey took his opportunities. Just as children will listen to a grandfather's reminiscences not so much for the stories themselves as for the gleam in the old man's eye, so we listened on Wednesday.

Prey was in excellent form. At sixty-eight he still has, in his looks and in his bearing, a youthfulness, and it is there in his voice, too. In his middle register there is a patch of sheer gold that time has had little effect upon. But there are the profits of maturity, too: often a phrase will emerge with the rich polish that comes, to voices as to wood, from repeated use. Above all, the mood is true. At the end of this long, uninterrupted recital he arrived at Schubert's very last song, and conveyed what he had called the 'eerie cheerfulness' that seems a response to imminent death. Here and all through the evening, his performances were a reminder of his powers, but they also had an impressive candour that was of the moment. He was singing of himself. Joseph Anderer was the mellow horn soloist in 'Auf dem Strom'. At the piano James Levine was, of course, a closely sensitive partner throughout, in tune with the twilight. (*New York Times*, 13 March 1998) [Prey died a little more than four months after this recital.]

Cathy Berberian

Those of us in these islands who have some care for the musical arts have but infrequent opportunity to taste of the exquisite, the true art which now flowers in the more fashionable salons of Paris. With what pleasure, then, did we attend, yesterday evening [at the Queen Elizabeth Hall], a soirée at which Mlle Cathy Berberian was present! Mlle Berberian gave a recital in the latest French manner, prefacing her selections with a motto: *A la Recherche de la musique perdu*, which, I am informed, refers to a French literary work.

Mlle Berberian began with Parisian novelties: a charming song by M Reynaldo Hahn and a most terrifying one, entitled 'Danse macabre', from the pen of M Saint-Saëns. Mlle Berberian's fluency in several tongues was much commented, and this was especially evident in a song by M Rimsky-Korsakoff, wafting us to the silken colours and heady perfumes of Araby. The recital also included some very beautiful songs which had been arranged, with great intelligence, from the works of Beethoven. How oft has one listened to the sonatas and symphonies of this master feeling that only words might bring their sentiment to its truest and most perfect expression! The truth of this was ably demonstrated in Mlle Berberian's delightful rendering of 'Through thou so blest', an arrangement by Zilcher of a tune from the Fifth Symphony.

In deference to her hostess Mlle Berberian most courteously included a number of English songs. Her performance of Purcell's ditty 'Nymphs and Shepherds' was extremely well received, although I considered that the voice was not here at its prettiest. Mlle Berberian drew tears with an affecting new song, 'There are fairies at the bottom of our garden', by Miss Liza Lehmann; and several of the gentlemen present were seen to lay aside their brandies, so heart-rending was her singing in 'Father's a drunkard' by Mrs E.A. Parkhurst. If one might venture to criticize Mlle Berberian, it would be for the lapse of taste which induced her to present a song from the Paris music-halls by M Erik Satie and one of M Offenbach's more improper airs. Mlle Berberian was accompanied at the pianoforte by Signor Bruno Canino, a very accomplished artist. We must hope that both will return to our shores ere long. (*Financial Times*, 18 October 1972)

Schnittke

Alfred Schnittke was the most prominent Russian composer of the generation after Shostakovich, and by far the most productive, especially during the decade after Mikhail Gorbachev's arrival in power (1985), when his music seemed to match the rapid pace of events, the surprise, and the sense of history peeling back. There were three operas from him in those years, and four symphonies, not to mention numerous other orchestral and chamber works. Since this was also the period when much of his earlier music reached the west for the first time, the onrush was startling.

Symphony No.1

If one wanted a nickname for Schnittke's First Symphony, which was played for the first time in this country last night, then perhaps it could be 'The Brezhnev', the work being vast, immensely powerful but supremely confident, jovial but chillingly mirthless, and only just credible as an example of human behaviour.

It is also, and here perhaps it departs from the late Leonid, a great mass of contradictions and incoherences. We knew already that Schnittke was a master of masked and faked voices, beguiling the ear with tales of long ago and nevermore while furiously shrieking at the same time, asking questions about identity and consciousness that may seem particularly acute in the Soviet Union but are by no means irrelevant elsewhere. The symphony now shows him capable of commanding immense resources over a span of eighty minutes, of creating musical ironies that combine explosive immediacy with a capacity to rumble on.

But we have heard the works in the wrong order. The First Symphony predates the chamber works and violin concertos that have established Schnittke's current reputation in this counrty: it was written between 1969 and 1972, and it fits uncannily well, given the composer's almost total isolation from the west at that time, into the scheme of music generally. In particular, its recognition of Mahler as crucial and of stylistic multiplicity as inevitable brings it into line with contemporary works by Berio, Maxwell Davies and George Rochberg. However, its force and assuredness in this area perhaps come from a nearer relation to Shostakovich, who may himself, in the enigmatic quotations of his Fifteenth Symphony, have been influenced by this work.

Schnittke's method, though, is more often to imitate than to quote, with the exception of one or two momentous passages. The second movement springs from the conflict of something totally blithe and early classical with military marches on the brass, and at its midpoint a circus band brings on a jazz break for violin and piano, here featuring two Estonian musicians, Paul Magi and Rein Rannap. Then at the end of this movement the wind players troop off, to leave the strings for an adagio where imitation, of late Mahler, seems to fade into individual expression, especially when the music's complex polyphony is cramped into the treble register. If there has been a death, it is more coarsely commemorated by the return of the wind playing a funeral march, more off than on Chopin's. The finale seems then to be a search for ways of closure, including a colossal diatonic apotheosis (perhaps from the official symphony that this certainly is not), huge music for organ and brass, and another mass exit referring to Haydn's 'Farewell'. But in fact the work ends as it had begun, with the orchestra coming on to the platform in chaotic improvisation. (*Times*, 18 December 1986)

Symphonies Nos.6–7

The first time I heard a piece by Alfred Schnittke was at the 1971 festival of the International Society for Contemporary Music, in London, when a short, chamber-scale cello concerto by him, *Dialogue*, was played. It seemed at the time a cautious blend of Shostakovich and Schoenberg—a piece that would not have been too remarkable had it not been written in a Soviet Union culturally stifled since the ejection of Khrushchev in 1964. We on the outside knew there were other composers swimming against the official stream, and among them Edison Denisov appeared a much more colourful fish, with his background in Stravinsky and Boulez. What we did not know was that Schnittke was then in the middle of writing his First Symphony, in which the Shostakovich-Schoenberg style was to be just one possibility in a great Ivesian circus. And what we could not know was that his subsequent symphonies, concertos and chamber works would instal him (it happened about a decade later) as the heir to Shostakovich, the musical voice of Russia.

I am not sure if Schnittke was present at that 1971 festival, or if memory has taken his image from a black-and-white photograph and placed him there, which it easily could have, for even in the indubitable flesh, as he was seen last month onstage at Avery Fisher Hall, he cuts a painfully exhausted, paled, monochrome figure. I certainly do remember encountering both Denisov and Schnittke at a reception at the British Embassy in Moscow in 1986: the former affable, broadly smiling, holding court, Schnittke standing alone in another room, hunched, in his habitual mid-grey suit, with his back turned—surely much less from discourtesy than from reticence—to deter approach.

Possibly I have held onto these mental pictures because they accord with a pre-existing concept of the music, but what is significant is that we all find ourselves forming such connections, that the music wants to scratch out of us some interpretation in terms of its composer, the conditions of his life, the recent history of Russia, or the decline and fall of western culture. Kurt Masur, speaking to the audience in Fisher Hall before conducting the first performance of Schnittke's Seventh Symphony (commissioned by the New York Philharmonic), referred to the music's 'harsh' qualities, and related a poignant anecdote about his first visit to the composer, in 1975, when it was necessary to go at dead of night, because foreign guests were not allowed at the home of one who declined to sing the Party tune. Masur's further reference to 'hope' in this music was not so useful: perhaps the reference was itself a gesture of hope, aimed at persuading the audience that, though they might have to sit through twenty minutes of strenuous discord, all would be well in the end. One must also wonder how the invocation of 'hope' (it was there, too, in a programme article) sounds to a composer who lived through—lived against, one might say—a time when 'optimism' was one of the official requirements. It would be an appalling irony if his music were now to be celebrated for precisely the attribute it refused to supply on demand in Brezhnev's Moscow.

The only sure hope in this music—one notes this more bleakly than gaily—is the hope it brings to the record business. With forty compact discs devoted exclusively to his works, Schnittke must be the living composer most frequently recorded (Philip Glass would be the nearest contender for that title); the figure also testifies to his productivity. Within the last decade, for instance, he has written five symphonies, four concertos, two full-length operas and numerous smaller works. But though one might think that this creative abundance would itself express hope, it does not quite work that way, largely because there is no clue in the music as to whether we are dealing with a Haydn, fluently composing to order, or a Hugo Wolf, tearing through sheets with his demons behind him. The clues can all be read both ways, and it is the thorough ambivalence of this music, down into its marrow, that is responsible for its disturbing unease—and that efficiently eliminates all hope of hope.

This ambivalence is a particularly Russian quality—Stalin's great gift to musical history. It is not the pearly ambivalence of a Boulez or a Berio, where the meaning is in the glistening of many meanings; it is an ashen ambivalence of enforced statement (joy, progress, affirmation, as it had to be for Stalin's composers) and dissident subtext (i.e., Don't you believe it)—an ambivalence that, in the case of Shostakovich, did not need spelling out in alleged memoirs. It did not need spelling out because the voice in Shostakovich's music is clear, and we feel we can tell what tone it has.

But the great point about Schnittke's music is that it refuses us this confidence. Schnittke has no voice, because he has no style. His name is legion. He can write radiant choral harmony in the Russian Orthodox tradition, as in his Concerto for chorus, or dark, brooding pieces, like his Viola Concerto, or gags and parodies, or Baroque pastiches, as in his several concerti grossi, or pseudo-Mahler, as in his Fifth Symphony. He can pile all these things up and put a jazz band on top, as he did in his First Symphony. He can clear them all away and leave just the wandering melody of a waltz, as he does at the end of the new symphony for the Philharmonic, which Masur was conducting. What he never tells us is what they all mean. One cannot just accept them at face value: a waltz in the 1990s cannot be simply a waltz, and the way Schnittke presents his waltz, as a solo line intoned in succession by three deep bass voices—tuba, contrabassoon and double bass—displaces any possibility of naive acceptance. We listen expectantly for the double meaning: this is how the music imposes its demand for interpretation. But what we are given is a sequence of blank cheques on which we can write what value we will, in the knowledge that afterwards we are bound to feel we have failed some test, or been cheated (though only if we think we have a right to certainties the music cannot offer and does not pretend to offer).

It may help a little to have some awareness of the Soviet background—to know, for instance, that the early-music revival of the 1960s and 70s had in Russia the special meaning of dissent, because it allowed musicians to steer away from officially sanctioned symphonic practice, and to do so unimpeachably. Hard to call Vivaldi to account before the Composers' Union. The harpsichord thus became a symbol of challenge, and dissident composers—like the energetic

Andrey Volkonsky (what became of him?)—found in the unlikely medium of Baroque continuo playing a way of voicing protest. Unapprized of this history, one might easily read Schnittke's frequent recourses to the harpsichord and to eighteenth-century style as merely rococo prettifications or images of lost content.

But they may well be those things too. Before the new symphony, the Philharmonic played the composer's *(K)ein Sommernachtstraum* (a deeply Schnittke-esque title, in saying only what the piece is not: apparently he had thought of calling his First Symphony *Kein Symphonie*), which begins as a Mozartian minuet conversation between violin with piano and flute with harpsichord, and which progressively occludes and refracts the innocent little air, until all we hear is a haze or a rude circus march. Is the piece, despite that title, a dream, like Ives's *Putnam's Camp*? Is it a joke? Is it a refusal of Soviet conformity? Is it—bearing in mind it was commissioned by the Salzburg Festival—a satire on the veneration of St Wolfgang Amadeus? This performance, which Masur teasingly let steal upon us directly after three minuets with bona fide Köchel numbers, quite properly left us with the questions.

(K)ein Sommernachtstraum was written in 1985, which is an awfully long way back both in Russian history and in Schnittke's catalogue. In his more recent music he appears to have moved away from fake Mozartiana and from the bustling pseudo-Brandenburgery of his first concerti grossi: the fifth in this series, which had its premiere at Carnegie Hall three years ago, is a fiendish, glacial violin concerto, composed for Gidon Kremer, and recently recorded by him. This more recent music is shocked and numb. It is still riddled with references, but they have retreated, become sketchy and doubtful. For example, the Seventh Symphony starts out with an unaccompanied violin solo, whose opening rise echos, though with severe attenuation, the same point in the Seventh Symphony of Bruckner. But the moment passes, and it is hard to know whether it was a planted allusion or a coincidence—a coincidence of the kind that happened in *(K)ein Sommernachtstraum*, when, in concocting what he thought was imitation Mozart, Schnittke came up with something like the melody of one of the minuets Masur selected for this program, K.104 No.3.

Saying we cannot be sure what is deliberate in this music is equivalent to saying we do not know what it means—not for reasons of difficulty or obfuscation, but because the ground has slipped from under our feet. It has slipped, too, from under the composer's. In a recent interview, he made a striking remark about his Sixth Symphony, saying: 'It's not clear if we've really heard it .' The reason for this would not be that the composer has not done his job properly, or that audiences so far have been uncomprehending; the reason would be that the ability of all of us—composer and audience—to make contact with the music is impaired. Schnittke is not in the business of writing us messages: the doubts and doublenesses in his music would make such presumption impossible. He is as distanced from his music as the rest of us, perhaps as puzzled by it. It is just that he has the responsibility of trapping these grey clouds, these ashes, for us all to inspect and ponder.

In an output not notable for good cheer, the Sixth Symphony—given its New York premiere by Mstislav Rostropovich and the National Symphony at Carnegie Hall a few days before the Seventh—is particularly desolate. It has the usual four movements, of classical dimensions, but the fabric is shot to pieces: long stretches of the opening allegro, for instance, are occupied by just a few brass instruments, or by the low strings, and much of the material is abrupt: idea, silence, idea. Often the fragments suggest religious music—chorale or chant—and one is reminded that Schnittke's two previous even-numbered symphonies were both muffled rituals: No.2 a hidden mass and No.4 an interweaving of Catholic, Orthodox and Jewish sacred melodies. But the wreckage of a church is pretty much like the wreckage of a liquor store, and what shouts loudest in this movement is the plain fact of brokenness. We may not have 'really heard it', but what we did hear was frightening enough. The many who piled out after the initial movement may have been the astutest listeners.

The Seventh Symphony—in three movements, playing for under twenty-five minutes—is less uncomfortable, but not by much. Again, a lot of the music spans thinly over great vacancies: in the opening violin solo, in the gaunt scoring and spasmodic gesturing in most of what follows, and in the final waltz, where eighty-odd people are sitting on the platform for minutes with nothing to do. (Schnittke is a great composer for silent musicians and, conversely, of invisible music. At the start of *(K)ein Sommernachtstraum* the difficulty of seeing who is playing heightens one's awareness that so many are not, and in the Fifth Concerto Grosso there is a prominent part for off-stage piano. The Seventh Symphony leaves some instruments cold except for the tiniest flicker of life: a scale and a chord from the eternal harpsichord; just a chord each from harp and piano. Perhaps one day there will be a Schnittke symphony in which all the music comes from unseen players, while an orchestra onstage helplessly waits.)

The third movement is by far the biggest, and includes episodes of extreme weirdness—especially some highly angular melodies from oboe and clarinets, brilliantly played by the Philharmonic soloists (and Eugene Levinson on bass at the end was outstanding: perfectly in control, whistling in the dark). The first movement is almost exclusively for strings, the second almost exclusively for wind and percussion, calling out German place-names in musical code. This geographical interlude was maybe a nod to Masur (Schnittke's Third Symphony, also written for him, had included similar ciphers for German composers), maybe an acknowledgement of the composer's ancestry and current abode. He must, too, have appreciated the irony that the German pitch names extractable from 'Deutschland' come perilously close to the DSCH motif with which Shostakovich inscribed himself in his music: though living in Hamburg, Schnittke remains a Russian composer.

The altogether excellent performance of the new symphony did credit to the Philharmonic and to Masur. They were lucky, though, that there were others around to pick up the Schnittke theme: not only the National Symphony at Carnegie Hall but also Yale Music Spectrum with two keyboard works at Merkin Hall, and Leon Botstein and the American Symphony Orchestra with the *Faust* cantata at Avery Fisher Hall. Without these additional events, the Philharmonic's 'Composer Week' would have been a rather meagre affair. (*New Yorker*, 7 March 1994)

how it was, maybe

Where 'early music' at the start of the 1970s had meant ensembles specializing in medieval music or Monteverdi, during the 1980s performers on period instruments, and conductors pointing to support for their interpretations in studies of period practice, gradually took on a large part of what had hitherto been in the repertory of standard symphony orchestras, notably Bach, Haydn and Mozart. Soon historically informed performance became the new orthodoxy, and dizzying discoveries came: the most familiar music was refreshed, the previously marginal magnified and the unknown—even the unnotated—brought to life after centuries.

Brahms

Time is being swallowed up and the race is on. Having cleared the century and more from Bach to Berlioz during the 1980s, leading exponents of period performing style are now well into the next generation. That was marked this week when Roger Norrington and the London Classical Players began the assault on Brahms. If they continue at this rate they will be on to Boulez by the end of the century, and then we can all forget about the music of the past. Everything will have been done. The LCP, the English Baroque Soloists, the Orchestra of the Age of Enlightenment and the rest of them will all be waiting eagerly for the next Brian Ferneyhough premiere so that they can follow with an authentic performance.

Enticing though this prospect may be, there is something a little worrying about the present gallop through history, and not least the implicit assumption that once a piece has been delivered onto compact disc it has been dealt with. A movement founded on retrieving the past thus finds itself instead consuming, or at least memorializing, and instead of constantly enlarging the possibilities of interpretation, which so far has been the most positive outcome of the search for 'authenticity', musicians may unwittingly be reinforcing the old myth of the definitive performance. Yet a further alarm signal is the evidence that the house style of each ensemble is becoming so strong, perhaps under the encouragement of competitive instincts, that it ceases to matter very much whether one is hearing Bach or Brahms: the image is the same. So again, a movement which started in opposition to accepted norms is generating its own establishment of star conductors, distinguished as much by their mannerisms as by their musical intelligence.

The Norrington style is unmistakeable: a matter of brisk speed, long crescendos, very clearly exposed woodwind solos, careful blending of small groupings but yet a coarse and wind-heavy tutti sound. It is dynamic, exciting, virtuoso. But as an instrument of musical unfolding it has its limitations. They were least apparent this time in the opening performance of the St Antony Variations, which came up shining fresh from the application of sharply contrasted tempos, contrapuntal lucidity and beautiful solo playing. Perhaps it helped, too, that the sounds were still, at this point in the concert, new: the intense but suavely phrasing oboe, the shadowed flutes, the wonderfully buzzing bassoons. The piece became a mid-nineteenth-century Young Person's Guide to the Orchestra.

After that came Mozart's C Minor Piano Concerto, given with a string body of the same size (forty players) and perhaps intentionally brought forward in time, since Melvyn Tan used the Brahms cadenza. However, this stretch of Brahms was the least successful part of this performance—not because it stood out stylistically, which it had every right to do, but because Tan's 1858 Erard sounded wonky and unbalanced when being asked to produce Brahms's fuller chords. Elsewhere the sounds Tan drew from the instrument were exquisite, especially in passages of extreme pianissimo that stole through the hall with breathtaking clarity. He is also, as he proved again, a master in the art of using the disciplines of period instruments as permission for an unashamedly Romantic, poetic style of interpretation. Norrington and his woodwind soloists responded similarly, with telling, if more obviously practised, shapes and gestures.

It was the Brahms First Symphony, after the interval, that opened all the doubts. Certainly there were marvellous things which depended on Norrington's tight control. But, with very fast speeds in the outer movements and a sense of intent propulsion even in the andante, rather too much was drilled and driven. Also, Norrington's platform layout—with horns on the extreme right, trumpets and trombones on the extreme left, and woodwind and timpani at the back—leads almost inevitably to a spread, unbalanced sound in loud tuttis. One may hear more of the orchestration, but one hears much less of the harmony. Sensational Brahms is hardly Brahms at all. (*Times*, 29 September 1990)

Rameau

Debussy, writing about a 1903 concert performance of two acts from Rameau's *Castor et Pollux*, mentioned among the marvels Pollux's air 'Nature, amour', a piece 'so unique in feeling and so novel in its construction that all sense of time and space is suspended'. The composer, he went on, 'seems like one of our contemporaries, whom we would congratulate as we left the theatre'. Many of us at the Brooklyn Academy of Music recently might also have been looking around for the tall, gaunt figure of M. Rameau to shake by the hand, after performances of *Castor* and of *Les Indes galantes* (Third-World Civilities, one might say) conducted by William Christie, with his group Les Arts Florissants. Both works have been recorded for Harmonia Mundi by the same outfit with almost the same casts; home listeners will miss only the excited atmosphere at BAM and the snazzy concert attire of the singers: Sandrine Piau's tightly-buttoned vermilion silk dress, erupting in the middle into a huge bustle; a modish tuxedo sported by one of the gentlemen of the chorus.

In style and daring and contemporaneity, the apparel matched the music better than wigs and crinolines could have done. Christie's ability to make old music sound new is well known here, thanks especially to his ensemble's performances of Lully's *Atys* at BAM last year and in 1989. Re-creating the distant art of the French Baroque is, for them, simply a matter of creating it perfectly, with the addition of particular perfections devised particularly for Rameau. Young, vibrato-free, well-tuned voices are crucial, but equally vital—and vitalizing to Rameau's line—is the ease with which both singers and instrumentalists include ornament as part of the phrase, so that the frequent mordents, trills and appoggiaturas are moments of suppleness in the melody and not encrustations.

Then there is Christie's way of wafting the music into the air. The tempting connection between Rameau and his coeval Watteau lies partly in the weightlessness of their figures, and Christie makes a fine show of Rameau's levitation by his sense for the exquisite, the momentary, in the harmony (Debussy on another occasion was to write of 'harmonic "moments" to caress the ear'), by the fluidity of his tempo and by the give, too, in how he draws together his ensemble. As if drafting the musical line with a pencil, he can make it precise and fine, as he has to do when he lets some of the dances dash off at the boisterous speeds they demand, or else he can use the flat edge of the lead, brush the voices and instruments along a little more relaxedly. The resulting slight spread in the harmony may on occasion produce a succulent sensuousness, as in the entry of Cupid in the prologue to *Castor*, imploring his mother Venus to bring Mars to heel; more generally the gentle arpeggiation suggests music which we catch as it is just moving into focus, music in formation, in the present.

We might also feel the music to be new, to be happening now, because Rameau, like Monteverdi, reaches us unstaled by a continuous history of performance: this is music that has only recently begun to come alive again. Other freshnesses, though, are inherent in what the music is, and in what these musicians reveal it to be. The performances are polished to complete transparency, letting through the vividness of the imagery and its range from monumental lament (the chorus with which the drama of *Castor* begins, done with a chilling slow tremolo on the long second syllable of 'gémisse') to seductive suavity (Hebe's attendants courting Pollux in the second act, their music falling in sweet sixths through gruppetti as they sing of chains of flowers), or to the harsh, jagged music of the demons in the next act. But the first surprise of the Arts Florissants performance, even to one familiar with the old Harnoncourt recording of the opera, is in the expressive immediacy, the way the recitatives, especially, respond so swiftly to movements of thought and feeling.

Castor is full of recitative dialogues in which changes of heart are brought about. In the first act Telaira, newly bereaved widow of Castor, persuades Pollux to repress his love for her and restore her lover to life. (This version of the story has it that, while both twins were Leda's children, only Pollux was the son of Jupiter.) In the third act Telaira at hell's gates presses Pollux to take the fateful step that will lead him down to Hades to change places with his brother, against the wishes of Phoebe, who is in pursuit of him. Pollux's discourse with the two women comes to rest on the high plateau of a marvellous trio of divergent emotions, where Christie leaves the voices to meander almost alone, supported by the barest touch of a cello on the bass line. The climax of the drama, in the fourth act, is a long scene between the brothers, in which Pollux's firmness and regret project a steady support for Castor's impressionable weave of feeling: joy at seeing his brother again, delight at the prospect of rejoining Telaira, horror that this means leaving Pollux once more and as his substitute, acceptance that only thereby can the twins—together in intention but eternally apart—best serve Telaira. Finally in the fifth act comes another long dialogue, where Castor insists that he must go back again to the Elysian fields and release Pollux, while Telaira swerves from felicity to fury to a bleak acknowledgement of human impotence in her marvellous line 'If they had loved, these gods, they would know what love means'.

The situations are moving, but it is Rameau's music that makes all this the dearest matter on earth—partly because the affect can be so nimbly altered by a new insinuation of harmony or rhythmic character, partly because the voices are often in deliciously unstable territory between the formulae of recitative and the phrases of song. The quickness of expression can perhaps be illustrated best by an example from *Les Indes galantes*, since in that work a whole story has to be unfolded inside each act, and there is not the leisure for argument. Phani, an Inca princess, is in love with Carlos, a Spanish officer, but afraid of her people's retribution. In a single passage of recitative, lasting only half a minute, she invites Carlos with warm, falling intervals, which lead her into an increasingly hectic enthusiasm before she stops, to a cautionary reminder in the harmony, and warns him not to come alone; then a brisk modulation enables her to race off again in imagining what might happen if Carlos were indeed to attempt an unaided abduction, and the sequence ends with an almost squeaked 'Ciel!'

There are problems of acceptance here, problems that the BAM surtitles did not address, and would not have addressed even if they had been free of solecisms. We need to be following, and feeling, Phani's mood shifts as they happen, not reading about them in a different time, and in a dismayingly informal translation. No wonder the audience laughed. And though laughter is not inappropriate, it ought to come from sympathy with the work's selfconscious outlandishness—with the fun that Rameau has with emotional quick changes, including some in a couple of wildly improbable recognition scenes. Maybe Louis Fuzelier's libretto for *Les Indes galantes* does creak at times, but a man who could write a line like 'Lorsque l'on aime, on craint toujours' (To be in love is always to be in fear) was not entirely useless as a poet of the emotions, and the swagger and the suddenness provided conditions in which Rameau's music could flourish.

Castor et Pollux differs from *Les Indes galantes* as classical from exotic. It lacks such bizarreries as the volcanic eruption whereby Phani's problems are resolved (fierce reiterated discords for the earthquake, followed by violin rockets to simulate the burning stones that the chorus sees shooting through the air), and has a simple integrity of tone and subject. But the two works are close in Rameau's output: *Les Indes galantes* was his second piece to be performed in the theatre, after *Hippolyte et Aricie*, and *Castor* his third, coming two years later, in 1737. They are also formally similar, for though the earlier piece is classed as an opera-ballet and the later one as a lyric tragedy, *Castor* has hardly any less dancing, and *Les Indes galantes* hardly any less display of emotion through song. Besides, these are not really distinct categories: some of the dances are choral numbers, and some of the songs are dances with voice.

The dance element is one clear impediment to staging these works, but it is also part of what makes them structurally, as well as expressively, special and contemporary. In Rameau's works opera has still not been released from its origins in festival, in telling a dramatic story for the purposes of celebration, and the dances repeatedly remind us that our contact with the myth is only through a theatre of artifice. But there are more levels than these two. The prologue of the gods, showing Venus's triumph over Mars, supplies not only a conventional nod to the recent ending of the War of the Polish Succession but also a frame for the entire ensuing drama; to that extent, it is well worth keeping. (Rameau removed it when Olympian allegories for the news went out of fashion, but Christie follows the original version.) Then, within the drama, two of the danced divertissements are entertainments that are provided for certain of the characters, and that we hear, such is Rameau's command of nuance, as if through those character's ears: the luscious but vain enchantment Pollux descries in Hebe's air and sarabande, the monotonous, flaccid sound that eternal bliss has for Castor alone in the Elysian fields.

In both these passages, and indeed in much of the opera, characters feel themselves to be in the wrong place: what motivates song in *Castor* is, beyond the much more usual conflicts between love and honorable conduct, a sense of alienation, a longing for somewhere else, for an abode where present frictions and frustrations would fall away. This again is something both Watteauesque and modern—modern because the resolution is to be found not within the story but in a leap from it onto another narrative level. Castor longs for the world when he is in Hades, and for Hades when he is back in the world. What settles both brothers, and stops their singing, is their final emplacement in the celestial realms of the frame, of the prologue, which is musically recalled when Jupiter arrives briefly in the second act and recalled again at the start of the final astronomical masque, in which Castor and Pollux are installed as a sign of the zodiac—with enticing possibilities, surely, for any production team.

The question is not why Castor and Pollux should, through three and a half acts, be feeling themselves in need of relocation, but rather why a story of displaced personages should have wrought from Rameau his finest opera. Perhaps *Pygmalion*, his finest one-act piece, may help us towards an answer, since the myth of the statue brought to life echoes something tremulous and wakening in Rameau's characters (something like the soft light that shines out of Watteau's). They are Baroque statues being made, by the power of a new musical art, to speak, and what they speak of most is the fearfulness they find in the human emotions they newly feel—a fearfulness that motivates, most explicitly, the air for Pollux that impressed Debussy. They might well wish to become statues again, to become silent, which is what Castor and Pollux eventually achieve.

If this betokens some consciousness in Rameau's characters that they are characters, such self-knowledge might have come from the composer's own extraordinary self-awareness in the act of creation. Like so many twentieth-century artists, but like few of earlier times, Rameau was a theorist too, and a theorist before he was much of a composer. He knew what he was doing, and why he was doing it. Writing, for instance, of Telaira's heart-stopping lament 'Tristes apprêts, pâles flambeaux' (Piteous rites, faltering flares), he pointed out the 'compunction' produced by the drop from tonic to subdominant on the fourth syllable, and the relief brought by the restoration of the tonic on the eighth. Few composers before the age of Stravinsky and Schoenberg, one imagines, can have found their tunes in quite that way. Rameau's characters are born into a world lit by a theory of how their singing works on the passions; that is the world in which they look around, understand themselves, and flinch.

For bringing these intensely touching characters into their plaintively reluctant life for the Arts Florissants performances, one has to shower praise on Howard Crook and Jérome Côrréas (the Dioscuri of high artistry combined with directness), on Mark Padmore (his bright tenor a trumpet to Crook's expressively virtuoso oboe), and on several diverse sopranos: Agnès Mellon for the purity and anxiety of Telaira, Claron McFadden for the welcoming voluptuousness of Hebe in *Les Indes galantes*, Sandrine Piau for several smart impersonations in both operas, and Véronique Gens for the arresting drama of Phoebe, who steps into *Castor* almost as a character from opera seria. More praise has to go to the darting violins, to the sensitive continuo team, to the bassoons of horn-like richness and warmth, and of course to Christie.

I end with Debussy's words. Moments of real joy in life are rare: I would not want to keep them to myself. (*New Yorker*, 22 March 1993)

Edda

Listen. This is how the story begins: 'Listen'. And the audience—at the Lincoln Center Festival show *Edda*, which opened on Tuesday night at John Jay College Theater—can do no less as the story unfolds.

Its language is remote: Old Norse, as written down in Iceland in the thirteenth century, at a time when the story was already many hundreds of years old. Its subject matter, too, is distant, telling of a prince who was turned into an otter and a fish that guards a hoard of gold, of a man who laughs as his heart is cut out, and of his sister who kills the man she unwillingly married.

But out of these double dark-age obscurities—of language and of magic and violence—it is pulled into a living immediacy by the *Edda* performers and the production made for them by Ping Chong. Three singers and two instrumentalists are dressed in costumes that hint at Viking home attire but would not cause comment on contemporary streets: shapeless black dresses for the women, who have the occasional braid in their hair, leather tabards for the men. Not only do they look the part of skaldic tale-tellers, they move the part as well—by not moving at all. They stay seated throughout, which strengthens their startling ability to create movement and drama with words and sounds.

Then, between episodes, their chairs slide slowly forward, backward and sideways, seemingly unaided, as the lighting changes. This serves the practical function of bringing the performers into different groupings for the different sequences, so that the story can wind on in the voices of one, two or three narrators, with or without the instrumentalists. But the magical sliding also gives these people a specialness, a strikingly effective replacement for the aura of the bard at the hearth. The story is related in a chant that can sound wild and strange: right at the start the two female narrators, Lena Susanne Norin and Agnethe Christensen, shoot their voices up through two wide intervals almost to the pitch of a scream. For the most part, though, the singers twine melodic formulae into the story in a way that gives it the strength and authority of a tale often told. Nobody can know whether this is how the story sounded more than a thousand years ago. It is thoroughly convincing now.

Also marvellous is the way Benjamin Bagby—the show's prime mover and principal narrator—delivers his material with such evident relish. Words of bargain and bloodshed slip from his mouth like polished jewels, and he keeps a fresh smile at the wonder of it all, while his one free hand (the other holds a lyre) stabs in quick gestures. The only problem is how to take one's eyes off him occasionally and look at the projected translation.

Norin and Christensen are, very suitably, all the while more grave, conveying the wisdom and sadness that are also there in the story. Norbert Rodenkirchen (on a skirling flute and a second lyre) and Elizabeth Gaver (on fiddle) are the expert instrumentalists. Christopher Caines mimes the part of a creature—six-breasted, blue, conical-hatted, goatskin-kilted—whose appearance at the start takes one into a world where the uncanny is normal. (*New York Times*, 12 July 2001)

Reich

Before the premiere of his *Music for Eighteen Musicians*, in 1976, Reich worked as a rock musician would—exclusively with his own band, on tour and in the recording studio, and outside the mainstream culture that had accepted the music of, for example, Carter and Boulez. By the 1990s, though, there were no more countercultures; Reich's music was one of the threads in a multicoloured tangle.

early steps

Steve Reich toured Britain two years ago; last night he returned, to the Queen Elizabeth Hall, bringing a programme of music composed since his previous visit. It is with his work as a whole as it is with each piece: the framework and the basic ideas remain constant while details fluctuate and change.

One principle of Reich's work is 'phasing', moving short rhythmic ideas into and out of synchrony. *Clapping Music* demonstrates this in the simplest possible way, with just two musicians using nothing but their hands. Well, not quite nothing: maintaining your own rhythm while listening closely to another requires concentration and training. Reich tours with his own performing ensemble, which has cultivated this double-mindedness to breathtaking perfection.

So much was evident in their playing of *Music for Pieces of Wood*. Five performers, each with a pair of claves, gradually build up a texture of similar rhythms jostling in a steady pulse. The effect is more fascinating than hypnotic, as the mind moves from one line to another, jumping back to the first to find it changed. This sudden discovery of the new in the fundamentally repetitive (like a fleeting pattern of ripples on still water) helps to give Reich's music its sense of simple wonder.

The quick-moving threads are not always solely rhythmic, though rhythmic shift is always paramount. When Reich uses pitched instruments, as in *Six Pianos*, he does so to glorify tonality. Ideas teem in brilliant D major, move into a Dorian E and then to B minor. Going through similar motions three times is another recurrent feature of Reich's work.

Finally, and most exultantly, *Music for Mallet Instruments, Voices and Organ* provides a warm glow of electric organ and women's voices while the mallet instruments—marimbas, vibraphone and glockenspiel—dash and twinkle. Again the processes of change are steady and straightforward; again there are so many of them that the listener is constantly being caught by surprise, as if watching an opal slowly revolve to reveal new colours and hidden traceries. (*Times*, 12 February 1974)

The Cave

In 1988, when *Different Trains* was played for the first time, Reich spoke of his hope that it would lead him to 'a new kind of documentary video music theatre'. Now we know what he meant—or at least now we can begin to perceive what he may have been hoping for, since *The Cave*, which had its first performance earlier this month in Vienna, is a remarkable adventure that feels more like a journey than an arrival, perhaps largely because of Reich's honourable reluctance to push his material towards a decisive artistic destination.

As in *Different Trains*, much of the material comes from recorded interviews—from fragments of speech, rarely exceeding a short sentence—which in *The Cave* are delivered by people seen on video screens, and are usually rerun a couple of times in the midst of imitations from instruments and sometimes voices. To take a memorable example, a recorded speaker in the third act of this two-and-a-half-hour piece tells firmly of Abraham's divine calling—'God says go, I'll tell you where later'—and the phrase becomes a musical theme: three strong beats, the last resting high, followed by a desinence of short notes, with each pitch approximating to the speaker's pitching of his voice. This theme can now be played by a violin, or sung by a tenor, or reproduced by any or all of an ensemble that includes four singers (two sopranos, tenor and baritone), a string quartet (a link to *Different Trains*, which was written for the Kronos Quartet), two woodwind players, and a typical Reichian assembly of percussion and keyboards, all precision-controlled by the conductor Paul Hillier to chime with the pictures. Word becomes note. Language is translated into music in a way that is both unusually direct and curiously automatic.

This is one expression of Reich's documentary faithfulness to the voices that he and his collaborator (also his wife), Beryl Korot, collected. Voices, voices—quilts of voices—give *The Cave* its being, and their utterances and musical echoes, beyond all that they immediately say, seem to be repeating the opening of St John's Gospel: 'In the beginning was the word.' It is a solemnly appropriate message to be hearing in a piece concerned with two word-centred faiths, those of Judaism and Islam. Words generate the musical ideas. Further words lie behind these recorded words, since what all the dozens of videotaped respondents are talking about is the gallery of stories associated with a name the voices differently speak as Abraham or Ibrahim. Reich and Korot put simple questions to the people they interviewed in Jerusalem, Hebron, New York and Austin during the four years of the work's preparation, asking 'Who is Abraham?', and the same with regard to Sarah, Hagar, Isaac and Ishmael. *The Cave* resounds with the different, sometimes discordant, answers that came back.

In that respect the piece fits its title. Listening to it is indeed like tuning in to words that have been spoken, and go on reverberating, in some great cavern: new words and old words, the words of living people and the words of the Old Testament and the Koran, quotations from both of which are interleaved with the fragmented interviews. *The Cave* is also a cave in its physical layout for performance. John Arnone's set is a functional metal scaffolding that provides a vertical checkerboard of five screens for video display and several apertures for musicians, with, down below, a cavity for the string quartet, two pianos and some of the percussion. But the title's most direct reference is to the cave of Machpelah, in the West Bank town of Hebron, which is reputed to be the burial place of Abraham/Ibrahim and Sarai/Sarah, and is the location of one of the few places of worship in the world where Jews and Muslims can pray together, or at any rate simultaneously. That place, built by the Byzantines as a little church on top of a massive Herodian structure, is the goal of each of the first two acts, in which the voices are Jewish and Muslim respectively.

The Jewish first act is almost as long as the other two put together, and the feeling of extension is increased by the fact that it is also—surely deliberately—discontinuous. Sections of interview material shuffle on and off to be replaced by episodes from Genesis and the Midrash that are either sung or else slapped onto the screens, syllable by syllable, in time with the pulses of percussion music. There are also segments of unaccompanied speaking, of chant, of unpleasant scrawling as roller-ball pens write out the 'Who is?' questions, and of engine noise as we move towards Hebron for the finale of this act.

Korot's video show follows the music in its course and in letting the raw material show through. The talking heads are not subjected to any questioning or editorial scrutiny, except occasionally and tacitly in the way they are juxtaposed. 'There is great power attached to this place', one speaker says of Machpelah. According to the next, 'The cave is for the dead, not for the living'. Meanwhile Reich's music makes no comment, but suggests only the attentive listening that was necessary to its composition. And though that listening may have been addressed principally to the manner rather than to the matter of the answers, the reiterated musical phrases implicitly reiterate the spoken words that gave rise to them, and indicate, like calligraphy on an Islamic bowl or archway or garment, that text is both sacred and the only legitimate source of ornamentation.

Where Reich is obliged to invent music to project words that come to him in written form—the words of Genesis, say—he adopts a style of plain, light declamation similar to that of parts of his last work with singing voices, *The Desert Music*, but without that work's embedding orchestral richness. This first act of *The Cave* is austerely wary of musical enrichment, and its severely sectional structure implies that the documentary intention is foremost, on two levels. What we are offered is a catalogue of evidence: the evidence of Jewish people, both living and long dead, as to the meaning of Abraham's mission, and the evidence of videotapes and written questions as to how the piece we are experiencing came to be put together.

Being so overt about its construction, this Jewish part of *The Cave* exemplifies the persistence and the frankness that have always been characteristic of Reich's work. There are no secrets. We are shown what is going on. And the showing is the piece. As he wrote of *It's Gonna Rain*, one of his early tape compositions, 'once the process has been set up it inexorably works itself out'. The essential difference is that the process in the first act of *The Cave* is not a purely aural one—of rhythms sliding against each other, or of notes gradually being sustained through intervening silences—but, instead, a process of assembling videotaped and written testimony, and one in which the music is subordinated to what is seen and what is heard spoken. It becomes apparent that there is a fierce conflict implanted in Reich's notion of 'documentary video music theatre'—a conflict not between video and music, since those aspects are so well conjoined, but between documentary and art. The musical replays and the video blowups teach us nothing about Jewish responses to the Abraham stories; the piecemeal documentary form repeatedly requires the music to stop and start again, and so opposes its inclinations to keep on going—to keep on repeating and pulsating.

That conflict continues into the second act, which moves from Genesis and Israelis to the Koran and Arabs. The structure is more regular: there is simply a slow alternation of interview material with Koranic chanting before we arrive, as in the first act, at Machpelah. However, Reich's participation is now limited to the interview sections, since Islam permits no musical accompaniment to the traditional intoning of the Koran. In order not to have his singers idle throughout this act, Reich has them singing the speech-derived melodies which, in the first act, were only interpreted by instruments. This is not a happy device. The soloists' sing-song repetitions suggest a Protestant world of hymns and choir-leaders, despite the exclusively Semitic origins of the spoken material, and despite the composer's own Jewish background (though here Copland provides a parallel—vividly close when, as often happens, Reich's bare string octaves recall *Appalachian Spring* in all its innocence).

In keeping, again, with their documentary idealism, Reich and Korot register the divergences between the Israeli and Arab acts without any emphasis or commentary. One speaker in the second act calmly insists that Abraham was a Muslim. We hear—or rather, in the case of those of us not versed in classical Arabic, we read, in English, German and French on the screens—the Koran giving its own version of the story of Abraham's sacrifice, one in which the saved victim is not Isaac but his elder half-brother Ishmael, the ancestor of the Arabs. At the same time, the discrepancies among the projected texts quietly signal the Koran's remoteness from Europe-derived culture. This is, for most of us, the other view. As if, though, to affirm the brotherhood of Isaac and Ishmael, the second act ends exactly as the first had done, with shots of Israeli soldiers slung with automatic weapons inside the Machpelah sanctuary, and with the string quartet picking up the A minor drone of the building's natural resonance.

But as Reich has said: 'We can't solve the problems of the Middle East.' Accordingly his third act, in which the faces and voices are from the US, spins away from controversy. The witnesses are now more various: black Christians and white atheists, a Jew and a Buddhist, a young man of Hopi descent and a woman Episcopalian priest, distinguished figures (Carl Sagan, Richard Serra, Arthur Danto) and students. As one might expect, the clashes are far more abundant and violent. A young black woman, speaking of the Bible, remarks: 'When people say to me it has nothing to say to us I think they've never read it.' To which Serra immediately and obligingly adds: 'Old Testament: never read it', with a change to the melody of those last three, shared words which speaks of a certain satisfaction. Where the responses of the Israeli and then of the Arab speakers moved in the same direction, albeit with occasional frictions, those from the US are all over the place. There is another difference. The people recorded in Jerusalem and Hebron, whether Jews or Muslims, were agreed on a principle about themselves: I have my meaning to the extent that I relate to history. Hence the importance of genealogy and tradition. But for the people recorded in New York and Austin, this principle is reversed: history has its meaning to the extent that it relates to me.

The diversity of the US material is, to Reich, a release from obligations to treat text as sacred, and his third act is at last a continuous and exuberant musical structure, combining the interviews with sung imitations as in the second act and with sung stories as in the first. This is where we hear of Abraham and Isaac, in a patchwork of Bible verses and modern comments ('The kid knows that something is about to happen') that moves away from the passivity of the first-act Genesis settings to achieve a mounting tension. This is also where we hear the story of Abraham entertaining angels unawares, with its beautiful Midrashic gloss about how he went into the cave of Machpelah 'and found Adam and Eve on their biers, and they slept, and lights were kindled above them, and a sweet scent was upon them'. In this act Korot's screens also become livelier, and move beyond dutiful presentation of the speakers to show us patterns and ribbons of colour created out of features of dress or background.

The brilliant success of this third act is possible because, as in *Different Trains*, there is a harmony between documentary and artistic intentions. In the quartet piece it was a harmony of live instrumentalists and reminiscing voices both travelling, both shuttling in pulsed rhythms, both moving along prepared tracks. In the last act of *The Cave* it is a harmony of rush and contradiction, in which the very inconsistency of the speakers seems to have allowed Reich to mix and match them as he musically pleased. Because this part of the piece is so much more pepped-up, it might be better to play the entire work continuously, instead of giving the audience a break just before things start to get interesting.

One could maybe object that the triumph of the third act is a triumph of life's vanities—colour, humour, animation—over the serious discussion of contending loyalties and traditions. One could also say that it is a triumph for optimism and the human capacity to begin afresh. We finally learn that there may be no real cave—nothing under the Byzantine church and the Herodian mausoleum, nothing to anchor people in inevitable enmities. Those were the wisest words: 'The cave is for the dead, not for the living.' Reich's work, in its last half hour, makes its escape from the cave of record. (*New Yorker*, 31 May 1993)

City Life

There is not much slow music in Steve Reich's output, nor in how he speaks, which is not just up-tempo, but engagingly balanced—again like the music—between cynicism and boyish enthusiasm. We are in his suite in a London hotel. Yesterday he was on the plane from New York. Tomorrow he goes to Metz for the premiere of his newest piece, *City Life*.

City Life is a kind of follow-up to his string quartet *Different Trains* and his first theatre piece, *The Cave*, which was performed in Europe and the US two years ago. That work proved itself a massive achievement, and—such is the world we live in—seems unlikely to be seen again in quite the same form, with an elaborate construction to hold the five video screens and seventeen live musicians. 'The fact that the economy now is so restricted simply must be a consideration. I think this is something everyone's realizing—and it wouldn't be such a bad thing if the result were to be a whole lot more things like Stravinsky's *Histoire du soldat*.' His next essay in video-music-theatre will, accordingly, be smaller and leaner, with just one screen and lasting maybe half an hour, so that it can be performed with other examples of what he sees as a coming new genre.

Economy is written, too, into *City Life*. The piece is scored for an economical orchestra, of just eighteen soloists, though that is not only for financial reasons. 'I'm interested in working with musicians who aren't afraid of microphones, of performing as soloists, of playing with electronic keyboards, and my experience with orchestras is that they are afraid of all the above. Also, I'm like the little boy who goes to a concert and says: Why are there eighteen people playing the same thing? If you amplify just one violin, you have quite a different animal—and one that can do things eighteen people can't.'

Among the things the amplified animals do in *City Life* is imitate and develop recorded sounds—the sounds, precisely, of city life: not just voices, as in *Different Trains* and *The Cave*, but also 'car horns, car door slams, boat horn, air brakes (that white noise. . .), sirens, pile driver, heartbeat'. What is different from the two earlier pieces is that now these sounds are played on sampling keyboards, not simply heard from a tape. 'The tape recorder gets you to think about sound in a certain way; samplers get you to think about sound in a different way.' For instance, when a fragment of recorded speech is controlled by keys, it is possible for the musician to alter the phrasing and tempo of the words, or to play 'chords' of words or bits of words. The result is a freer way of handling the source. 'Obviously, you don't feel as reverential to someone saying "Check it out" as you do to the words of a holocaust survivor I used in *Different Trains* or the Abraham story I used in *The Cave*.'

So is this a comedy? 'The first of the five movements is maybe streetwise, funny, but then the mood turns darker. The second movement for me has something to do with the mechanization in that Chaplin movie *Modern Times*, and in the third movement, which uses noises I recorded at a demonstration outside City Hall, there's an imminent violence. The fourth has long boat horn sounds: my wife calls it "the intensive care section"; it has images of water, of souls going out over water, of death. The last movement starts out very fast, and ends with a chorale that came in the first movement but wasn't completed there. It's in three flats, and as it starts to settle down into C minor various other chords are placed over it, rather as in some of Ives.'

City Life is a celebration of New York, where Reich was born, and a farewell. 'I'm getting to dislike the city. It's increasingly difficult to live there: the city's increasingly noisy and increasingly dangerous. We have a place in Vermont, and I think when our son finishes high school we'll move out.'

Meanwhile, his music's moving out from the city to the world village of *Proverbs*, the piece he is writing for this year's Proms. 'I want to go back to writing as I did in the seventies, so that the music is much thinner, a lot simpler.' Scored for just six singers with two pianos and two percussion, the new work will set proverbs from a great international encyclopedia of them and from Wittgenstein. As I leave, Reich is paused over his choices. Say little and do much. Think on the end before you begin. How small a thought it takes to fill a whole life. . . . (*Classic FM Magazine*, May 1995)

celebration and ceremony

Things both change and do not change. That is perhaps the central lesson of Steve Reich's music, and through matching concerts he gave with his regular musicians at Miller Theater on Thursday and Saturday evenings, the lesson zigzagged through many dimensions.

The four players intent on a pair of xylophones in the first part of *Drumming*—Bob Becker, Russell Hartenberger, James Preiss and Reich himself—were there when the music was new nearly three decades ago, wearing similar plain outfits of white shirts and dark pants. Time might have silvered and thinned the hair on their heads, but the music they were making now was as young as ever, exuberantly rattling through processes of growing complexity and changing pattern against a stable pulse and a stable repeating frame.

Yet that identical music has altered in its implications over the years. Where once it started a piece lasting not much more than an hour, now it opens toward half a lifetime of music. In other ways, meanwhile, its focus has concentrated. Connections with Ghana, where Reich had recently studied when he wrote these notes, have relaxed; the music is now more personal. Particularly—since *Different Trains*, the 1988 piece for string quartet and recordings that was also played at these concerts—the regular click-clack rhythmic appoggiaturas of Reich's music, weak-strong, have gained another history in his childhood experience of rail travel across the United States.

The two concerts—given to a packed and enthusiastic audience for the most part younger than *Drumming*—were devised around the presentation to Reich of Columbia University's infrequently given and prestigious William Schuman Award. The events thoroughly achieved their celebratory objective. Both opened with a classic—the *Drumming* introduction on Thursday, the intellectually sparkling and physically exciting *Music for Pieces of Wood* on Saturday—and then moved through the dark 1980s (Sextet and *Different Trains*) to arrive at the joyful 1976 of *Music for Eighteen Musicians*.

Joyful, too, were the performances of this final piece on each occasion. The work went around the world in the late 1970s in the form of a recording, but it gains a lot from being experienced in live performance. One can see and hear how the vibraphone player chimes signals, like courses of bells from a tower, to which the others respond with a gearing up or down of harmony, or how musicians move from one instrument to another to bring about changes in the texture. Watched as well as heard, *Music for Eighteen Musicians* is a kind of ceremony, voiced in repeating bits of tune, in harmonic progressions, in sumptuous sonorities, in time.

A ceremony enjoins submission to order, and *Music for Eighteen Musicians* looks and sounds like human clockwork. But this is not frightening. When engaged in with full heart, vigour and alertness by everyone, as here, the detailed plan is not a confinement but a recipe for exuberance. The wheels of the clock go around smoothly at their different rates: a few seconds for a bar, an hour for the giant cycle that is the entire work. And the passing of time is not baneful but exhilarating. (*New York Times*, 26 September 2000)

Three Tales

Three Tales, the big new live-music video by Steve Reich and Beryl Korot that had its world premiere here on Sunday night in the

Museumsquartier at the Vienna Festival, is going to excite a lot of controversy. These two artists did that with *The Cave*, which started out in the same place nine years ago and considered the common ancestry of Judaism and Islam. But where *The Cave* researched roots, *Three Tales* examines destinations. And where *The Cave* reached a bright US optimism in its finale, *Three Tales* mounts to a clamour of warning.

The three tales are presented as one in the sixty-five-minute performance, tightly and excitingly given by members of the Ensemble Modern and Synergy Vocals under Bradley Lubman. *Hindenburg*—much improved since it was first done four years ago and now smoothly taking its place as prologue—uses film clips of the fire that swept over the eponymous airship as it landed in New Jersey in 1937. *Bikini* similarly takes off from newsreel images of preparation leading up to the 1946 testing of an atomic bomb.

In *Hindenburg*, musical processes are paramount. The opening sequence is a slow deceleration for the ensemble of vocal quintet, string quartet, piano duo and four percussionists, so that the sung sounds lengthen to join with the appalled whine of the reporter who was there. After this, while the building of the airship is shown on screen, recorded and live percussionists construct with the pervasive rhythm from the anvil-driven Nibelheim interlude in *Das Rheingold*, and the pianos purloin two chords from Wagner's score.

Bikini has much more of a sustained sweep in which sound and screen are conjoined. The cross-cutting of images—islanders leaving, a plane in flight, streaming numbers, a radar display—mirrors Reich's agile manoeuvring of different textures and harmonies, while his pulsings actuate the forward drive implicit in the story. *Hindenburg* began with the airship already in flames; *Bikini* keeps up the tension of countdown, a tension that extends, through the firestorm in the palm trees, into the beginning of the third and final episode.

Titled *Dolly*, this has to do not so much with the cloned sheep of a few years back as with the larger matter of genetic engineering and also with artificial intelligence. *Hindenburg* and *Bikini* were both disaster stories, and Korot and Reich do everything in their formidable power to suggest in *Dolly* a disaster waiting to happen. The faces and voices of scientists are grotesquely stilled and replicated: Richard Dawkins is a particular target as he expounds the machine nature of life. His speech and those of others are at times frozen into a rumble that sinisterly recalls the engine whirrings heard earlier from the Hindenburg and the plane approaching Bikini. Also, an MIT device called 'Kismet', with wobbling fake eyeballs and rubber-tubing lips, is chosen to speak for the robots. Meanwhile, the contribution of a rabbi, Adin Steinsaltz, is treated with great reverence, and the screen keeps flashing up words from Genesis, as it had in *Bikini*, with instruments sounding the voice of God.

What is troublesome here is not just the loading of the argument, not just the dubiously helpful appeal to religion, but that the mechanism of debate becomes the problem, or rather two problems. In the first place, Dawkins, Steinsaltz and the others are not dramatic characters; they are speaking for themselves, as themselves, and they bulge out of the frame of the artwork. We are in the real world now. We are called upon to agree or disagree with the talking heads directly, so that Reich and Korot are moved to the sidelines of their own creation. They are also bumped by a machine of their own making, for artistic content is drowned out by the awesome and easy potency of large screen images and rapid editing when combined with amplified music. In *Hindenburg* and *Bikini*, points are made with some subtlety. Reich's take on Wagner is a fight between freshness and monumental authority, and the outcome is ambiguous. Korot's slow blurring of the Bikini islanders makes them look like a Gauguin and places the bomb test in a history of western encounters with island paradises. But *Dolly*, the unappealing triumph of the sound bite, invokes anxiety not about the cloning or robots of the possible future but about audiovisual persuasion as we have had it for some time.

The best of Reich's music has always involved a tender touching of natural and electronic, human and mechanical, spontaneous and repetitive. That happens in this piece, for instance when the singers in the hall, live but wired up, join their voices to that of the 1937 announcer. Here is a quiet truth, that of sympathy across barriers of time and medium. Here is an artist from whom one can expect technological stories of far finer nuance, positiveness and accomplishment. (*New York Times*, 14 May 2002)

tracks in Allemonde

So precise in its emotional colours, so clear in its levels of subtext, so innately itself in every gesture, Debussy's opera *Pelléas et Mélisande* is nevertheless endlessly interpretable, by conductors, singers and stage directors. The situation could hardly be simpler. Pelléas is a prince, in the lost realm of Allemonde, and Mélisande the new young wife of his elder half-brother Golaud. The two fall in love, or more drift. Golaud's jealousy mounts—frighteningly, as he forces his young son Yniold to spy for him and violently challenges Mélisande in the presence of his aged grandfather, Arkel. He kills Pelléas, whereupon Mélisande declines, via childbirth, into death.

Welsh National Opera 1992

Not quite. Or perhaps not yet quite. What was widely expected to be one of the year's outstanding operatic occasions was indeed an evening of many marvels, but there was a sense at Friday's opening performance in Cardiff of a production still moving loudly in the clanks and bangs of the scene shifting towards a possibly glorious fruition, and a sense of great minds thinking not wholly alike.

First of those great minds is, of course, that of Pierre Boulez, and it is a proud coup for Welsh National Opera to have secured him to conduct his first new opera production since the premiere of the three-act *Lulu* in Paris in 1979. Ten years before that he conducted an intensely remembered production of *Pelléas* at Covent Garden, one that placed Debussy's opera in a momentous realm between Wagner and *Wozzeck*, between sweeping magnificence and sudden gestures of shock and violence. This is still where we are. The Wagnerian breadth is maybe even surer; certainly much of the music in the opening acts is slower and calmer. One is reminded that Debussy's score is full of warm, flowing string music as much as gauzes and aerations, and in this relatively small theatre it all sounds wonderful. There is also a fierce immediacy to the more Bergian side of the opera, which Boulez finds in its treatment of Golaud's wrenching jealousy. The aggrieved husband's urgent questioning of his dying wife, in the last act, is underscored with tortured directness (as well it might be, given Donald Maxwell's acute involvement), and the interlude after his taunting of Mélisande has the same function as the great D minor interlude in Wozzeck. This is music pulling away from the drama to voice its passionate protest and sympathy straight at the audience.

For this all to work properly, though, the heroic orchestral performance will have to be joined by heroic silence backstage. And this is where another two of the great minds come in. The production fulfils Boulez's long-standing dream of working with the director Peter Stein, who in turn fulfils another dream of seeing something of the work of Karl-Ernst Herrmann in this country. Herrmann's designs, pastel sketches on black paper, look stunningly beautiful and right as they are reproduced in the programme, inhabiting a world somewhere near Odilon Redon and Munch (the Nordic atmosphere, of extreme emotion mummed, also comes across in echoes of Ibsen and Strindberg in Stein's direction). But the translation of the designs into three dimensions is not altogether happy. Some go right: Yniold's solo scene is magic. The child (a charming performance by Samuel Burkey) skips about in tan trunks like an Arthur Rackham Puck on a Japanese lacquer-box lid of black with muted gold and silver. Some go wrong: the tower is a blank and shoddy construction. But most of the stage pictures frustratingly allow the intention to be seen through a not very satisfactory deed: a giant rising sun as Pelléas emerges from the depths, an opening at last of the castle to the air as the music reaches rest. One effect of having a different set for almost every scene is to evaporate what portion of solidity these characters retain. They have no home. But that seems to be Stein's intention, to focus on the emotional moment, and to do so in a literal way. It is rather a surprise these days, and almost quaint, to see operatic characters doing what they say they are doing. When Pelléas first comes in, Geneviève remarks that he has been crying and sure enough, there he is with his hankie. But when this literalism extends to the use of a real dove to fly from the tower (and exasperatingly to flutter about the theatre for the next half hour) and even a real sheep, it becomes trivial.

Much, much more to the point is Stein's, and his cast's, forceful projection of feeling and character through posture and movement. Penelope Walker as Geneviève sings well and acts the widow who has carefully put away hope. Arkel, an Old Father Time with a spindly crown and a senile tremor, is an apt creation, and Kenneth Cox gives him a voice of majestic sureness and musicality that fully coexists with the frailty, as egg with shell. Pelléas is also finely presented: a quick innocent, a straw-hatted Martin Pippin in his first scene alone with Mélisande. Neill Archer gives him a voice of appropriate lightness, a winged whisper, though maybe there could be occasional rapture and radiance too. As for Mélisande, she covers a range of detachment from fairy glaciality to something like the drumming smothered sensuality and cynicism of a Hedda Gabler. There is a similar untethered agility to Alison Hagley's singing, glancing through a tone of extraordinary, sprite-like purity. Maxwell's grim, strong Golaud has no answer to this: singing with vigour, making every word tell, he is waiting for the world to make sense around him. (*Times*, 24 February 1992)

Bouffes du Nord 1992

'Simplicity is paramount in *Pelléas*—I spent twelve years removing from it everything that might have slipped in *parasitically*.' This was Debussy writing to Edwin Evans at Covent Garden on the occasion of the first performance of his opera there in 1909. The letter, apparently unknown hitherto, is in the programme book for Peter Brook's new production at his own theatre in Paris—a fitting place for it to come to light, since Brook is at one with his composer in his ruthless excision of the unnecessary. Debussy goes on to remark that he had 'tried to prove that people who sing could stay human and natural', by contrast with the usual course of things in opera, whose means are 'equally false as grandiloquent'. This view, too, would surely gain the full assent of a director whose dissatisfaction with conventional opera perhaps has less to do with the common complaints of conventional audiences, uncooperative singers, limited rehearsal time and short runs than with the size of the enterprise: the demand for big gestures and bold relationships. Rhetoric, for Brook, gets in the way.

More than thirty-five years have passed since he bade farewell to the opera house after staging *Eugene Onegin* at the Met, at the end of a controversial decade that had also seen a *Salome* in Salvador Dali's designs at Covent Garden and a *Faust*, again at the Met, in which he had tried to respond to the irony—the 'art of the wink'—of a composer using waltz time to set the most hallowed treasure of German literature. It was only after he had created his own theatrical laboratory—in the picturesquely mouldering Bouffes du Nord, a small nineteenth-century auditorium close by one of the main Parisian rail stations—that he found the means to return to opera in his own way, with a cut-down version of *Carmen* in 1981. The new *Impressions de Pelléas* follows from that, with the same principles of multiple casting (so that performances can be given every night, over a long run, by one of three different teams taking the roles of the central trio), treating the score as a guide more than a recipe, cutting out the chorus, and reducing the accompaniment to a pair of pianos. In other, more essential respects, his treatment of Debussy's opera follows directly from what he was doing at the Met and Covent Garden forty years and more ago, since always, in all his work, there has been this belief in the soul of a text, waiting to be found and awakened. His aim, he has said in connection with *Impressions de Pelléas*, is 'to seek to reach the source of the author's inspiration, which lies beyond the overt form'.

It is a dangerous adventure—and a lonely one, in an age when musical and theatrical performances tend to justify themselves either as re-creations of former events, exact and faithful in every particular, or as radical reinterpretations. *Impressions de Pelléas* is an undoing of the text, but totally without the intention of undercutting or subverting the original. On the contrary, this is a remarkably uncritical evening—uncritical, that is, in its response to the piece, whose qualities of freshness, delicacy, mystery and immediacy it seeks to honour and cherish. We are not being invited to contemplate Debussy's work as an object in its time and place, to understand it as a 'case': a handling of the femme-fatale theme so common in literature at the turn of the century, a response to Wagner, an essay in symbolism, a contribution to the emergent study of the subconscious. Anything that belongs to the opera by virtue of period, nationality or genre is likely, rather, to be removed or avoided; anything that diverts our attention from the emotional action, or pretends to limit or explain the emotional action, is, according to Brook's artistic morality, a mask, a counterfeit. He is not interested in the work as an exercise in tradition and language, only in what, 'beyond the overt form', it says and what it is.

These beliefs and priorities account in part for his priorities. If nothing is gained by considering *Pelléas* as a specifically French piece, then awkwardness in pronunciation is unimportant, and might even be construed as an advantage, in implying the irrelevance of medium and manner. Brook's casts are international. If at one performance the French Pelléas (Gérard Theruel) was impeccable, the Chinese Mélisande (Ai-Lan Zhu) and Polish Golaud (Wojciech Drabowicz) were both evidently singing a foreign language. On the other hand, matters that Brook judges to belong to the opera, rather than to its mode of presentation, are accepted without question, and naively. Mélisande tells Golaud in the first scene that she comes from 'far away'; O.K., let her appear in a kimono, and be portrayed by an east Asian singer. (The two other interpreters of the part come from Japan and Korea). Or again, Brook is content to lose the scenery and the orchestra of the original, but accepts the libretto as the voice of Debussy's intentions, and not only of Maeterlinck's in the superseded play. The whole production rests on the assertion that not only is the substance separable from the means, but the characters' words may be a truthful signpost to the substance.

However, one can recognize Brook's untested assumptions and still be stunned by the result he achieves—or not so much stunned as infected, infected with a slowly developing surprise which grows after one has left the theatre. The production is so simple as to appear absent. Just about the only new slant comes in the scene that has Pelléas and Mélisande meeting at the well, where Pelléas in this version surreptitiously finds the wedding ring that Mélisande has just lost, and straightaway throws it back into the water. Afterwards one realizes that modification and addition were not the point, that the point was honest transmission and subtraction—removal of the 'parasitic'—in the interests of honesty. One realizes, too, how much one was required to notice in the course of a performance condensed to little more than a hour and a half.

The geometry of the Bouffes du Nord allows Brook to make of it a single room in which all are present, actor-singers and audience together. There is no separation between stage and auditorium: the performing space is a small amphitheatre in front of the proscenium arch, and a high darkening cave behind. So the theatre itself, without scenic illusion, can actualize the contrasts of light and dark, openness and enclosure, presented in the dialogue and the stage directions to echo the conflicts of aim and motive within the internal drama. Also, because of the dimensions of the place, no spectator is more than a hundred feet or so from the action—close enough to touch, as it seems by comparison with the customary scale of opera houses. Under these circumstances, every movement of a cheek muscle tells, so that the performers have to be thoroughly in control of their bodies as well as their voices. And it is through that control, as much as through the physical intimacy, that the audience is made not only to watch but to witness.

Contact is intensified further by the removal of any pretence that the action we are called to concerns the royal family of medieval Allemonde in an old castle set in a park by the sea. Instead, the stage picture is a formalization of the true conditions of the performance: we are at a musical soirée, where people are singing around the piano. Just one of the two grands in use is visible towards the back of the stage, across a floor covered with Turkey carpets and otherwise empty except for a few pieces of furniture, a couple of lamps and a large goldfish bowl—the only concession to symbolism, besides providing a reminiscence of one of Debussy's most familiar piano pieces. The characters, apart from Mélisande, appear as people from the period of the opera's composition, the 1890s: men in dark chocolate three-piece suits (except Arkel, who wears the light jacket of an old man sitting in the sun), Geneviève in a long dress of deepest Burgundy. Mélisande's oriental apartness is that of a discordant note in the harmony. Another dislocation is the presence of two shallow rectangular pools of water on either side of the amphitheatre area. Mélisande and water: these are the two external elements that the drama must try and fail to accommodate. (The setting already suggests the failure: the imprisonment of the goldfish bowl is the only solution this place can find.)

The production's design, by Chloe Obolensky, is beautiful and satisfactory; it also reintroduces, on another, more interesting level, the vagueness that a straightforward realization of the stage directions might find in medievalism. The people we see and hear are precisely placed as members of a family gathering, or possibly a house party, a century ago. What is not at all precise, and certainly not so stable, is the degree to which they are involved in their roles. On a singer's face, in a singer's voice, emotion can leap like a lightning bolt from charade to reality: for instance, from the double enactment of Theruel playing a sensitive young fin-de-siècle gentleman playing Pelléas, to the immediacy of a feeling quite independent of character. The outstanding value of Maeterlinck's text, in answering Debussy's prayer for a libretto made of 'things half-said', is revealed as its open invitation to create, through music and secondarily through gesture, a play of fierce, nimble emotions liberated from human subjects. The people of the drama are hopelessly irrelevant; they will be caught in the same trap of love, uncertainty, blindness and jealousy whoever they are. Perhaps this is what Debussy meant when he spoke about reaching 'the naked flesh of emotion': emotion revealed of itself, without its clothing in character.

This requires from the singers a nakedness of their own: a transparency, a candour, an ability to act as glass vessels, showing feelings without holding onto them, and without trying to manipulate them in order to create characters for themselves. They are fearfully exposed. They have to give the impression that they sing, immediately, whatever comes into their heads and hearts, but also that singing is no effort to them, that every movement of chest or throat or lip (and little can be hidden in this theatre) is prompted by expression, not by the needs of vocal technique. Everyone involved in this performance—Bernadette Antoine was the nicely watchful Geneviève, Roger Soyer the disillusioned Arkel—rose to the exacting demands of Brook's theatrical practice, even if only Theruel also contributed a distinguished account of the music.

The general modesty of the singing made one feel this was a performance that ought to be seen not in great cultural capitals but in small towns, in places where full-scale opera would never be possible. This seems to have been Brook's view, too, when eleven years ago, soon after his reduced *Carmen* had opened, he remarked in an interview that although the orchestra was one of the glories of Debussy's opera, 'one could start afresh with a version for piano and still do a *Pelléas* of great vitality. There are many towns that will never have performances of opera because of costs, but people would be delighted to meet small groups around a piano'. His new production exhibits the 'great vitality'; the irony is that it will be seen not in opera-less towns but, after the end of its run at the Bouffes du Nord later this month, in Glasgow, Barcelona, Lisbon, Vienna, Berlin, Frankfurt. The hope must be that it will stimulate others, in other places, to do likewise.

In Brook's realization of his dream, the cast's double presence—as people of the 1890s and as creatures in a legend—heightens the sensation of a drama under observation, since the observers include not only the audience but also some of the singers, overseeing, as comfortably placed ladies and gentlemen, the others taking part in the sung action. Yniold's role is particularly important in this regard. Through his child's-eye view we all the more easily accept the fluid movement between the reality of the musical party and the illusion of Allemonde, and his response to the drama delicately expresses its curve. Beginning as the ally and companion of his father Golaud, he gradually loosens those links to associate himself more with Pelléas and Mélisande, and yet his demeanour is always grave and simple. Brook's casting of this role again suggests what qualities he finds most urgent in the opera: the boy was vocally frail but exactly right in how he stood and moved with impassive calm.

While the production uses the possibility of people being present for scenes in which they do not sing (Yniold at the side of his wounded father, for instance), the production is also extraordinarily responsive to the power of entrances—and, indeed, of non-entrances, of points where a character is already in place as a scene begins. Such responsiveness is attainable partly because successive scenes are not set off from each other by changes of decor or lighting: the only mark is in the regrouping of people. (An exception to the even flow is the scene in the vaults, done in general gloom by the light of a lantern, which Golaud holds, and shines into Pelléas's eyes in order to emphasize the interrogation.) The changelessness of the stage picture also has an effect on how the music is heard, placing it not with the scenery, which stays the same, but with the people, who move and feel and alter. The score is less a description of light, leaves, wind and surrounding sea sounds, more a witness itself of the human drama, and in that way it, too, seems to notice entrances more vividly—especially the entrances of Pelléas, who bursts into scenes more often than anyone else, and does so each time to an outbreak of joy and eagerness in the accompaniment.

That transfer of the musical intention, from nature and depiction to people and passion, may be aided by the keyboard adaptation, which not only removes the evocative colour of the score but gives it a more bodily, muscular rhythm. The percussive sound world is a reminder of Debussy's fascination with Javanese music, while the presence of instrumental performance alongside the action suggests Asian theatrical forms that the composer is unlikely to have known, but which certainly seem no more distant from his work than the operas of Verdi.

A further effect of the soirée setting is to situate the performance at a time when the piece is not quite finished. We know that Debussy composed the opera in the form of a draft, and that he would play through scenes at the piano for his friends: this is the world into which we are invited by Brook and his musical collaborator Marius Constant, with whom he also worked on *La Tragédie de Carmen*. One can believe, certainly for the duration of the performance, that this is even a truer way in which to be hearing the opera. Debussy's recitative becomes newly agile and expressive when, with only background pianos in support of the voices, one can hear not only every word but the forming of every word. (The few moments that do not work in this version come when the work makes compromises with conventional opera, in the passionate climaxes to the two scenes in which Golaud comes upon Pelléas and Mélisande in passionate communion.) The voice-piano format also suggests how Debussy may have been led to the possibility of *Pelléas* through his experience as a song writer, and especially through the experience of the *Proses lyriques* he composed to his own prose poems as he was beginning the opera.

As in song, a whole imaginary world can be conjured by a vocal phrase or a fleeting moment in the accompaniment. *Pelléas* is an opera infiltrated by nature, but it matters not at all that nothing of the natural world—except for the immured goldfish—can be seen in the theatre during this production. Golaud only has to sing the word 'forêt' to bring memories and images rushing into the empty space, and this confidence in the power of words, or of words and music, respects the confidence of the opera's creators, demonstrated explicitly in the first encounter between the title characters, where Pelléas points out to Mélisande things that the audience cannot see, and that would be grotesquely redundant if the audience could see them: a great ship out to sea, lighthouses sending beams through the mist. Brook simply goes a little further. The love play of the tower scene, where Pelléas is supposed to tie Mélisande's hair into the branches of a willow, is done in a stylized way, with a white veil for the flowing locks: it is obviously a difficult scene to achieve in a production otherwise so artless, but even when less than thoroughly convincing it can still suggest the two playing lovers drawn into a shared fantasy, whose sources are in Mélisande's oriental elsewhere.

Brook and Constant achieve their conflation of the work by eliminating two scenes (the only two that could be eliminated without damage to the narrative thread: Pelléas and Mélisande in the sea cave, and Yniold and the sheep) and by trimming others. After the prelude we move straight to Geneviève's narration at the start of the second scene (Constant is responsible for the smooth musical joins as well as the two-piano reduction), and the first scene opens out of that, as if to illustrate what Geneviève is reading in Golaud's letter about his first meeting with Mélisande. This is where the spectral unreality of the characters is taken a step further: they are not only figures being played in a drawing room but figures being played to illustrate a story being told in a drawing room.

The intercalation of the second scene into the first is the only major change to the original dramaturgy until the ending, where, since there is no chorus, Brook is obliged to cut the last two or three minutes. Characteristically, though, he makes a virtue of necessity. 'But the sadness, Golaud,' Arkel sings, 'but the sadness of all one sees. Oh! Oh!' And as he sings those gentle sobs, the accompaniment turns the page on Debussy's text to become a quiet chiming, which collapses the characters—characters in a drama or in a reading—into the gentlefolk, and calls them all off to bed. (*New Yorker*, 18 January 1993)

Netherlands Opera 1993

Where Peter Brook had implied that the orchestra of *Pelléas* is packaging, Simon Rattle, in a new production staged at the Netherlands

Opera by Peter Sellars, has us acquiesce happily in his belief that the score is the place where the drama really happens—that the subject is sound, and the sway of sound over creatures whose understanding of their predicament is pitifully inadequate. These are not people who can seize the musical initiative, launch a line and make the orchestra follow them. Instead they are flotsam on the eddies and swirls of the orchestral current, to which they can do no more than listen.

Maeterlinck's play is full of listening, which must be one of the reasons for its appeal to Debussy as a libretto. Golaud, the hunting prince lost in the forest right at the beginning of the opera, hears the sound of weeping, and so discovers the terrified runaway Mélisande. Later in this opening act, Mélisande first becomes aware of Golaud's young half-brother Pelléas by hearing him approach before what is, for us in the audience, their initial encounter, and the two of them then join together in exercises of the senses: they listen to the wind rising on the sea, and watch a ship sail off through the darkening shine that comes from a lighthouse. Watching here becomes listening, since all these phenomena of sea, ship and light are present in the theatre as purely aural images, created by the magic lantern of the orchestra. Similarly, later in the opera, the characters hear not only sounds but also sights: the quiet sleep of the water at the spring in the castle grounds and the shadows of the trees, the noise in the sea cave and the darkness of the vaults. At the climax Pelléas, with Mélisande in the park, hears the slam of the castle gates being shut against them, and at last realizes he is hearing the sound of his own fate. Then in the closing scene—with Pelléas, the opera's most acute listener, gone—the old king Arkel remarks on how Mélisande's death has passed silently, unheard.

A reason for the opera's present ubiquity is possibly this inability of its characters to understand the kind of world in which they exist, even though they may be aware, intensely, of the noises it makes. Debussy's score is a stream of information—a gorgeous stream as Rattle makes it appear—and one that the people onstage can detect and parse: among the casts of operas, they have the most discerning ears. And yet they fail to recognize the relevance to them of what they hear. The world is clear to them, and opaque. It is a situation that may be as familiar at the end of this century as it was at the close of the last.

Rattle's success is enough to make us all, with Pelléas and Mélisande, listeners, and listeners of the kind this work requires: enraptured, but also quick and fresh, and taunted by our inability to act. There is that cruelty to the beauty. The treat is also, in this performance, lustrous rather than lush; it has to do with immediate sensation and swift movement. Sometimes the sensation is so immediate that one is left more aware of the print on the memory than of the present experience: the orchestra flashes with the suddenness of lightning. The speed is only partly a matter of generally fast tempos. Equally important is the feeling that the music is always moving somewhere, that it is in perpetual acceleration, as it almost can be when periods of motion are either chopped by changes of thematic subject matter or overlaid, so that a level of slower music can come forward to take over from faster music that is close to spending its force. Rattle is particularly good at achieving the polyphony of speeds Debussy often demands; he is also good at showing how musical movement can come about not through speed and changes of speed but rather through the progressive alteration of a repeating motif. Something smooth and rounded can gradually crack open towards splinteredness, or it can subside into the background.

There is a commanding musical intelligence at work here, and also a commanding sensibility. Everything matters, and the tragedy—of characters who know that it matters, but do not know how it matters to them—is for that reason the keener. But this is to describe the performance in terms that are perhaps too abstract, not giving sufficient weight to how beautifully and exactly it realizes all the effects of sound and light the main characters hear, or how it presents a choreography of their movements and feelings. Pelléas's impulsiveness is in the music that pushes him onto the stage; so is Mélisande's stillness in the music that keeps her there. (Pelléas makes three appearances mid-scene; Mélisande is there at the start of any scene in which she appears.) All the many details that Rattle brings forward are keyed into the drama, either as representational items (the throbbing secondary line that could be the boy Yniold's fearfully fast heartbeat in the scene where Golaud forces him to spy on Pelléas and Mélisande) or as elements in a musical tide that is the more dangerous for the strength and complexity of its undertows. What we have here—superbly played, superbly blended—is obviously the result of a passionate partnership between Rattle and the Rotterdam Philharmonic.

Sellars's production could almost have been designed to give their work together its most appropriate foil: a staging that demonstrates its own irrelevance. While the score is pressing upon us all we need to know—all the characters' actions and gestures, all the vistas and effects of light they see, and, most obviously, all the sounds they make and hear—here are four conspicuous sounds that Sellars intrudes: Mélisande's high heels clattering as if on some paving in the first scene; the chink of spoon on bowl as Arkel is fed by his nurse;

Golaud's groans in the last act; the click of the handcuffs that the two cops fasten on him in the final seconds. Where the music is saying everything, these things are beyond everything, have no place. The groans sound not like Golaud's but like Willard White's. The other noises similarly relate only to the accidents of this performance and stay outside the opera.

Only the most literal-minded will object that in almost every scene Sellars directly counters the libretto. The opera's stage history is full of Golauds who, when they assure their Mélisandes in the opening scene that they will 'stay here by the tree', totally lack the arboreal wherewithal. For White in this production, the tree's place seems to have been taken by a sewage outlet, which three scenes later will serve as the spring—the spring that used to cure blindness—beside which Pelléas and Mélisande meet. None of this is necessarily absurd. The ostentatious ignoring of the libretto can be taken, rather, as a signal of how the music has surpassed the particulars of the story that gave it birth. However, a director spoils his case if he takes advantage of the vacuum to substitute a story of his own.

Sellars's story depends, typically for him, on a resiting of the piece in the contemporary urban US—though in this case the police officers, the street people and the sewer underlie a Fallingwater-like house set into a cliff over a bay of coloured fluorescent tubes that undulate in intensity. The tubes remain from his last opera production, the Salzburg revival of Messiaen's *Saint François d'Assise*, which had the same design team of George Tsypin for the set, Dunya Ramicova for the costumes, and James F. Ingalls for the lighting. The problems of matching the lighting to the music's rhythm are also still there, with occasional delights of luminous consonance—particularly when the tubes are in pearly harmonies of white, pale blue, lemon and pink—to hint at what might be possible. Returning from *Saint François* too are the video monitors, though these are considerably fewer, monochrome, and presumably present only to compensate for the poor sightlines into the several interiors of the cross-section house.

The cutaway view makes it possible for the production to show three scenes at once. At the moment in the second act when Mélisande is visiting the injured Golaud, Arkel is being bathed by a nurse and Geneviève, Pelléas's mother, is keeping watch at her sick husband's bedside. This makes a powerful image of symmetry and contrast: three women, in different parts of the house, are tending three weakened men, but Golaud's weakness is superficial and transitory, and he is capable, as his father and grandfather are not, of exerting a savage authority over the woman on whom he depends.

Striking as this picture is, though, it is disabled by the fact—the inescapable fact in this performance—of the score's omniscience. Anything the music does not register—any person, any action, any feeling, any sight—simply fails to happen in the theatre, but remains half-happening, as Sellars's parallel scenes remain half-happening, in a limbo of superfluity.

This can be disturbing. People for whom there is no music are in an important sense not there, even though the singer may be physically present on the stage. Sellars's production is full of such sad apparitions that are all flesh and no spirit: Yniold in the last scene of the first act, Geneviève in numerous scenes after the only two in which she sings (never before can a Geneviève have had six costume changes), Pelléas's father, and of course the police officers. It is a measure of the music's power—compelling in this performance—that we trust our ears rather than our eyes, and that therefore all these people are extraneous. In the world of Debussy's score there are no mute characters until the final scene, when the arrival of the silent maidservants is—or should be—an alarming sign of irreversible change. This effect the composer created, consciously or not, when he excised earlier scenes in which the servants appear and even speak. Sellars brings back an allusion to one of those scenes, that of maids washing the castle, as one of his many mimed additions. In his production the strangeness of the silent is a sign that has been flashing on and off since the postlude to the opening scene, and so the maids' arrival to witness Mélisande's death is nothing special.

Nowhere, though, do mutes so get in the way as in the music after the shocking scene of Golaud's rage against Mélisande. This interlude—like the only comparable passage in opera: the adagio after the death of Wozzeck—brings forward a generalized slow cry of sympathy and complaint as the music swerves around from presenting the drama to looking back at it and commenting on it. All we need to see are the two characters who remain after Golaud's distracted departure: Mélisande, abused, and Arkel, helpless to act. Perhaps an empty stage would be even better, suggesting that the music is concerned not just with Mélisande's sorrow and Arkel's impotence but with the whole world of which they are a part—with Allemonde. What we do not need is a quartet of slightly sinister nurses coming on to calm the king and his granddaughter-in-law, and to create, by their particularity, a brutal dissonance with the music's universal voice.

The specific voices of the Amsterdam cast are variable. White as Golaud is outstanding: his solemn and coldly open-toned bass projects a violence forced on the prince by despair, but at times there is a gleam of light—anguish or hope—reflecting in bright upper overtones he can bring into play through the darkness of his sound. He is a fine actor. He frankly provides what Sellars asks: a man wresting himself from suicide, picking up a weird girl he soon stops trying to understand, being engaged in some kind of uneasy truce with the police, and finally falling victim to these opponents. But his noble vocal carriage and his expressive power make all this seem pretty trifling.

Philip Langridge as Pelléas makes us all spectators at a contest of art with nature. He neither looks nor sounds like an immature young man, and the part has no use for his distinctive gifts—notably the catch in the voice, the slight rasp that can intimate something unpleasant being hidden or ignored in, for example, how Stravinsky's Oedipus or Schoenberg's Aron or any of Britten's leading tenor characters present themselves. Pelléas is not hiding anything, and what he ignores is not some malignant secret but the entire universe outside himself. Such naivety is not an easy prize for artistry to attain. Langridge goes down fighting. But at the same time there is a rightness in how this Pelléas is overcome by the rising orchestral vehemence he unleashes through his challenge to fate in his final scene.

Robert Lloyd's Arkel is immensely solid and accomplished, and his rapport with Rattle is enjoyably sure. Quite against the foolish sentiments of his words, he sounds like an oracle: the only character who hears, in the orchestra, what is going on. Felicity Palmer is clear and forceful in Geneviève's narrative; Elise Ross, if vocally pressed on opening night, looks good as a Mélisande in ice-blue track suit and sneakers (nothing abnormal about the hair). Gaële Le Roi's trim performance as Yniold shows up the anglophone French of the others, though the part does need a boy.

Inconsistencies in the casting are, however, of minuscule importance against the orchestral magnificence and precision. While writing the opera, Debussy played with the remarkable notion of putting some of the orchestra onstage for Mélisande's death—an idea that perhaps came out of his concern for effects of space and texture dependent on the relative positioning of the instruments. Rattle's performance cares for all those effects, and makes the orchestra not just part of the scenery but the evening's object. (*New Yorker*, 28 June 1993)

Met 1995

That it is not impossible to present *Pelléas et Mélisande* in a huge theatre is proved by some few things that go right in the Met's new production. One of the gleams in a sad fog of misdirection and imprecision is the general audibility of the words. The singers—all North Americans with the exception of one Briton—enunciate with the syllable-by-syllable clarity of people speaking a foreign language, with the result not only that the words are heard but that they are heard as strange, which is apt. The syntax of Maeterlinck's play is elementary: the characters speak a kind of high school French, as if there might be some other language in which they would be able to express themselves more freely. Debussy's discovery was that this other language could be music.

At the Met the music is not swamped by the scale of the place: on the contrary, the orchestra, under James Levine, often sounds too loud—especially the timpani in the interlude leading up to the scene where Golaud is in his sickbed. This is one place where, not too surprisingly, Levine enjoys finding how much Debussy learned from *Parsifal*. The wounded Golaud becomes a cousin of the wounded Amfortas, and later, in the big interlude after the scene of Golaud's violent attack on Mélisande and the ancient Arkel's impotent pity, the weight and the march rhythm of Levine's performance point to a kinship with the transformation sequences that lead in Wagner's opera to the grail chapel. This mighty adagio, as Levine makes it, rears up from the pit as a display of music's power, but also of music's powerlessness to help the characters embroiled in it. The moment cannot quite be spoiled by the busy scene-change that goes on at this point: Levine touches magnificence. However, Debussy's music more commonly is that of a man who can change his mind every quarter of a second, and Levine, in his effort for grand design, is often obliged to stop and restart. The music of silence is not what this conductor is about.

Nor is it very much what his cast is about. Frederica von Stade's Mélisande was always firmly human; maturity has only increased her tendency to plant the character in a low register of rich tone and expressive fullness. Yet she commands ambiguity. In the tower song, which was her triumph at the opening performance, she started as if singing out of a sob in that warm and distinctive mezzo reach of hers, but then one began to feel that the sob might be a chuckle. This was moving and excellent: Debussy's world is one in which, as he said of the effect of his Sonata for flute, viola, and harp, one does not know whether to laugh or cry, and it is good to have a Mélisande who can display her dislocation by simultaneously and full-heartedly doing both. What is more questionable is her occasional exaggeration when the emotion is simpler, as in her line 'Je ne suis pas heureuse' in the middle of the second act. This is not someone bewailing her misfortune; this is a person tentatively beginning to understand what unhappiness might feel like.

Even von Stade's most defiant directness is, though, exceeded by Victor Braun's as Golaud. To a degree, this is just. Golaud is a blunt man surrounded by people who are disengaged; hence the drama. But his bluntness is all there in his music: he does not have to rage into the line, as Braun does, and virtually speak or shout whole phrases, suggesting a man who is impatient with, not through, what he has to sing. One cannot fail to be touched by Braun's portrait of jealous frenzy, suspicion and grief. But he is wrong. And because he comes to a climax of fury in the second act, rather than in the fourth, he raises the unnecessary question of why Golaud's behavior should suddenly be so sinisterly calm when, early in the third act, he discovers Pelléas wrapped in Mélisande's tresses.

The Met's Pelléas is also a man of solid emotional substance, but in his case by virtue of the tessitura and type of his singing voice. Debussy wrote the part for a high baritone, and it sounds well on a tenor, who can bring a brightness to the occasional high-lying phrase ('Ce sont des autres phares', for instance), as if for most of the time he were inhibited by shyness, or as if his voice would intermittently, like an adolescent boy's, skid out of control. Dwayne Croft, a chestnut baritone, is no adolescent. He makes Pelléas sound not so distant in colour and range from Golaud—if far distant from this Golaud in his consistent nobility of tone, roundness of delivery and musicality of phrasing. Where Mélisande's choice is normally between the conventional Golaud and the poetic Pelléas, here the action is turned around, and Pelléas is a rather proper young man who falls victim to Golaud's primitive urges.

Whether this is by accident or design on the part of the director, Jonathan Miller, is a moot point. Miller has asked us to see the opera as having a link with French novels of the period—Proust, *Le Grand Meaulnes*—though the look of his production is, especially where Clare Mitchell's costumes are concerned, more Merchant-Ivory than Alain-Fournier. It is asking a lot to present Mélisande in a wide Edwardian hat; nor does von Stade look happy so bedecked. Also regrettable is the decision to flesh out the social background. Pelléas's father is one of the great characters in opera exactly because he is never seen: it is his absence that puts a question mark after every sentence in the text, because we have to ask how things would be differently spoken, differently felt, differently done were he around. Miller wheels him on in an invalid chair. We also get to see Yniold's nurse, a couple of gardeners, a butler, a footman, and various maids, all long before the finale, where servants are supposed to appear, and by their silent appearance mark Mélisande's and the opera's passing. It is a foolish trend in this opera to use supernumeraries when the issues of who is onstage and who is not singing are so crucial.

Not so foolish is the transfer of the action to the period when the opera was composed, though the device is by now a bit commonplace, and certainly it has been better done—notably by Harry Kupfer in a London production more than a decade ago, and by Peter Brook in his drawing-room containment of the piece. By comparison with those predecessors, Miller's vision is tepid. There is too much dithering, in place of the strong gestures that could really communicate indecisiveness. When the characters do actually do something, they banally replicate the text: Mélisande's hand strays to her head at the thought of her lost crown, and what is potentially mysterious comes crashing to the ground as mundane. The one good visual idea is the gradual reassembly of the high beige walls of John Conklin's set. At first they are astray, with little architectural logic, and with the possibility of a tree in what might be a room. But as they rotate for each new scene, an order begins to assert itself, sufficiently for there to be a propped-up ruin or a construction site (it is nicely unclear which) for the scene in which Golaud threatens Pelléas in the castle vaults, a comfortable salon in the next act, and a completely rational bedchamber for the finale. The opera is drawn inexorably into normality, which is death.

This production also follows what has become common practice in casting a boy as Yniold, and good and true though Gregory Rodriguez is, nobody should have expected him to cope with singing in a theatre of this size. The tail end of his solo scene disappears under the orchestra, though this charming suspension of the tragedy has already been thoroughly throttled by Miller, who has Yniold sing it from bed. Bad idea. The drama is not in the dreamer but the dream: the stone the boy cannot lift, the passing sheep and shepherd, the way he skips off 'to tell somebody something'. Bringing Yniold on in other scenes as silent witness, too, works less well on this stage, deeply shadowed, than it did in the clear intimacy of Brook's version.

Robert Lloyd, as Arkel, was worryingly off the note and muffled (by his beard?) in his first scene, but came more into focus. Marilyn Horne, as Geneviève, was there right from the start, as this character rather has to be, since she vanishes after the first act. Horne made her letter recitation a masterpiece of experience, authority and musical intelligence, bolstered by bottom notes that now have an almost Heldentenor strength. This is a wonderful part for an old trouper—perhaps one for von Stade in the next Met production, which is now an urgent hope. (*New Yorker*, 17 April 1995)

Glyndebourne 1999

The new production at Glyndebourne of *Pelléas et Mélisande* belongs squarely in a modern tradition of locating Debussy's opera not in a land of crumbling castles and fairytale princes but in the here and now, or at least the here and then. Graham Vick and Paul Brown, the director and the designer, have everything unfold within a grand salon from around the time of the opera's composition. A spiral staircase rises in the middle of the room, and under the undulating glasslike floor are thousands of red, orange and yellow chrysanthemums, aptly symbolic of confinement and death. Such a set cannot respond to the important distinction between interior and exterior scenes in the libretto: how Pelléas and Mélisande like to meet outside, in the presence of natural light and flowing water, whereas the other characters are indoor people. On the other hand, in this version a potent effect can be created when the two central figures sing of the sea from within their sombre room. It is as if their reality, like their love, is something they are creating together.

As Christiane Oelze sings the part, Mélisande is the instigator of that love. Oelze's tone is bright and pure but also subtly inflected; she combines naivety with canniness. Everything she sings seems to have two or three layers of ulterior motive, and she is not as shocked as the audience when the ancient Arkel, the king, gives her a more than grandfatherly kiss. At that moment and elsewhere Vick and his cast richly convey the queasy feelings of a stifling family existence—an existence documented by reminders of the sickroom in which Pelléas's unseen, unheard father lies, and by having characters around when they are not directly involved. The quick scene that Pelléas and Mélisande snatch together at the start of the fourth act, for instance, is begun by Pelléas's rising from the dinner table to catch Mélisande as she comes downstairs. This makes it clear that the initiative is his and that he has begun to feel the need for secrecy, whereas before he had seemed not to understand the jealousy of Mélisande's husband, his half-brother Golaud.

This Pelléas, appealingly played and sung by Richard Croft, is a boy. This Golaud, John Tomlinson, is a man. His lack of sensitivity to his son, Yniold, is startlingly portrayed in the scene where he pumps Yniold for information about Pelléas and Mélisande. Tomlinson makes a big, scouring sound that is graphically expressive of anger, and Jake Arditti is excellent as the child vainly trying to mollify his parent until the point arrives where his fear overcomes him and breaks through. Always cruel, this scene is here almost terrifying and in many ways the climax of the drama. Golaud's destructive impulses are now let loose. The deaths of Pelléas and Mélisande become inevitable.

What makes the scene work so well is not only the dramatic intensity on the stage but also the passionate, driving, monomaniacal ostinatos coming out of the pit, where Sir Andrew Davis conducts a performance in which sonic beauty, of which there is a great deal, always has expressive implications. Often one thinks of this score in terms of marine blues and greens, but the flowers and the copper walls of the set give it the colour of a radiant sunset in this production, and Davis gets a corresponding fullness and glow from the orchestra. (*New York Times*, 5 June 1999)

Met 2000

Debussy's opera, which was revived at the Metropolitan Opera on Wednesday, tells us at once not enough and too much. There is no clear information about time, place or even the precise relationships within the family of wandering solitaries that is being observed. And much of what they say is vague or off the point. It is the power of Debussy's music, though, to reveal how remarks that seem stray and almost meaningless, or questions that appear idle, can be tight little burning bombs, fired by one person at another with exact control in games of love and cruelty.

Everything is in the subtext, and much of the subtext is in the orchestral score. This was beautifully presented by the Met Orchestra under James Levine, with fine string textures, gleaming brass, excellent woodwind solos, colourful harps and timpani gestures unusually full of character. Levine's tempos were generally slow, but often with the possibility—and sometimes the actuality—of a sudden or gradual acceleration, conveying an intensification of emotion. The impression was of a frozen lake that could crack at any point to reveal the water beneath boiling.

The whole penultimate scene—the last of six scenes between Pelléas and Mélisande but the first in which they speak directly to each other, with catastrophic consequences—was one long accelerando toward passion and violence. Speed went with fury, too, in the terrifying scene in which Yniold is forced by his father, Golaud, to spy on his stepmother and his uncle, Mélisande and Pelléas, together in an upstairs room. This scene's turning point was tellingly marked. Yniold, seeing the state his father is in, tries to get away. No, says Golaud: you stay with me. And the line was intoned by José van Dam with the sullen, irrefutable force of a man turning into an animal, backed by low sounds in the orchestra having the same tone. Then, with his father holding Yniold up to the window, the orchestra's fast brilliance communicated simultaneously the boy's rising fear, the father's mounting suspicion and perhaps the growing poignancy and even embarrassment the audience must feel in witnessing these events.

Van Dam's performance was strong all through. His singing was heightened speech, the notes and rhythms always making a direct expressive effect, across a range from care to anger to, in the last act, dumb bewilderment mixed with an emphatic wish still to get to the truth (a word he sang with the tremolo of bursting emotion). And his body language matched his singing.

The last act was also important for the orchestra and Levine. With more characters onstage than in any previous scene, and with the action moving to a standstill, it seemed the lead was being taken by the orchestra, playing music as sweeping and rapturous as *La Mer*. The people, on the point of departing, were being revealed as the playthings of their inner life, a life to which they had no conscious access. That is the work's keenest tragedy.

Its great gifts here are in the splendid cast as well as the superb orchestra. Susanne Mentzer provides a magnetic and dark-voiced Mélisande, projecting a sensuality of which the character seems unaware, caught up as she is in feelings of disaffection and melancholy. Dwayne Croft is full and ardent as Pelléas, aptly veering between the radiant confidence of shining phrases and softer insecurity: he makes everything sing as much as Van Dam makes everything speak. Robert Lloyd shows the grandfather, Arkel, still in complete possession of the lyrical genes that went to Pelléas. Nadine Denize is the bit-part mother and James Danner a spirited Yniold. (*New York Times*, 2 October 2000)

Birtwistle

Harrison Birtwistle's was the great creative story of the 1970s and 1980s in London, where most of his major works were introduced, and where he thrived with institutions that shared his sense of music's steady progress, notably the BBC and the London Sinfonietta. By the late 1980s he was a world figure.

Earth Dances

Quite how the Festival Hall could have been half empty for one of the most exhilarating concerts of the season is bewildering. Here was Stravinsky's grandest late monument, *Threni*, a fascinating double piano concerto by the master of expressionist surrealism, Bernd Alois Zimmermann, and the first big orchestral piece for fourteen years by Harrison Birtwistle.

Bruno Canino and Antonio Ballista were the quick-witted soloists in Zimmermann's *Dialogue*, which has a vast orchestra flickering with keyboard figuration, as if issuing from a dozen rainbow pianos, before the awesome entrance of ghost quotations from Debussy and Mozart. After a masterly exposition of this score Peter Eötvös conducted a beautifully calm performance of Stravinsky's liturgy of chance, dances and magic letters for the church of the lost god. Then came Birtwistle's *Earth Dances*, a thirty-five-minute sprawling, lumbering giant of a score that makes a quick verbal sketch more than usually irrelevant. It is like his *Silbury Air* and his *Secret Theatre* multiplied together, a work of long groundswells, of strange unending melody (especially for the woodwind ensemble), of cascading clockworks from tuned percussion, of densly worked string textures and huge heroic fanfares: often of all these things together, with the addition of something new in the dance element that keeps trickling over the surface, frequently speaking rather curiously with a Latin American accent, though not in the climactic and tumultuous 'Danse sacrale'. A lesser composer would have followed precedent and stopped here, but Birtwistle successfully goes on into a slow, quiet coda, to leave his audience staring (like Parsifal) after an opaque ceremonial of magnificence. (*Times*, 17 March 1986)

The Mask of Orpheus

Birtwistle's second opera has been a long time with the shadows. Murmurings of it were first heard more than fifteen years ago, followed by the more tangible evidence of associated works and glimpses of the libretto. Parties from Covent Garden and from Glyndebourne were sent back to bring the thing into the light, but evidently both looked over their shoulders at the fateful moment, and it has been left to the English National Opera to reveal a work of immense power and fascination. After such a wait, expectations have been running exceedingly high, and there must be many who have been grappling to form their own impressions of what the eventual opera would be like. It was a situation almost made for disappointment, and yet *The Mask of Orpheus* turns out to be both a richer and a more single, strong and dynamic experience than one had dared hope. Birtwistle's *Punch and Judy* used to be the one perfectly satisfactory reinvention of opera since Stravinsky. Now there is another.

It does not, however, show its purpose all at once. The rhythm of the opera is one of increasing tension as the wheels of circular events are swung into ever-faster motion. This makes for a relatively slow and diffuse first act, where what we see onstage seems partial and makeshift: there are things happening beyond, of which we hear amplified whisperings, and the whole impression is of dramatic and musical elements being weighed and assembled. Some of those elements are striking. There is a love duet of ice-cold eroticism where the partners chant on each other's names, and then a rampaging entry for the priests, with the noise of wood and drums. Later a 'yawn aria' for Euridice is a vocal flower that quite avoids the waiting bathos. But it is only at the end of the act, with the hysterical coloratura of the Oracle of the Dead and a quite extraordinary procession of deep wind chords as Orpheus remembers his future journey, that action and music are gripped as one.

The second act offers musical repetitiveness to power a relatively straight unfolding of Orpheus's travel to the underworld and back: the generating symbol is that of a system of arches, each a station in the myth, and each presented in the same musical form of sung narration and mimed enactment. The doubling of the main roles by singers and mimes, which in the first act had been a source of indecision, now has a straightforward function, though the orchestra retains its powerful place, dependent on the stage but not bound by it. As Orpheus moves towards the inevitable loss, for instance, the orchestra builds up a huge movement that intensifies the mythic force of the moment, but then the actual turn is hardly noticed in the music.

The gyrations of an orchestra that is in the same place but not doing quite the same things become more overwhelming still in the last act, where both music and action move in cycles of different repetition: the governing image is now that of tides, each one shifting the arrangement of details in multiple re-enactments of Orpheus's death. There are again many extraordinary details: the great electronic clang that keeps shivering the auditorium, the urgent orchestral manoeuvres led by brass marching upwards from the bass, a fantastically strange soprano-tenor duet for Orpheus as oracle. But the mind is gripped throughout by a work that has hit the centre of its territory. In the first half of this century it was possible for artists like Stravinsky, Eliot and Strauss to deal with myth on terms of familiarity. Birtwistle, on the other hand, shows us something alien, even barbaric, but terribly important. Or the comparison might be made with other times in operatic history when a new version of the Orpheus legend was called up to answer a new vision not only of opera but also of the nature of the self: Birtwistle's work is nothing less.

And it is admirably presented. Philip Langridge uses his anxious lyricism to great effect in the long central role, and Jean Rigby and Ethna Robinson are well matched as alternative, darkly-voiced Euridices; Marie Angel gives a startling performance as the Oracle of the Dead. The orchestral score, with all its dense brooding, ceremonies, alarms and ticking mechanisms, sounds magnificent under the direction of Elgar Howarth and Paul Daniel, though the wind need to be brought up to the level of the amplified percussion. Barry Anderson, who assisted Birtwistle in the composition of the very important and awesomely successful tape sections, is in charge of the electronics. David Freeman produces, and Jocelyn Herbert designs, a staging that mightily activates the savagery of Greek culture with potent help from Mesoamerica, and the mime artists, led by Graham Walters as a highly sympathetic Orpheus Hero, dance as if from Attic vases. The world afterwards is different. (*Times*, 23 May 1986)

Yan Tan Tethera

The clocks of Birtwistle's muse have been spinning madly forwards and backwards to chime together, bringing within recent months the premieres of his massive, majestic orchestral piece, *Earth Dances*, then of his *Mask of Orpheus* by English National Opera, and now of another opera, *Yan Tan Tethera*. As compositional time passed in fact, *Yan Tan Tethera* was written after *Orpheus* and before *Secret Theatre*, the London Sinfonietta piece which preceded and made possible *Earth Dances*. The new opera uses a similar orchestra to that of *Secret Theatre*, and there are similarities of musical substance. Both works make much of a strong melodic line, driving hard and sure like a chisel, and used in the opera to project Tony Harrison's version of Wiltshire folktale. Both, too, combine and measure the melodic impetus with pulsating accompaniments: *Yan Tan Tethera* is coloured with bell sounds, with xylophone clatterings, and with the stressful ease of repeated chords from strings and harp. Birtwistle's own description of the work as a 'mechanical pastoral' is more than a Polonianism: it points to the twin, inseparable aspects of the piece as a reiterative machine and as a fresh song of the fields.

The Mask of Orpheus was in this sense a mechanical pastoral too, and there are shades of that old myth in the new opera when the hero is immured underground for expecting music to turn back the passage of time. The single, ninety-minute act of *Yan Tan Tethera* also bears some resemblance to the last act of *Orpheus*, in length, in style, and in its construction as a continuous thrust moving through and over cycles of repetition. But it is a simpler piece. One might think of it as an astronomical clock, but with music rotating instead of heavenly spheres, and with the puppet figures replaced by human actor-singers in their own circlings. Watching it has some features in common with watching a clock. There are stretches where very little happens and time hangs heavy, but then suddenly the mechanism springs into life, and one recognizes that all the counting was necessary in order to reach the golden numbers, such as the devil's dance halfway through or the moment near the end when the hill opens to release the boys pent up for seven years.

The counting, with its references to the natural world of annual cycles and population growth, is perhaps what attracted Birtwistle to the story, but the fact that the hero is an honest northerner, feeling alien in the south and the victim of underhand machinations planned by his southern colleague, must also have struck a chord with both composer and poet. The northern shepherd prospers; the southern shepherd is jealous and summons the devil to his aid. But good wins through, and the northerner is left not only with a fecund flock but also with a wife and four boys. That is all that happens, but the story has to be so elementary when it is effectively the accompaniment to the music: the Opera Factory London Sinfonietta production rather gets this the wrong way around by placing the orchestra at the back, behind a screen. It would have been good to see the instrumentalists—always there, like the dolmens and standing stones of David Roger's set. But at least one has a good view of Ariane Gastambide's marvellous masks for the sheep, whom David Freeman has chewing, pawing and nuzzling in a thoroughly ovine way: the individual differences within the similar mass are a perfect complement to the score's habit of throwing out variegations of sameness. The cast is led by Omar Ebrahim, who sings strongly, with northern vowels to accord with the dark modality of his music; he also never wastes a movement. Helen Charnock is equally resolute, despite the wife's music being more excited, and Richard Suart is a serious villain. Philip Doghan ably doubles on fife as the devil; Elgar Howarth conducts. (*Times*, 8 August 1986)

Endless Parade

A commission from Paul Sacher is almost the Nobel Prize for composition: it means joining the ranks of Stravinsky, Bartók, Strauss, Boulez and, among British composers until now, only Britten and Tippett. That Birtwistle should be summoned to the elect was a happy honour, and it has brought from him a happy response in *Endless Parade* for trumpet, strings and vibraphone, which was given its first performance by Håkan Hardenberger and the Collegium Musicum Zurich under Sacher's direction.

As Birtwistle has remarked of this and other pieces, the musical parade is not only endless but beginningless. Of course, it has to begin, and does so arrestingly, with the trumpet striding up through a great swirl of tone, but the effect of this start is to suggest one has entered a process that is already under way, turned a corner to meet a festive procession in midtrack: this is the composer's own metaphor, the piece having its origins partly in his experience of a fiesta in Lucca. Among other origins is his own decade-old *Melencolia I* for clarinet, strings and harp; or rather one might say that both pieces are expressions of a model music for chorus-leader, chorus and shadow. The solo part is colossally challenging, exploiting the instrument's full extent of pitch and dynamic range, and also demanding the ability to sustain long, bursting phrases throughout a twenty-minute period; but it is not an exhibitionist role. This is a concerto in mask: the soloist is not a showy individual but a spokesman for the group, and for the musical imperative. And the vibraphonist is not a second soloist but the provider of a luminous, resonant continuo, adding depth and largeness to the sonority.

The parade itself is of many sorts, bringing forward a great variety of fascinating string textures and of different balances between trumpet and ensemble. There are some figures that return: notably a little four-note descending motif, coming back repeatedly as a comma, and the long upward ride of the opening. But at the same time new discoveries continue to be possible, and they include Birtwistle's discovery for himself of a relaxed smile. The piece is, of course, utterly his from non-beginning to non-end (the orchestra here frozen with bows in the air), but the abundance of melody in it is new, and so is the magical fantasy of a section in glissando: memories of Britten's *Midsummer Night's Dream* here were overwhelmed by the thought of how excellently Birtwistle himself is now equipped to deal with Shakespearian wonder. That he can incorporate savage fanfares and sensuous delight in the same piece, and intermingle rather than juxtapose them as he had in *Punch and Judy*, is itself a wonder and an immense excitement.

Sacher's conducting was understandably cautious at this first performance, but Hardenberger, perhaps even more at the final rehearsal than at the premiere, made the piece a grand act of assertion. (*Times*, 5 May 1987)

Salford Toccata

In 1973 Birtwistle provided the brass band with the work it probably did not know it had been waiting for: a sustained grim lament filled with slowly wandering melodies, echoes of tolling bells, broken chorales and the chippings of clockwork mechanisms winding down. That was *Grimethorpe Aria*, and magnificent it was. Now suddenly we are asked to take this as only the first part of a triptych, whose second section, *Salford Toccata*, was ambitiously commissioned by the Salford College of Technology and given its first performance by the college brass band on Wednesday night. It offers a very different view of the same scenery. *Grimethorpe* ends with its lumbering, mumbling progress bearing on, and then *Salford* bursts in with wild triumphant gestures, much more in the brass band tradition, though, of course, eminently Birtwistlian. In the florid cornet writing one is reminded at once of the recent trumpet concerto, *Endless Parade*, and the hocketing of soloists and ensembles, which is a strong element in the work's eruptive presence, recalls the composer's orchestral version of Machaut's *Hoquetus David*. There are moments when all the ebullience and positive thinking go off somewhere, and one is left with a grey expectancy not so far from *Grimethorpe*, but the essence of the new piece is brilliant instrumental virtuosity and fast motion, leading up to a surprisingly Boulezian chase of semiquaver stuttering before the coup of the ending, where a large bass drum (marking the entry of percussion after half an hour of brass choiring) stops the music short, and the piece breathes its last in the depths of the double bass tubas. *Salford* is such a powerful shock after *Grimethorpe* that splicing the two together, as Birtwistle apparently intends, seems a mistake: the quiet ending of the aria demands a pause, and it might almost be better to play the toccata first. But perhaps the scheme will justify itself when it is completed by *Accrington* (or wherever) *Fugue*. (*Times*, 14 April 1989)

Antiphonies

Here was the composer, sitting on the stage of the Festival Hall in London an hour or so before the performance of his latest big work, *Antiphonies* for piano and orchestra, a massive, wild and wonder-filled half-hour commissioned by donors for the Philharmonia and Los Angeles Philharmonic orchestras. He was there for a panel discussion—plainly not his favourite means of expression. His two hands on his lap pulled at each other stiffly, fist jerking over one finger, then another, while he waited, and while others spoke. They all seemed to know so much more about his music than he did. James MacMillan, the young Scots composer who was chairing the exchange, talked about the way Birtwistle's music gives the impression of being at once proudly new and defiantly ancient. Joanna MacGregor, who was to play the solo piano part in the new piece, described the music's density. Pierre Boulez, the evening's conductor, analysed how that density is made up of layers: 'tiled' music, he called it, where thematic material could jump up or down from one layer of tiles to another, so that there could be continuity and disjunction at once. But foremost, said Boulez, was the power, 'a very strong way of telling things, and of telling things which are very personal'.

All of this was sure and true. None of it, though, eased the embarrassment of the composer, whose hands continued their anxious dry washing of themselves, except when he was called on to speak, and so needed them to hold and show and measure his music in the space in front of him. Even then his words were faltering and his wit awkward. Introducing a few sections he had picked to have played during this introductory session, he said he did not know why he had chosen some bits rather than others: 'They were all equally good.' When he had to talk specifically about his first example, he lapsed almost into incoherence.

'OK, well . . . we're going to play the first page of the piece . . . and . . . [sigh] . . . really . . . [sigh] . . . really to explain music is very hard. Um . . . it's, it—I suppose an analogy would be, is, is like, it's like opening a door on something that's already happening.'

There it was at last: the sudden window onto the piece. Birtwistle still finds words bothersome, for all the length and scale of his success, and for all the magisterial command over language he shows in his operas and songs. In a public forum, or even sometimes in a private conversation, he can appear like a fish out of water—or more, given his strong, rounded shape, stillness of posture, and rough beard, like a bear at bay.

In his music, miraculously, the labouring effort to communicate and the flash of articulacy happen both at once. This is music that typically sounds heavy with its own birth, struggling to bring something to expression. And yet the struggle, the heaviness, is what is to be expressed. There is not, as there is when he speaks, the sense of a blocked message. The blockage is the message. The feeling in the best, biggest pieces—of which the new *Antiphonies* is certainly one—is that we are waiting for something momentous to take place, and at the same time experiencing that momentous thing. Both are possible because of the power to which Boulez alluded: the power that creates both immense impedance and the force to overcome it. The impedance is principally harmonic thickness and lethargy; the force comes from urgent, pushing rhythm, or from insistent repetition, or from music's being squeezed through at the extreme edges, in the acute high treble or the lowering far bass.

Until quite recently there was another obstruction in the way of Birtwistle's music: the scarcity of recordings. But that has been alleviated, so that *Antiphonies* has an audible context. For a composer whose concert works are as dramatic as his operas, that context begins with his two previous pieces for a similar cast of soloist plus orchestra: *Melencolia I* for clarinet, harp and strings, and *Endless Parade* for trumpet, vibraphone and strings. Parallel in instrumentation, these are dark and light sisters. *Melencolia I* is an almost continuous monologue for the clarinet, a monologue of long, brooding melody and fierce outbursts, with the harp as companion (ally, rival or persecutor) and the strings as a landscape for the two figures—or perhaps rather a seascape, in moods variously of complex turmoil and wide calm. It is one of Birtwistle's finest achievements, and the recorded performance does it proud. *Endless Parade*, written a decade later, in 1986–7, is similarly a soliloquy, but one made up of fanfares and brilliance from the trumpet, gilded by the vibraphone, with the strings now more subserviently placed as foil and audience.

Antiphonies is different again. To take account of the multifacetedness of the new soloist, the orchestra is enriched to full symphonic proportions; also, the relationship between solo and ensemble is much more complex. Where the clarinet and the trumpet in the earlier works stood quite apart from their backgrounds, as singers from a chorus, the piano of *Antiphonies* is integrated into the orchestra. It is aligned with harps, vibraphones, bells and glockenspiels, whose bright resonances can connect further with the sounds of high woodwinds and violin harmonics; it is also joined to a wood-percussion group of marimbas and temple blocks to make a clattering orchestra within the orchestra. But the piano is seen too as separate: an alternative space in which ideas can appear and develop as if in monochrome form.

This is how a great deal of the antiphony of *Antiphonies* takes place: in transfers of thematic material between orchestra and piano. On the opening page, for instance, the piano flickers into life with chords that are doubled or imitated by orchestral ensembles. Subsequent interchanges concern more substantial bodies of music, such as a four-part counterpoint that swivels between airy woodwind and busy piano soon after the beginning, or else involve more sharply characterized entities, like the brusque, rising interjection that is the trombones' only contribution to this initial phase of the work, and that the piano obediently repeats each time, seemingly with increasing irritation.

The motif soon disappears. As Birtwistle remarked during the discussion beforehand, 'I tend to use musical ideas like a child playing with toys: when I get bored with them I just forget them.' Of course the casualness is disingenuous: we lose the trombones' brutish interruption just when it is threatening to become intolerably nagging. But at the same time, this is a composer who does seem to make his music with ideas and decisions that are in some ways capricious, while being in other respects absolutely precise. The trombone signal is a case in point. It is always the same in rhythm, shape and prominence, but the notes are subtly changed each time, for no obvious reason. Rigid repetition, as so often in Birtwistle's music, is combined with haphazard alteration. There is a middle level of obvious pattern—the level of repeated notes, or chords, or motifs—while the lower level of detail and the upper level of large-scale form provide no simple answer to scrutiny.

The formal complexity has to do with those tiled layers of which Boulez spoke. There are strata in *Antiphonies* that seem to be always present, even though they may in fact come into hearing only intermittently. One is the slow, deep song of the tuba, a song that may be taken up by other instruments of the distant bass. Then there are events that happen only once, appear to come almost from nowhere, and contribute to the feeling of constant, turbulent self-renewal and discovery. One is a sequence of huge deflations, where fortissimo chords for the entire orchestra lapse towards silence through downward slides. Another is a set of quiet, lifting gestures for the strings, divided into thirty parts to create widely spread harmonies at once monumental and mysterious. Yet another is the unison middle-register A that arrives to signal the end of the race of incidents, and still another the beginning of that end, with a long melody confidently breezing in high woodwind while the piano has been left behind to idle.

There was a time when Birtwistle's forms were episodic, like those of Stravinsky or Messiaen, as some of his early titles suggest: *Refrains and Choruses*, *Verses for Ensembles*. In *Antiphonies*, though, it is as if the pellucid fragments of those earlier works were being piled on top of one another, or as if a simple verse-refrain structure, an elementary antiphony, were being refracted through a musical prism. Some of the examples in the pre-concert demonstration were given with the layers laid bare: with just the wind and percussion playing, or just the strings. And they sounded so much clearer that way. But the essential challenge of this music is that of monitoring more hectic musical traffic, and in that respect *Antiphonies* is a successor not so much to the two earlier solo-ensemble pieces as to Birtwistle's magnificent last piece for large orchestra, *Earth Dances*. What *Earth Dances* was to *The Rite of Spring*, *Antiphonies* is to *Petrushka*.

The comparison with Stravinsky is justified on grounds not only of mosaic structure and objectivity (Birtwistle has talked about wanting his music to have 'a formal voice') but also of drama, of what Birtwistle has often referred to as 'role-playing' for instruments. Where Stravinsky in composing *Petrushka* saw 'a puppet . . . exasperating the patience of the orchestra with diabolical cascades of arpeggios', *Antiphonies* presents multiple characters: the tuba humming to itself, the first trumpet remembering the assertive, instigating force of *Endless Parade*, the piccolos revolving slowly around each other in high air they share only with the top of the piano and with the violins. In other cases there is more than one role, and especially for the solo piano, which seems to switch voices in order to outwit the orchestra in a running game to gain possession of the musical material. (The part cries out for the strength and the focussed intelligence of a Pollini.) Except for moments of luminous truce, the game between soloist and orchestra is played with canniness, pouncing speed and bared claws: the composer's reference to child's play is apropos.

What further validates that image of the composer and his toys is the external nature of the musical playthings he picks up, handles and discards through *Antiphonies*, the sense that they enter the piece from outside. Often they do: Birtwistle has always snatched ideas from one piece into another, and *Antiphonies* includes more than one reference to the arresting way *Earth Dances* starts, with a quake and a collapse in the orchestra's bass grounding. But there is also a personal outsideness, that of a composer who has been able to keep himself apart from the traditions, so that he can come to a conventional medium, the piano concerto, as if it were as alien as Mayan temple architecture. There is, too, an externality intrinsic in his ideas, a matter of the detachment with which they are made and used. Just as he is more the committed observer of his own music than the voicing origin, so we feel his instruments to be vehicles of action rather than expression. They do not propose the music, but rather the music is proposed through them. Players can be passionately involved and yet still not be singing for themselves, being rather buffeted by musical forces that are as alien and unpredictable as the weather.

The sense of enactment in Birtwistle's music is thus fully compatible with its struggle into existence, and also with its unusual combination of lucidity and ignorance, expressed in the coexistence of pattern and randomness. The musical weather—the meteorology of harmony most of all—he treats as an intractable given; he then makes his instruments play in it as best they can. There was some suspicion in his opera *Gawain* that he had begun to know how to create his own storms: the music was often unusually selfconscious in its drive to illustrate the libretto. *Antiphonies*, however, affirms a return to the older manner, in which the music's purposes are not so easily defined, and in which the composer seems to be tackling enormous forces that he and his players can only learn to live with, not control.

As Birtwistle continues his progress, so his strategies for living with upheaval become more precise. *Antiphonies* is his most virtuoso piece of orchestration to date, having a fastidiousness of effect that entered his music in the late 1980s (the Rilke song 'An die Musik' marked the change) and appears now in an orchestral concert work for the first time. Aligned with this delicacy is a new accuracy and speed in the instrumental role-playing, which is a feature too of a piece written immediately after *Antiphonies*: *Five Distances* for wind quintet. One waits eagerly to hear how this keenness of instrumental drama will transfer into the theatre in Birtwistle's next opera, *The Second Mrs Kong*.

Back at the introduction to *Antiphonies*, he finally told a story that said everything about his robustly practical but slantwise approach to composition, his fidelity to his material, and his ability to pursue a task logically without enquiring about premises that anyone else might find hopelessly and vexingly arbitrary. 'I began by going to the piano, and putting my hands down, and playing a chord. Then I investigated it, and learned how to make more of it.' He held up his hands to show us. That was how it was done. (*New Yorker*, 19 July 1993)

Exody

Birtwistle was in New York for Christmas, having made the visit, so he said, to see the new Richard Serra sculptures at the Dia Center for the Arts. 'I prefer seeing sculpture in enclosed spaces,' he explained. 'These are like dinosaurs in a cage.'

His music has some of the same qualities as Serra's work: monumentality, weight, severedness, the sense of an alien presence that is both extremely ancient and as new as today. Recently he completed a big orchestral work, *Exody*, which will be given its premiere next month by Daniel Barenboim and the Chicago Symphony. It is, he said, 'a celebration of leaving. Its full title is *Exody 23:59:59*, the second before midnight. So it's about the ending of the century, but also about leaving in general.'

Further than that he was unwilling to go. When asked how a half-hour piece could express a particular instant in time, he would say only: 'Well, it can't do that, can it?' And to the remark that there must then be some sense in which the music relates to the moment before midnight he replied: 'Mmm, there is.'

After a long pause he went on. 'The piece is like a journey. When I describe my pieces, they all come out sounding the same, and perhaps they are. But having said that, I think there are some very different things in the way *Exody* speaks, in what the journey is. It's very much a journey into a labyrinth and out again. Where you enter therefore has to be where you leave, and the piece begins and ends with the music that ended my last orchestral piece, *Antiphonies*: the widest C possible on the orchestra. There are also other points where it comes back to a place where it's been before.

'I'm interested in the whole notion of what a journey is. Whenever you're travelling, there's the prescribed place you're attempting to get to, but there's also the moment where you are within the journey—the scenery, if you like. Even more interesting for me is the question of right and left, the fact that when you're looking at something, along the journey, you're all the time cutting out other things. You can't see everything all the time. And so the question of continuity and discontinuity also interests me—how you make discontinuities that in another way add up to a continuity.

'I like to think the continuity is given, and it's a matter of where you choose to put the eye—or, in the case of music, the ear—to make the continuity fractured. For instance, I made some things in the piece that are like frames. They have no context. They just happen, and then they're gone again. It's as if you open a trapdoor and see something else going on underneath. But it's very difficult to know how to make a sort of logic out of the illogicality. That's the problem. Francis Bacon said something interesting about that, that he'd always wanted to make pictures that were very formal and yet falling apart, in a state of disintegration.'

Much of this does indeed make *Exody* sound like a number of Birtwistle's other works and invites the question of whether he has favourites among his output. 'I don't have favourite pieces. I have favourite moments, as I do in all music. But what I can never do is recreate a favourite bit in another piece, because the moment depends on the context. For instance, there are four bars in *agm* I've tried to emulate once or twice and not succeeded. They're special to me because they do something in moving from a very fragmented texture, a lot of notes, to a unison. It's like a sudden jump into focus. But you can't take that as a technique and do it again. It's like when a performer will show you some tricks. I can never use them. I feel threatened by them. The virtuosity has to arise out of the music.'

Right now Birtwistle is writing for a virtuoso performer, the British pianist Joanna MacGregor, for whom he is composing a set of four solo pieces. 'I read that book, *Longitude*, which is about a clockmaker who made just four clocks and was called Harrison. So I'm writing these four pieces called *Harrison's Clocks*. They're mechanisms—rather elaborate toccatas, I suppose. At least, the two I've written are. I don't know what the other two are going to be, so I can't answer for them.'

Next on the agenda, after these final clocks, is an opera, *The Last Supper*, to be written for Glyndebourne. 'I want to set it for just thirteen blokes and not a very big orchestra, with a chorus among the players. They'll probably sing the mass, in Latin, and respond to what's happening in the action.' The casting of the central role is already clear. 'He has to be a baritone. I don't think Jesus can be a tenor. But Judas is certainly a tenor—not a countertenor, because they don't have any dramatic qualities. I'd like him to be like Mime in *Siegfried*—muscular, streetwise.'

'The form is interesting,' he added. 'That notion of twelve people, as a chorus but also with independent opinions. And one thing that interests me about the subject is that they go to celebrate one ritual, which is Passover, and he invents another one in the middle.' (*New York Times*, 31 December 1997)

◆

Birtwistle's music, so new, seems at the same time to be coming to us from very long ago, as if it were music written in Hittite. Some of its expressions are so basic as to make an immediate effect—indeed an effect especially immediate by reason of the strangeness of the context. In his half-hour orchestral piece *Exody*, which gained a vivid and thoroughly prepared first performance from the Chicago Symphony under Daniel Barenboim on Thursday evening, some elements had a sudden presence: trumpet fanfares and peals of bells, massive accumulations and sudden dissolves, solo instrumental songs and percussion pulses. But the whole language of western music appears not yet to have been formed. Birtwistle, entering his fifth decade of mature creativity, has developed his own way of speaking. His rhetoric was always forceful; now he can tease out his arguments with extreme sophistication. *Exody* is a triumph of the self-made and, in its ignoring of customary ways, an instant relic, gigantic and magnificent.

An appropriate metaphor for it might be that of a ruined city. Birtwistle likes to speak of his works as journeys, and for *Exody* he has evoked the image of a labyrinth: there is one entrance point—an open doorway of orchestral space, from the lowest possible C, in double basses with electric piano, to the same note six octaves higher, in violin harmonics with glockenspiel—which has to be found again at the end. But more than a route the piece impresses as an entity—an animal entity. Imagine it as some large creature with a plated or sculptured hide: Dürer's rhinoceros or a triceratops. And on its hide, growing out of the fleshly substance of it, are innumerable clocks. It stands. It moves. It bellows. And the voice of the work, as so often in Birtwistle's music, is low, rooted in two tubas and several low woodwind instruments. It is seen right up close and then in long shot. And all the while there are these clockwork tickings and throbbings.

The merging of animal and machine is a merging of times, of the smooth, continuous time in which we feel ourselves to exist with the abrupt, indistinguishable instants in which time seems to issue from a clock. Our time gains its shape from memory, which allows us to reconsider stretches of passed time as if every moment in them were in the same now. In Birtwistle's music the power of memory is the power of melody, which similarly makes us experience the past (previous notes and intervals) as belonging to the present, and *Exody* is full of melody, urging and exalting. But the clocks are a constant counterweight and threat. At one exemplary moment most of the orchestra falls silent, to leave just gong and drum strokes, lightly coloured by tubas, harps, electric piano and basses. The scene is being set for a threnody; Mahler is close. And a slow melody duly begins, on all the violins, violas and cellos in unison. Almost at once, though, a piccolo starts rotating notes in regular rhythm, 'like clockwork', as the marking in the score has it. Song, striving to make meaning through time, is checked by mechanical action in which all moments are identical and nothing can be learned.

Majestic and angry, light and obscure, *Exody* keeps its clocks and its melodies going right to the end, where, now outside the rediscovered doorway, the melody finally falls a tone in the Romantic sound of a solo horn, magically perpetuated by muted cellos playing harmonics. The song here is again elegiacal, and the recurrence of lament in the piece enforces in a passionately human way the leave-taking implied by the title. But there is also here the clock's unnoticing second in which a death or a departure happens. (*New York Times*, 7 February 1998)

The Shadow of Night

The adventure goes on. Birtwistle, now sixty-seven, has been carving out enormous chunks of exploratory orchestral music for four decades, irregularly. *The Shadow of Night*—which the Cleveland Orchestra and Christoph von Dohnanyi commissioned, played for the first time last weekend and will bring to Carnegie Hall on Friday—is like all its predecessors: something strikingly new but heavy with echoes from the past and, indeed, the future. This is music made to speak now, authoritatively, and (like little else in our time) made to last.

Birtwistle's earlier orchestral scores have lasted well. *The Triumph of Time*, written in the early 1970s, is a grand, slow procession, bearing melodies and signals like heavy banners. *Earth Dances*, of the mid-1980s, has a more geological sound, weighty with low brass and percussion, as musical layers move over one another with the ruthless determination of rock strata while woodwinds fuse in lament. If anyone wants to know where are the great symphonies of our time, here are two of them.

Dohnanyi and the Cleveland players performed *Earth Dances* a few years ago; they also made an impressive recording. In a recent conversation at the Royal National Theatre Studio in London, where Birtwistle was working on a production, he described how those Cleveland performances had led to a productive conversation with Thomas W. Morris, the orchestra's executive director and a great friend of new music: 'He asked me what else I wanted to do, and I said I had a piece in my head that was a sort of nocturne.'

The title, *The Shadow of Night*, comes from a poem by George Chapman, a contemporary of Shakespeare probably best remembered—thanks to Keats's poem—as a translator of Homer. Birtwistle was alerted to him by reading one of Frances Yates's books on Renaissance hermetic philosophy: 'She wrote a very good essay on "The Shadow of Night". It's in a book where she also talks about melancholy and the Dürer print.'

Dürer's engraving *Melencolia I* prompted one of Birtwistle's most moving scores, a piece of the same name for clarinet, strings and harp. That was a quarter of a century ago. He wanted to go back there, he said. 'It's another side of me that I wanted to unearth.'

Not that he has been so far away in the meantime. Indeed, robust as his music is, much of it lives in a shadowy realm. His fantasy opera *The Second Mrs Kong* unfolds partly in the world of shadows, where the dead live. Another work from the same period, the early 1990s, is *Pulse Shadows*, a sequence of Paul Celan settings and interludes for string quartet. But *The Shadow of Night* is exceptional in its concentration. 'It lasts about half an hour', Birtwistle said. 'I bet it's longer than that, and it's all slow. I tried to avoid using fast music just for the sake of variety. It's quite horizontal in its thinking. It's very linear. But I get worried describing a piece, because what I'm talking about is what I'm trying to do, not what I have in fact done.'

For Birtwistle music comes from an interior domain, another world of shadows, where even he is working in the dark. The conscious mind makes certain preparations and manoeuvres, and may afterwards come up with certain explanations, but the important work of thought and creation is coming out of the unknowable. This was one of Chapman's themes. Early in his poem, published in 1593, he calls on his readers to move with him into the night:

> All you possest with independent spirits,
> Indu'd with nimble and aspiring wits,

> Come consecrate with me, to sacred Night
> Your whole endeuors, and detest the light. . .
> No pen can any thing eternal write,
> That is not steept in humour of the night.

For Yates this Chapman poem was emblematic of a whole culture of melancholy in late Elizabethan and Jacobean England. Sadness was only part of it, the door. Sadness was regret for the absence of day, but true melancholics, followers of one of the four principal humours governing the human soul, found themselves most fully alive when they could, in the strength of their internal sombreness, disregard the illusions of daylight.

By tradition the goddess Melancholy was black; her light, as Chapman explains, was all inside: 'There is thy glorie, riches, force and Art.' The melancholic—as student of the night, penetrator of the undisclosed, commander of the unseen—was in the advance guard of humanity. Hamlet was one such, walking around Elsinore with his head swathed in night. But Birtwistle's example is a musician: Dowland.

'I think there's a certain lyrical melancholy that's in Dowland, and I don't think it's expressed in any other music. It's in his most famous songs: "In darkness let me dwell", "Flow, my tears". I thought about that when I was writing *Melencolia I*.'

Dowland was of the same generation as Chapman and Shakespeare. But unlike them he spent most of his young manhood travelling in mainland Europe, returning to London only in 1606, when he was in his early forties. Rediscovered in the twentieth century, he has been proposed as the model for another of Shakespeare's melancholics, Jaques in *As you like it*: a not unlikely guess, since Dowland and Shakespeare could have met in the early 1590s, when Dowland seems to have been in London briefly, and Shakespeare was surely aware of Dowland's first book of songs, which attracted a lot of attention when it was published in 1597. When Birtwistle wrote music for *As you like it* at the British National Theatre, he duly made Jaques sing pastiche Dowland. In *The Shadow of Night*, though, the engagement goes much deeper.

'A layer of the piece is a sort of meditation on Dowland. The start of "In darkness let me dwell" just goes up a semitone and down again: there's a long "in", as if the word "in" is going into the song, and then it goes up and back down on "darkness". I've used this, and it proliferates through the music. It's in a lot of different forms. For example, there are chords that come out of chords and go back in again, as if they were breathing.'

Birtwistle is also attracted by the image of the lone singer: 'There are all these real parts in the music, but they all converge in the one voice. Also, you have to think that he wrote the words, and he sang the songs, and he played them.'

But this is Birtwistle talking in the daylight of words. The real substance will come in the dark and unspoken world of musical communication, where a composer of the early twenty-first century finds himself speaking of the things that excited and troubled an ancient colleague. 'Where night's black bird her sad infamy sings', we can imagine Dowland singing to his own lute accompaniment in 'Flow, my tears', 'there let me live forlorn'. The black bird and the infamy are still with us: Birtwistle sings of them in his own way.

It is a way that was waiting. The score of *The Shadow of Night* carries an epigraph that comes not from Dowland but from another poet of the period, John Danyel:

> No, let chromatic tunes, harsh without ground,
> Be sullen music for a tuneless heart;
> Chromatic tunes most like my passions sound,
> As if combined to hear their falling part.

Here, four centuries ago, was someone who seems to have heard Birtwistle's music. (*New York Times*, 20 January 2002)

Pulse Shadows

'There are still songs to be sung on the other side of mankind.' The words are those of Paul Celan, and they come singing now near the start of a magnificent hourlong sequence of songs and interludes by Harrison Birtwistle, collectively titled *Pulse Shadows* and newly available on record.

Finding those songs, those still songs, was the work of seven years for Birtwistle—longer than he has spent on any other project besides his immense and complex opera *The Mask of Orpheus* (1973–84). And the process of finding, of searching and travel, is vividly present in the final work. There are also connections with that Orphic opera. The 'pulse shadows' are in part the shades in the underworld, still pulsing with life however feebly, and the music's effort is to bring at least one of them up into the light.

Any encounter with Celan must have to do with death, for reasons that spring from the precise detail of his work, from the context of that work as a meditation in the sombreness after 1945, and from the trajectory of his life—which so easily seems also the trajectory of his work—towards suicide, after a quarter-century of increasingly splintered, intense, ringing poems. His life and his work both rose to a pitch of supreme mastery, from which the ground was suddenly pulled away. It is a gesture that, perhaps coincidentally, recurs here and in other recent works by Birtwistle: the gathering of musical energy into a sure, firm note, and then the deflation in a downward scale.

Since Celan's death his collected poetry has become not only a book of almost biblical stature for scholars and explicators but a rich source for composers, especially for composers coming out of the tradition of German expressionism, composers for whom Celan's words provide a way of voicing a shriek. That is not how Birtwistle proceeds. His songs come not from piling on the pressure but from looking somewhere else, to where the poet knew songs could be found.

As so often happens Birtwistle was probably not looking at all but just hit on Celan and a new kind of song. The work began in 1989, when he wrote a single song for an anthology concert presented by a British group, the Composers Ensemble, which stipulated the unusual but—as he was to discover—extremely versatile and suggestive lineup of voice with two clarinets and a low string trio (viola, cello and bass).

The song he contributed was 'White and Light', a setting of a Celan poem not in the original German, which perhaps would have made expressionism unavoidable, but in one of Michael Hamburger's brilliant, close-fitting translations. In this form the poetry, while as observant as possible of the German text's meaning, sound, etymology and word order, comes a little towards an English world of natural observation and uncanny riddling: 'Sickle dunes uncounted. In wind-shadow, thousandfold: you.'

'White and Light' is a beautiful song. In it Birtwistle is at once at home and a stranger, on a shore—the poem's shore—where what is anciently familiar is the same as what has just been washed new by the last wave. The music wanders around a walking tempo and at one magical point almost comes to rest before being tautly pulled onwards again. The two clarinets spill and slip around the voice—now a little ahead, now behind—while the strings go their own way: the texture reappears often in *Pulse Shadows*. And when the poem speaks of sleep there comes an enfolding into D major, a warm gesture of comfort completely refreshed.

Still, what is perhaps most remarkable is, simply, the poised height of the vocal writing. Birtwistle starts out, as he often does, on an E, this time the E at the top of the treble staff, a tricky note between the soprano's middle and upper registers. It is an awkward point of entry and an awkward place to stay. Yet in this song it is not only awkward but right. The E has regular tendencies: up to F, down to D flat. In this difficult, elevated and uncustomary world, the vocal line behaves like a folksong, filling out its mode.

Birtwistle returned to pretty much the same manner when, in the 1990s, he added to 'White and Light' eight more Celan songs, three starting on the same lifted E. Almost everywhere the flow of the line is, as in that first song, wonderfully free and flexible, and the movement through steps and small intervals is voice-friendly and fully lyrical. But this is a lyricism not quite like anything ever heard before. The line is a little strange, a little strained, as if squeezing around an obstacle or through a blockage: coming, indeed, from 'the other side of mankind'. What also estranges the voice is the fact that the accompaniment is at the same time intimately close—as the clarinets are close in 'White and Light' and elsewhere—and objectively distant, travelling on its own musical plane. The world from which the soprano sings is one that knows tenderness and dispassion, and not the least of her music's lessons is how to tread a wary course between the two.

Two years after 'White and Light', Birtwistle wrote a short movement for string quartet—again an occasional piece, composed for the ninetieth birthday of Alfred Schlee, the former director of his publishing firm. Again, too, more followed, in one or the other of two styles. There were 'friezes', like the original movement, normally with three different things happening at once: a slow melody winding on and on, a faster chugging around within a confined pitch-space and a figure being repeated over and over, like a cog in a musical machine. Then there were 'fantasias', in which the four instruments behaved in a more unified manner, although fantasias could break down into friezes, and friezes congeal (or, in terms of the effect, warm up) into fantasias.

At some point Birtwistle realized that his two cycles, the Celan songs and the quartet pieces, could go together. The string quartet movements, in a medium made for pensive and personal expression, would fit well into the Celan landscape, and the songs could suitably spring out of a more monochrome environment. Songs and instrumental pieces might seem to be preparing one another or, to cite just some possibilities, interrupting, ignoring, lapsing into, fighting against. Meanwhile, on a practical level, gentle pauses would allow the singer to glide through the half-hour song cycle as if it were one breath.

In the recording Claron McFadden gives a spectacular performance. She hits the notes spot on, no matter where and when they arrive, and superbly sustains the music's long lines with sound that is simultaneously pure and rich, suiting the music's tones of fierce involvement and oblique chanting. Her impeccable diction makes the melody seem to flow from the words. She is the perfect singer for this music, sensuous and oracular. The musicians of the Nash Ensemble provide evocative support, encouragement, protest and contradiction, with mellifluous clarinets. Reinbert de Leeuw conducts, with audible emphasis at times. The Arditti Quartet can rarely have played better. Everyone seemed to know this was an important occasion.

In Monteverdi's Orpheus the story begins with a bouncing toccata and an introduction sung by Music herself. In everybody's Orpheus the story effectively ends when the light of day first falls on Eurydice's face and her lover turns in that light to look. *Pulse Shadows* similarly starts with fast reiterations, moving from instrument to instrument in the opening fantasia and eventually moving aside to let the first, dedicatory song come through: the song about songs. And it ends with a climb toward the word and the idea it has been rooting for all through: 'light', now with no slippage back. (*New York Times*, 14 July 2002)

a departure

Karajan's last London concert

The maestro enters. He has come to the edge of the platform on the arm of an assistant, and now stands. Like a cat observing his prey, he has his eyes fixed on the podium, which seems challengingly distant at the tempo of his approach. Like a man walking through water, he rolls, supported by a chain of hands held out in alternation by his first violins and violas. At last, the destination reached, the leader moves forward to offer the baton. The whole process takes perhaps no more than fifteen seconds, but it has established the aura: this is charisma holding on with fierce tenacity into its ninth decade.

The performance of Schoenberg's *Transfigured Night* is valedictory, as if projected out from the love music at the end of Mahler's Third Symphony to presage the death song at the end of his Ninth. The moments of tension and drama register strongly; the dialogue of double basses and upper strings for the voices of the lovers is graphic; and the variations of texture make their full effect. Yet the speed generally is slow; phrases are followed into their fading; and the superb blending of the Berlin Philharmonic strings produces a richly sombre colour, even in the appeased coda. The maestro does not seem to generate the music so much as to preside over it: except for a moment close to the finish, when he turns to encourage the first violins in their last high melody, he keeps his head still, towards the cellos in the middle, and his gestures are level, just sufficient.

Brahms's First Symphony is quite different. He moves a little more, but the impression of aloofness, even disengagement, is no less powerful. What has changed is the behaviour of the orchestra, for this is Brahms done with driving passion: the sound, which in the finale reaches a loudness extraordinary even for this orchestra at full size (quadruple wind, strings to match), and the intensity might better go with the balletics of a Bernstein. They hardly connect with this dispassionate figure, so that it seems the orchestra is making an offering to him, striving to sound as intent, as committed and as beautiful as they know how. And they do so as one. Even the solos for oboe (a lovely mellow sound, as golden as the instrument in the player's hand) and clarinet in the slow movement sound like particularities of a versatile but single sounding substance. Even the hard, metronomic beats of the timpanist in the explosive opening to the first movement are part of the whole. Even the uproar of the horns in the finale is embedded.

The maestro, perhaps with the faintest trace of pleasure as he turns to the audience, leaves. (*Times*, 7 October 1988)

further reading and listening

Carter

Oboe Concerto, Holliger/Boulez, Paris, December 1988 (Erato 75553, 1990; 98496, 1995) compact disc.

Partita, Barenboim, Cologne, 1 June 1994 (Teldec 99596, 1995; 81792, 2000) compact disc.

da lontano

Mozart: *Die Entführung aus dem Serail*, Salzburg production, 1997 (Image Entertainment 9312, 2003) DVD-ROM.

Amjad Ali Khan et al.: *Sarod for Harmony*, from Carnegie Hall concert (Navras 0160, 2002) compact disc.

a handful of pianists

Sviatoslav Richter: Bartók: Three Burlesques, from London concert (Philips 442 459) compact disc.

———: Mozart: Sonatas K.282, 310 and 545, from London concert (Philips 442 583) compact disc.

Purcell 1995

Adams, Martin: *Henry Purcell: The Origins and Development of his Musical Style* (Cambridge, Cambridge University Press, 1995).

Burden, Michael: *The Purcell Companion* (London, Faber, 1995).

———: *Purcell Remembered* (London, Faber, 1995).

Campbell, Margaret: *Henry Purcell: Glory of his Age* (London, Hutchinson, 1993).

Duffy, Maureen: *Henry Purcell* (London, Fourth Estate, 1994).

Holman, Peter: *Henry Purcell* (Oxford, Oxford University Press, 1994).

Keates, Jonathan: *Henry Purcell: A Biography* (London, Chatto & Windus, 1995).

King, Robert: *Henry Purcell* (London, Thames & Hudson, 1994).

Westrup, Jack: *Purcell* (Oxford, Oxford University Press, 1995 [first edition 1937]).

King Arthur, Les Arts Florissants, 1995 (Erato 17351, 1997) compact disc.

being in Assisi

Saint François d'Assise, Paris production, 1983 (Cybelia CY 833/36, 1988; Assai 222 212, 2002) compact disc.

———: Salzburg production, 1998 (Deutsche Grammophon 445 176, 1999) compact disc.

Boulez

Le Marteau sans maître and *Notations*, from 1985 Baden-Baden festival (CBS MK 42619, 1989) compact disc.

Bartók: Dance Suite, etc, Chicago, 1992–3 (DG 445 825, 1995) compact disc.

Debussy: *La Mer*, etc, Cleveland, 1991–3 (DG 439 896, 1995) compact disc.

Messiaen: *Chronochromie*, etc, Cleveland, 1993 (DG 445 827, 1995) compact disc.

Webern: Concerto Op.24, etc, Paris, 1992–4 (DG 437 786, 1995) compact disc.

Mozart 1991

Banks, C.A. and Turner, J. Rigbie: *Mozart: Prodigy of Nature* (New York, Pierpont Morgan Library, and London, British Library, 1991) [exhibition catalogue].

Branscombe, Peter: *W.A. Mozart: Die Zauberflöte* (Cambridge, Cambridge University Press, 1991).

Eisen, Cliff: *New Mozart Documents* (London, Macmillan, 1991).

Gruber, Gernot: *Mozart and Posterity* (London, Quartet, 1991).

Heartz, Daniel, edited and with chapters by Bauman, Thomas: *Mozart's Operas* (Berkeley, University of California Press, 1990)

Nagel, Ivan: *Autonomy and Mercy: Reflections on Mozart's Operas* (Cambridge, Mass., Harvard University Press, 1991).

Rice, John A.: *W.A. Mozart: La clemenza di Tito* (Cambridge, Cambridge University Press, 1991).

Rosenthal, Albi and Tyson, Alan, eds.: *Mozart's Thematic Catalogue: A Facsimile* (London, British Library, 1990).

Stafford, William: *Mozart's Death* (London, Macmillan, 1991).

Todd, R. Larry and Williams, Peter, eds.: *Perspectives on Mozart Performance* (Cambridge, Cambridge University Press, 1991).

operatic passions

Rihm: *Die Eroberung von Mexiko*, Hamburg production (cpo 999 185, 1995) compact disc.

Holliger: *Schneewittchen*, Zurich, 1999 (ECM 1715/16, 2000) compact disc.

at the movies

Hommage à Andrei Tarkovsky, Vienna, 27 October 1991 (DG 437 840, 1997) compact disc.

Prokofiev: *Alexander Nevsky*, Temirkanov, St Petersburg (RCA 61926, 1995; 68642, 1996; 60867, 2004) compact disc.

Glass: *La Belle et la Bête*, 1994 (Nonesuch 79347, 1995) compact disc.

Schoenberg on the stage

Moses und Aron, Boulez, 1995 (DG 449 174, 1996) compact disc.

five British composers

Simpson: Symphony No.9, Handley, Poole, 7–8 February 1988 (Hyperion CDA 66299, 1988) compact disc.

Lachenmann

Mouvement (vor der Erstarrung), etc, Klangforum Wien (Kairos 1220, 2001) compact disc.

Stockhausen

Mantra, Kontarskys, 1971 (Stockhausen 16) [LP DG 2530 208, 1971] compact disc.

Stimmung, Collegium Vocal Köln, Cologne, 30–31October 1969 (Stockhausen 12) [LP DG 2543 003, 1969] compact disc.

Indianerlieder, Helga Hamm-Albrecht and Karl O. Barkey (Stockhausen 20) [LP DG 2530 876, 1977] compact disc.

Montag, Milan production (Stockhausen 36) compact disc.

Freitag, Leipzig production (Stockhausen 50) compact disc.

behind the rusting Curtain

Jeney: *Spaziosa calma*, etc, Castellani, 1987 (Hungaroton 32050, 2001) [LP SLPX 12971] compact disc.

———: *Cantos para todos*, Twelve Songs, etc, Castellani, 1989 (Hungaroton 31653, 1996) [LP SLPX 12971] compact disc.

Verdi at the Met

I lombardi, Metropolitan Opera (Decca 455 287, 1997) compact disc.

how it was, maybe

Rameau: *Castor et Pollux*, Arts Florissants, 1992 (Harmonia Mundi 901 435/37, 1993) compact disc.

———: *Les Indes galantes*, Arts Florissants, 1990 (Harmonia Mundi 901 367/69, 1991) compact disc.

Edda, Sequentia (Deutsche Harmonia Mundi 77381, 1999) compact disc.

Reich

The Cave, première production (Nonesuch 79327, 1993) compact disc.

Three Tales, première production (Nonesuch 79662, 2003) DVD-ROM.

tracks in Allemonde

Pelléas et Mélisande, Welsh National Opera production (DG 440 073 0309, 2002) DVD-ROM.

Birtwistle

Pulse Shadows, McFadden/Nash Ensemble/Arditti Quartet (Teldec 26867, 2001) compact disc.

Index

Eastman Studies in Music

(ISSN 1071–9989)

Music's Modern Muse: A Life of Winnaretta Singer, Princesse de Polignac
Sylvia Kahan

The Pleasure of Modernist Music: Listening, Meaning, Intention, Ideology
Edited by Arved Ashby

The Poetic Debussy: A Collection of His Song Texts and Selected Letters (Revised Second Edition)
Edited by Margaret G. Cobb

Portrait of Percy Grainger
Malcolm Gillies and David Pear

The Sea on Fire: Jean Barraqué
Paul Griffiths

"Wanderjahre of a Revolutionist" and Other Essays on American Music
Arthur Farwell
Edited by Thomas Stoner

The Poetic Debussy: A Collection of His Song Texts and Selected Letters (Revised Second Edition)
Edited by Margaret G. Cobb

Concert Music, Rock, and Jazz since 1945: Essays and Analytical Studies
Edited by Elizabeth West Marvin and Richard Hermann

Music and the Occult: French Musical Philosophies, 1750–1950
Joscelyn Godwin

"Wanderjahre of a Revolutionist" and Other Essays on American Music
Arthur Farwell, edited by Thomas Stoner

French Organ Music from the Revolution to Franck and Widor
Edited by Lawrence Archbold and William J. Peterson

Musical Creativity in Twentieth-Century China: Abing, His Music, and Its Changing Meanings (includes CD)
Jonathan P. J. Stock

Elliott Carter: Collected Essays and Lectures, 1937–1995
Edited by Jonathan W. Bernard

Music Theory in Concept and Practice
Edited by James M. Baker, David W. Beach, and Jonathan W. Bernard

Music and Musicians in the Escorial Liturgy under the Habsburgs, 1563–1700
Michael Noone

Analyzing Wagner's Operas: Alfred Lorenz and German Nationalist Ideology
Stephen McClatchie

The Gardano Music Printing Firms, 1569–1611
Richard J. Agee

"The Broadway Sound": The Autobiography and Selected Essays of Robert Russell Bennett
Edited by George J. Ferencz

Theories of Fugue from the Age of Josquin to the Age of Bach
Paul Mark Walker

The Chansons of Orlando di Lasso and Their Protestant Listeners: Music, Piety, and Print in Sixteenth-Century France
Richard Freedman

Berlioz's Semi-Operas: Roméo et Juliette *and* La damnation de Faust
Daniel Albright

The Gamelan Digul and the Prison Camp Musician Who Built It: An Australian Link with the Indonesian Revolution
Margaret J. Kartomi

"The Music of American Folk Song" and Selected Other Writings on American Folk Music
Ruth Crawford Seeger, edited by Larry Polansky and Judith Tick

Portrait of Percy Grainger
Malcolm Gillies and David Pear

Berlioz: Past, Present, Future
Edited by Peter Bloom

The Musical Madhouse (Les Grotesques de la musique)
Hector Berlioz
Translated and edited by Alastair Bruce
Introduction by Hugh Macdonald

The Music of Luigi Dallapiccola
Raymond Fearn

Music's Modern Muse: A Life of Winnaretta Singer, Princesse de Polignac
Sylvia Kahan

The Sea on Fire: Jean Barraqué
Paul Griffiths

"Claude Debussy As I Knew Him" and Other Writings of Arthur Hartmann
Edited by Samuel Hsu, Sidney Grolnic, and Mark Peters
Foreword by David Grayson

Schumann's Piano Cycles and the Novels of Jean Paul
Erika Reiman

Bach and the Pedal Clavichord: An Organist's Guide
Joel Speerstra

Historical Musicology: Sources, Methods, Interpretations
Edited by Stephen A. Crist and Roberta Montemorra Marvin

The Pleasure of Modernist Music: Listening, Meaning, Intention, Ideology
Edited by Arved Ashby

Debussy's Letters to Inghelbrecht: The Story of a Musical Friendship
Edited by Margaret G. Cobb

Explaining Tonality: Schenkerian Theory and Beyond
Matthew Brown

The Substance of Things Heard: Writings about Music
Paul Griffiths

Paul Griffiths here offers his own personal selection of some of his most substantial and imaginative articles and concert reviews from over three decades of indefatigable concertgoing around the world. He reports on premieres and other important performances of works by such composers as Elliott Carter, Sofia Gubaidulina, Karlheinz Stockhausen, and Steve Reich, as well as Harrison Birtwistle and other important British figures.

Griffiths vividly conveys the vision, aura, and idiosyncrasies of prominent pianists, singers, and conductors (such as Herbert von Karajan), and debates changing styles of performing Monteverdi and Purcell. A particular delight is his response to the world of opera, including Debussy's *Pelléas et Mélisande* (six contrasting productions), Pavarotti and Domingo in Verdi at New York's Metropolitan Opera, Schoenberg's *Moses and Aaron*, and two wildly different Jonathan Miller versions of Mozart's *Don Giovanni*.

From the author's preface:
"We cannot say what music is. Yet we are verbal creatures, and strive with words to cast a net around it, knowing most of this immaterial stuff will evade capture. The stories that follow cover a wide range of events over a period of great change. Yet the net's aim was always the same, to catch the substance of things heard.

"Criticism has to work largely by analogy and metaphor. This is no limitation. It is largely through such verbal ties that music is linked to other sorts of experience, not least the natural world and the orchestra of our feelings."

Paul Griffiths's reviews and articles have appeared extensively in both Britain (*Times, Financial Times, Times Literary Supplement*) and the United States (*New Yorker, New York Times*). He has written numerous books on Bartók, Cage, Messiaen, Boulez, Maxwell Davies, twentieth-century music, opera, and the string quartet, and is the author of the recent *Penguin Companion to Classical Music*. He is also author of *The Sea on Fire: Jean Barraqué* for the University of Rochester Press (Eastman Studies in Music).

Praise for *The Substance of Things Heard* by Paul Griffiths

"If, as I think, a music critic should be distinguished by three features: an informed and passionate involvement with new music, an imaginative and civilised turn of the phrase, and the readiness to warmly appreciate, Paul Griffiths has to be counted among the leading lights of this precarious trade. Just look up his piece on a performance of Giulio Cesare. It makes the reader delight in the writer's generosity—a generosity that never loses its focus while praising each performer on his or her own merit."

—Alfred Brendel, pianist and author of *Alfred Brendel on Music: Collected Essays* (Chicago Review Press)

"Music criticism in the English language has been fortunate in attracting distinguished writers, such as George Bernard Shaw and Ezra Pound. Nowadays, Paul Griffiths comes closest to filling this ecological niche. Future musicologists will have to take Griffiths's responses into account in mapping the relation between music and culture in the twentieth and early twenty-first centuries."

—Daniel Albright (Harvard University), author of *Untwisting the Serpent: Modernism in Music, Literature, and Other Arts* (University of Chicago Press)

"A fascinating read."

—operatic tenor and recitalist Ian Bostridge

"No critic gives so interesting, complete, judicious and readable an account of the world of music as Paul Griffiths."

—Charles Rosen, pianist and author of *Beethoven's Piano* Sonatas (Yale), *The Romantic Generation* (Harvard), and *Piano Notes: The World of the Pianist* (Free Press)